PRAISE FOR BARBAI...

The Lost Girls of Devon

One of *Travel + Leisure*'s most anticipated books of summer 2020.

"A woman's strange disappearance brings together four strong women who struggle with their relationships, despite their need for one another. Fans of Sarah Addison Allen will appreciate the emphasis on nature and these women's unique gifts in this latest by the author of *When We Believed in Mermaids*."

—*Library Journal* (starred review)

"*The Lost Girls of Devon* draws us into the lives of four generations of women as they come to terms with their relationships and a mysterious tragedy that brings them together. Written in exquisite prose with the added bonus of the small Devon village as a setting, Barbara O'Neal's book will ensnare readers from the first page, taking us on an emotional journey of love, loss, and betrayal."

—Rhys Bowen, *New York Times* and #1 Kindle bestselling author of *The Tuscan Child, In Farleigh Field*, and the Royal Spyness series

"*The Lost Girls of Devon* is one of those novels that grabs you at the beginning with its imagery and rich language and won't let you go. Four generations of women deal with the pain and betrayal of the past, and Barbara O'Neal skillfully leads us to understand all their deepest needs and fears. To read a Barbara O'Neal novel is to fall into a different world—a world of beauty and suspense, of tragedy and redemption. This one, like her others, is spellbinding."

—Maddie Dawson, bestselling author of *A Happy Catastrophe*

When We Believed in Mermaids

"An emotional story about the relationship between two sisters and the difficulty of facing the truth head-on."

—*Today*

"There's a reason Barbara O'Neal is one of the most decorated authors in fiction. With her trademark lyrical style, she's written a page-turner of the first order. From the very first page, I was drawn into the drama and irresistibly teased along as layers of a family's complicated past were artfully peeled away. Don't miss this masterfully told story of sisters and secrets, damage and redemption, hope and healing."

—Susan Wiggs, #1 *New York Times* bestselling author

"More than a mystery, Barbara O'Neal's *When We Believed in Mermaids* is a story of childhood—and innocence—lost and the long-hidden secrets, lies, and betrayals two sisters must face in order to make themselves whole as adults. Plunge in and enjoy the intriguing depths of this passionate, lustrous novel, and you just might find yourself believing in mermaids."

—Juliet Blackwell, *New York Times* bestselling author of
The Lost Carousel of Provence, *Letters from Paris*, and *The Paris Key*

"In *When We Believed in Mermaids*, Barbara O'Neal draws us into the story with her crisp prose, well-drawn settings, and compelling characters, in whom we invest our hearts as we experience the full range of human emotion and, ultimately, celebrate their triumph over the past."

—Grace Greene, author of *The Memory of Butterflies* and the
Wildflower House series

"*When We Believed in Mermaids* is a deftly woven tale of two sisters, separated by tragedy and reunited by fate, discovering that the past isn't always what it seems. By turns shattering and life affirming, as luminous and mesmerizing as the sea by which it unfolds, this is a book club essential—definitely one for the shelf!"

—Kerry Anne King, bestselling author of *Whisper Me This*

The Art of Inheriting Secrets

"Great writing, terrific characters, food elements, romance, a touch of intrigue, and more than a few surprises to keep readers guessing."

—*Kirkus Reviews*

"Settle in with tea and biscuits for a charming adventure about inheriting an English manor and the means to restore it. Vivid descriptions and characters that read like best friends will stay with you long after this delightful story has ended."

—Cynthia Ellingsen, bestselling author of *The Lighthouse Keeper*

"*The Art of Inheriting Secrets* is the story of one woman's journey to uncovering her family's hidden past. Set against the backdrop of a sprawling English manor, this book is ripe with mystery. It will have you guessing until the end!"

—Nicole Meier, author of *The House of Bradbury* and *The Girl Made of Clay*

"O'Neal's clever title begins an intriguing journey for readers that unfolds layer by surprising layer. Her respected masterful storytelling blends mystery, art, romance, and mayhem in a quaint English village and breathtaking countryside. Brilliant!"

—Patricia Sands, bestselling author of the Love in Provence series

WRITE
MY
NAME
ACROSS
THE SKY

PREVIOUS BOOKS BY BARBARA O'NEAL

WRITE MY NAME ACROSS THE SKY

a novel

BARBARA O'NEAL

Text copyright © 2021 by Barbara Samuel
All rights reserved.

Published by Lake Union Publishing, Seattle

www.apub.com

Amazon, the Amazon logo, and Lake Union Publishing are trademarks of Amazon.com, Inc., or its affiliates.

ISBN-13: 9781542025997 (hardcover)
ISBN-10: 1542025990 (hardcover)

ISBN-13: 9781542021647 (paperback)
ISBN-10: 1542021642 (paperback)

Cover design by Shasti O'Leary Soudant

Printed in the United States of America

First edition

For my aunt Lisa, who was a belly dancer,
and traveled the world, and speaks five languages,
and brought matzo to my grandmother's Easter dinner
to share Passover ideas with her nieces and nephews,
and breathed possibility into my heart from day one.
I would not be who I am without you, Auntie.
Much love and thanks.

Chapter One
Gloria

I am setting up a photo shoot when I hear the news that Isaak has been arrested. For a long moment, it doesn't sink in. My body reacts ahead of my mind, warning me with a long ripple over my spine as I tweak the red shoes sitting beneath a lady's slipper orchid in the soft green environment of the conservatory.

Then his name penetrates my brain. *Isaak Margolis.* I lift my head and look at the radio, as if it will show me his long-lost face. My heart pauses, as if bracing to be shattered all over again, then starts up again with a hard thud.

Isaak.

All these years I've been waiting for the other shoe to drop. Now it falls like a meteor into my world, when I have finally relaxed into this rich, ordinary life filled with music and my Instagram photos and monthly luncheons at the Russian Tea Room with the dwindling numbers of former flight attendants I've known for more than fifty years.

I sink into a chair nearby the table, my legs too shaky to support me, and listen to the BBC announcer explain that the suspected art thief and forger was picked up by Interpol in Florence at the end of a decades-long search for missing works of art. The art world is electrified because he was found with a Pissarro that's been missing since before World War II.

All this time. All this time. For long moments, I allow panic and regret and longing to roar through my veins, emotion surging through me in ways I'd forgotten. I think of Isaak's hard, long face and lovely hands, think of our shared history—our mothers, who suffered both mundane and unimaginable tortures during the war; our desire to shake off that history and live unencumbered. I think of desire, the air crackling blue when we came within a few feet of each other.

I think of the very real possibility that I will spend the declining number of my days in prison.

I think of his body. His rough voice. The connection that bound us from the very first moments we met. So long ago, and yet, in a way, as recent as last night. Memory is strange that way.

I stand, take a calming breath.

And I wonder, How long do I have?

Chapter Two
Willow

As I ride the train to Gloria's on a rainy February evening, I am shivering in my flowered dress and thin jacket, clothes that worked in LA but are no good in this weather. My neck is cold even beneath my hair, and I'm going to have to get a scarf. Not something in floaty silk but a real scarf, knitted and thick. I'm a little embarrassed to be so naively underdressed.

Not that I had much of a choice. I'm carrying everything I own.

My aunt Gloria called yesterday to ask me to house-sit while she jets away to the second home of one of her old TWA buddies. I've done it fairly often the past few years, watching over the apartment and her cats, but the job is really about the greenhouse on the roof and the hundreds of plants she's nurtured for more than two decades.

It would be impossible to say how much of a relief her call was. My last gig finished with a whimper, and I've been couch surfing much too long, thanks to my asshole ex, who locked me out of his Malibu house after a big fight. When my album failed, he had no more use for me, which I should have expected, but it stung. Now, I'm down to $549 in cash after buying my dinner at LAX last night and hiding in the back of a Panda Express to eat it, and to say I have my tail between my legs would be a major understatement. "Midnight Train to Georgia" has been running on a loop in my mind, Gladys Knight singing her mournful song about giving up. LA proved too much for me too.

Am I giving up? The thought gives me a pain beneath my ribs, but to be honest, I'm thirty-five. How much longer can I possibly live the life of an itinerant musician? By now, I thought I'd be rocketing across the heavens like my mother did. I really believed it, and that's as embarrassing as the failure itself.

Not a failure, says the eternal cheerleader in my head. *Just a setback.*

Whatever. It's getting harder and harder to believe her. The evidence is pretty overwhelming in the opposite direction.

The train stops, and I feel a rush of relief at the familiar sight of the subway tiles looking faintly green in the fluorescent light. People get off. People get on. A blonde teenager with a startling anime tattoo across her neck; a woman in a blue hijab holding the hand of an impish toddler; a remarkably tall, bald white man wearing a bowler hat; a pair of weary-looking middle-aged Latinas with shopping bags on their laps.

It feels right. Welcoming. Nothing could say *home* more than this mix of peoples. LA is a wild blend, too, but everybody is so spread out you're working with a patchwork quilt more than a stew. Relief runs up my spine, and I relax my hold a bit on the Johnny Was bag on my lap, a tote I bought when the album first came out, a celebration of success.

The embroidered bag is now packed to the brim with my earthly goods. I am wearing the handmade cowboy boots that once belonged to my mother and have now become my trademark. I wish I had some leggings, but I forgot how cold the February rain would be. The mark of an outlander, a tourist. I am neither.

At the subway station at 72nd and Broadway, I get off and climb the stairs to greet the pouring rain. That, too, feels like home. Sometimes the sunshine in California can start to feel oppressive. Huddling in my cloth coat, rain dripping down the back of my dress, I hold my violin case close to my chest and hurry home to what is, in summer, one of the

4

prettiest streets in the neighborhood. By the time I reach the six-story prewar building, I'm soaked clear through.

Jorge, the burly, aging doorman, greets me with a joyful cry. "Willow! Where's your winter coat? Why don't you have an umbrella?"

I'm shivering and exhausted. "I know." I squeeze his arm. "We'll talk, but I'm wiped out."

"Sure, sure. She's up there, waiting for you."

I nod wearily. My boot heels clomp over the marble entryway, and I punch the button for the old elevator. It's been upgraded, but it's still slow and tiny. It carries me to the top floor, number six. The hallway smells of dinner—meat and aromatics and even a note of baking bread—from the other apartment. My stomach growls. I hope she's shopped.

Jorge must have rung her, because before I reach the door, it's flung open and my aunt opens her arms. She's wearing turquoise, of course, because that's her signature color. Today it's a silk caftan printed with peacock feathers, belted tightly to show off her tiny waist. "Willow," she says. "You're soaked! Where is your umbrella?"

"I forgot I might need it," I say wearily. In fact, I can't remember when I last owned an umbrella.

"Come in, come in," she says kindly. "Go get in the shower right now."

Beneath the shards of light falling in patches to the worn, once-fabulous parquet floor, I drop my bag and violin and wiggle out of my boots. I turn them upside down to drain on a thick braided rug Gloria keeps for this purpose. Water drips from the ends of my hair. "Will you make some tea?" I ask.

"Absolutely." She has produced a thick towel, a vivid pink, because she sees no point to having anything that isn't filled with life in some way. I wipe my face, and one of the cats comes tripping joyfully in to greet me. She's a pretty black and white with long hair and yellow eyes. "Hello, Eloise!" I say, reaching down to stroke her tail. She trills.

"Sam said she'll be around tomorrow," Gloria says. "She had a soiree tonight for the release of a new app."

Sam is my older sister, a dazzlingly successful game designer who finds me unbearably ridiculous. She'll only show up out of duty and probably won't be particularly cheery, but I've never really overcome my hero worship, and a part of me will be glad to see her anyway. "She said 'soiree,' did she?" I ask dryly.

"No, of course not." She waves toward my bedroom. "Let's get you in a hot shower. Are you hungry?"

"Starving."

She grins. "There's my girl. What do you want?"

"A Reuben from Bloom's."

"I'll call it in right away." She pats my shoulder, then picks up my bag. "Good God. What've you got in here?"

Everything, I want to say. "Not everyone can pack a year's worth of clothing into a handbag," I say, referring to one of her many talents. As she was a TWA stewardess in the swinging seventies, she is an astonishingly good packer. Shouldering my violin, I follow her out of the foyer into the hallway that runs the length of the building, east to west, and all the way to the end, where she opens the door to my corner bedroom. Windows to the west and south show dusk falling, lights springing up yellow and blue and red all the way to the horizon. Within is my four-poster bed, hung with mosquito netting when I was a teen, and a painting of the Faerie Queene in blues and greens that takes up a lot of space on one wall. Photos of me at various competitions hang next to a copy of my album cover, which is next to the most famous of my mother's.

Home.

It's a word as fraught as any I know, but this spot is one of my favorites in the world. Here, I can let the space ground me, hold me, give me some time to figure out what's next in my mess of a life.

The Reuben is the most glorious thing I've sunk my teeth into for months. Everybody in the world thinks they know how to make a good one, but you just don't know if you haven't had the real thing, with real pastrami from a deli where they've made it authentically for generations and then layered it with fresh, crisp sauerkraut and swiss cheese, all of it grilled on true rye bread. I've never cared for the dressing, which Gloria remembered.

"This is *stunningly* delicious," I manage after a few bites. I set the sandwich back into its wax paper wrap and wipe my fingers, feeling the sense of home and comfort expand, deepen, spread through my body.

"I wish I had your metabolism," she says for probably the millionth time, and that, too, is comforting. "Your mother was the same. She could eat anything."

"Luck of the draw," I say and push the potato chips her way. She adores them but will only eat two. "You look fit and happy."

She turns her head away from the small television, where a twenty-four-hour news channel plays on a shelf of the poorly lit kitchen. This is a new habit. "Sorry, I wasn't paying attention," she says and turns it off with a remote.

"Did something happen today?"

"Not really." She swings her foot beneath the caftan. Her toenails are a candy-apple red. "It's just noise."

I nod. I wonder if she's been lonely, but that's not really in character. All my life, she's been very sure of herself and her needs and perfectly able to meet them. I offer her another chip, and she takes it distractedly. "Where are you going this time?" I ask.

"Sorry?"

I raise my eyebrows. "Your trip? Isn't that why I'm here?"

"Oh. Yes. Dani is going to the islands and invited me to come stay at her guesthouse."

"That sounds good. February in the tropics."

"Yes." Her gaze drifts back toward the television, and I notice she hasn't put down the remote.

"Is everything okay, Auntie?" I ask.

"Of course!" Again, she seems to refocus, pouring fresh tea into my cup from one of the pots she's collected in her travels around the world. This one is green enamel with white leaves, and I know she chose it for the green tea on purpose. "I've missed you, sweetheart. Tell me about everything."

But I can tell she's still not really with me. Something is definitely off.

Chapter Three
Sam

The release party for *Ganymede's Ghosts* is held at Hops and Heads in Brooklyn, a leathery place masquerading as a hip brewpub so that all the aging boy wonders can reassure themselves they're still cool. I'm only there because Tommy Gains, the designer, is one of my oldest friends in the business and he personally called to invite me.

I hate these gigs, but I polished myself up and wore a belted yellow tank dress that does wonders for my boxy body, and some heels that make me stand a full head above most of the guys. Ever since I was thirteen, people have asked if I was a model. Not because I'm beautiful, because I'm not; it's just the only thing they can imagine a woman of five feet eleven would do, especially if she has "strong" features like I do, a bold nose and heavy eyebrows and a super-wide mouth that gives me a ridiculous number of teeth when I smile, like Jerry Hall to the twelfth power. I make it a practice not to smile and paid an optometrist to fit me with several pairs of geek-girl glasses, horn rimmed and round wires and some very cute pairs of colored acrylic. Just donning a pair of glasses awards a woman an extra fifty points of intellect. As a woman in the competitive field of computer games and game apps, I need all the help I can get.

The noise is frenetic, with an electronic beat thrumming through the room, not too loud, not too soft. My goal is to find Tommy, give him a punch in the arm, and get out. I don't want to see the pity in the eyes of those who know what's going on with my company, and I also don't want to fake it with those who don't.

I'll be forced to do both, of course. The faster I go, the less I'll suffer.

One of the things that surprises me as I make my way through the crowd at the pub is just how many women there are in the room. Since Gamergate in 2014, major companies have overtly recruited women and invited them into the circle, which has led to more females in college programs and showing up on the staffs. A few of them notice me, give me a chin lift.

One earnest girl with rainbow tips in her long hair swings around, and her mouth drops open. "Oh my God! Sam Janssen! You're the whole reason I'm in this field. I absolutely loved *Boudicca* when I was a little girl."

When I was a little girl. "Thanks. What's your name?"

"Ashley Madrid."

"Nice to meet you." I shake her hand and start to move past her, but she's got some grit and moves her body a little to keep me there, sliding a card out from somewhere, one that she presses into my palm.

"Look, I know I'm nobody, but I would seriously love to talk to you. Just coffee?"

"I'm kind of—"

"I would intern with you for free, for whatever. I would bring your tea or run errands or whatever you wanted, just for a chance to see how you work."

It's hard to resist a pitch like that, with her big brown eyes full of hope and the surety that Big Things Await. "Maybe," I say and tuck the card in my pocket. "I'll think about it."

She gives me a namaste bow. "Thank you. Have a good night. I saw Asher over by the snack table, if you're looking for him."

Asher.

A jolt burns through me, happiness and sadness all mixed up together. Asher is my oldest friend, my erstwhile business partner, and one of the people I love most in the world. Once upon a time we would have shown up here together, amusing each other with snide remarks. "Thanks."

What I should do is steer clear, but some ancient part of me makes a beeline for the snack table.

Before I reach it, I run smack into Jared Maloney, a big hale guy with very little hair left on his head and a bushy blond beard to make up for it. His jeans are up to the minute and the paisley button-down is painfully hip, but no matter how much money he makes, it'll never hide the miserable adolescence he suffered. His voice is always just slightly too loud, and he doesn't respect personal space.

"Samantha!" he says, using the full form of my name even though no one in our world does. I know he does it to remind me that I'm female. "Just the lady I wanted to see."

Lady. "How are you, Jared?" I say without inflection.

"Very well, thank you."

"Good, good." I look over his shoulder to see if I can spy Asher. Surely he'd rescue me if he saw me standing here with Jared, who has one main theme, which starts in . . . three, two, one:

"I just scored a prize bit of Billie Thorne memorabilia—a poster from her first show at CBGB."

My attention snaps around. "CBGB?"

"She played there." He sips his beer delicately. "You didn't know?"

"I have to admit I didn't." There's no rescue in sight. Sometimes, just giving in to his desire to rave about his favorite rock star, my mother, is enough to buy some goodwill. And for all his wretchedness, he is a very powerful guy in my world, known for aggressive takeovers and splashy buyouts. I have no doubt I'm on his list of upcoming acquisitions. "That sounds like quite a prize."

"Yes," he says. He tells me the songs she played for the gig, the people in her band at the time. It was early on, for sure, before she made the album that sent her star skyward, *Midnight Morning.* "I found a photo," he says and scrolls through his phone, one finger in the air to pin me in place. "Here it is." He swings the phone around.

It's my mother at age twenty, skinny and still blonde, her hair in ribbons over her shoulders, her nipples poking out of a T-shirt, seven necklaces ringing her neck, her arms full of bracelets. A cigarette is burning in her right hand. She's punky and hippie and beautiful—and I've never seen before how much my sister Willow looks like her. A year or two after this shot, she chopped off her hair and dyed it black, turning herself into Billie Thorne instead of Billie Janssen.

"Great, isn't it?" Jared says and looks at it again.

I feel pierced, seeing her so young. Untouched. For a while when I was very small, she grew out the black pixie. A memory slips through my mind, me brushing her hair over her shoulders as she sits on the floor. An entirely too familiar sense of loss breaches my walls, and I have to take in a deep breath to make it recede, staring off into the crowd so that he can't read anything.

I give a nod. "Yeah."

"You're lucky you knew her," he says, and I know he means it most earnestly. "She was one of the best singer-songwriters to ever live."

"She was definitely something." A junkie, a lost soul, never really a mother at all.

He drops the phone in his pocket and looks at me. I'm instantly on alert, his body language transmitting something my body picks up on but my mind is slow to recognize. "Sam."

I raise my brows. "Jared."

"I'm hearing rumors."

Fuck. Here it is. "About?"

"Boudicca's in trouble."

I turn at the mention of my company, ready to flee, now urgently searching for a face I know. "I'm not talking about this."

He touches my arm. Just touches it, right above the elbow. "I want to help."

I plant my feet, fury rising through my spine, stiffening it. "Help? Don't you mean take over?"

"No, no, no! It's not like that." He spreads his hand over his chest. "I swear on Billie Thorne that I would never do that."

Weirdly, I believe him. Or maybe I'm just desperate enough to entertain any kind of possibility. "What, then?"

"I would like to sit down and talk with you about the company. I have some ideas."

He is probably going to offer to buy Boudicca, where it will be absorbed into the massive brand that is Arrakis, his game company. Even the thought of it creates stars of fury behind my eyes. And yet Boudicca *is* in trouble. I wait.

"Dinner, tomorrow?"

Something has to be done, and I don't have to say yes to anything he says. "Sure." Instantly, my temple starts to ache.

"I'll have my assistant send the deets."

Then I'm standing there in the crowd where I don't know enough of the players anymore, feeling 150 years old, a has-been at 40. I realize this is probably how my mother felt when she went on the road that last time, after a flopped album and a half dozen stints in rehab for a heroin habit that started probably right around the time that CBGB photo was taken.

Just give me one more chance. It's not a prayer because I don't believe in God, but maybe something is listening anyway.

I make my way to the bar. I miss beer deeply but haven't been able to drink it in ages, and at the best of times, I'm not a big drinker. I've just never seen the point. But right now, I need something to take the edge off this headache. "A vodka soda with lime, please."

The bartender, with muscles popping from below his shirtsleeves, says, "A woman who knows what she wants." He pours the drink and passes it over with a wink. "Good health." His accent is Irish. He's really quite hot, and how long has it been since—

Nope. He can't be thirty, and I haven't yet started seducing boys. "Thanks." I raise the glass and face the room, promising myself I only have to make the rounds once, find Tommy, and get the hell out. I take a sip and stand there, searching the room for my points of entry.

"Didn't expect to see you here," says a familiar voice in my ear.

"Asher!"

He smiles his big, happy, welcoming smile. His glasses are not fake prescriptions but correct a very serious nearsightedness, which he has always claimed is the mark of a brilliant mind. His hair is wild as ever, loose black curls he never bothers to tame with product, and below it is the most welcome face on the planet.

Before he can put up his guard, I dive in for a hug, and before he can remember not to, he hugs me back. He smells of fresh air and Safeguard soap and a note of cinnamon that marks him completely. "It's so good to see you," I say, inhaling. Feeling.

He doesn't immediately let go, which I take as a hopeful sign. His arms are tight, and I can feel the density of his torso. "Ditto." He disentangles himself. "I thought you and Tommy fell out a couple of years ago."

"We did." He posted a thoughtlessly sexist comment about female gamers on social media, and I sliced him into little tiny pieces. "And then we worked it out." I give him a level look, trying to use telepathy to say that's what I want to happen with us. I punch his arm lightly, and even as I do it, I think it's stupid. "How are you?"

"Good. You?"

"Great."

Then we stand there awash in an ocean of things. Things we can't talk about. Our long friendship, our ill-fated night, our broken relationship. "How's your mom?" I ask.

"She had the flu that's been going around, but she's fine now. You should go see her. She misses you."

"It's just been busy." A lie, but I missed the way things had been so much the last time I visited Deborah that I just can't do it. It underlined all the echoey emptiness that is my life these days. "I'll make it happen soon."

"How's Gloria?"

I give him a half smile. "She's Gloria. Her Instagram account has two hundred fifty thousand followers now. She's a bona fide influencer."

He laughs, showing his big white teeth. "That's great. Give her my love."

"You should do it yourself. You know you love her. Willow's home too."

"To stay?"

"Doubtful. You know Willow."

He nods. "She's a free spirit."

He swivels to pick up his beer from the bar. We squeeze down to let a trio of twentysomethings belly up to order drinks. "I feel about ninety-seven years old in this room," he says.

"Right? When did we become the older generation?" I shake my head. "A girl who played *Boudicca* when she was a 'little girl' offered to be an intern."

"Ow. But also, that's a good thing, right?"

"I took her card. What are you working on now?"

"New game," he says and mimes zipping his lips. "It's at that embryonic stage."

"I get it."

"You?"

"A couple of things," I lie. My business is in trouble entirely because I've had a dearth of ideas since Asher left the company. "Still on the AI app. Just can't quite get it right."

"Anything you want to talk out?"

I look up. His familiar brown eyes meet mine. In them, I see patience and kindness, qualities I have undervalued my entire life. "She still feels like an annoying, needy girlfriend. The opposite of what I'm going for."

He chuckles. "That's a time thing, right? Training."

"Yeah, probably." I sip my drink and think of a million ways to express how awful life is without him. I choose the simplest sentence. "I miss you, Asher."

"Me too, Sam."

"Can't we just have lunch or even just coffee sometimes? Go to a movie?" We often spent Saturday nights watching anime, a habit we'd started way back in grade school, long before anime was hip. I aim for a lighter note. "It's kind of hard to talk adults into picking up the anime habit."

He bows his head. "No. I'm not there yet."

I swallow. Give myself a minute so I won't sound as intensely emotional as I feel. "This is crazy. We've been best friends for thirty years. How am I supposed to just go get another one?"

"I don't know." His mouth twists with regret. "I'm lonely too."

"Then why—"

His jaw sets. "No. Sorry."

"'Kay." If I don't get out of here, I'm going to make a big scene, and that's not going to do me or my business any good. "I have to go."

He catches my arm. "I'm sorry, Sam. I wish I could."

"Me too."

I walk away.

Chapter Four
Gloria

I've been online since dawn, trying to figure out exactly what's happening with Isaak, googling and following links down rabbit hole after rabbit hole. It's still not clear what he's charged with, exactly, or where he will be tried. It pains me to think of him in a cell, wearing rough cotton, eating horrible food. He has always been so careful with his clothes, so particular about his food.

I'm standing over the sink peeling a boiled egg and drinking black coffee when a news story pops up on the small television planted on a shelf in the corner. Willow is still asleep—poor girl looked even more waifish than usual last night—and I plan to let her sleep as long as she likes. I've had a few suspicions about that manipulative boyfriend of hers, and by the haunted look in her eyes, I'm not wrong.

The announcer says, "France has announced that they will extradite Isaak Margolis for trial. The suspected art thief is connected to dozens of paintings that were lost during World War Two, which Margolis is suspected of selling during a flurry of activity in the late seventies and early eighties. Interpol is still seeking several accomplices. It is not known if the paintings were actually the lost masterpieces Margolis claimed or forged reproductions."

My heart whirls into a staccato rhythm, and I wonder if I'll have a heart attack and be spared all the decisions I need to make. I press the heel of my hand into my breastbone.

"Two masterworks in particular are thought to be among the lost paintings, a Renoir and an early-medieval masterpiece stolen from a hidden cache of Nazi holdings in 1947. In other news—"

I click it off. Stand here trying to think through the noise in my brain. Will he be prosecuted? Will they trace things back to me?

Carefully, I brush my fingers clean and walk through a swinging door into a small butler's pantry that smells of dust. At the other end is another door, nearly always propped open, into the formal dining room where none of us ever eat.

It's a very formal room, with wood-paneled walls and parquet floors covered in properly faded arabian rugs. An enormous table, left by the former owners, is carved of dark wood and surrounded by twelve matching chairs. It dominates the center beneath a rather plain chandelier. I moved the ornate crystal beauty that used to hang here into my bedroom, where it would be enjoyed rather than hidden away.

On the walls, all the walls, are dozens of paintings, which Billie collected on her travels with a casual fanaticism that always surprised me. Few of them are better than average, but she made a couple of brilliant purchases over the years—an early Lee Krasner, a surrealist drawing that turned out to be an Escher, a remarkable sketch by David Hockney that's probably worth a small fortune. She had wide-ranging tastes in art, just as she had wide-ranging tastes in everything. Music, sex, food, drugs. Most drugs she could manage, but heroin brought her down, just as alcohol brought down our mother.

I wander into the parlor, also filled with art. Hanging in plain sight among all the others, the abstracts and landscapes and sketches, is a small square painting in need of cleaning, but I daren't take it in to have it done. Even beneath all the grime of decades of New York City soot, it's a bright landscape, wheat and trees and a row of poppies very much in the style of Renoir.

Because it is.

An actual Renoir.

I cannot sell it, of course. No one has ever noticed it on the wall among all the other paintings and imitations, and I hope it will remain this way.

But there is much to connect me to Isaak. Will Interpol come after me too? Our love affair was quite well known in our group, and Interpol will certainly pay attention to the fact that I was a flight attendant, flying internationally for nearly two decades, so could easily have carried contraband.

I am also the subject of many of his own paintings, a fact that will come to light sooner rather than later. If I know anything about the inflammable nature of the internet, Isaak's work is about to be splashed everywhere.

Perhaps it will become valuable. That would be a bittersweet angle to his story.

Or maybe I'm just being paranoid and dramatic. Honestly, it's been decades—why would they bother?

Except—here is the Renoir. Should I move it, or would that make it look more suspicious? I can't very well claim I had no idea it was real if I hide it.

If I do hide it, where will it be safe? I've always planned to leave instructions about it in my will so that the world will have it again after its long loan to me. It was a gift from Isaak, late in our shared caper.

Where shall I hide it?

A certain tension begins to fill my throat, a sense of urgency and the very real fear that I must take steps to secure my freedom. The emotions freeze me for a moment, and then I straighten my spine. I will not indulge panic. Instead, I march myself smartly into the shower. One never accomplishes anything without a clear mind.

I need to decide on a plan. The last thing in the world I want to do is flee—leave my home, the girls, my life—but worse would be prison. A vision of Isaak locked behind bars in some grim jail makes my stomach hurt.

I have to figure this out. Probably the first thing I need is a lawyer, a criminal lawyer who knows something about international law and art forgery. My regular guy probably won't know much about that, but I know somebody who will, or will know who to recommend.

Chapter Five

Willow

Light trickles into my bedroom early, filtering through the curtains and onto the dusty Turkish carpet. For a moment, I lie there, grateful for my bed and my room. I'm lucky to have a place to land and I know it, but that doesn't really help the bottomless sense of failure that also arrives, right on time, five seconds after I open my eyes.

I roll over onto my back, hands on my ribs, and let it come all the way in. *Go ahead, get it out,* I think to the voice that so harangues me.

She dives right in with the same litany I've been hearing on repeat for months now. *You're too old for this. Your music is too offbeat for the masses. You should have known you'd never really make it.* And the worst: *You've let everybody down. Some prodigy.*

I wait, but the harridan seems to be finished.

With a sigh, I roll out of bed, shake it all off, and slip into a pair of yoga pants and an old 3 Doors Down sweatshirt. My violin sits by the door, and I pick it up and carry it with me into the kitchen. Gloria is an early riser, but there's no sign of her as I make a cup of tea. Maybe she's in the greenhouse.

The kitchen is where the age of the apartment shows most vividly. A window over the sink is framed in faded yellow curtains, and the cupboards have so many layers of paint you can see the decades in chips showing through the slippery white top layer. The linoleum floor is from some era I can't even name and is so battered that Gloria keeps it covered with an area rug.

And yet the counters are plentiful, a butler's pantry provides a generous amount of storage, and the view through the window is of the Hudson, eternally moving slowly to the sea.

The best of the room is the back door that leads to the rooftop garden and the old-school greenhouse built out there. When I was a child, I played in the mostly neglected greenhouse, dancing my dolls along the shelves, enjoying the dappled light coming through the mossy, dirty windows. My mother was flush through the eighties and early nineties and paid a gardener to come in twice a week to tend the trees and the flowerpots, so they sometimes overwintered a few things in the greenhouse. Mostly, I had both the garden and the greenhouse to myself, a magical place in the mornings, no parties or grumpy sister to ruin my pleasure.

Carrying my cup of tea and my violin, I step out that back door into the misty morning and the splendor of what Gloria has created from the wreckage of my mother's life. The potted trees of my childhood have grown tall and leafy, though of course they're bare limbed in February. Pathways lined with pots lead to a cozy nook furnished with a table and chairs, and then to a semicircle overlooking the city to the south. In the distance, I spy the Empire State Building to the left, the pin in the map of my world.

Last, the path leads toward the door of the greenhouse, a wrought iron structure leaning against the wall of the house. I duck inside, breathing in the scents of earth and moisture, letting them work their miracle of release along my neck.

It's a huge space, but every inch of it is filled with a fecund outpouring of flowers and greenery. Bougainvillea winds in splashy magenta over the ceiling, and orchids bloom in pockets, along with a multicolored selection of begonias with showy leaves. Lettuce, spinach, and radishes fill a raised bed against the cold wall, and on the warm end over a radiator is a cherry tomato plant covered with fruit. After Gloria came to live with us, tomatoes were the first thing she planted out here, and my childhood was dotted with the harvesting of cherry tomatoes. I pluck a ripe one and pop it in my mouth, covering my tongue with explosions of flavor, and I close my eyes for a moment. Store tomatoes do not taste like this at all.

I thought Gloria might be puttering out here, but it's empty. I settle my tea between a blooming red-and-white gloxinia and a sturdy Martha Washington geranium, then pick up my violin and tuck it under my chin. The harridan slinks away to her cave, silenced by devotion.

Because I am devoted. Devoted to music, and violin, and the part of me that burns to create. For a single moment, I allow myself to be just there, ready to begin, on this lovely morning back in my childhood home.

Then I tune my beautiful instrument, face the audience of plants, and let music rise in my body, allowing whatever wants life to tickle my fingers. It's both practice and pleasure, discipline and joy, a daily habit I've rarely skipped. In a little while, I'll work on the piece I've been composing, but for now there is just this. Morning practice, and then again in the evening if I don't have a gig. Twice a day, every day.

This morning, the first to emerge is an easy Mozart sonata that allows my body to warm up. The acoustics are fairly good, and music swirls around the plants in soft lavender notes, spreads along the glass panes of the ceiling in pale clouds. I can sense the plants turning their heads and leaves toward the sound, drinking it in and offering me back the gift of oxygen. I fill my lungs with it, fill my body, and close my eyes.

And as so often happens in various places in the apartment, I sense my mother, a presence that's just beyond my physical senses, memory or imprinting on the space or a ghost. I don't know; I just know I like it. I keep my eyes closed and play for her, imagine her faint smile, the pride she took in my abilities, abilities she nurtured deeply.

The sense of her fades slightly as I finish, and I open my eyes to the plants and soft green air. My skin feels softer already. A rex begonia, with a spiral swirl of red on her ruffled leaves, moves slightly as a waft of air touches her. I move my finger along the edge, pick up the violin again. "What would you like to hear, my beauty?"

I fancy I hear the answer, though of course it's only my own mind. *Lindsey Stirling! Of course! So much energy!*

The weaving of Celtic and electronica is one of my favorites. Some have compared my compositions to hers, and that's fair, but I'm very much my own artist and a composer working on my own ideas. Her music now pulses a sense of energy and passion into my body, pushing away the past, the struggles I'm facing with my career, the choices I have to make sooner rather than later.

There is only now. This. Music and plants and potential.

When I'm finished with that, I shake out my shoulders and allow the new composition to fill me. It's not quite a concerto, not quite a sonata, not quite a single song. It's layered and wild and rich, and if I can get it right within the next few days, I can enter it into a music competition that carries a substantial prize, $10,000, and a lot of great exposure within the industry. The piece isn't finished, and I can feel holes in it as I work. Something in the middle lacks some essential magic, the fairy dust that takes a composition from good to fantastic, and I can't figure out what's missing.

From the corner of my eye, I see Gloria slip in, her short white hair gelled into a sharp, ultramodern style, sleek on the sides, swirling longer on top. It sets off her cheekbones and jeweled eyes, always her best features. This morning, she wears a simple turquoise cashmere sweater and silk trousers that I could not get away with. She waits for me to finish, her head swaying along, and shoots a series of photos with her phone. This is something I've grown used to. She'll post to Instagram, but I never mind. Sam hates it.

When I finish with a flourish, Gloria claps. "Fabulous!" she cries. "And look at the plants! They're so happy."

"It does seem as if they like it." I pick up my tea. "Are you going somewhere?"

"In a little while. I'm meeting the girls for a special lunch."

The "girls" are a gang of septuagenarians who met in flight school for TWA back in the sixties.

"A birthday?"

For a moment, she looks confused. "A birthday? Oh, no. We just felt like it. Not getting any younger, you know."

I nod. "So when are you leaving?"

"Not for a couple of hours." She pats her wrist, which gleams with a rose-gold smart watch on a mesh band.

"I mean for your trip."

"Trip?"

I raise my eyebrows. "I'm here to house-sit?"

"Oh, that." Her hands fly around. "Not sure. I have some things to work out. Are you in a hurry?"

"Not at all." There's something about her face or her posture that makes me cross the small space between us and envelop her in a hug. She's taller than me by several inches, and my head falls exactly into the hollow of her shoulder, the place of safety I most needed as an orphaned child. Now her body feels taut, and I wonder what's going on. Her arms eventually come around me, but not in the usual way. "Are you okay, G?"

She pets my head, but in a sort of distracted fashion, like she needs to get moving. "Fine, sweetheart."

I think not, but I release her and step back to examine her face carefully. Slight blue circles that can't be fully hidden beneath meticulous makeup reinforce my sense of unease. "You know the 'lean on me' thing goes both ways, right?"

She barely seems to hear me, looking at her phone. "I'll leave you to it," she says and bustles away, already opening an app.

Curiouser and curiouser.

Chapter Six

Sam

It's raining lightly as I start my morning run. My joints are a little achy, and I feel like I might be catching a cold, so for the space of a few minutes, I consider not going.

But I'm already in my running clothes, and I have the right gear for the weather, a lighter-than-air raincoat that can fold as small as the palm of my hand, performance layers underneath, and what my aunt Gloria calls my foreign legion hat, with long tails to cover my neck.

I've also arranged to meet my father at a coffee shop near his apartment as a last-ditch effort to find the funding I might otherwise have to get from Jared. I could skip the run and just take a cab, but truly, running is the only thing that keeps my anxiety in check, and I have a lot of it this morning. I toss back a couple of Advil and head out into the day.

It's Sunday, still early, and I warm up with an easy jog from my Harlem apartment down to the Hudson River Greenway. Not many people are out, and most of them are like me, runners. When I hit the path, I pick up the pace until I hit my natural stride, pretty solid eight-minute miles. In my ears is a playlist of the hip-hop I grew up with, Tupac and N.W.A. with a mix of others. I had a major crush on Tupac as a teen and had a poster of him on my bedroom wall. He and my mother died within a couple of years of each other. I cried much harder over him than I did over her.

The rain is more of a mist down here. The river is a restless dark gray between me and the buildings lined up in New Jersey on the other side. It's not long before I feel the click, that moment a mile or two into every run, where I feel all the tension in my body slide out and I'm suddenly looser, moving easily. I forget about the aches and pains and find the place where I can think about whatever problem I'm trying to work out.

This morning, it's Boudicca and the cash flow issues. My last two games have not done well at all, and if I don't come up with something spectacular, the company will sink like the *Titanic*. When I saw the acquisitive hunger in Jared's eyes last night, it underlined the urgency. If he knows, everyone knows. I have to find a way to fix this.

The problem is that Asher and I worked very well together as a *team*. I'm great at story conception and design, and I can code as well as the next person, but Asher's the Michelangelo of coding. No one can touch him.

And without him, I'm struggling to get my concepts—which are still strong; I feel that in my gut—into the shape I need them to be. If we were a music duo, he'd be Lennon and I'd be McCartney, a good writer but not the genius.

Of course, he always said it was the other way around—my stories gave his tech wings. Whichever way it was, we were an amazing team, and I completely wrecked it.

A rise of tension builds through my chest, and I pick up the pace until it subsides again. Boudicca is my baby, founded when both Asher and I were nineteen years old. We created one of the first video games aimed directly at girls when we were kids ourselves, funded with the money my mother left me, and became literal millionaires overnight.

But that was more than twenty years ago. The game didn't translate well to new platforms, and what seemed cutting edge in the late nineties seems lame by today's standards.

Maybe I've lost touch. Or lost *my* touch. Maybe the reason the business is in trouble has less to do with bad investments and more to do with my slipping grasp on the industry, where the players seem younger by the minute and 40 feels like 102.

Tupac sings "When Thugz Cry" in my ear, and I wish I could cry myself over the mess my life has become. I swing around a young mom jogging with a vinyl-draped stroller and give her a wave as I pass, then wipe water off my face with a bandana.

I really don't want to sell. I'm angry with Asher for taking our personal rift into the business realm. We'd been struggling for three or four years about the direction of the company too—he is wildly interested in open-ended building games, while I've been trying to drill down to what girl gamers want now.

I'm also enchanted by the great leaps in AI and have been working a lot on an app featuring a robotic sort of best friend. Which I haven't been able to perfect yet. It's either too needy or too robotic, and there's a problem with shared memories—memories shared between the AI and the user—that is more important than I expected. To feel real, a robot needs to know and understand the time and history of the user.

The trouble is, I've been spending far too much time on that and not enough on developing ideas for new games. My last release was a dud, and I need to get something new out there sooner rather than later. I need resources, and at the moment, I just don't have the cash for them.

I might give the young woman from last night a call, see if she's serious. I've had an idea for a new game swirling around in the back of my imagination, and with an extra pair of hands and a brainstorming partner, maybe I could get something together.

Time. I just need to buy myself some time. Long enough to develop the idea into something concrete. Thus the meeting with my dad to see if I can get a short-term loan to pay the bills until I can get another game to market.

Without an influx of cash from somewhere, I'm going to have to close my doors.

I try to leap over a puddle and instead land right in it, my entire foot getting soaked in cold, probably disgusting water. But it's nearly mile four, and I don't care.

By the time I reach the coffee shop, I'm soaking wet, and I duck into the ladies' room to dry off a little. My hair has been protected by the hat, so I shake it out and comb it with my fingers, dry my face with paper towels, and shake the water off my gear. Not perfect, but it will do.

I spy my dad in the corner, already holding a coffee and a pastry in front of him. He's a handsome guy in his early sixties, with a full head of hair and square shoulders. He stays trim playing racquetball twice a week and still does fifty push-ups and sit-ups every morning. It has paid off, because he's married to a woman almost thirty years his junior who has given him a pair of honestly adorable little boys.

He glances at his watch and peers out the window, looking impatient, and I rush over. "Hey, Dad. I'll just get a coffee and be right back."

"I got one for you." He pushes the paper cup over the table, as well as the pastry.

"Oh." I push the pastry back. I can smell it, sugary and yeasty, with cherries shining in the center. My mouth waters. "I can't eat those anymore."

"Still off gluten, huh? You don't need to lose weight."

I take a breath to calm my irritation. His casual criticisms are annoying, but I'm used to them. "It's not about weight. I'm a celiac. I'm allergic."

He lifts an eyebrow and pulls the danish back to himself. "It's still weird that happened, just out of the blue. You loved doughnuts and bread and pasta as a kid. I worried that you'd grow up and get fat."

He takes a bite, and I can hear him chewing it, a horrifying set of mouth noises, squishing and soft smacks, that practically brings tears to my eyes. It isn't that he is a rude eater, just that I can't stand mouth noises of any kind. I press the button on the earphone in my right ear, and Tupac comes on, just loud enough to drown the sounds.

"How's it going, Dad?" I ask, sipping the coffee. This is right. Milky and sweet and strong, just the way I like it.

"Good, good. Britt just sold a penthouse in Tribeca, so we're going to take a little jaunt to Italy over Christmas."

"Nice. And the boys?" My half brothers are sweet kids, and they worship me in a way that's wildly satisfying. We don't spend much time together, but I make it over for most birthdays, for holidays and the odd party.

"Great. Nathan is reading at a sixth-grade level—did I tell you that? Five grades above his age. Some of his teachers think he should skip, but that was hard on you, wasn't it?"

I nod, ducking my head. Grade school was not the easiest time. I was skinny and too tall, even two grades up, and I had food allergies even then, to eggs and shellfish and, weirdly, melons of many kinds. Which my dad figured out through an elimination diet. My mom could never really get with the program to stick with the four-day testing periods. "It's hard to be the smart kid no matter what, but it's easier if you're a boy."

He focuses intently on my face. It's one of his gifts and has made him famous for a certain kind of in-depth, revealing interview that gets at the heart of a person. It was how he met my mother, an interview for the *Village Voice*. The first big piece for both of them: Billie Thorne, the up-and-coming punk star, and Robert Janssen, the rising journalist. "I guess it would be. If you were Nathan's mom, what would you do to make it better for him?"

Of course he's not interested in me particularly. This is for his child, the one he won't leave the way he left me. But I'm willing to indulge some give-and-take. I take a breath. "Maybe don't make too much of it; let him just have a lot of interests and be a normal kid."

"But he's not."

"I know, Dad. He has a ridiculous IQ. But it's not going anywhere. He'll always have that brain. Let him be a kid."

"That sounds like we didn't let you be a kid, and I think we tried hard to make life feel as normal as possible for you."

"You did. I know you did." I feel the same creeping shame I always do when I'm with him, that sense of not appreciating enough what has been done for me. The lengths he went to. A little burn is starting in my gut. I duck behind the same story I always do. "Not everybody is the kid of a rock star."

"Yeah." He leans back, the pastry evidently forgotten, thank God. Looks at his watch again. "So what's up, Zelda?" It's his nickname for me, for one of the games I loved madly as a kid. It's one of the things he does to endear himself to people, give them nicknames, and even though I know that, I feel seen.

Until he follows with, "I have brunch in half an hour."

I press my lips together. Maybe this was a bad idea, but I'm running out of possibilities. Baldly, I say, "My business is in trouble, and to avoid having to sell to a competitor, I need to raise some money to give me time to finish a game."

He waits to see if there's more, but I can't come up with anything else.

"It's not the best time," he says. "Even though I just said we were going to do this little trip, that's Britt's money, not mine, and we just paid tuition for the boys, and—"

I raise my hands, palms out, to stop him. "Never mind, Dad. It doesn't matter."

"Why don't you sell that apartment of your mother's? I'm sure Britt would give you a very good deal on the fees, and even in the state it's in, you'll bring in a fortune."

This again. He aches for the commission his wife would earn from the sale of the apartment, but I also think he longs for the place on some other level. Maybe because he was happy there once upon a time, or maybe it's just the New Yorker's longing for that elusive perfect apartment.

It's annoying but irrelevant to the discussion at the moment. "I don't need millions. I just need a short-term bridge to keep the business afloat for a few months, until I can get a new game out in the world."

He gives me a regretful expression. "Wish I could help. But seriously, think about the apartment."

Did I really expect him to help me? Even though he has a history of not really showing up unless it works out for him? "Gloria lives there. And so does Willow at the moment, even though I know you don't care."

"I have no feelings about her one way or the other."

A gigantic lie, even all these years later. He adored my mother, worshipped the ground she walked on. The happiest years of my life were before the age of four, when my parents curled up together with me, when we took walks in the park and sailed paper boats at the ponds. When I was four, my mother gave birth to a beautiful blonde baby with a sunny disposition, a baby that was not her husband's.

"Whatever. Doesn't matter." I stand and shove my arms into my rain jacket and pull on my hat. Maybe I think he'll feel bad and offer something else, but of course he doesn't. "Thanks for the coffee."

I head out into the drizzle once more.

Water splashes down from the brim of my hat to my face, momentarily blurring the world. I'm getting a headache and rub my fingertips against my forehead, trying to ease the muscles.

Sell the apartment.

A part of me aches at the possibility of it being out of our hands. I mean, it's a fantastic place, even if I personally find it heavy and dark and overwhelmingly in need of updates.

Another part of me wonders, *What if?* My share of the money would be plenty to pay salaries and rent until we can get a new game out in the world, and I wouldn't have to sell my soul to Jared.

Would Willow be willing to listen? Could Gloria be enticed by the possibility of some sleek, modern place where things aren't constantly in need of repair?

The greenhouse, rioting with color and scent and humid possibility, runs over my imagination. My aunt created that oasis. She won't leave it.

But—the thought is traitorous but distinct—it doesn't belong to her. It belongs to me and Willow, the legacy our mother left us, supported by royalties from her music. Gloria has no legal claim at all.

Except the very simple reality that G gave up everything—her career and a life of adventure—to come back to New York and take care of us after my mother died.

That little detail.

As for Willow, she flutters in and out between gigs, between relationships. Willow of the flowing golden curls. Willow of the delicate wrists. Willow of the million talents, who is wasting her life on chasing dreams that have constantly eluded her.

My sister drives me crazy. She drifts along like dandelion fluff, letting people take care of her. She makes terrible choices: the wrong jobs, the wrong men, the wrong apartments, everything. She's like the manic pixie dream girl on steroids, all light and sparkling charm and sweet sexiness wrapped up in disaster. Even her name. Willow Rose. A delicate little flower of a person, in need of love and protection and champions.

I mean, I love her. She seriously is a wildly talented musician, which plays nicely into that MPDG thing in the worst (best?) way. How could any man not fall in love with all that pretty hair and a voice like something that fell out of heaven and her energetic fiddling, which sometimes makes the world just turn colors, like flames that come right off the strings and drift around lighting fires in everyone listening?

And oh my God, can she cook! I have never known anyone to think so little about what to cook and just make these amazing things. It was a miracle when we were kids and our mother didn't want us to get fat, so she starved us. That sounds like an exaggeration, but it isn't. We were hungry all the time, and Willow could rustle up a half stick of butter with some spices and milk and a snap of her fingers to make a soup that sang. I wish I could cook like that, but I'm a city woman, born and raised. My fridge is filled with take-out containers.

I love her, and I get it—she was damaged too. But I also think it's time for her to drop the manic pixie thing and get on with her life. She's thirty-five. That's not going to play forever, and then what will she do?

Maybe it would be good for her to live somewhere else besides the apartment, to leave behind our ghosts and start fresh. There would be plenty of money for all of us, including Gloria.

At the corner, getting soaked, I'm indecisive. Should I head down there to talk to them about this, or maybe just say hello? I told Gloria I would come by while Willow was here. As one does.

I let the light change, looking first to the north and Harlem and the space I've created for myself, then west to the hospital, where my ex works. Sometimes, even now, I run by there. Just in case.

In case of what? I hear my therapist ask in a weary voice. *In case he walks out of the hospital and falls instantly in love with you? Sam, that's akin to emotional cutting, wouldn't you say?*

It was such a good line I fed it to the AI app, and at this moment, it brings into focus the hollow, pounding ache in my gut. For some reason, I go back to Eric, over and over, venting my sense of loss and grief over the other things in my life on him. If I do the emotional cutting there, with the man I thought I was going to marry, then I don't have to feel the pain over my dad. Or Asher. Or my mother, my therapist says, but I think that's overstepping.

I really didn't have much luck with the males of the species before Eric. I'm too strange and too weird looking for most guys, but I met

Eric at a race, a virologist who loved the fact that I could outrun him easily and bragged to all his brainy friends about my brains.

For my part, I was completely dazzled that this gorgeous Viking of a man fell for me. We were together four years, and I really believed we'd get married. Instead, after a trip to Vietnam, a trip I thought was really deep and beautiful, he left me and joined Doctors without Borders to go study Ebola and other terrible diseases.

That was almost three years ago. I was completely insane for a solid year. The kind of crazy girlfriend who makes a movie painful and funny and awful. I hate remembering it.

Not today.

I take a breath, pull out my phone—still eyeing the northward path to home—and punch the simple drawing that marks the AI I've been working on for over a year. "Hey, Suzanne," I say. "Do I run west by the hospital or south to visit my aunt?"

"Which one will make you feel better at dinnertime tonight?" she asks. Her voice is middle aged, a little bit deep, with highly educated undertones. It took months to find just the right sound, but this is really it. She always makes me feel calmer.

But she's never asked me this particular question, which is a success from a programmer's point of view. To keep her learning, I reply, "Good question."

"Thanks. What's the answer?"

"Definitely better to go see my aunt."

"Do that, then."

Chapter Seven

Willow

I'm in the kitchen, huddled over a bowl of deli tomato soup, when Samantha arrives. I have spent thousands of happy hours at the small table, eating whatever Gloria imported or had delivered, or practicing violin, or chopping herbs for my experiments. No one in the family likes to cook except me, and they think it an odd manifestation, like an extra toe or double-jointedness.

I'm enjoying the soup, which is deep tomato with hints of basil, thickly pureed with plenty of onion and garlic and some spice I can't quite name that gives it an exotic undernote. Sumac, maybe? Lime? Not sure.

When my sister bursts into the room, I find my shoulders tensing instantly.

"So you're here."

Sam is four years my senior and a full seven inches taller and carries the will and presence of a hurricane. Also, she has resented me since the day I was born, and nothing I've done since has done much to change her mind.

She's wearing her running gear, which shows off her skinny, long legs and broad shoulders. Her thick hair, the richest color of cinnamon, is pulled back in a short, messy ponytail. She looks pale, even for her.

I love her more than I am able to express, with no justification whatsoever, the curse of a younger sister. Long, long ago, in the days before my mother died, she could be completely magical, creating entire worlds for us to play in with our stuffed animals and dolls. Her attention turned on and off, but it was on often enough that I was trained to adore her. "Hi to you too, Sam. Gloria needs a house sitter."

She raises a brow. "Nothing to do with the flop of the album, huh?"

"Wow." I shake my head. "Couldn't you just say hi and leave my shaming for five minutes?"

She shrugs. "I'm not shaming you. It's just an observation."

I press my lips together, and to my utter fury, tears sting my eyelids. I could say that she didn't pick a reliable career, either, but I can't trust my voice, and honestly, she's been successful. Wearily, I say, "Not all of us are superstars at twenty."

"Mom was twenty-three."

I look at her. "I was talking about you."

She glances away, out toward the river. "Whatever. I'm sure you'll find a guy to rescue you soon enough."

I shake my head, defenses crumbling. Is she right? Is that how I live? From guy to guy? I definitely leaped when David dangled a record contract in front of me, but—

Stop. I'm not going to let her do this to me. "I really don't need your bitchiness, Sam."

"Where's Gloria?"

"In her bedroom, I think. Please go find her."

She pauses. "I was only kidding, Willow."

I sigh. "That's what people always say. It's really quite passive aggressive."

"Whatever."

As fast as she came, she whirls away, her feet creating busy noise even in running shoes. You'd think a runner would be light on her feet, but Sam sounds like a moose stomping over the wooden floors.

I ladle a spoonful of soup, which I automatically eat very carefully, even if Sam isn't in the room. She has a condition that makes it painful to hear people eat. I feel six years old, trying not to mind her sharpness, wishing she'd get the fuck over it already. I had no control over the adults who made me, nor did I have any over the father who deserted her when he'd found out his wife was cheating on him.

Shocking that a rock musician, on the road half the year, would cheat. I know *I'm* astonished.

The mental sarcasm is unbecoming and not accurate. I know lots of musicians in committed, long-term relationships. My mother, however, was never one to skip a delicious morsel just because there was cake at home.

I stare out the window at the drizzly day, feeling lonely. I should get in touch with some of my local friends. I pick up my phone and scroll through my email out of habit. Almost nothing is there, except one message.

My heart sinks.

The sender is Music Holidays around the World, and the header reads, *Great fit!*

Of course. In desperation two weeks ago, I applied at the travel company to see if I could at least get some travel out of the gig. A friend from Ren Faire days had sent me the link and recommended the people highly. She'd made good money with them but had met someone and was settling into a suburban life in Maine somewhere now, and she'd told them about me.

My thumb hovers over the email, and then I punch it quickly before I can chicken out.

Dear Willow,

I was so very pleased to receive your resume. I have several trips coming up for which you'd be a great fit, and I'd love to talk to you as soon as possible. Your main duties are not onerous, involving 1-2 classes per day to vigorous older adults with a passion for music, leaving you plenty of time for exploration on your own or with others in the group. The pay is competitive.

Please let me know when we might be able to talk.

Sincerely,
Marta Platten

PS The samples you included from your album were so wonderful I ordered the CD immediately.

Tears sting my eyes, and I shut the email app instantly, looking up to ease the emotion. I was feeling lost and desperate when I sent the application, but maybe if I get my feet under me here in the city, I won't have to take what essentially is a tour guide job.

Which wouldn't be so bad, except that I have always believed, all the way to my bones, that I was meant for something else.

All the more reason to double down on the competition.

Meanwhile, I need to get out of my head. Most of my friends here are also musicians or actors, people I met in high school at LaGuardia School of the Arts. A couple of them have made the big time—a dancer who has done well on Broadway, and an actor with a name so famous I try never to drop it, even though we were part of the same little group.

Most of us, however, are like me. Modestly successful in our fields, but always scrambling for the next gig, the next influx of cash. My mother's royalties used to cover a lot of my life, but they've dwindled dramatically the past few years. There's really only enough to cover the fees and upkeep on the apartment.

But I don't mind the life of a musician. Not everyone loves the insecurity of it, and I have to admit it gets old, but what can you do if that's what your very blood insists you're meant to pursue? Nothing feels like music does, and I can't imagine what my life would be like without it.

Empty. Not really a life at all.

In another room, either the dining room or the parlor with its long windows overlooking the street below, Gloria and Sam are arguing about something. I try not to pay attention, standing up to carry my dishes to the sink, and wonder what to do with the rest of the day.

Gloria appears at the kitchen door. "Will you join us, sweetheart?"

I follow her down the dark-paneled hallway to the parlor. It's smaller than the living room, with a pleasant fireplace and carved wood everywhere. The rain outside obscures the view, making it all gray and misty, blurring out the buildings in the distance. Sam is perched on the edge of a wingback chair that must be older than either of us, one leg flung over the other as it swings back and forth, a sure sign of irritation. Behind her on the wall are gatherings of paintings. One of my favorites, an evocative and colorful rendition of a Middle Eastern market, hangs right over her left shoulder.

"What's up?" I ask, curling up on the sofa. I pull a pillow over my middle.

Gloria gestures with one hand. "Why don't you share with Willow what you suggested to me?" Her voice is much too calm.

Sam sighs. "I want us to talk about selling the apartment."

"What?" I leap to my feet. "No!"

Gloria looks smug. She would never leave this place. "That's what I said."

As if she is the most long-suffering martyr in all of time, Sam sighs. "It's a dinosaur, you guys! Look around you. It needs so much work!"

"What the hell, Sam?" I'm eyeing the purple shadows beneath her eyes and suddenly remember when she first broke up with Eric. I left the Ren Faire band to come home and check on her, which ended up being one of the best things that ever happened to me, because it was on that trip home that I played a gig where I caught the eye of a music executive with some actual power to do something for me.

Which led to my album. And a relationship, and a nice stint in a great house in Malibu.

And getting locked out of that house.

Best *and* worst things that ever happened to me.

It was also one of the better times I've shared with my sister. In her loneliness, she let me in, let me cheer her up. I thought maybe we were overcoming the tensions of our childhood. No such luck. A year later, she was as mean as ever, shutting me out when I came to visit after her friend Tina got married.

She doesn't really deserve my attention, but old habits die hard. "Is something going on with you, Sam?"

She frowns irritably. "No. It's just time." She looks around the room. "It's a mausoleum."

"It's not your taste," Gloria says. "Which is fine, since you don't live here and haven't for more than twenty years. I'm with your sister: What's going on with you? You don't look good."

Sam ducks the hand Gloria reaches out and defensively smooths her hair, even though Gloria never even got close. The movement exposes her collarbone, which is perfectly defined, the skin dipping away from it on both sides. I frown. She's a bitch, but I'm also the only sister she has, and therefore it's my job to pay attention.

I say, "Why all of a sudden, right now?"

"It's not all of a sudden. I've been thinking about it for months."

"Why?"

"None of your business!" she bursts out. "I have my reasons, but I don't know why I have to share them with you."

Mildly, Gloria says, "Well, maybe because both of us actually *live* here and you don't."

"Willow lives in LA."

"Not anymore," I say.

They both look at me. "I thought you were house-sitting," Sam says.

"I am." I hold the pillow close to my chest, not wanting to get into the whole mess, throw blood in the water for my sister the shark. "I'm tired of LA, and I'm also moving back here. I miss New York. I miss my friends." I gesture, taking in the paintings, the carved fireplace, the big mirror that's gone smoky, the view of the rooftops out of the windows. "And I *love* this place."

Gloria's phone vibrates on the coffee table, which I'd love to say is an authentic antique, but it's just an ordinary glass-topped table with a dusty coffee-table book about my mother on it. She sneers from the front cover, her dyed-black hair chopped into a long shag, her guitar in front of her braless chest. I've seen the photo a million times, but for the first time, I realize that she was younger than I am now.

Gloria picks up her phone and turns off the alarm with her manicured fingernail, painted glossy coral. "I have to go. I have lunch plans and can't be late." She stands. "Willow and I are not interested in selling the apartment, Sam."

"It's not *yours*," Sam says furiously, glaring up at Gloria.

A vivid hush falls. There are things families never say, and in ours, this is one of them.

Gloria doesn't even flinch. For a long moment she stands where she is, imperious at almost five feet ten, her blue eyes sparking. Once upon a time, several New York agencies tried to get her to model, but she loved flying and thought models had boring jobs. The swoop of cheekbone and the clean jawline have stood her in good stead, because at seventy-four, she is still beautiful.

And as able to stand up for herself as ever. "I don't know what's going on with you, Samantha, but maybe if you're honest, we can find another way to help you." She waves. "See you later, Willow."

She's gone. I sit where I am, waiting for Sam to speak up. Instead, she grabs her paper cup off the table and takes a swig. "Wouldn't you like to live somewhere more modern?"

"No! I don't even know what you're talking about right now." A pulse of distress thuds against my throat. "I've lived lots of modern places. This is better."

Her mask slips for the slightest moment, showing weariness. "I saw my dad this morning."

"Yeah? I didn't think you were seeing him much these days." I try to resist, but she isn't the only one who can be mean, and I add, "Since he has that lovely new family and all."

She rolls her eyes in acknowledgment. "I hadn't seen him in a while."

I nod, waiting. Whenever her dad is involved, trouble follows. He has a gift for dangling things in front of her, then snatching them away, and I'm sure she sort of knows that, but we all have an Achilles' heel.

A kaleidoscope of emotions moves over her face, and she digs her hands into her hair at the temple. When she still says no more, I prompt, "And?"

"I don't know." She sighs, allows a tiny glimpse into her real feelings. "I just keep expecting him to be someone else."

"How's that going?"

To deflect, she asks, "What are you really doing here?"

"I'll tell you if you tell me what the hell is really going on with you." She stands. "Nothing."

I shrug and stuff my story deeper into my chest, even though I would really like to tell her the truth, that my life in LA was absolute crap at the end. I ran out there with such high hopes, riding on David's promises, choosing to not see or to ignore the fact that he really only had one value: money.

Talk about people who offer one thing and deliver another.

But Sam gathers herself. "If you're living here, I'm sure I'll see you more often."

"Will we?"

Again she rolls her eyes. "Don't be dramatic. I've gotta go get a shower."

I want to ask how she could be so mean to Gloria, but it's not that strange for her to be a bitch. I don't move as she lets herself out. Eloise leaps up into my lap and butts her head against my hand as I slump in my chair and look toward the rooftops. Her purr gives weight to my sense of homecoming.

The sky is a pale gray, the windows smeared with rain, and a shimmer of light flashes yellow, then white, against the glass from some invisible source. Inside, paintings my mother and Gloria collected, along with family photos—some professional ones, most of them snapshots and amateur favorites—line the walls. A carved mantelpiece frames the fireplace, and a mottled mirror hangs above it, reflecting the windows and the paintings and the ceiling. If I close my eyes, I can feel myself at five playing with the zoo of stuffed animals I adored, and at nine, my head pressed against the window as I wondered where souls went, if my mother could see me standing there. I am twelve, listening to Gloria's varied and sometimes-shocking guests laughing and trying to outdo each other with outrageousness. Everyone sat at her table—the opera singer from downstairs, and her flight attendant friends, and drag queens, and bankers, and art-gallery owners. More than one of them died of the scourge of HIV. Others survived. I played my violin for all of them and learned to tell a good story to earn my place at the table.

Home. It's so good to be home.

My mother bought the apartment with cash in 1978. The money was from her first album, a pop/rock/punk mix-up that sold modestly well. One song, "Write My Name Across the Sky," still plays regularly on radio stations around the country, though most of the rest of her work has slid out of the public eye.

Anyway, at the time, the nine-room, sixth-floor-with-a-garden apartment cost $85,000. I recently priced it on Zillow, and the equivalents were in the four-mill range or better. It has never been upgraded, so it's all original, the parquet floors and wainscoting and charming windows in bathrooms and skylights and of course the greenhouse, which is either the greatest selling point of all time or a big headache to be filled with somebody's leftover junk.

My mother's public persona was that of a bad, bad girl—Joan Jett meets Janis Joplin. She sang hard, loved hard, partied hard.

But she loved this place. At home, she was kinder, easier, quieter, especially during the periods when she was clean, which was more often than the press would have you believe. It was going back on the road, back to the hungry, hungry crowds, that sucked her under. She needed them, craved their attention, but she also couldn't really manage them or the demands of fame.

The apartment was her refuge and getaway. The building has always been filled with creative people: The ancient opera singer who still lives in Apartment 4-A; a professor in 2-B who wrote a sweet allegory that rocketed to the bestseller lists, freeing him forever from any kind of material concern; an artist who turned the master bedroom into a studio and played mournful classical music late at night right below us. Next door to us, sharing a wall to the rooftop garden, was a married couple in their eighties who'd escaped Europe after the war and spent the rest of their decades living like it could all end at any moment.

For me, the apartment is simply home. It's always here, reliable and peaceful. I don't know what's on Sam's mind, but there's no way I'd even think of selling. It's the only place I truly feel I belong.

Chapter Eight

Gloria

Every week for the past forty-five years, except for the sad four years it was closed in the early aughts, I have met with my friends at the Russian Tea Room. Depending on who was in town or who was flying or who had married, there was a fluctuating number of TWA flight attendants, all of us trained in the midsixties, when girls still had to quit when they turned thirty-two or married or gained too much weight. That last one took a while, but we managed to get the other rules changed in time for all of us to fly as long as we wished.

Today, there are only five left out of the thirteen we started with. Some of us have died, of course, and one is too frail to make the journey into the city anymore.

Once upon a time, it was a point of pride for me to walk the thirty blocks, enjoying the constitutional, which gave me the chance to work off my treats. Today, Jorge hails my cab, and I take a photo of him through the rain-dotted window, his figure smeared and regal, standing under the awning. A good shot for later, perhaps.

At the iconic tea room, I find three of my friends assembled around our table, a booth three-quarters of the way back, beneath one of the firebirds flying from the ceiling. It gives me relief simply to walk into the place—the reds and golds, the sense of a time long past, of my own history, lived here at these tables for so long. A thousand conversations I've had hang invisibly in the air around us.

"Good morning," says Miriam, the one of us who worked the longest, until just four years ago. She is wearing her usual crisp navy pantsuit. Her silver hair is short and tidy, her cheekbones giving her face as much beauty as it held in her twenties, when she'd reminded all of us of Sophia Loren. "You don't look as if you've slept much."

I slide into the booth, brush snow from my shoulders. "No."

Fran is next to me, a shrinking version of herself, growing tinier and tinier every year, her bones starved of nutrients for too many years. She looks ten years older than she is, too, her skin similarly starved, and she's had dentures for decades, all the price of what we now know is bulimia. "How was the trip to Antigua?" I ask.

She shrugs. "Fine. I just wish we'd stop traveling."

I pat her hand. "I know. We've done our miles, haven't we?"

On the other side of her is Dani, a vigorous woman who has slightly darkened the shade of red she dyes her hair but otherwise has kept up the fight against time with excellent results. Everything has been tucked and plumped and exercised to exquisite tone. If you passed her on the street, you'd think her midforties, and her ice-blue eyes still capture every man within a hundred miles. She's been married for decades to a very wealthy man who worships her. "I loved the slipper/slipper shot on Instagram."

"Thanks."

The knowledge of what we are all avoiding lies around us, thick on our shoulders as fog. "Is Angie coming?" I ask, turning off my phone.

"She hasn't said she wasn't," Dani says, sipping her coffee carefully. "She's the one who is going to freak out the most. She's waited a long time for a grandchild. The baby is due next month."

"Nothing is going to happen to any of you," I say firmly. "You've done nothing wrong. It's all on me, and I will take responsibility for it."

I know they're going to worry, but they truly have no reason. None of them carried stolen art or forgeries, and although they don't know it, they didn't buy lost masterworks either.

Which is not going to sit well with my old, old friends. I squirm a little, thinking of how to tell them the truth.

"Well, it's not like we didn't know what we were doing," Miriam interjects. "There's Angie."

We watch her cross the room, unhurried, graceful. In another tale, she would have been the duchess. In this one, she is ice blonde and patrician, wearing a St. John coat with three brass buttons and a cute flare at the hips. As she sits down, she signals the waiter and asks for a glass of rosé, which is her water of choice. "French, not Californian."

Then to us, she says, "This is a pretty pickle." Her voice is husky from years of smoking, which she gave up ten years ago when it became intolerably politically incorrect. "What are we going to do?"

Everyone looks at me. "Nothing," I say. "There is nothing that needs to be done right now. Once I figure things out, I'll let you know."

"What if our husbands divorce us over this?" Fran says.

"What if we go to jail?" Angie says sharply. "That would be slightly worse than divorce."

"I can't do jail," Dani says.

Miriam all but rolls her eyes. "None of us can 'do jail.' We'll figure things out. Just because Isaak was arrested doesn't mean we'll be implicated."

"Except Gloria," Fran says.

"Thanks for the reminder." I actually carried stolen and forged paintings, which at the time seemed like a thrilling caper, rather than an international crime. My stomach flips, but I still don't tell them they're off the hook, because that would mean confessing that the paintings they paid tens of thousands of dollars for were all nothing but sincere imitations. They're going to hate me.

I hate myself for it now, but back then it seemed like a big lark. Their husbands could afford it, and they thought they were getting away with something.

I pick up the menu. "Can we order before we start planning our doom?"

The waiter arrives as if he's been eavesdropping, which makes me remember that we need to be more careful.

The orders never really change—Angie chooses the caviar and blinis; Miriam loves the chicken salad in summer, beef stroganoff in winter; Fran has never learned to eat so has the appetizer salad; and Dani loves borscht and lamb dumplings, for which she saves calories all week. I'm usually very careful, but today, I'm in need of substance to ground me and get me through the challenges. "I'll have the kulebyaka."

He smiles at me happily.

"Separate checks," Fran says.

"Yes, dear, I remember."

As he hurries away, I take out my phone and illustrate. "Turn it all the way off. Not just airplane mode."

Dani narrows her eyes. "That's not paranoid or anything."

"It might be," I say, "but I had ads for Allbirds following me around all week after our discussion about them, so better safe than sorry."

"She's right," Miriam says. "I've been reading a lot about privacy issues. Phones are a big gray area."

With varying levels of reluctance, they all turn their phones off.

"Now," says Angie. "What exactly is going on?"

I lean in. "All I've been able to discover is that Isaak has been on Interpol's list for decades, and they must have finally found some evidence that linked him to a particular crime."

"Forgery?" Miriam asks archly, because she's the only one who knows the truth. She was burned once by a glorious forgery he'd painted of a Morisot, but it was only because she had a degree in fine arts before she started flight school that she figured it out. It wasn't that the painting lacked authenticity, but she spotted an error in the story of how the painting was found. "Or theft?"

"Theft. They found a Pissarro in his apartment."

Isaak's gift was for producing paintings that were exactly what an artist *might* have painted, and he made a brilliant living out of painting "lost masterpieces," such as the Morisot.

I rub my temple. Will the penalties for actual theft be higher than for the forgeries? He was—perhaps still is—one of the best forgers who ever lived. His downfall is that he was in love with original art, as well, and in a handful of cases, he couldn't let the originals go. Because nearly everything he copied or sold on the black market was art previously stolen by the Nazis, he felt it justified his choices.

And perhaps, in a way, it did. His mother, like mine, spent the war at the mercy of the Nazis—mine in France, his in Poland—and worse.

"Was he living in Rome?"

"Florence."

"The city of art," Fran sighs. "Of course that's where he'd be."

I exchange a glance with Miriam. Fran suffered a painful, long-term crush on Isaak, something she tried and failed to hide.

"Have you heard from him?" Angie asks.

"Not in years."

"I always thought you'd end up with him," she says, taking a sip of her wine.

"So did I," Dani says and touches her throat. "When the two of you walked into a room together, you could feel the fire thirty feet away."

I smile, touch her arm. "To be young again."

"That's not youth," Miriam scoffs. "That was chemistry."

I'm unexpectedly filled with the sense of him, all around me, his voice rumbling into my ear, his hands and smile, the smell of him— tobacco and spice and man. It was chemistry, certainly.

But I think, too, of our long walks on a beach or in a market, talking and talking, about ideas and books we'd read and history and time and everything. I'd never known anyone in my life who thought so much the same as I did. "It was more than chemistry," I say quietly.

"It was a long time ago," Angie says. "The point is, What are we going to do now?"

I can't help looking over my shoulder, but there's almost no one else in the restaurant. "I haven't had time to do any research, but I'm probably going to need a really good lawyer." I direct this to Dani, whose husband will know exactly whom I should call.

She nods.

"I'm not really sure what's going to happen, but if I have to leave New York, I called Willow to stay at the apartment."

"That's good," Miriam says. She butters a slice of bread meditatively. "We all should . . ." She pauses, chooses her words carefully. "Find new homes for old pets."

"What do you mean?" Fran asks plaintively.

"Never mind, dear," Dani says, patting her hand. "I'll tell you later."

Miriam means that everyone needs to get rid of the paintings on their walls. Some of which they might believe are the real McCoy.

It's complicated. "None of you need worry," I say, and it's true. All they've done is buy copies of supposed masterworks. I'm the one who trafficked in stolen art. And more. "You don't. For reasons I'd rather not get into."

Miriam knows the truth, that none of the paintings they own are originals. Shame burns in my cheeks—what seemed harmless back then now seems a really wretched betrayal, and I know they'll feel the same way.

At least for a little while. Surely they'll forgive me when they realize they won't be sent to jail.

The other three look at me with varying degrees of skepticism. I raise a hand, meant to be calming. "I've got this. I promise."

"Okay, now can we talk about something else?" Fran says.

"Oh," I say, "how about this? Sam waltzed in today and just announced that she wants to sell the apartment."

They're all properly aghast, and we spend an hour on children and grandchildren and nieces and dogs, as we always do.

I listen to their voices with a sense of bittersweet longing, a ghost of the hungers that are waiting for me. If I have to flee, I will miss them desperately.

Please, I offer up to whatever gods might be listening. *Let me stay.*

Chapter Nine

Sam

Jared Maloney's assistant sent me the time and location of our dinner meeting. I'm not familiar with the place, and it's a hidden spot with just a name on the door, nothing to indicate what it is. Inside, it smells of leather and grilling steak with an undernote of bourbon. As if that weren't enough branding, the chairs are heavy and gigantic, and the colors are all muted browns and greens, like an old-school steak house. It is, not ironically, a steak house. Meat, meat, meat. As the host shows me through the room, I pass knots of men in deep conversation, all of it presumably very important.

I only see two other women in the room as I'm seated in the over-size chair, which is not oversize for me because I'm tall enough to handle the space. My sister would look like a tiny doll, Alice lost among the giants. Jared has not yet arrived, and I order a sparkling water with lime in a highball glass, trying to compose myself.

He saunters into the room, stopping here and there to shake hands, clap a fellow on the shoulder, making a show of how important he is. I wish I'd been late to miss it, but he was probably waiting in the wings somewhere for me to arrive, so he would have made this show no matter when I got here.

Or maybe that's cynical.

I don't stand when he comes to the table. "Sorry, love," he says, as if he's British. "Traffic." He bends in to kiss my cheek, and I endure it. He slides into his chair. "Thanks for meeting me."

I nod.

The rest is up to him. All of it.

"So how are you, Sam?"

"Fine," I say. "You?"

"Good. We've had our best year ever, thanks to *Mirror Land*."

"It's a great game," I say without rancor, and I mean it. "Hannah Canter's work, wasn't it?"

"Her brainchild, for sure." His blue eyes sharpen. "Bet you wished you'd grabbed her when you had the chance."

I shrug. "She's an excellent game designer, but our styles would have clashed." She's a genius programmer, but she has a mild demeanor I would have run right over and, as often happens with the milder-mannered women, a taste for extreme violence, which is not part of my games. I sip my soda, carefully, as if it's strong, set it back down.

"Ah, the woman conundrum. Two women is one too many, am I right?"

"Not at all," I return, hiding my exasperation. "Hannah and I just see games differently."

He shrugs, leaning back to allow the waiter to place a brown drink in front of him. "Fair enough."

A silence falls between us, and I struggle to come up with a new thread, but he beats me to it, leaning forward on one arm to say, "I'm sorry about *Purple*."

The game that flopped six months ago. I thought we'd managed to bring out something completely fresh and original, and instead it just fell flat. Players found it slow. "Win some, lose some."

"But you haven't had a win in a long time, have you?"

Damn. I'm not even going to get a meal out of this, am I? "Why don't you just get down to business, Jared?"

"Let's slow down, have a drink, a good dinner."

I rub a spot over my eye that's starting to ache. I'd rather not prolong the misery, and I've never understood why you need a whole dinner to talk about business anyway. Again, I miss Asher, his smooth manners and calm ways. He was the one who managed the social side of things.

But I'm the only one who can save Boudicca now, and I take a breath, channel my aunt Gloria, who could make friends with a snake.

Ha, snake, I think, smiling to myself—and an image flashes over my mind of a pink snake in a business suit. For a moment, I let it float there as I stare sightlessly at the menu in my hands.

I flash on the steely way she looked at me before she left, her laser beam eyes looking right through me, as always. I hear myself spit out, *It's not yours!* A coil of shame winds up my throat.

Then I'm back, here, with Jared. "I'd love to split an appetizer, if you're up for it."

"Sure. Nothing too carb heavy, if you don't mind."

I read the entries, and it's an actual old-school steak house, with olives and stuffed celery and marinated herring in the offering. "So vintage!"

"Right?" He grins. "I love it. I grew up in Kansas, and you can take the boy off the farm, but you can't take the farm out of the boy. This was the height of fancy for our town."

I raise my head, and I can see through to the kid he must have been—bespectacled, like Asher, a misfit with his brain, not great with girls, his bedroom papered with posters of Billie Thorne. At least Asher was born in New York, a world where misfits come in a variety of forms. "Did you always know you'd come to the city?"

"Yeah, way back. I didn't really know it would be games, but life takes you all kinds of places, right?" He pauses. "Would you be up to giving the steak tartare a try?"

"Why not? And some olives, please."

We order the appetizers and entrees, and when the waiter departs, I feel myself struggling to make small talk, then remember his favorite subject. "My mother would have loved the food in this place."

He brightens as if a spotlight shines from his eyes. "What would she have ordered?"

"I don't know that much, really, but the redder the meat, the better." A memory surfaces of the three of us, my mom and Willow and me, along with Gloria, somewhere in Manhattan. Willow and I drank Shirley Temples, while the adults drank gin and tonics. "She loved steak Diane."

He leans closer. "What else?"

I think back, back, back. I spent so much time angry with her that it's hard to remember things like that. "Milkshakes. Peaches. Doughnuts." I think of us at a bakery on the Lower East Side somewhere, gritty back then, and a white bag full of fresh doughnuts, glazed and chocolate frosted, and even apple fritters. I smile. "She really loved doughnuts."

"Yeah? That's cool." He shifts his napkin on his lap, and I can feel the energy it takes for him to rein in his curiosity. "How'd you like the party?"

For a few more minutes, we make small talk. The waiter brings the appetizers, and I suddenly realize steak tartar is going to be right in the middle of my texture revulsions. Hummus, oatmeal, all those mushy but slightly grainy things. I'll pretend to eat it. Pretending has carried me a long way.

What would Asher do? I think of his genial expression, his calm way, but it doesn't help ease the nervous anticipation tangling in my gut. "Why don't you tell me what's on your mind, Jared?"

"All right." He is remarkably quiet as an eater, and I relax a little bit. "I've been watching Boudicca for a couple of years, and I don't mean to be a bastard, but it's clearly in trouble. You've struggled since before Asher left, but it's been more obvious since the breach."

I choose an olive from the plate. "Common knowledge."

"What happened to you two? I expected you to be married by now, with a couple of cute kids wearing glasses."

"The relationship was always platonic." At least until it wasn't.

He cocks his head. "Was it, though?"

"We've been friends since third grade," I say. "I was practically engaged to someone else for over a year."

"Sorry." He studies me for a long minute. "I got it wrong, I guess."

Irritation buzzes along my neck, spreads around my forehead. "What do you want, Jared?" I know I'm desperate, but he doesn't. Bravado has carried the day more than once, and I hope it will again. "I am not going to let you absorb Boudicca, and you must know that, so what do you propose?"

"Fair enough." He dabs his napkin over his fingers. "I'd like to be a silent partner. Bring in some cash, get the company over the hump. You'd maintain control, but I would get a voice on the creative side."

I want to reject it instantly—even the thought of him messing with my ideas makes me feel homicidal, and our tastes are not at all the same. But I don't have that luxury any longer. "How much of a silent partner? And how much of a voice?"

His shoulders are still entirely relaxed when he says, "I want fifty percent and final veto on any major project."

I roll my eyes. "You know I won't take that."

"I knew you'd say that," he says, pointing a finger at me. "But have you thought about why? What would you really be losing?"

"My company!"

"But you wouldn't. It's still yours. You still develop the games you want to write, but the cash will mean you can bring more people in to get the coding done."

"Why the veto?"

"You've made some errors in judgment," he says unflinchingly. "*Purple* should never have gone to market the way it was. It needed more time and more depth."

He's not wrong. I was anxious to get it out, to get some better cash flow going, and overlooked some red flags. It was humiliating and frustrating. I knew better, and now I'm paying the price. My headache beats a tempo over my left eye, but I don't say anything.

"I'll send a formal offer via email," he adds, "but I'm guessing you will need quite a substantial sum to carry you into a new era." He names a number that is far above what I would have expected.

It's daunting. It's depressing.

It is possible he is quite correct.

And yet. How can I give up the one thing that belongs completely to me? Give up without a fight? "That's a very generous offer, Jared, but I just—"

"Take some time," he says. "Think it over. Talk to Asher and see what he advises."

As if I could just pick up the phone and call him, no big deal. "I'll think about it," I say, but something in me howls in protest.

There has to be another answer.

Chapter Ten

Gloria

After lunch with my friends, I stop by my local church to bring some day-old bread I picked up for the soup kitchen and meet with a friend I have there who can maybe help me get a passport in a new name. I walk home, aching with the possibility that I might really have to flee my life here. I might lose this very walk, which I take nearly every day. My chest is filled with anxiety, my mind with a swirl of thoughts, regrets, hope, despair.

Something is going on with Sam, and Willow is like a pillow without its stuffing. They need me right now, and if I have to leave, who will they lean on? Will their always-volatile relationship burn up, leaving them with no one at all in their corners?

When I arrive home, Willow has gone out. She's left a note: *Don't wait up. :-) Out with friends.*

Worry loops around my chest, raises my blood pressure enough that I can feel it pulsing in my throat. I take a breath, let it go. It won't do to make myself sick.

I shed my slacks and blouse and trade them for a pair of ancient silk pajamas. The fabric is cool and soft against my skin, making me remember pleasures I've not had much of in recent years, maybe won't again. I only loved one man, Isaak, and it took me nearly a decade to get over him. Men are a lot of trouble, honestly, and unlike many of my friends, I find no need to have one in my house, though I miss having one in my bed now and then. For quite some time, I had a lovely arrangement with a film critic in 3-C, but he died a couple of years ago, and I haven't bothered to replace him. A young couple with an air of lifelong entitlement moved into his apartment.

Never mind.

Until I get new papers, there's little I can do to move the process along. In my uneasiness, I head for the greenhouse and keep my hands busy with the work of tucking geranium slips into potting mix so they'll be ready for spring.

My mind is free to wander where it will. Rain patters down on the glass roof, an appealing music, healing, along with the notes of soil and greenery in my nose. My thoughts wander to Sam and her tense, faintly hostile bid to sell the apartment. My elder niece has never walked easily in the world—she's prickly and easily offended and yet so very deeply vulnerable to hurt. I worry about her, far more than Willow, who has always walked an easier path. Sam didn't look good today—pale and tired—and I wonder if there's a problem with the business. Snapping lower leaves from the stalk of a clipping, I make a mental note to google it.

Once the clipping is tidily tucked into its little pot, I brush my hands off and pick up my phone. The light is excellent, pale and soft, tinged with green, and I focus on the ruffled edge of the leaf, the blue tone of the glass behind it. A good shot for a gardening-day story. It calms me.

I know Willow is bewildered that I'm not bustling around to get ready for a trip, and I haven't even come up with a story to tell her. It's just that I needed her to be here, in case. In case I am arrested. In case everything truly does fall apart.

I open my Instagram account to post the photo. A tiny bump tells me there's a private message on Instagram, from a name I don't recognize, which is not at all uncommon. Mostly, they're new followers who just want to connect a little bit. I answer all of them if I possibly can, honoring the whole purpose of communication. I touch the name and it opens.

Ma bichette, do not worry.

As if I've been doused in icy water, my limbs freeze. *Ma bichette* was Isaak's endearment for me. The wildness of emotion that's been running under my every moment now swells and overflows, filling my eyes with tears of . . . what? Longing? Loss? Remembrance?

Hope?

I stare at the single line.

Ma bichette.

How can I so suddenly, fiercely miss someone who hasn't been in my life in decades?

But if he's in prison, how can he write to me? How did he find me?

I tap on the account name, David Levy. The page shows a seascape in the profile photo. The bio is in Hebrew, which I can't read, and it's marked private. David Levy is about as ordinary a name in Israel as John Smith is in the US.

I return to the direct message, tap reply, and type quickly, *Who is this?*

There is no answer, no matter how long I stare at it.

Over lunch, Angie said, "How did we get into this mess anyway? What were we thinking?"

Dani rolled her eyes. "We were not *thinking*, sweetheart."

I hadn't been thinking. I'd been feeling. Feeling the sun on my skin on the sparkling coasts of North Africa. Smelling the spice and heat of the markets, hearing the call of voices in a dozen languages, feeling the thrill of discovery and the delight of freedom.

Oh, how free we felt!

In those days, there were not nearly as many flights overseas, not a dozen carriers sending multiple planes per day to every port in the world. When we flew to Casablanca or Cairo or Hong Kong or some other faraway place, we often spent two or three days on a layover, waiting for the next scheduled flight.

For most of us, it was the very best part of the job. The airline paid for a room for us to share in a nice hotel, and we all knew the best bars and restaurants. Pilots and businessmen were eager to take us out, buy us martinis in hopes of a tumble, which many of us were happy to indulge. It wasn't the myth of a swinging stewardess we indulged but our own appetites, liberated by travel, by the heady power of freedom.

So much freedom! It was an astonishment to me, coming as I did from a small, provincial town in upstate New York, that little town where my Parisian mother shrank into an embittered pickle of herself.

One of my favorite routes was the New York to Casablanca trip, which gave us a three-day pause in that most storied of cities. I adored the movie with Humphrey Bogart, and I couldn't believe it when I was actually scheduled for a flight there. The first time, I was giddy all the way over the Atlantic, for once not minding the hands of businessmen wandering too freely over my backside as I served their drinks and steaks, chattering with my friend Nancy in the galley as we prepared the first-class meal of steak au poivre and served champagne and cocktails. I couldn't sleep at all, and when we landed, late on a Wednesday afternoon, I couldn't wait to get out and see it.

See it, eat it, drink it up. I gobbled up the world then, eager for whatever it wanted to offer me. Outside in the dusty, hot street, with the music of voices and commerce and cars honking and motorbikes roaring and men shouting and people calling back and forth, I saw a monkey running along the edge of a stall and stopped dead, laughing.

Alive.

Here I am, Mama.

She would so have loved a life like this, full of travel and new sights and the possibilities of adventure! As the daughter of a wealthy middle-class family, her father a professor, her mother an opera singer until her marriage, she'd been primed to expect it. My mother had been a brilliant pianist with her eye on the stage and both the talent and the beauty to pull it off.

Instead, the war had marched into Paris. By the time it was over, she leaped eagerly into the arms of my father, whose provincialism was obscured by his dazzling good looks and her desperate need to escape. She lived the rest of her life in a farm town of nine hundred, teaching piano and slowly souring into a bitter caricature of herself who smoked herself into an early grave at the age of forty-one.

She breathed into her daughters, me and Billie, the urgency of never settling, of dreaming a big dream and following it. She gave us her old-world manners and taught us the value of good looks and made us both promise to never, ever marry for comfort.

Imbued with her dreams, I applied at TWA as soon as I was old enough. And on the streets of Casablanca one sunny day in 1975, I bought a brightly patterned scarf and sampled *kefta* and mint tea and buttery *harcha* in the market and soaked in all the sights and sounds and smells of that fabled city. I wrote a postcard to my sister, who shared an apartment with four other people as she tried to find her place as a musician.

For Mom, I wrote.

It was perhaps a year later, when I'd learned the best restaurants and most interesting alleys, that we arrived after a rather turbulent flight. All of us were exhausted but overwrought. A terrible crash at JFK just a few weeks before had left us soberly aware of just how dangerous the job could be. My nerves were taut, and I wanted a martini and a good meal as soon as possible.

My girlfriend Nancy and I got ready for an evening out. I wore a turquoise silk sheath, sleeveless, custom made on a trip to the East, with a loose white scarf draped around my neck and shoulders. I knew I looked good as I entered the hotel lobby, poised and polished and world traveled, and carried that assurance with me.

I saw the most extraordinary man standing nearby the door as if he were waiting for me. Not particularly tall but beautifully proportioned, with wide shoulders and a nipped waist shown off in a tropical white linen suit. He had beautiful hands, the hands of an artist, long and brown and well tended, with oval nails and strong palms, not that I saw all that right then. I saw his dark, glittering eyes and his slow, almost invisible smile as he watched me enter the room. He was both intensely masculine and urbanely polished. European, I thought then.

Israeli, as it turned out. He reminded me of Leonard Cohen, whose new album had been playing constantly in my apartment and upon whom I had a massive crush. I felt him watching me, and at the right moment, I looked at him long enough to let him know I was intrigued.

He didn't take the bait, and I simply kept walking with my girlfriend. We walked to a restaurant not far from the hotel and sank gratefully into our meal. A band played music, and a few couples danced. Nancy and I spoke little, until she said, "I think I'm done flying."

"Because of the turbulence today? That just happens, Nance, you know that."

She speared her steak and looked out over the crowd. "No, it was the man in 8-A. Mr. Harris." A brunette with a staggeringly good figure, Nancy was a magnet for the type of traveler who believed stewardesses were just a version of Playboy Bunnies, ready for a tumble with just about anybody.

"Ugh." I rolled my eyes. "He did give you a pretty hard time."

"He stuck his hand all the way up my skirt." She shuddered. "*All* the way."

"I'm sorry. We should have cut him off sooner."

"That's no excuse. Other men were drunk, or at least tipsy, and none of them did that. It shouldn't be allowed. What gives him the right?"

The airline, I thought, but I didn't have to say it. She knew. We all did. The tone of advertising offered stewardesses up on a platter with slogans like *Come Fly with Me* and *Ready When You Are*. I touched her arm. "I'm sorry. It's humiliating."

"It is," she said. "And I am not willing to put up with it anymore."

"But what will you do?"

"I don't know. Find Gloria Steinem and join the movement."

"Burn your bra?"

She laughed, gesturing. "That might be a little dangerous. I wouldn't want to hurt anyone!"

We both laughed.

"Pardon me, ladies. May I interrupt?"

I looked up to see the man from the hotel. Up close, his eyes were green and mesmerizing, his face a little more rugged than it first appeared. He had a scar along one cheekbone and a wide, generous mouth. My skin rippled, head to toe. I met his gaze.

"Will you dance with me, mademoiselle?"

I was already sliding out of the booth. On the dance floor, he kept a respectful distance, his hands in their proper places, which I appreciated more than usual after the conversation with Nancy. It was wearing at times to fend off the advances of passengers. "My name is Isaak Margolis," he said. "What's yours?"

"Gloria Rose."

He smiled, very faintly. "Lovely. Where are you from, Gloria? What do you do? Tell me everything about you."

His voice was deep and smooth, words lilting with an accent I didn't recognize. "New York City," I said. "I'm with TWA."

"A stewardess?" he said. "Really." He inclined his head, as if this was a surprising confession. "You seem . . . much more than that."

"More? Whatever do you mean?"

"You're not a shallow woman."

I laughed. "How in the world could you possibly know that?"

A flash crossed his face, and he stepped ever so slightly closer. "You have intelligence in your face. In your eyes." He looked at my mouth, and it was as intimate as a kiss. "I saw it in your bearing at the hotel."

I raised a brow. "Perhaps I only think of silks and capturing a wealthy husband."

His fingers moved slightly, respectfully, along my waist. "No, I do not think those are your goals. You want freedom."

It startled me, that he could see into my soul so clearly. Lightly, I tossed off, "That's the dream of every man, isn't it? A woman who hungers for freedom?"

His wide mouth cocked upward, only on one side. "I suspect most wish for quite the opposite."

"A servant?"

His shrug was so very continental. Again, that shiver from eyebrows to toes, back and front. I felt myself spellbound, as if he'd woven invisible ropes around my body. To shake it off, I straightened and asked lightly, "And you? What do you do? Are you the rich husband I seek?"

He laughed softly. "Afraid you will be disappointed on that score."

"Husband or rich?"

His gaze caught and held mine, and our legs brushed. "Neither."

"Are you married?"

"No." He swung me slightly, and I responded to the spin, and he caught me on the way back. "I'm an art dealer. From Tel Aviv."

"Israeli?"

"Yes, does that surprise you?"

"Not at all." In fact, I didn't really care where he was from. The chemical stew of our bodies burned at an incandescent temperature. He smelled intensely masculine, some sort of heady aftershave and sweat and skin. I did not look away from his green eyes, lashed so heavily they softened the harshness of his face. When he stepped closer, smoothly bringing our bodies into contact, it was as if an actual current connected us.

It rattled him. I could tell. "Your perfume is extraordinary," he said. "What is it?"

"I'm not wearing perfume," I said, eyeing his mouth and moving my body closer. "That's only skin."

"Perhaps I should deliver you back to your friend before the air around us ignites."

"Perhaps you should," I said, but it was the last thing I wanted.

Instead, he took me to his room, and we had the most explosive sex of my life. Intense, sweaty, fall-off-the-bed sex. Everything from the sensual way he kissed to the knowledgeable way he moved his hands on my skin was at least a few steps beyond anything I'd imagined it could be, and when we lay in the dark, sweating and naked, our breath returning slowly, he said, "I have never had sex like that, ever."

"You're lying," I said, with a laugh.

"I am not." He rested a palm on my belly. "But I hope to find out it can be even better."

Like a moth to a flame, I flew, right into the incendiary blaze.

Chapter Eleven

Sam

The next day, I have a headache from tossing and turning all night, but I pull myself together and head down to my Brooklyn office anyway. Looking at the small, loyal crew I've assembled over the years, I think about Jared's offer, about the failure of *Purple*, and about the games we have in development now, none of which are going to bring the deliverance needed.

It's not a big company, only twenty of us. Last year, I lost three coders to pregnancy and attrition and two more to moves west, but many of the others have been with me for nearly twenty years. Looking at them, working in an open-concept space, some singly, some in groups of two or three, I realize there isn't a single person under thirty, and however much I try to keep the numbers even, there are always more men than women.

The card for the young woman at the party is in my pocket. I think about her youth and eagerness, her desire and belief in that Shining Future. Maybe she can help. I dash off an email asking her to come in and talk to me.

I need to do more of that. More shuffling. More exploring of new ideas. More—everything.

Some of it will cost money.

But not all of it. Taking out a large notebook, I start brainstorming ways to freshen the labor pool without spending money. Interns are one way to start, but maybe it's not so much age and talent as a need for fresh ideas. I call my assistant into my glass-paneled office. "Jenny, let's schedule a meeting for next week, all hands."

She taps her tablet. "Tuesday at nine a.m.?"

"Great."

"Are you feeling all right, boss?" she asks. "You're looking a little under the weather."

Why do people ever ask that? "I just have a headache. No big deal."

"I'll bring you some tulsi tea."

"Great, thanks." I flip a new page in the notebook and write, *Incentivize new game ideas, ask for brainstorming new ways to do things.* I pause for a moment. *Be honest,* I write, *and ask for honesty in return.* I need to let my coders and designers be totally real with me. I haven't always done that—again, that was a role Asher took on, and I've not been able to step into his shoes the way I'd like. It's very difficult for me to listen to criticism.

But without it, without my openness to the discomfort, Boudicca will go under. I can't give up until I've explored every option.

By midafternoon, the headache sends me home. It's gone far beyond a tension headache and blasted right past the ibuprofen I took, and just after lunch I'm forced to give up, handing the day over to my assistant. She gives me a wry smile. "Everything will be all right without you for a day or two, boss."

Now, I've given in to my favorite silk pajamas, a luxurious habit I picked up as an adolescent under Gloria's sensual tutelage, and a schleppy sweater that is my own contribution, and I'm curled up in my apartment eating ice cream. I should really make a run to the market, since there's almost nothing in the kitchen except coffee and a stale box of Cheerios.

And ice cream. I run a lot, affording me plenty of my favorites. Ben & Jerry's Cherry Garcia is my poison of choice. Sometimes I cheat with Half Baked, but that's rare, and tonight, I need comfort food. It's raining steadily, making the open layout of the rooms feel cold, even when I crank up the heat.

The cold is the one downside to the space. I wrap myself up in a blanket and enjoy the other aspects—the enormous windows with a view of treetops, bare at the moment, but they're beautiful all summer and fall. The kitchen is up-to-the-very-minute modern, with full-size appliances and gleaming granite countertops. Brushed-steel lights hang down over the breakfast bar and the range.

Not that I cook. But I'm pretty sure that one of the reasons Eric fell for me was that he was smitten with my kitchen on sight. He loved experimenting with all kinds of cuisines.

The apartment is the exact opposite of Gloria's, my gift to myself at age twenty-two when the game sold so many copies, a badge of honor.

Like my mother buying her place, I think now, for the very first time. How could I never have seen that before? Billie's purchase was even more bold than mine, a single woman buying a place on her own—not the easiest thing in those days.

A worm of distaste squirms through me as I remember what I said to Gloria this afternoon—that it isn't hers. Technically, it isn't, but it *is*, because she's lived there for more than twenty-five years. My mother died in 1994, and Gloria moved in to take care of Willow and me. My mother didn't always do the best job with that.

My comment was a meanness she didn't deserve, and I honestly can't believe I said it.

The story of my life: blistering someone with my fury, only to regret it later. Shame lodges under my ribs, rough and painful. Somehow I'll have to make it up to her.

A text dings on my phone. It's my friend Tina. Wanna FaceTime? Baby is asleep.

YES! I pick up my tablet and balance it on my knees. In a moment, she rings through, and I open the app to see her big-eyed face, one of my favorites in the world. "Hey!" I cry. "It's so good to see you!"

She runs a hand through her loose, greasy hair. "As you see, this is the super-polished me. I've got no makeup on and can't remember the last time I had a shower."

"I wouldn't care if you had smears of axle grease on your face, sweetheart." I gesture with my arms. "As you see, I'm also in glamour mode."

She peers into the screen. "I'm a fine one to talk, but are you okay? You don't look good."

"A headache. Not sleeping that well." I shake my head. "Still struggling with business issues, but it's nothing to worry about. How is motherhood?"

"I know I'm a mess, but oh my God, Sam, he's the best baby in the world. So funny and cheerful and adorable."

Jay is almost three months old, a round little creature with his mother's giant sparkling black eyes and his father's thick black hair and a toothless grin that makes my ovaries hurt. "I'm so glad."

"I miss you," she says and touches the camera with a fingertip. "I'm making do with the other moms, but they're just not my people."

I am so lonely it's like acid on my skin. Tina left and Asher stopped talking to me, and they were pretty much my entire world after Eric, but I'm not going to drop that in her lap. She's as happy as I've ever seen her. I force myself to say, "Maybe you'll run into somebody working on a doctoral thesis about game theory who also knits the perfect afghan." She's a big knitter, a hobby I admit bewilders me.

"Maybe." She laughs. "How's your world?"

"My sister is in town, and I stopped by to say hello."

"Really."

"Well, kind of." An ice pick stabs through the top of my skull down through my neck, and I wince, slapping my hand to my neck in defense. "Whoa. Sorry about that. I did stop in to see Gloria about some things, and Willow was there. Also—" Another stab, this one so sharp it feels like broken glass.

"You okay?"

I blink hard. "Fine. Have you talked to Asher at all?"

She nods, and there's something hesitant in the gesture.

"What?" I ask, my heart freezing. "Is he getting married too?"

"No, no. I don't even know if he's dating. He hasn't said. But he's up for an Origins Award. Didn't he tell you?"

A sudden sting of tears fills my eyes, and embarrassed, I look away. "No. I saw him at a party for a new app, and he didn't say a word."

"I hate this, for both of you. I'm mad at him for being so stubborn, and I'm mad at you for letting it go. You guys have been friends for decades! And I don't like either one of you being so alone. You need to fix it!"

"It's not up to me," I say, plucking at the edge of my sweater sleeve. I haven't told her everything that happened, out of respect for my longer relationship with Asher. She only knows that we had a falling-out after her wedding, now just over a year ago. "He wants to keep his distance, so fine. Let him."

"You're cutting off your nose to spite your face," she says, one of the proverbs she loves. She has a million of them, which I suppose will be great tools for motherhood. "He's your best friend."

"No, *you* are my best friend."

"He was there first."

True. We met in third grade and bonded immediately over our geekhood, which led to creating a very successful video game ten years later, one of the first with a devout following of girls. The main character, Aline Alice Bright, was our dual creation, and she made us both quite wealthy.

And now I've fucked up both the friendship and my part of the business. My headache slams harder.

Tina says, "I wish you'd tell me what really happened."

"I know. I just can't . . . betray him." What happened to us is private, a thing just between us, so intimate that it would just be wrong to share it with another person, even Tina. A stab of pain goes through my eye. "I hate to say it, love, but this headache is killing me."

"No worries. I just heard Nuri come in. Text me and tell me how you are tomorrow, okay? I'll worry about you."

"Promise!" I kiss my fingers and wave them at her, and she does the same. Holding the phone, I fall sideways on the couch.

Asher. It was sex, the thing that ruined everything. After thirty years of being strictly friends, we slept together during the highly romantic week of Tina's wedding in Hudson. I still have no idea why we tumbled over the line, except that maybe both of us were tired of being the single friend at the dance.

It was also . . . something else. I close my eyes, rubbing my forehead, and remember that moment.

Asher wore red, along with the other groomsmen, and it set off his pale skin and dark eyes. I'd seen him in formal wear before, of course, but he'd been volunteering at Big Brothers, playing a lot of basketball with the kids, and he'd taken on a sheen of health, maybe a little muscle, his cheekbones tan from being in the sunshine. He wasn't wearing his glasses, which I like, actually, but it made his whole face more . . . accessible. Right before the declaration of "You are now man and wife," I glanced over, and he was looking at me. He smiled, very slightly, and I thought, *How have I never realized how hot he is?* The recognition swept away my lingering broken heart, along with anything to do with anyone but Asher. And me. Me and Asher.

Even now, I can feel that recognition in my belly, my thighs, as if the chemistry between us had suddenly switched *on*.

I close my eyes against my headache, trying to make myself get up and take some ibuprofen. Instead, I fall asleep, thinking of three days of happiness that ruined absolutely everything.

Chapter Twelve

Willow

After feeling so horrified over the music teacher / tour guide offer, I've put out the word to my local friends that I'm up for any kind of short gig. I need time to finish the piece for the contest, but I also need an influx of cash, and the more I'm out there, the more chances I'll have to find something satisfying.

I'm known for Celtic fiddle and electronica, but my training was broad enough that I can do almost anything. A friend is playing at a pub in Brooklyn and says there might be people there who know about work, but maybe it would just be nice to get out and play. She says she'll give me fifty dollars, and it's enough to get me moving.

I wash my hair and let it dry at its wildest, then dress myself up in an oversize white peasant blouse and a silk patchwork skirt that I found at a Ren Faire a few years ago. Also my lucky boots, of course, which belonged to my mother and fit me like Cinderella's slippers. The heels make an agreeably solid noise as I walk to the 81st Street station to catch the C train. It's busy, and I'm lucky to find a seat. A plump middle-aged woman knits on one side of me, and a guy in leather from head to toe nods his head to his earphones. I hold my violin on my lap.

It's been months and months since I played in public. The album was released early last year to a great thudding silence, and for a few months I was embarrassed and didn't want to show my face, and then things went downhill with David, who blamed *me* for the spectacular failure instead of all the dramas that were happening in the world right after that.

David. My mouth twists as I think of him, but mainly because I'm annoyed with myself. He was too old for me, in his midforties when we met, and kind of corporate in his dress and attitudes. I knew that, going in, but it was thrilling to be admired so deeply, and he treated me beautifully until he didn't, and he did have power, the power and resources to help me get my album made and out into the world. He invited me to live with him in his Malibu house, all glass and ocean views, and I walked right into the lion's den under my own power.

Because he was also controlling. At first it was subtle, but over time it became more and more overt. I found myself disappearing, unable to leap until the album came out, unable to break free until I found myself.

In most families, growing up to get married and have a family is the norm, but neither my mother nor Gloria believed in marriage. I think Gloria had a grand love affair with a man she doesn't talk about much, but she never married him, and although my mother briefly married Sam's dad, that was the extent of her long-term relationships.

I've also managed to keep myself unentangled. David was the anomaly—he just promised so much!

And proved himself to be a total dick when my album didn't thrive. We'd started having trouble by then anyway, as I found subtle ways to resist and reassert myself. When he threw my things out, I was as relieved as I was unsurprised.

And yet here I am, riding the train to Brooklyn to play a gig with an old friend for pennies. Pennies I need.

I toss my hair out of my face and watch the lights go by as the train emerges out of the dark into the evening. I am a musician. Musicians play.

I miss it, playing for people. It's one thing to play for myself, to let out the music that's singing through me, to show up and hold my instrument, give it the respect of practice.

But music is meant to be shared. It's communication. The music itself taking life through an instrument or a voice, then reaching into the hearts and bodies of other people, and coming back. I never feel so alive as when I'm playing for people, with them. My heart lifts a little.

My first memory is about music. My mother was writing a song at the piano, in a room that would have been a bedroom anywhere else but was a music room here. She kept all manner of musical things there, a piano and flutes and finger bells, a guitar and a violin, and even a set of conga drums she sometimes used to pound out rhythms. It was my favorite room in the house, and I knew it was hers too. When she was home, I hung around the edges of the room, hoping to catch her eye.

The windows looked south, sunny during the day, full of sparkling lights at night. That afternoon, a bar of light fell through the glass, making an elongated yellow square on the floor and my mother's hands. She sat at the piano, one hand working through a series of notes on the keyboard, over and over, while the other scribbled notes on a piece of paper propped up on the music rack. She hummed under her breath, *Lala-laLA, mmalala.* Paused, ran through a series of notes on the keys. Wrote something down, came back to the keys, singing under her breath.

I sat in an oversize burgundy velvet chair that I thought of as the Grandmother because of the way she held me. I played with a doll but mostly watched my mother, listened to her running through the notes over and over. *La-la-la-la-lala-la-LA!* Never quite right. I climbed down and stood beside her, waiting while she ran through the sequence. Then I brought my finger down on the right key. "That one," I said.

She frowned, then played through it again, using first her notes, then mine. Mine were right, and I waited for her recognition.

"How did you know that, Willow?"

I shrugged.

She scooted over and swept me up to sit beside her, a thrilling move. "Let's try something, shall we?" She played a series of notes, and I heard the building tension, unfinished when she stopped. "What's next?"

I heard it in my head but didn't know the places on the keys. I sang instead. "La la la."

She smiled. It was an expression we didn't see from her very often, but I knew it was good. I knew it was for me, and I would have done anything to see it again.

All these years later on the train, I can feel the pleasure of her approval, but what I felt more was the sound of the right note, the note she kept missing. She told the story over and over, the discovery of her prodigy.

Not such a prodigy now, I think, but that's the sad part of every prodigy's story, isn't it? Once you're no longer eight years old, playing Verdi, you're just another violinist. Which I'd made peace with until David stirred up my ambitions all over again.

Or maybe that's just a convenient excuse. I can't blame my ambition on him. Like my mother, like my sister, even like Gloria—who inspired my mother's song with her big career, her desire to stay unencumbered, and is still building fame at seventy-four—I'm driven. The family code is ambition, which is not the most comfortable quality if you're female.

At the pub, the crowd is substantial. I've never been here before, and it's much better than I expected, a very big space with a raised corner dais that's set up for the band. I ask the bartender, a round woman in her forties with snapping black eyes, for Paige, and she smiles. "She's in the back over there."

"Willow," I offer and shake her hand.

"Willow Rose?" she echoes. "I know you! I *loved* your album."

"You did?" I laugh, astonished. "Yes! I'm so pleased that you know it."

"Girl, the day will come you'll be so famous you'll never play a little place like mine, mark my words. Let me buy you a drink."

"I hope you're right. Just water with lemon for now, please."

"You've got it."

I lift the pint glass in a cheer. "Thanks."

Paige is bent over the table, scribbling, alone, when I find her. Her long auburn hair trails down her back and over her shoulders, and her attire is much like my own, a little hippie, a little Celtic, a lot Ren Faire. "Hey, you," I say and touch her shoulder.

"Willow!" She jumps up and hugs me, hard, rocking me back and forth. She smells of strawberry oil and green forest. "I have missed you so much."

I rock her back. "Me too." We've been friends since ninth grade, when we walked into our violin class at the very famous high school, scared to death, and sat down side by side. My mother had always planned to send me there, and Gloria followed her wishes. It was a great fit.

"Come sit with me," she says.

"Where's the band?"

She mimes smoking a joint.

We spend a half hour catching up, trading gossip and newsy items about people we know. The Very Famous Actor we never say we know to anyone else, the woman who is conducting the Houston Symphony, the poet who killed himself, the guitarist who was arrested. "What about you?" I ask.

"Eh, you know." She shrugs, gestures around the bar. "Not exactly what I thought I'd be doing at thirty-five."

I look out at the crowd, think of my dreams of packed stadiums and me under the spotlight. It felt so close for a moment, and now it feels further away than ever.

But if I give up now, the one sure thing is that it will *never* happen. To give us both a pep talk, I say, "The thing is, we're still doing it. Making music. We always said we would never give up, and we haven't."

"I guess. But why?" She shakes her head a little. "I'm just starting to get tired of it. Maybe I want the ordinary things, you know, like a family and breakfast and school days for the kids."

It startles me. I peer at her. "Really? Like . . . settling down?"

"I know." She pokes at a mark on the table, not meeting my eyes. "Sounds like selling out, right?" She looks at me. "But can you imagine doing this night after night in ten years? Twenty? What kind of life is that?"

Something twists in my chest, resistance and terror. "I don't know." I think of the trickles of music swirling over my nerves when I played in the greenhouse this morning, the elusive notes I've been trying to track down. I think of mornings practicing, and evenings playing or listening to others play, and contrast that against the vision she's described of busy mornings of packing lunches and gathering homework. It makes me want to weep. "I'm not ready to throw in the towel."

"But you had an album! That's way more than I've had."

I roll my eyes. "An album that failed."

"No." She leans forward to put both hands over my forearm. "No, Willow. No! It *didn't* fail. It went out into the world and found listeners and became what it is."

The black hole of devastation I carry around with me, a black hole I barely admit even to myself, shrinks. A lot. "Thank you. It helps to remember that there's more than one way to measure an artistic project."

"The money man always wants more money," she says.

"And they want artists who will make that money." I take a breath, centering myself. "I don't know that I'm ever going to be that person. I'm just too niche."

Paige glances to her right, and I see the guys coming in, all long haired, dressed in poet shirts and vests. One dark-brown man, styling himself after Hendrix with a big soft Afro tied back around his forehead and a silky purple shirt, lifts his chin. I can tell he fancies himself a lady-killer, and he has the pheromones for it, but I'm so not into men at the moment, not even for quick sex for the fun of it. That's how all these things get started, and then everything falls apart.

"That's Josiah," she says. "He's not as terrible as he looks."

"Pass," I say. "Pass on all of them."

And yet something nags me. Have we met somewhere? He seems familiar.

She lifts one eyebrow. "Wait until you hear him talk. But never mind that." She squeezes my arm tightly. "Hear me, Willow. The compositions and arrangements on *Rosebud* were amazing. It was a first album. You will find your audience. I know you will."

I have to look away to hide the sting of tears in my eyes. So embarrassing. "Thanks, my friend. And thanks for the gig."

"Are you kidding? I miss you like crazy when you're gone." She gestures toward the guys, and they fall into places around the table. "What d'you feel like playing tonight?"

"Me?" I say. "I'm here to follow along."

Josiah has taken the place at the end of the table. "I loved the arrangement you did of 'The Devil's Questions.' Would you lead us in that?" His voice is the deepest possible bass, as resonant as an entire orchestra. I feel it moving along my skin, down my spine, as stirring as fingers. All the music centers in my body go on high alert.

I glance at Paige. She has a ghost of a smile on her mouth.

"Uh, sure," I say. "I'd love it. Do you know the male part?"

"I do."

And for a minute, I realize that he's a little . . . dazzled . . . by my music. Not me. The music. It makes me sit a little straighter.

Chapter Thirteen
Gloria

It's quiet in the apartment with Willow gone. I've spent the day trying to get my affairs in order, and I'm exhausted. I spoke with Dani's husband, Matthew, retired but still a master of the universe, and he sent me to a friend of his for counsel. We spoke over the phone, and he's going to dig into the case and the background and get back to me in the morning. I did some research into various escape locations, too, but it just depressed me to imagine any of them. I'd be alone. Away from everyone and everything I love.

I tried to take down the Renoir, but it proved to be too heavy. I had a rotator cuff injury a couple of years ago that means I can't lift my left arm over my head. Maybe I'll make up some reason for Willow to help me get it out of sight.

Exhausted and anxious, I control my environment by changing into ancient silk pajamas, then carry my tablet into the parlor and pour two solid fingers of twelve-year-old scotch into a highball glass with ice. No soda or water. I learned to drink it straight and savor it one small sip at a time.

My chair is waiting, and I settle with a sigh. Lamplight spills over my shoulder from an art deco lamp I found antiquing with Dani over a decade ago. She lives in a gorgeous old brownstone, and for years, we took trips to scavenge for lovely things for our homes.

When I first moved in with the girls, the apartment was thinly furnished. A few things had been left behind by the former owners: the heavy, long dining room table with its even dozen chairs; a couple of bureaus that were scuffed but well made. Billie had furnished the rooms with the tastes of the eternal teenager she was—cheap sofas and bland accoutrements and knockoffs of every variety. The four-poster in Willow's room was an exception, and somewhere Billie had found a Tibetan altar that graced the parlor, and of course, her music room held a good piano, but the rest was tacky and hard to look at. Our mother had grown up amid beauty and luxury, then lost it all in the war. Living on a farm in upstate New York had done little to restore the life she'd known, but she taught us both an appreciation of art. Billie was always torn between her longing for the bourgeois beauties of art and the apartment itself, which our mother would have adored, and the bohemian world of her music.

I had no such conflicts. Thanks in part to my excellent salary, then pension, and the money that came in through Billie's royalties for a long time, I furnished the apartment properly. I hung the paintings my sister had collected and left leaning against the walls, and shopped for antique furnishings that I could reupholster in delicious fabrics like plum velvet and forest-green silk. I bought appropriate side tables and beds and bedding.

The whole place is getting quite worn, it must be said. Water damage has infected some of the cornices in a couple of rooms, and the parquet floors need to be stripped and refinished. In the bathrooms, the tile work alone will take thousands to restore—if the art deco tiles can even be matched. The responsibility has become heavy, and a very tiny thread in my heart wonders if Sam might be right. Someone else could come in, bring a fresh infusion of money, and fix it all up.

The trouble is, we'd never be able to be sure anyone could love it as much as we would.

As much as I do. How can I possibly leave it?

This room is my favorite. The paintings whisper among themselves just beyond the circle of yellow light, and from my chair, I can see out to the rooftops across the street and the skyline winking beyond. The chair is covered in rose velvet that's gone a bit shiny over the years, but the ottoman still fits me perfectly. The scotch goes on the side table, my feet cross on the ottoman, and I plump a pillow on my lap for the tablet.

It's a nightly ritual to check the messages from Instagram. I often check things many times a day, clicking a heart to like something a viewer says, offering a quick comment, reading through the feeds of other people. Tonight, however, I'm hoping for another message from the mysterious man who sent the direct message yesterday. I sent another query last night.

There's still nothing.

I'm stuck in a holding pattern in all directions, which is the thing I hate the most. My entire being wants to take action, *do* something, anything, and I'm forced for now to sit still and await advice.

To give myself some peace, I read the messages and emails that have become such a framework in my life. In the four years since I started the G-L-O-R-I-A account, I've made true friends online, women my age and both older and younger. They write to me DMs and emails, and I am sometimes staggered by their stories. There is Harriet Allen, who was a nurse only because her father would not let her study to be a doctor, who retired from nursing early when her husband died and left her a large sum of money. She was at loose ends when we "met," just turned fifty-five and feeling as if life was over. She insisted it was my influence that caused her to return to school for her MD, but I think she would have made it there anyway.

There is Paulina, who took up a paintbrush for the first time at eighty, and sold her first painting a few months ago; Rita, who walked away from a long marriage at the age of sixty-three; Mary, who is spending her retirement traveling to every state in the US.

Not every story is a big one. Some have made small steps, to stop drinking wine or eating sugar, to be kinder, to be aware or start meditating. Some women have come into my life and then died, which I truly hate, but I'm glad we crossed paths this way.

Tonight, I read through the DMs and requests, and it's the usual mix. Trolls dressed up as doctors and military men of a certain age, and other trolls who take me to task for various crimes against humanity like feminism and frankly sexual comments, as if women our age have simply given it up forever.

As if.

I wish there were another message from Isaak. He's been so much in my thoughts, and I've been feeling that whisper along my nerves today. That longing for kisses, for hands on my body, for my mouth on a man's belly.

His belly. His hands. I close my eyes for a moment and call up the details, my fingers on my lips as I remember his kisses. I have never known a man who could kiss as well as Isaak, as if all of life could be found in my lips, in the well of my mouth, and he could not help but explore every bit of it.

I do hope he's all right. He must have access to some help or less grim circumstances if he can send a DM. Or perhaps he's given someone else—a lawyer, a friend—encouraging words to send my way.

I scan the internet for one of the photos of him being arrested, and although he's older, as I am, he is still so much himself. That craggy face, his crisp trousers. With the edge of my thumb, I touch his mouth.

Enough.

I open my photos and look for a shot that will express my mood on Instagram, and laugh when I find it—a soft green-and-pink amaryllis bud, just beginning to open. There's a drop of water trembling at the tip.

I post it with the caption, **All the flowers in nature know one thing is very important. And you definitely don't need a partner. #natural #sexytimes #flowers #thisisseventy**

If Willow reads it, she will laugh. If Samantha does, she'll be so embarrassed. Maybe I need to buy her some funny sexy toys.

But mainly, I wonder if Isaak will see it. If he will know I'm thinking of him.

I've just started running water in my bath when the phone rings. It's on my night table in the other room, and I am not in the mood to talk to anyone. My thoughts are tangled, and the places in my neck that get stiff at the slightest whiff of worry are starting to warn me. A hot bath with my favorite lavender oil will help stave off a torturously painful neck. If it's one of the girls, they'll leave a message, and I'm not going to be in the bath that long.

One more beautiful thing I will desperately miss if I have to leave. I adore this room. It's enormous, large enough for a dressing table beneath a glass-brick window that fills the space with light. I've placed begonias with showy leaves on shelves and counters around the room. One old Boston fern sits where a dressing table might have gone, right where diffuse light will shine on her leaves. She's been there fifteen years, an annoyance for the cleaners, who have to vacuum up leaves that she sheds, but a deliciousness for me, as I love her fluttery sturdiness and the oxygen she breathes out.

The tub is long and deep, now filled with slightly purple water that fills the air with a natural lavender scent. I'm particular about the form of lavender—artificial forms are tinny and horrific, but true lavender is one of the most beautiful scents in the world, relaxing and soft.

I'm about to discard my robe when the phone starts to chime again. This time, I feel a sense of slight dread. It's possible someone has died, but I feel in my gut that it's something to do with Isaak. Straightening my shoulders, I leave the steaming bath and pad across the soft carpet into my bedroom and pick up the phone.

"It's time to run," says a man's voice. I don't recognize the voice, but before I can say a word, the connection is cut.

I stand where I am, phone in my hand, my mouth dry. It was a code phrase between Isaak and me, back in the day, in case something had gone wrong. Back then, we each had a plan and a circuitous route that would bring us together on the far shore of hiding.

Now, I have no plan, no hope of reuniting, only loneliness and exile awaiting me.

The alternative is that I will be arrested and spend my days locked up in a cell, without beauty or music or anything to bring me joy. A flash of myself in a prison jumpsuit, meeting with Willow and Sam at some grim metal table, knocks the air out of me.

And if I'm in trouble, I really don't want it spilling over on my nieces. They've done nothing to deserve it.

I have to get things in order here as fast as possible, then get myself the hell out of Dodge. Leaving the luxurious bath to go cold, I pick up my tablet and open the internet.

And then I worry that the authorities will be able to track me this way, through my wanderings online.

How else can I find the information I need?

Time to run.

Chapter Fourteen

Sam

When I wake up, I bolt upright, feeling panicky. What time is it? Have I slept all day and wasted all those hours? Rain is still falling, and it's really cold in my apartment, and I have the most massive headache I've ever had in my life.

It also takes concerted effort to swallow past the razor blade in my throat. I need a cup of tea with honey. And I'm not really hungry, but eventually, I will be. I need to order some food before it's too late.

It's hard to focus. I think of the work I should be doing, the emails I was meant to send, and then I'm lost in my headache for long moments.

I do have to pee, which is a good thing. Once I dehydrated myself so badly with the flu that they had to give me intravenous fluids. I roll over onto my side with great effort and look across the ocean of hardwood. The bathroom is about five or six miles away.

This is the worst part of living alone. No one to bring you a cup of tea when you're sick or open a can of soup for you or press a hand over your steaming-hot forehead. I really didn't think I'd *still* be alone now, my eggs withering, my heart turning so hard it's like a walnut. I think of Willow, floating through our mother's apartment, hanging out with Gloria, and fury flickers through me. Or maybe it's jealousy. Or maybe even longing.

I wish somebody were here.

C'mon, Sam. I force myself up. One step at a time, and I cross the vastness of the apartment.

I pee and wash my face and hands, carefully because bending over makes my head hurt worse.

A snippet of a game world races across my mental screen, electrifying and vivid, an avatar of a woman, tiny and blonde, under a spotlight. Not quite anime but . . . I try to capture it by staying very still, but it disappears with a pop. Still, it was something strong; I can feel it.

In the kitchen, I look for Advil. There are only two left in the bottle, and I put the kettle on for tea.

I remember that I need some food. I pick up the phone, suddenly afraid it's too late to order anything, but it's only nine. I've been asleep for five hours.

Huh. Am I really sick, or is this just me feeling sorry for myself? As a child I often caught a cold or the flu when I felt out of control, and to my eternal shame, it has continued into adulthood.

I put my hand to my head, and it feels hot, but I'm not sure if that's just my imagination or if I actually have a fever. It seems like a lot of work to cross the room again for the thermometer. If I even have one. Do I?

And really, I'm probably overreacting because I'm stressed. I'll order some food and sleep it off.

The girl in the game world of my imagination plays a chord, a hard chord, too loud, and I press fingers to my left ear, realizing that it aches. Not just aches, burns. Shit. I'm really coming down with something.

Sleep. Sleep is the thing. Opening a delivery app on my phone, I order two vats of chicken soup, two liters of 7UP, and extra crackers. *LOTS,* I write in the little box.

Order will arrive in 20 minutes.

The kettle whistles, and I list toward it, dizzy when I stand up, and pour water over a tea bag. While it brews, I find I'm shivering and pull the sweater around me more tightly. My neck is getting stiff from tension, and I lift my shoulders up and down a couple of times to try to shake it loose.

Such a headache!

Maybe, I think vaguely, I should call someone.

But it's late. I don't want to bother anybody.

I pick up the tea and head for my bed. I'll just rest until the food gets here, then have some soup, and by then the Advil will have kicked in and I'll be a little better. Watch something on my tablet.

It makes me think of Willow again, when she showed up with all the things to try to cure my broken heart after Eric, the full set of seasons from *Felicity*.

Poor Felicity should never have cut her hair. Who knew hair was so important?

The girl in my imagination cuts her hair, dyes it black. "Who takes a blonde seriously?" she says.

Pulling the covers around me like a cocoon, I drift off, and the girl on the stage stands up and walks toward me. I lean in to listen and I'm gone, into her world like Alice in Wonderland.

Gone.

The next time I surface, the rain has stopped and it's much quieter. My phone is on the other side of the room, so I don't know what time it is, but the tea on my bedside table is cold and untouched. Man, I really went out.

The headache is much better, but I can tell I don't want to swallow. I know I need to drink something, however, so I force myself into a sitting position, very slowly so as not to awaken the wasps in my head. The tea is cold and too strong and unsweetened, but I gulp it down, and it only hurts a little.

Good. Maybe the worst is over.

The food!

I pad over to the door and open the locks, and there it is—a big paper bag with the soup and bottles of soda and—it makes me smile—about fifty packets of saltines. I close the door and carry the bag to the counter, pick up my phone.

There are three voice mails, two from Willow and one from Gloria. Huh.

I listen to them and realize that they're responding to phone calls I made, phone calls I have zero memory of making.

My cheeks flame. How embarrassing! So needy!

But now it's twelve thirty, and I'm not going to call back and wake them up. I'll give them each a call in the morning.

The game world buzzes to life in my imagination again, and between when I take a bowl out of the cupboard and when I pour in some soup, my brain offers up a dozen ideas, images and snippets of direction in words and code. A shiver runs up my spine. This might actually be good. I heat the soup in the microwave and find a big spiral notebook with grids—I have dozens—and start to scribble down some of the ideas that dance through my feverish brain. It's about the girl, the avatar, on a stage. But not just on a stage. There've been a million games about becoming a star. How will this one be different?

She can be anything. Make her own avatar. Be a rock star or a senator or a billionaire designer, taking her place shoulder to shoulder with the guys.

The microwave beeps, and I pause to get the soup and force myself to eat some of it, staring at the drawings and notes and bits of coding that popped up—just a line, here and there. I can feel the tone and atmosphere, even a sense of what the music should be. Music is powerful. If I hear the notes from *Zelda*, I'm transported instantly to an era, age eleven, sitting with Asher in his room or mine, more often mine, since he has four younger siblings and they could be annoying, interrupting us all the time.

As I'm staring at the page, I see an elegant piece of design, put the bowl aside to sketch it out, and fall into the shape of the emerging game, filling page after page with sketches and notes, downloading all the crazy stuff and all the workable stuff and all the recycled bullshit onto the paper. I'm so into it that I fall asleep on the counter and only awaken when the headache has roared back to life and my neck is stiff as hell and I'm frozen solid. I pick up my phone and stumble back to bed, thinking I should drink some water.

In a little while.

I'm inside the game, trying to make my way through a forest of trees drawn in prism colors, like Mylar, beautiful but blinding. I look at my arms, and they're dusky purple, and I have a sword, but not an actual sword. A sword of words. I peer at them and see that it's code, code as elegant as Asher would write. No one ever appreciates code, no one ever sees it, but our peers know the difference between ordinary and elegant. Asher is the best.

The best.

I wake up and stumble to the bathroom and realize again that I'm really sick. I can't find any more Advil, so I drink as much water as I can, hoping it will wake me up again soon. I fall back into bed, and my phone is under me. I peer at it and see that my sister called again, and Gloria, but neither of them left a voice mail, and even if they had, I don't have the energy to listen to them. My skin hurts. It's burning. My head feels like it's going to explode.

Asher writes the best code. How did I lose my best friend? He's the person I would call. He would always answer.

No more.

—— ⟨⟩✦⟨⟩ ——

In my dream, I am in a very midcentury modern sort of living room, but softer. I know I'm in Brooklyn, but not exactly where. Asher's sister, Roda, lives not far away, and we planned it that way because we want the kids to grow up close to their cousins.

I forgot about this!

Here are my children—two little boys with his dark eyes, and the oldest one already wears glasses at five. They're playing LEGOs on the dark-gray carpet. I smell food, something savory with lots of healthy vegetables cooked in ways that the children will eat, and I can see the kitchen, with pale-gray shimmering tiles, like water, and granite countertops (marble is too cold) and a Wolf stove. We must be making a lot of money, I think, and Asher comes in the room. He's starting to bald a little bit, so he wears his hair very short now, and it suits him, makes him look lean and focused, though the rest of him is a little plump. He looks like a dad. Like the dad of my children. Like the dad I always wanted.

And then I'm in the iridescent forest again. The sword says *The Way to Greatness*. I think, very loudly, it should be *Write My Name Across the Sky*.

No, not my mother's song.

A blinding pain shatters all the dreams, and I find myself leaning on my counter, trying to remember what I'm doing there. Why am I standing here?

Damn, damn, damn, I'm so sick. I was ordered not to do this again, and here I am. I can barely see the screen of my phone. What time is it?

I don't know. I'm going to fall on the floor if I don't go back to bed.

I go back to bed. My head feels like it's going to explode.

I need help. I really, really need help, and I can't think how to call anyone. They're all so far away.

Chapter Fifteen

Willow

The first set is rousing, with Paige and me playing off each other as we always have—we must have played together a thousand times, her long, elegant bowing weaving through my intricate fingering. We never could keep a band together, for no real reason that made sense, even though we tried for years.

I know she's had this group for more than five years, and they're tight. Paige is clearly the leader, with her lilting vocals and lithe dancing, every inch the professional onstage. I can't imagine how she thinks she can walk away.

We sing a duo together, a ballad meant for two voices, and Josiah comes in behind, improvising a bass line, and the result sends gooseflesh over my arms. The crowd loves it, too, cheering and shouting, some of them standing up to double the power of their cheer. When we're done, I glance back at him and nod. He half smiles and gives me a thumbs-up, his dark eyes shining. The part of me that is composing music all the time, even when I'm eating, when I'm dozing, nudges me again. *Music!*

Paige moves aside, taking support as Josiah steps up to the mic, sets his acoustic bass down, and picks up a Les Paul. I cover the mic. "I don't have my electric violin. I thought we'd do it acoustic."

"Use mine." Paige takes my acoustic and supplants it with a very high-end electric. I plug it in, pluck the strings, run the bow over it, tuning and getting a feel for it. Into the mic, I say, "Hey, everybody, we're going to try something here, an arrangement of 'The Devil's Questions' that was on my album *Rosebud* last year."

A whistle comes from the back, and I wave. "Josiah and I have never done this together, but you all just heard him sing, right, so—"

The reaction this time is much more enthusiastic. He grins at me, white teeth and glittering eyes, and a spark arcs between us. Equal parts heat and music, a frisson of power I can feel in gooseflesh down the backs of my arms.

I raise my violin, wait for him.

"The Devil's Questions" is one of the classics of the Child Ballads, an enormous number of English and Scottish folk songs collected by Francis Child in the nineteenth century and given new life by the folk movement in the sixties and seventies. "This one is for my mother, Billie Thorne, who loved the Child Ballads but liked them a little rough."

We start to play, and the band picks it up quickly, drum and flute lacing through the dark melody set down by my violin and my voice. A woman meets the devil disguised as a knight on the road, and to escape him, she has to answer nine riddles.

My voice is not my strongest musical point, but it's clear and true, and melodies like this one bring out the best points. Josiah's voice is intensely thrilling, bending the words into a molasses depth of seduction that hushes the room. My body is thrumming by the end, every cell plumped by musical magic, and I'm sure I'm not alone.

This is why I am committed to music, moments like this, when I am plugged into something bigger than me, something enormous and wild and full of life, a thing that flows through me and into the world, into the other bodies here, spilling out into the street, offering hope and healing and sparks of joy.

Lost as I am with Josiah in the music we are making, I suddenly capture a piece of the sonata I've been composing—a new depth I have never heard before. As the crowd whoops, I meet his gaze and bow in gratitude. When I straighten, he gives me a courtly bow and, in a bit of theater, presses a kiss to his fingers and flings it toward me.

I laugh, catch it in the air, and mime tucking it into the top of my blouse. The crowd loves it, and I wink at him.

At the break, I wash my face in the bathroom and go out the back door to get some air. It's shivery cold with a February wind that cuts right through my blouse. The guys are smoking, but Josiah isn't with them. Away from the noise, I check my phone and see a couple of voice mails, which is kind of unusual. The first is a spam call from LA, the voice mail just empty.

The other is from my sister. Weird times ten. Sam *never* calls me. It came in at nine thirty, more than an hour ago. "Hi, Willow. Sorry to bother you, but I'm having a bad night. Call me when you can."

A bad night? What does that mean? Urgently, I press the return button, and it rings and rings and rings. I try again, worried now, and she still doesn't pick up. "Hey," I say. "I'm at a club, so I can't hear the phone. Text me if you want me to come by in a little while. I'm happy to do it." I pause. "Sorry you're having a bad night. Call me back if you want, anytime."

Then I wince. Too much.

But it's too late.

"Willow!" Paige calls from the door. "Let's talk about the next set!"

We finish the last gig at just after midnight. I'm sweaty and happy and full of the effervescence that always fills my body after a live performance. Some musicians like studio work, and I've done it to make ends meet, but the pleasure of playing for a crowd, seeing their faces and reactions, amping them up, is unmatched for me. My fiddling and singing meshed brilliantly with both Paige's and Josiah's, and as we start packing up, Paige is as high on the whole thing as I am. "That was brilliant!" she cries, lifting her hair off her neck. "I'm so glad you came. The crowd loved it, don't you think?"

"Absolutely. I love singing with you, always."

"We sound good together," she agrees and points with her bow at Josiah. "But seriously, you and Josiah should put something on tape. You have amazing stage chemistry. That was outrageous."

I nod. "It was *really* good."

"You can come play with us anytime," she says. "I mean it."

"Thanks. I might take you up on that, but I've got to find something that pays substantially."

"I totally get it. I'll keep an ear open." She stops and frowns. "Seems like I heard about somebody who needs a violinist for a baroque group. Interested in that?"

Baroque means a quartet playing chamber music for upscale parties, which is not my usual pleasure, but I'm in no position to be choosy. "If it pays, I'm interested."

She grins. "I'll look it up and text you."

"Thanks." I hug her, smelling the same faint sweat in her hair. "Let's get a meal soon and catch up for real."

"How's your aunt doing?"

"Oh, she's great. Get this: she's an Instagram influencer. G-L-O-R-I-A," I say, spelling it out.

"Like the Van Morrison song?"

"Exactly."

"God, she's a hoot. I'm going to look her up."

"Hey," I say, swinging my case over my shoulder.

"Yeah?"

I think of us at sixteen, planning futures of stardom. The stardom that hasn't materialized for either of us. "Don't give up yet."

She tsks, looks away. "Not quite yet. But I'm not you, Willow. I don't have that thing, whatever it is. The magic."

The word sparks against the flint of my sense of loss. I feel it, know it's true. There's something alive and longing for expression in me that wants outlet through music, and I can't imagine what my life will be, who *I* will even be, if I have to give it up. The idea causes physical pain in my ribs. "That's not—"

"Please." She holds up a hand, and I see that she's tired, really tired, and I wonder what it would be like to play a club six nights a week, month in, month out. "I'm pretty clear about who and what I am." She hands me a thin packet of folded bills. "It's all good."

"Thanks." We hug again, quickly, and I head out, still buzzing. Out on the street, I'm a little turned around and pull out my phone to check the location of the closest subway station. There's another message from Sam, and this time, she sounds very drunk. "It's all for nothing, right?" she says. "I need to order some avocados, and there are none in the forest."

I frown. "What the hell?" My stomach squeezes. This is so very unlike my self-sufficient sister. The message came in just a half hour ago, so I punch the return and call her back.

No answer. I call again, and a third time. It just goes to voice mail.

Damn. I need to swing by there, but I'm not sure the same train goes to Harlem.

"Where are you headed?" says an unmistakable voice.

I turn, and Josiah is standing there, looking much less alternative in a black camel hair coat and a hat that covers his hair. He's donned a pair of horn-rimmed glasses that give him a more serious aspect. "Upper West Side. How about you?"

"Morningside. Want to share a cab?"

I wave a hand. "Ugh. No. I'm taking the train."

"Nah, c'mon." A taxi rolls up, and I realize he must have already ordered it. "My treat." He opens the door, and I don't really want to take that long train ride, so I duck into the back seat. He slides in after me, gives an address. "You?"

I give my aunt's address. He raises an eyebrow. "Fancy."

"My mother bought it when she had a hit album, back in the late seventies."

"Ah, you said. Billie Thorne is your mother."

"Yes," I say with a smile. In the close confines of the cab, he seems longer, broader. He smells of hair oil and a nearly worn-away cologne and the heat of our performance. It prickles along the edges of my nerves, filled no doubt with pheromones, and I realize it has been months and months since I've had sex.

No. I slam the door.

He measures me for a moment. "That's quite a legacy."

"Yeah. It's a lot to live up to."

"I can see that. But you're an entirely different kind of musician."

"Not really. She was electric guitar and rock and roll, but the roots are the same."

"Yeah? In what way?"

I take a breath, looking out toward the dark expanse of the river, lights sparkling in buildings on the other side, both cold and inviting, life and challenge. "So many things, but the main thing was that she loved the Child Ballads and they informed most of her songs. Not in the same way they inform what I do, but in that sense of the doomed lovers and women having to twist themselves into pretzels to escape some terrible fate."

"Oh, yeah, yeah. 'The Wager,'" he says, referring to one of her songs. "I can see that."

It's hard to get used to that voice, so very deep and resonant. Every word sounds a hundred times more important.

"What was she like as a mom?"

"I was only nine when she died," I say, dodging. People always want this information, but I worry that I'm going to lose the small bits of her I actually remember. "My aunt raised me for the most part. And my sister." I look at the phone, but there's nothing from Sam. To shift the conversation away from me and my family, I ask, "Where are you from?"

"Northern California originally. Grew up on the circuit of Ren Faires."

"Ah! That's why we meshed so easily onstage!"

"You grew up in Faires?"

"No, but I spent almost ten years touring with them, a band called MoonDance Fiddlers."

"After my time."

I incline my head. "Did you like it? Hate it?"

"It was good. The whole family had gigs. My dad was a juggler. My mom was a serving wench and dancer, and my siblings and I had an act singing ballads. I can play recorder like a champ."

I laugh, and it's the kind of belly laugh that loosens all the tension. "I bet you were a hit."

"Thank you. I like to think so."

"I loved the Faires," I say.

"I did when I was small. It's a free way of living, and we were homeschooled, so I had a prime education." He shrugs. "It gets old after a time."

"I can see that. Are your parents still doing it?"

"No, my dad got cancer about ten years ago, and they settled down in Marin County. My mom grew up around there, and she's really happy to be back, I think. My sister lives nearby and looks out for them." We're crossing the Brooklyn Bridge, and lights flash over his face, illuminating a cheekbone, the edge of his jaw. "My dad's fine now, goes fishing like a proper old man."

"That's the kind of childhood I longed for. So normal."

He laughs, and that sound, too, is deep and evocative. "In Ren Faires?"

"No. Two parents. Siblings. A dad who goes fishing. That sounds pretty stable to me."

"I have to admit it was pretty good. I have a good family."

"How did you end up in New York?"

He looks at me. "You ask a lot of questions."

"You don't have to answer," I say with a shrug. "Just making conversation."

"Mmm." I hear the rumble along my wrists, the edge of my collarbones. "Deflecting, I think."

I meet his gaze. "Maybe."

"All right, Willow, daughter of Billie, I'll play. I won a scholarship to NYU for undergrad, and the minute I got here, I knew it was my place."

"Did you study music?"

"Literature. I'm a writer."

It's my turn to measure him. "It wasn't heartbreaking enough to just have one creative passion?"

He laughs softly. "It's not so bad. The music is play, and I've never expected the writing to make money."

"Ah, so you have a day job." It's something I might have to figure out if the contest doesn't pan out. I almost have to win rather than just place. Anxious little gremlins scurry around my body, and I shove the thoughts away.

"Not a day job," he says. "My main gig. I'm a professor."

In Morningstar Heights. "At Columbia?"

"Yes." That's all, just that simple affirmation.

He waits for my reaction, and it does take a couple of seconds to rearrange my assessment of him. The wild clothing is a costume, the music for play, the Ren Faire childhood. I try to imagine him in a blazer and jeans, or maybe a suit. "With all that entertainment background, I bet you're a great teacher."

He smiles, eyes as sleepy-dangerous as a tiger's. "Hope so."

My sister's dig runs through my mind. *I'm sure you'll find a guy soon enough.* I force myself to look away.

A news story on the back seat console shows a man in handcuffs in some European setting, being led away by police in black uniforms. The voice-over says he has been arrested in connection with a number of missing pieces of art. I've heard the news a few times, but this time they flash four photos of still-missing pieces, and the second one electrifies me. A Renoir landscape worth millions.

I stare, mouth dry.

The screen shows a well-tended woman of a certain age being arrested in Amsterdam, then flashes back to the man in his late seventies. His hair is thick and wavy, and I can imagine that he was quite the thing years ago.

"This is a pretty interesting story," Josiah says. "Have you seen it? All the elements. Art, theft, Nazis, romance."

"Romance?"

"Dude was a bit of a player. Women carried the paintings for him. This lady here was arrested because of a painting that's been lost for over three hundred years."

"Huh."

"You look like you've seen a ghost."

Maybe I have. I know that Renoir.

It hangs in the parlor.

My phone vibrates in my hand, and I turn it over, hoping it's Sam. Instead, it's Gloria. **Have you heard from your sister? She left me a weird message.**

"Sorry," I say to Josiah. "My aunt." I'm already typing. She left me a weird message too. I'm on the way home. Should I stop by her apartment?

If you wouldn't mind.

Done.

"Change of plan," I say. "I need to check on my sister. She's on One Hundred Twenty-First Street. We can drop you first."

"No, no. My original offer stands—we'll drop you first." He glances at his phone. "It's getting pretty late. Why don't I wait?"

I realize it's nearly 2:00 a.m. I hesitate. "No, I have an app."

"As you wish, good lady."

"Thank you, kind sir," I say in my best Ren Faire accent. But I'm calculating now how much of that fifty dollars I'm now going to spend on cab fare.

As for the painting, it can't possibly be real. I'm just getting carried away. Why would my mother have a Renoir? How would she have connected to some suave Romeo? Not really her type.

Unless it wasn't my mother.

Maybe it's *Gloria*. I mull this over in silence, staring out the window at storefronts and rain-shiny sidewalks reflecting squiggles of light. Is this why she seems so distracted?

At Sam's building, I check for my phone and purse and violin, then open the door. "Thanks." I pause. "I'd love to jam with you again. That was some magic on that stage."

"Definitely. Do me a favor, will you?" Josiah asks. "Text me when you're home safely."

"I will."

He holds out his hand for my phone, and I give it to him. I watch him type in his number, trying not to notice his long, graceful fingers, his broad palms. He hands it back. "Be safe."

"Thanks." I close the door and suck in a lungful of cold air to cool off. He's just one of those men. I'm sure every woman—and no doubt plenty of men—he meets has at least one tiny moment of awakening in his presence.

I have the code to the main door and let myself in, then take the elevator upstairs. All is silent. At Sam's door, I listen for any sounds, and apart from the television across the hall, there's nothing. I knock and wait.

Nothing.

I don't want to pound too much because of the other people on the floor, so instead, I knock again and call her on the phone at the same time. When her voice mail picks up again, I say, "Hey, I'm outside your door. Open up. Gloria is worried about you. So am I."

Nothing. I call again, and again, but even as I do it, I know how futile it is. She hates the noises the phone makes and keeps it entirely silent, relying on a flashing screen as if she has a hearing issue. I knock and wait. Knock and wait.

Should I go down and wake the super? I imagine myself rousing some old guy who comes to the door with his hair all sticking up and then see myself with him at Sam's door and Sam opening it with fury.

Maybe she just doesn't want to be bothered, and I'm just being an idiot.

But those messages. I chew on my lip, pound one more time. "Sam!"

Nothing.

With a sigh, I head back downstairs, pulling up the taxi app as I enter the lobby.

But Josiah is waiting. I see the cab through the front doors. I should be annoyed that he got all protectively macho on me, but I wasn't relishing the wait and really, really didn't want to spend the money. I keep resolving not to accept rescue, but here I am, doing it again.

He opens the door. "Sorry. I know it's paternalistic, but it's really late. I didn't want to think about you stranded way uptown."

I slide in and close the door behind me. "It *is* paternalistic, but I'm grateful anyway."

He smiles, and I'm glad he waited.

As we drive through the dark, lonely streets, I'm aware suddenly of a thread of music winding through my mind. I hum it under my breath, looking at the empty sidewalks, and I'm thinking of being onstage, the great performance chemistry we have, and the music gets louder. I hear his voice winding through my violin, and a whisper moves through the empty spaces in the composition I've been working so hard on. Urgently, I open my phone and make a few notes.

"Not to sound too pushy, and it sounds like you have a really full life and maybe even a family—"

"No family," he says. "Just me."

I half smile and let him see it. For a moment, there is just this space between us, smelling of a wild wood, of magic. "We should play together again soon," I say. "I really feel like there might be something good here. Do you have time?"

"Maybe. Evenings are challenging, because of the band."

"Afternoons? We have a music room. And a rooftop garden if the weather turns nice by some miracle."

"All right." He has an odd expression on his face.

"What's wrong?"

"Not wrong," he says, inclining his head. "I just keep thinking we've met somewhere. I can't place it."

"Me too. I thought that too. Maybe at a Faire?"

"I haven't been to one since I left home." Light edges his cheekbone, his lower lip, and a shimmer of attraction shines right through my walls.

For a minute, we only look at each other. Then, "I'll send you a text when I can check my calendar."

"Good." The music winds through my mind, then repeats.

We pull up in front of my building. "Thanks, Josiah. I really appreciate your help."

He simply salutes.

As I head up to the apartment, my mind swirls with the music, with the sound of his voice, a single element that brings something in the music alive. I've had it happen a handful of times before. Sometimes it's not a person but a particular place, the mood of a room, or the way the light breaks somewhere. I spent months driving up to a certain rise in Santa Monica to feel the way the light hit the trees and the watery horizon in early evening. It gave me one of my best arrangements.

This time, it's Josiah's voice. That rumbling, that resonance. I let myself into the apartment, and I'm still humming, caught in the music that's unreeling, something new layering in.

I forget completely about Sam or the painting, filled only with notes in colors, painting themselves over my imagination.

Chapter Sixteen

Sam

Asher is bent over me. "Sam, come on, honey; you need to wake up for me."

I blink. "I thought that was a dream."

"It's all right. Can you sit up?"

I realize that my body is complete putty. "I don't know. Even moving a finger seems like a lot."

"We need to get you to a hospital."

"Oh, no. I don't need the hospital. I hate the hospital. And all those poor nurses and doctors, so sad . . ."

"I know. I'm going to try to help you up, okay?"

I'm already drifting off a little, but I can smell him as he bends in, and it brings me closer to the surface. He loops my arm around his shoulder and circles my torso with his arm, and then I'm upright, leaning into the solid strength of him. "Sam, stay with me, okay?"

I try, but there's nothing but quiet if I close my eyes, and now that I'm not so afraid, I can go to sleep. "Don't forget the notes," I say. "I need my notes."

"I need you to focus for a minute, Sam," he says.

I'm suddenly, blurrily aware that there are other people in the room, bustling around. "We're going to get you to the hospital," a kind-sounding woman says.

"That's okay. I think I'm just dehydrated."

"I think it might be a little more than that," she says, and I feel her hands on my neck.

It *hurts*. I bolt upright, banging one of the others in the head, which sets off a gong in my head. I fall back down, clutching my skull. "I don't want to go to the hospital," I cry. Or maybe I only think that, because I can't really make words around this noise. It feels like someone is slamming my head with a sledgehammer.

"It's gonna be okay, Sam," Asher says, taking my hand, and I blearily surface to see his face, his glasses reflecting the light.

"Thank you," I say, clinging to his fingers. "I have such a bad headache."

"I know," he says and presses his palm to my forehead. "Does that help or hurt?"

"Helps." I suddenly think of the children. "Who's with the boys?"

"Boys?"

"They were playing in the living room," I say, eyes closed.

"Mmm. They'll be okay on their own for a little while."

My eyes fly open. "No! They're too little! Call your sister. Your sister will do it."

"Of course," he says soothingly. "Try not to worry."

"Okay." I close my eyes. "Why can't I remember where we got married?"

He says nothing, and I'm worried that he's upset, but now my neck and my knees are joining in the pain fest, and I am swept into it, a steady, throbbing red wave. And then even that disappears, and I'm gone into the trees again.

—— ❧❧❧ ——

The trees are transformed into a grove in Central Park, where I would take Willow when I was charged with babysitting. She made it into a fairy tale, all of it, the different trees, imbuing some of them with magical properties, the bridges and ponds where trolls lived. Our mother had taught both of us a vast number of the folk songs that influenced Billie's writing so much, dozens and dozens of Child Ballads, many of them recorded by singers with flutelike voices. My mother's voice was much more robust, more Janis and Aretha than Joni Mitchell, but Willow could match the sweet sopranos exactly when she was ten and eleven, and she would spin the ballads out like gossamer between the trees. I sang harmony, a passable alto, and imagined myself to be the queen of the grove, ordering soldiers out to defend the ramparts and serfs to gather food into the storehouses for the coming battles. It was a complicated world, built over years of wandering the same groves with my sister's sweet voice weaving through it. Almost all of it ended up in the first game Asher and I created, the one that made us famous.

Willow. Where is Willow now? The thought hauls me out of the dream and dumps me into a cold, sterile room. I startle so violently that a hand falls on my arm. "Shh, Sam. Everything is okay."

Asher. He's still here. His hair is tousled in the way that I know means he's been running his fingers through it. He looks very tired. "Willow is fine. She sends her love. They don't want anyone else in here right now because you might be contagious."

"What's wrong with me? Is it some weird flu?"

"No, no." He brushes my hair back from my forehead. "It's meningitis."

I peer at him, struggling to focus. "That's weird."

"Rest, Aline Alice."

I smile at the reference to our game character and grip his hand hard. "Don't leave. I don't want to be alone."

"I promise you won't be alone."

"My head hurts so much."

"I know." I feel his mouth on my knuckles, and for some reason, it makes me want to cry.

"Where did we get married, Asher? I just can't remember anything about it." A detail surfaces. The river, shining with its little island. "Wait. Hudson, right?"

He swallows and strokes my forehead, a smile that seems somehow sad on his mouth. "Shh. Don't worry about it right now. You need to rest."

So I do.

Chapter Seventeen
Gloria

While I wait for Willow to come home after checking on Sam, I sort through my belongings, trying to decide what to take and what to leave behind. I have to do it without detection, so I fetch a suitcase from the maid's room, which is really only a storage room now, and start packing things into it. It's too hard to imagine I'll never see any of my beautiful things again, so I imagine I'm just packing for a long trip. A few months, around the world. I'll need practical things and my favorite things and pictures and—

When I've done as much as I can bear, I tuck the suitcase into my closet. I'll have to leave tomorrow, once I get directions from the lawyer. I curl up in the bed I love so much, with all my excellent pillows and the duvet I found on sale. Another woman might have wept. I forbid it and doze off.

Hectic dreams of being chased jerk me awake at four, still full dark in February. I pad down the hall in my slippers. Willow's door is closed, so she made it home, and I hesitate, aching to see her. Very, very quietly, I turn the door handle and peek in. Light spills over her from the window, casting a bluish tint over her blonde hair. Her body is so slight she barely lifts the covers.

She is coming back here to live. The thought shatters something in me. I've missed her so much since she left home. Sam, too, but Sam is close, and Sam is prickly and aloof, and once she found Asher, she never seemed to need me.

I close the door softly and head for the kitchen. The apartment is so much fuller when Willow is here. I'm so very aware of her when she returns home, as if she is suddenly eleven or fourteen or seventeen and I am again in charge of making sure she is safe and fed and emotionally supported. I came too late to Sam's life to be much of anything but a guardian to her, but Willow was only nine when her mother died, and even before that I'd stayed with them often, taking up the slack when Billie was training or touring.

Or in rehab. So many rounds of rehab.

Which is simply to say that Willow is largely my daughter. More of a daughter than I had a right to expect. I am the woman who has been present in her life, there to buy her first bras and tell her about menstruation and hold her when she cried over mean friends.

In the kitchen, I turn on the television to monitor the international news, and before I can get sucked into my worry, I pull my phone out of my pocket and send a text to Sam. **Are you ok? Pls text me back ASAP.**

Eloise must have heard me moving around, because she suddenly jumps up on the counter, her fluffy tail high. "It's not breakfast time yet," I say quietly, petting her. Her fur is silky soft, her yellow eyes half-slanted in love. The thought of not having her and Esme in my daily life sends a knife blade through my ribs. I bend my face into her neck. "Willow will take care of you, baby."

There must be another way. I cannot bear to leave her either. "Perhaps a little tidbit." As my water boils, I scatter a few cat treats on the floor. She leaps down with aplomb and applies herself, ears tucked slightly away from her face as if she doesn't want to get them dirty.

A good Insta post, I think, pleased by the turn of phrase, and I take my phone out of my pocket to shoot the photo. The light is not great, too many shadows and a greenish cast to it all, but I can fix that. Cats are always a hit, on the internet in general and my feed in particular. My followers love cats and often tell me about their own.

It's the best part of this surprise influencer business, the pleasure I find in the connections with strangers. Women, almost entirely, who want to believe their lives are still valuable and still have meaning, even if they're seventy or eighty or, in some cases, ninety. I help them feel seen.

And in turn, it makes me feel seen myself. Being seen is a hard thing to give up when you've been mainly feted for your looks your entire life. That was what started the Insta feed—I found myself dancing around the kitchen to the Van Morrison song "Gloria," and inside, I felt as sexy and slithery and . . . *exhilarated* as I ever had. That was always my theme song, *G-L-O-R-I-A, Gloria,* and the idea for the Instagram came from that. I liked Insta, followed my girls, quietly, and a bunch of houseplant influencers, and a couple of old-lady fashionistas.

But I didn't want to be a fashionista. That wasn't really my speed, and they were already doing it better than I ever could. What I wanted was to celebrate being seventy, which is what I was at the time. Seventy and G-L-O-R-ious. Seventy and happy and fully alive. I wanted to celebrate my everyday life, my plants and my cats and my teapots and my conservatory and this wonderful, amazing apartment and my beautiful friends. All of it.

It was surprising how fast it took off. From the start, I made a point of responding to every commenter. If they took time to comment, it seemed the least I could do was communicate in return.

What next, eh, G-L-O? My digs in federal prison? A lump grows in my chest, and I pour a glass of water and drink it down to dislodge it. Through the window, I can see the lights on the other side of the river, the darkness between the two shores as murky as my future.

The voice from the phone call comes back to me: *It's time to run.*

I pour my tea into a thick clay mug, letting it brew while I find my coat, and then I wander out to the rooftop, where all my lovely plants and bushes and trees are still hibernating. I've just begun to plan what tasks to perform for the spring awakening, what seedlings to start growing in the greenhouse. At the possibility that I might not be here to take care of them, I feel a physical pain. I'll need to talk Willow into taking the job over.

But is that fair?

The air is still, not terribly cold, and I settle on a bench between two trees, with a view to the south and the buildings of Midtown. *Time to run.* My beloved town.

I didn't recognize the voice, but the message came from Isaak, no matter whom he'd found to deliver it. It was our catchphrase, a warning he'd insisted I memorize. In those days, I'd found it exciting, and I had a plan fully ready for execution at any moment, complete with currency for various escape spots, a fake passport, and a bag packed and ready for departure. It felt like a movie.

It still feels like a movie, a film I saw long ago.

And it feels like yesterday.

And I'm transported, back in time, to a flat with doors open to the hot, bright day, where Isaak is standing in silhouette against the light, his chest bare as he paints.

The air was utterly still and hot, the fingers of a furnace pressing heavily on my body, which was nearly naked on the bed, my hair a tumble on my shoulders. Lassitude filled my limbs, a laziness born of jet lag and sex. It was late afternoon, and I'd landed this morning. I had four days, a luxurious stretch of time, and felt no need to do anything but lean on my arm and watch Isaak paint.

He was a vigorously physical man who hiked and swam in the ocean and kept himself fit a hundred ways, and it showed in the taut lines of his body. He was never the most beautiful man I'd ever seen, but there was something about his elegant movements or his scent or maybe just the way he looked at me that made every cell in my body hum. I watched the muscles of his back move as he painted now, bending sideways to check the angle of something, cocking his head. His thick black hair caught the light, and even the back of his neck, darkly tanned from the hot Moroccan sun, gave me a sense of awareness. I never tired of looking at him.

He painted a dove. It had once stood on the balustrade overlooking the city, and he'd sketched it quickly in charcoal, from this angle and that, his fingers flying over newsprint. Those reference drawings now were taped to the wall, and the painting was nearly finished. He painted quickly, with lots of thick brushstrokes adding texture and depth, along the wings and the tail, on the rough wall, in the shape of the clouds.

"You should show your work," I said.

"No. I have tried that route. It is not for me, scrabbling, hungry." He wiped his brush with a cloth stained many colors. "The public only wants art that's like all the other art it has seen."

"That's why you do reproductions?" A room off this bedroom was a studio, stacked with canvases, some freshly stretched and primed, some painted. One side of the room held his own paintings, the vivid captures of the city or women's bodies or birds or the sea. All of them were filled with energy and passion and texture and vivid, intense colors. The others were imitations, or rather flawless reproductions, of mostly work of the Orientalists, which sold briskly to tourists.

"Among other things," he said. He wiped his hands and came to stretch out beside me.

"Other things?"

His long brown hands were dappled with the ghosts of the colors he'd used today, and the finger that traced my ribs, the dip of my waist, the rise of my hip, was faintly green. I wondered if he would mark me, my skin. "I will tell you one day, but not now, hmm?" That finger slid toward the center of me as his lips met mine. I gave myself up to pleasure, the pleasure of being twenty-five, the pleasure of a man who could kiss for hours, the pleasure of his hands on my body, and then our connection, deep and strong and athletic.

When we were finished, he lingered, pressing tiny kisses to my chin, my shoulder. "Your skin smells of twilight," he whispered. "I think of it when you are not here. I don't want my sheets washed, so I can smell you on the pillowcase."

My heart skipped a beat, but I was well versed in the wiles and ways of men. He had many women, and I tried not to think about them. We had promised each other nothing. Unlike many of the other girls, I had no desire to retire into the comfort of marriage, not after the unhappiness I'd seen in my mother's.

But his words stirred me. Stirred my growing feelings. I told myself those emotions were nothing but our powerful chemistry, the lusty connection of two bodies that fit together exactly right. I arched a brow. "That must be awkward when the next woman is in your bed."

He brushed my hair from my face. "I do not bring other women here. Only you."

A hush rippled through me. I looked up at his green eyes, the lush lashes, and saw something I had not glimpsed before. *Don't fall for it.* "I'm not sure I believe you," I said and smiled, tracing his mouth with my finger. "But it doesn't matter."

"I confess there are other women," he said, and jealousy plucked my heart viciously, surprisingly. "I see them elsewhere. In my home, I only see you."

"You don't have to do this. I know the rules."

"Rules?" He captured my fingertip and sucked on it, running his tongue over the tip. "Are you so jaded, my love, that you cannot see this is something remarkable between us?"

I shook my head. "Don't, Isaak."

"What? Do not tell you that I've never felt anything like this with anyone else? Because it's true."

I pushed him away, rolled from beneath him, and sat up, pulling the sheet over my breasts. "Don't make it more than what it is. I don't need that fantasy to enjoy this."

He sat up too. "Are you sleeping with other men?"

I met his gaze, lifted my chin slightly. "That is not your business."

He flinched but then nodded. "That is true." He picked up my hand, kissed my knuckles. "Forgive me."

I pushed him, toppling him backward, then climbing astride him, casting the sheet aside. "Let me tell you about my mother," I said. "She was beautiful, the kind of beautiful that makes people stop and take another look."

"It is no surprise to me that you had such a mother."

I nodded, not in vanity, but I knew my own worth. "Far more than I, but that's not the point. She was born and raised in Paris, and she had great talent as a pianist and expected to have a life in music. In another time, she would have toured and played and perhaps married a wealthy man. Instead, the Nazis invaded."

To my deep surprise, his eyes filled with tears, and he sat up, blinking, and brought us to an equal posture once again. "Go on," he said quietly.

"Her parents were killed, and she survived by trading on her beauty. She never told me the whole story, but I could piece it together. In the beginning, she was the mistress of a powerful man, but something happened to him, and she spent the rest of the war starving."

His fingers traced my skin.

"When the Allied forces liberated the city, she met my father, a GI from upstate New York, and married him to flee the city."

"And your father, was he a good man?"

"He is a good man," I said. "Kind and easygoing, but also a very simple kind of person. A farmer. He couldn't talk about music or art or the world of letters. He kept to himself, tending the land and animals, and she was absolutely miserable." I paused, thinking of my father's way of turning his face away from her sharp words, staring off toward the horizon. "They both were."

"She's gone, then."

This was still difficult. She had only been gone five years, and for all her whirling bitterness, her unfilled longings, I missed her. "Lung cancer."

"Which is why you do not smoke."

"Yes."

He bent his head, traced the line of my shin from knee to ankle, lost in thought. "My mother was born in Poland before the war."

I knew that he'd been raised in Israel, but not the circumstances. "Go on," I said, echoing his words.

I saw his throat move, and he stared for a long moment at the connection between his hand and my ankle. "She survived Treblinka. Not terribly well, I'm afraid. She was frail the rest of her life, but she did find some happiness with my father when she came to Israel."

"Is she still alive?"

"Oh, no. She died when I was a child."

"How old were you?"

"Ten."

"I'm so sorry."

He met my gaze then, and I saw something hard, shimmery, in his cut-glass eyes. "I have found my way to make peace. Perhaps what I do will help you make peace too."

"I didn't tell you about her because of the Nazis but because she should never have married my father. She should have stayed in Paris and joined the rebuilding and taken up piano again."

"You judge her very harshly. She suffered things you will never understand."

"I'm sure. But that was ended, either way." I struggled to find a way to express my deepest conviction—that had my mother been a man, she would have found a way to stay and fight for her life, the life she genuinely wanted. "She loved books and music, art and museums, all the things that make up an educated life. She married into a family that was suspicious of all those things, had no use for them."

He was listening carefully. "And she planted the love of freedom in her daughter."

"Both of us. My sister is a singer. She's going to be a star someday, I know it."

"Her dreams live in the pair of you." He kissed my wrist. "That's beautiful, no?"

"Yes." I took both of his hands in mine. "But listen, Isaak. Even if I fell madly in love with you, to the point that I could not breathe without looking at your face, I couldn't leave my work and my life to be with you. I won't."

He looked away. My declaration hung in the air, and I worried that it was too harsh. I worried that I didn't even mean it. I worried that I was only lying to myself about my feelings being simple lust.

"Very well," he said. "I will never ask that of you." He met my gaze. "If it becomes a thing that you want, you must tell me. Will you promise to do that?"

"Yes." Tears stung my eyes, and I blinked them away, but not before he saw them.

"Oh, my sweet Gloria," he said, curling his palms around my face. "It costs you to make that stand."

I swallowed.

"I am in love with you. And you, whether you say it or not, are in love with me. Can we stand in this moment of light for now, together?"

He kissed me, and I breathed in the scent of him, the rugged feel of his hands. "Yes," I whispered.

"Now, let's wander out, shall we? Find some elegant supper and have a walk?"

When I slipped into the bathroom to wash, I saw in the mirror that his fingers had indeed marked me, with smears of soft purple and green.

In New York City on a February morning nearly fifty years later, the faintest pale light begins to limn the buildings.

A movie, a romantic adventure. It still plays that way in my imagination.

And yet, unlike in a movie, I will now pay the consequences of my foolish actions. So many years later, when I have finally begun to offer something of value to the world, something that heals the wounds of time and life, I will have to flee, leave it all behind.

I can't bear it. Worse, though, how can I bear prison? Either way, I will no longer live the life I so love. A tear stings my eye. I don't want to give this up. This home, these nieces of mine, my Instagram world, this full and satisfying life.

Wallowing has never been my style.

But . . . where will I go? Who will be there when I arrive?

In the dark, I let myself shed tears of regret.

My phone rings in my hand, startling me. The screen says *Asher*. My heart drops. "Asher? Is everything all right?"

"Sam is in the hospital. Intensive care."

And suddenly the vistas of faraway lands disappear, and I see myself in prison gray, because I cannot leave my niece. I won't. "I'll be right there."

Chapter Eighteen

Sam

The next time I awaken, my headache is vaguely less horrific. It's still there, pulsing around the skin of my brain, and I feel dizzy and strange, but I can also actually see a little bit. There are no windows, so I can't tell what time it is. An IV pumps drugs into my arm, and a machine beeps my heartbeat.

I swing my head carefully to the right, and there is Asher, sound asleep. He looks terrible, his skin pale and greasy, his hair unkempt. The vision from my dream pops up, of him balding and older, our two little boys, and it breaks my heart in three directions. I was so happy that he was my husband, and we're not even friends anymore. I ruined everything with my evil, evil tongue. Tears fill my eyes.

I must make some noise, because he bolts up. "Sam!" He's at my side, taking my hand, touching my face. "How do you feel? You look better."

"I feel awful." Tears leak out of my eyes, and I'm embarrassed, but I can't stop them. "But not crazy."

"Do you know where you are?"

"Hospital. I think you came and called an ambulance? Or did I dream that?"

"No, that was real." He laughs softly and, for one second, drops his head to my shoulder. Everything is in the gesture. Fear. Gratitude. I feel the skin of his forehead against my neck, and my tears flow even harder. When he straightens, he notices. "Don't cry. It's going to be okay. We got you in time."

"How did you know I was sick?"

"You sent me an SOS."

"I did?" It's our signal to come *right now*, like the Bat-Signal against the sky. "How did you get in?"

"You left the door unlocked."

"Whoa."

"Yeah. Let me call the nurse, and maybe she can bring you something to drink."

"Apple juice."

"I'm sure they have that."

"It's such a little-kid drink."

He smiles, but there's something guarded in it, and I suddenly, humiliatingly, remember my questions about our marriage.

"I'm sorry about the wedding stuff. I just—"

He cuts me off. "It's okay. We don't have to talk about it."

Heat floods my cheeks. "Sorry."

"Don't be sorry. You were delirious. You had a fever of one hundred and four."

The word surfaces. "Did you tell me it was meningitis?"

"Yes. You were dangerously close to dying."

My heart squeezes. "I don't remember texting you. Thank you for coming."

"Of course."

The apple juice arrives, and the nurse checks vitals. "One hundred and one," she says of my temperature. "Much better." She pets my forearm. "What can I bring you to eat, sweetheart? Oatmeal? Yogurt? Soup?"

I shudder. "Not oatmeal. Yogurt." My throat is still pretty sore, and I sip the juice. "And hot tea?"

"You've got it." She bustles out.

The exchange has wearied me, and I close my eyes for a minute. Visions of the game world dance through my head—the girl and the trees and the mood. The swords. I look at Asher. "Did I tell you to bring my notes?"

"Yep." He picks up my notebook and hands it to me. "New game?"

I start to nod, but my neck really does feel stiff. "Yeah. It just showed up. I kept dreaming things about it." I look at the notes, afraid that I'm going to find gibberish, but the sketches are solid, reminding me of details that I'd lost a little bit. The sword is there—the way to greatness. I flip through the pages, lots of pages, far more than I thought. "This is not bad," I say with understatement. "Did you look at it?"

He shoves his hands deep in his pockets. "No . . . I mean . . . I wasn't going to, but I was sitting there with nothing to do, so . . ."

I half smile. "So yes."

"Yeah. Sorry." He tilts his head. "I can't figure it all out, but from what I can see, it's really good, Sam."

"Really?" A sense of hope cuts through my fear. Maybe if it's good enough, it will be enough to save the company. I glance through the pages. "I keep seeing this forest of trees. Iridescent, but living."

"I love it." His fingers move on my shoulder. The backs touch the side of my neck, and I want to hold them there forever. "You deserve a big win."

How can it be so easy between us and so very, very hard? I'm suddenly very tired. "Tina told me you won an Origins Award."

"Nominated. Not won."

"Yet."

He tilts his head.

"You could have told me. It's a really big deal."

124

"I didn't want you to feel bad. I mean—"

The words are like that giant broadsword in my game vision, slicing right through my heart. "Because you know I've been floundering," I say without question. "Everyone knows. Jared Maloney wants to buy Boudicca."

"What? No! He'd ruin it."

I look away. The headache is coming back. I'm going to need to call Jenny and tell Morgan, who is lead coder, what's going on so they can take over running things while I'm out. "I can't think about it right now."

"Right." He takes my hand. "Look, I need to go, Sam. I have a meeting tonight, and I just wanted to be sure you were over the hump. Gloria has been in the waiting room for a couple of hours, waiting for you to wake up."

Tears, humiliating and copious, spill out of my eyes. I want to say, *No, stop, don't go.* But I only nod. "Thanks for helping me."

My tears spark his, and he squeezes my hand. "See you around, Sam."

Then he's gone, and I feel like all the light has left the world.

Chapter Nineteen

Willow

I am awakened by the buzzer, insistently calling me to answer. Stumbling to the house phone, I say groggily, "Yes?"

"Miss Willow, there's a gentleman here from the FBI. Should I send him up?"

Blinking, I stare at the intercom. "Uh, yeah, I guess so."

I have enough time to splash my face with water and shimmy into a pair of leggings and a sweatshirt before they're knocking on the door. My heart is pounding, and I can barely hear for the rush of blood in my ears. Is this about the painting? It makes my stomach flip, and as I hurry up the corridor, I wonder if I should move it.

Then sanity rights itself. It's not a Renoir. That's ridiculous. I hurry to the door, toss my hair out of my face, and open it. "Hi, how can I help you?"

It's a single guy, not much older than me, the kind of person who blends into the furniture. Conservative haircut, balding a little in front, beige raincoat. "I'm Agent Balakrishna, and I was hoping I could speak to Gloria Rose."

An electric ripple zaps down my spine as I remember the news story in the cab last night. "I don't think she's here. I just woke up." *Be accommodating. Nothing to hide, nothing to see.* "Do you want to come in for a minute, let me check?"

"Sure, if you wouldn't mind." He gingerly steps into the foyer, which is flooded at the moment with jeweled geometrics from the skylight.

He looks up, looks at his feet. "Incredible," he says.

"I know, right?" I cross my arms and stand beside him, my bare toes turned blue by a bar of light. "I always think I'm remembering it better than it is, and it turns out I don't remember it well enough." As we stand there, my brain suddenly goes blank. Is the Renoir in the parlor? In the music room? Dining room? There are dozens and dozens of paintings on every wall in all those rooms, and some in here, too, which is where his attention flows next. To the paintings in the room. "Wonderful," he says. "Who is the art collector?"

"Both my mother and my aunt," I say. My palms are sweating, but one of the things you learn as a performer is to smile through anything.

"This is magnificent." He points to a whirling abstract of dots and lines and motion, violets and blues with splashes of yellow.

"A woman named Eleanor Parrot, a friend of my mother's. We have quite a few of her paintings."

"I know Parrot. Died of a heroin overdose when she was in her early thirties, right?"

"Yes. Are you a collector?"

"I'm afraid I don't have the resources. PhD from the University of Chicago."

My throat dries, but even so, I'm wondering how a person goes from that kind of intense academics to the FBI.

As if he gets the question often, he glances at me. "It is quite difficult to find a professorship these days."

"I can imagine." I find my fingers weaving together and force myself to let go. Hands on hips. Nothing to see here.

His gaze wanders over the rest of the paintings in the circular foyer, skimming most of them, stopping now and then, now at an original Dr. Seuss sketch, framed and signed—"Nice"—and a small, exquisite painting of a dove on a windowsill. "What about this one?"

"I don't think it's anyone famous," I say, and my mouth is so dry I have to lightly bite the tip of my tongue to trigger a saliva response before I can continue, and as I do, I tilt my head to see if I can read the signature. It's a stylized scrawl. Morgol? Margal? "I've always loved the light in it, though," I say, creating unity between us. Maybe. "The opalescence of those gray feathers, the detail in his eye."

He looks at it for a long time. "Do you mind if I take a photo?"

My stomach twists. Is this a problem? But I wave my hand like I have no idea why he'd do it. "Sure." I point toward an upholstered bench against the wall. "Why don't you have a seat, and I'll just run and check if Gloria is here."

I know she isn't here. I don't even know why I'm engaging in this charade, except that fear is pouring rivers of sweat down my back and I need to move to ease it even a little. I can feel the difference in the air when Gloria is around and when she's not, but I pop my head into the rooms along the corridor, parlor, dining room, kitchen, then green-house. Not anywhere.

And then I suddenly worry that the guy will start exploring on his own and see something more. I dash back in, and sure enough, he's wandering down the hallway, his head cocked as he looks at the paint-ings. "Gloria's not home," I announce, blocking his way.

I touch his elbow, gesture him back toward the foyer, spilling its brightness into the hall. To my relief, he responds to the directive and amiably moves back toward the foyer.

"It's a remarkable collection." He stops again, seemingly entranced. "I'm envious," he says, with disarming honesty.

I smile and see him as the nerd he is. A guy in love with art who has to work for an investigative team.

And then I realize that he's turned the tables on me. He's creating sympathy with *me*. The sweat on my body kicks into high gear, and I have to lift my hair off my neck. I can't even think of what to say, and I swallow the dryness in my throat again, wanting him just to go so I can call Gloria.

"Do you think I could have a drink of water?"

He's looking for a way to see the rest of the paintings, and I'm not going to leave him on his own again. Luckily, the place is set up for servants. "Right this way." I head for a door just to the right of the front door. We enter a narrow, plain hallway that ends in the butler's pantry, which also goes into the dining room, but I stand in front of the exit and, like a game show girl, direct him into the kitchen.

Nothing to see here. The small television. The old linoleum, the ancient countertops. I open the cupboard, feeling the twenty million layers of paint under my fingers. "Ice?" I ask politely.

"No, thank you." He stands right where I directed him and waits for me to fill the glass from a Brita in the fridge. Maybe he's just thirsty.

"What made your mom and aunt do all the collecting?"

I shrug. "For my mom, I think she started because she knew a lot of artists, and she was always on the road." I lean on the counter. "My aunt . . . no idea."

"This is your aunt?" He points to a photo on the shelf of Gloria winning an award for a begonia with a vivid yellow-and-green leaf a few years ago.

"Yes. She came up with a new hybrid." Again, I feel that sense of being played. "Is there anything I might be able to help you with, since Gloria isn't here?"

He sips his water. "No, not really."

"Can I tell her what it's in regard to?"

His bland brown eyes go entirely blank. "No, I'll just stop back another time." He drains the glass and gives it back to me. "Thanks. You've been very kind."

Hmm. "Sure."

I walk him back to the front door, braced for one last zinger of a question: *So, when you found the knife . . .*

But he doesn't. He walks out the door, and I close it behind him, leaning on the wood with my forehead until I hear the elevator doors open.

Immediately, I dash back into the living room, scanning all the framed paintings for the one I thought I recognized. It's not here, and I move to the parlor, where paintings hang in masses up to the ceiling.

These are some of the best. The light is good but indirect. An impressionistic landscape drenched in light, another of the mystery painter's works, Marwhoever, of a castle rampart or something, maybe in Spain, with a white bird and a peacock.

And there, framed without fanfare, is the one I saw in the cab. I've seen it a thousand times, a million, a small landscape with trees and a light-drenched sky.

Is it really a Renoir?

Heart pounding, I move toward it, trying to decide how I would know if it was real. The paint seems real, but wouldn't it seem so if it was a copy? I touch a swirl of paint with a fingertip, feeling the swoop. I remember something about brushstrokes and shift my position so that the pale, revealing light lends depth to the paint. It's not all one way or another, not up and down, but what does that mean?

Whatever is going on, it seems like one thing I can do is move it out of sight. I take it down, surprised at the heaviness, and carry it into my bedroom. It's nearly impossible to move my bed, but I can pull the mattress back a little and slide the painting, which is not much larger than my shoulder span, behind it. It won't do much good if there is a search warrant, but for the moment, it will keep unexpected eyes off it.

In the back of my brain, where music grows, I hear the bar of a melody, tinged with the faraway, the . . . something. I stare sightlessly out the window for a moment, not paying the notes attention but creating space for them. A pigeon lands, flutters his wings, and flies off. I think of the painting in the foyer that caught Agent Balakrishna's attention.

My heart is racing with adrenaline, and I snatch my phone off the table. The screen shows two missed calls from Gloria, and I punch one of them to call her back without listening to her messages.

"Willow! Thank goodness."

"Gloria, where are you? There's been an investigator here."

A single hushed moment of pause. "What kind of investigator?"

"FBI. And he was very interested in the paintings."

"I see." Her voice is calm, reveals nothing. "You can tell me about it when you get here. I'm at the hospital with your sister."

My heart drops. "What? Is she okay?"

"Not exactly. She has meningitis."

"Meningitis?"

"She's in intensive care."

I imagine Sam lying beneath white sheets, and it makes me feel hollowed out. I press my hand to my belly. "Is she going to be okay?"

"I don't know. Did you stop by her apartment last night as I asked you to?"

"Yes! She didn't answer. I didn't think I should get the super and barge in." Guilt thuds in my heart. I should have. I squeeze my eyes tight. I really, really should have.

"You're right." Her voice is thin. Sad. Kind of . . . old sounding. "It's not your fault."

"I'll be there as soon as I can, G. Do you need anything?"

"No. Just come. I need you."

———— ❦ ————

I throw on some jeans and a sweater and, on impulse, stop at Bloom's for some food. Not sure what Sam will be able to eat, but Gloria sounded so wan I know she probably hasn't had anything but tea today, and I can't even remember the last thing I had to eat. Waiting for my order, I wonder how long Gloria's been there, when and how Sam got to the hospital.

Meningitis. The word scares me, especially in relation to Sam, who has the best brain of anyone I know. I think my mom was probably really smart, too, but then she mated with a really smart guy and produced Sam, magnifying her genius. She mated with a musician for me, and that produced a lot of music in my mind, but I don't think being creative is as hard as it is to be really smart. I mean, I know how much the ordinary dumb people of the world annoy me, so it's hard to imagine how much worse it would be if you thought at the speed of light and everyone else thought at the speed of a tricycle.

She skipped two grades in school and still had fights with teachers all the time. She wanted to prove to her dad that she was worth something, so she doubled down on achievements, and it worked . . . for about five minutes at a time.

He's a total dick, that guy.

And yes, I'm using *mated* deliberately. My mother was not a faithful woman. Her only real love was for music, for the stage, and unfortunately, her twenty-year affair with bad boy heroin killed that by killing her. A story that's been told too many times.

I shift from foot to foot, anxious to get to the hospital. My heart beats out a tattoo: *Sam, Sam, Sam, Sam.*

Please be okay.

A guy behind the counter calls my number and hands me two paper bags of bagels, cheese, and boiled eggs, and I snatch them out of his hands and dash outside to hail a cab. "Columbia Presbyterian," I tell the driver. He's talking on the phone to a woman in a language I don't know. It sounds like Arabic, and I think about where he might be from, a landscape like the backdrop of the other painting this morning. The cadence of the language weaves itself into the bar of music I heard earlier, and I think of the dove and the orange sky and hear in the distance a call to prayer in the early dawn. Gooseflesh rises on the backs of my arms.

Something is really building here.

I deliberately ignore it, bending my nose into the bags to smell the bagels, and I see a flash of the agent bending in to look at the painting of the dove.

What is he after? Is Gloria in trouble?

Does she *know* she's in trouble?

Chapter Twenty
Gloria

As I enter Sam's hospital room, I'm feeling shaky, which I tell myself is too much coffee and worry over my niece, but it's coming mostly from Willow's comment that an investigator was at the house. Was he going to arrest me?

But right now, there's room for nothing but my Sam. She lies much too still in the hospital bed, looking pale as mushrooms under the greenish hospital fluorescents. Her eyes are closed and the lids are pale blue. Her lips are chapped. I don't want to bother her if she's sleeping, so I place my purse and sweater on a chair, prepared to just sit as long as she sleeps.

My girl, my girl.

Once they told me what she had, I immediately googled meningitis, and it terrified me that she'd been alone and out of her head until Asher had checked on her. He said she'd been very, very sick when he found her, but the IV antibiotics are doing the trick.

"Hi, G," she says in a craggy voice. "How long have you been in here?"

I leap to my feet, take her hand. "Only a minute." I smooth her dark hair away from her face, feeling her fever against my hand. "You're still so hot, my darling. How do you feel?"

Her eyes open a crack. "Like the coyote after he dropped an anvil on his head."

Even sick as she is, so clever. Tears of relief spring to my eyes. "Willow is on the way."

Her eyes close again, then pop open. She squeezes my hand. "G, I'm so sorry about the other day . . . yesterday?"

"Shh, no worries."

"No, that was mean. It *is* your apartment. I know that."

I lift her hand to my cheek. "Don't worry about it. I'm pretty good at taking care of myself, you know."

Her smile is wan. "I wish I were."

I touch her face, her temple. "I do too."

"I have to keep my eyes closed," she says. "The light is killing me."

"Let me turn them off, then." I have to search awhile to find all of them, and I can't seem to find the switch that will turn off the one at the head of the bed, but it's much darker.

"Thank you," she says, blinking. "I don't know why my eyes hurt so much."

I make a cold compress from a washcloth and gently lay it across her closed lids. "How's that?"

"So good." She touches her fingertips to the cloth. "Asher rescued me; did he tell you?"

"He called me."

"I dreamed we were married, and then I guess I thought he should be the one I called." The sound of tears is in her voice. "I completely humiliated myself."

"Honey," I say as gently as I can, "you're very sick. Maybe let everything go for a couple of days. Let us take care of you. Me and Willow, and Asher too. We all love you. You don't have to hold up the tent."

She pulls the cloth off her eyes to look at me, and there are so many tears rising. "My dad didn't come. I called him, and he didn't come."

Because he's an asshole, I want to say. Over and over, he's disappointed her. Left her, chased after some woman or dream interview or whatever was in his selfish head, never seeing the little girl who adored him, who needed him. I brush my hand lightly over her hair. "Shh. Let's listen to a podcast or something, shall we? Or maybe I can read to you. *Daughter of the Forest?*"

Her body visibly softens. "How did you know that was my favorite?"

"Maybe because you carried it around with you for an entire year?"

She gives me a thin smile. "I did." She raises her hand, drops it on her chest. There's something so vulnerable in the gesture that it half rips my heart out. "Would you? Read it, that is?"

"I absolutely would." I settle on a chair and pull up my digital account and order the book. On the screen of my phone is a news alert about the art world reeling, and I know exactly why. My chest squeezes again, warning me this is all coming to an end.

But for now, I'm here. With Sam, who needs me.

By the time Willow arrives, texting me from the waiting room, Sam is in a deep, restorative sleep. I nag the nurse to turn off the light over her head, and the room turns into a pale-gray cocoon. I use her phone to turn on a soft classical playlist to block some of the hospital sounds and tiptoe out.

Willow looks frazzled, her curly hair springing out wildly, overshadowing her small shoulders and boyish figure. "How is she?"

I sit down next to her and accept the bag of bagels she offers. "Very sick, but they caught it in time, and she's on IV antibiotics, so she should be okay."

"How long does she have to stay in the hospital?"

"Could be up to a week, they said, less if she responds well. We should get the guest room ready for her." I spread the bagel with cream cheese, half an inch thick, to hell with the calories. The first bite is 100 percent comfort, like arms around me, and I'm suddenly seven, with my mother in Syracuse, a town not far from our little upstate village, sitting at a storefront bakery with bagels and cream cheese and cups of tea. My mother was French, and she didn't think anyone in America could make proper croissants, but she'd grown up with bagels in her neighborhood in Paris, and they gave her happiness.

One of the few things that did.

A nudging of memory, Isaak and our long talks about our mothers and the things they suffered, pushes at me, but I push it back. There are times to think, and there are times to savor. I choose to savor this perfect bagel and the memory of my very pretty mother enjoying one with jam so many long years ago.

"Are you okay, G?" Willow asks softly.

I realize that a tear has escaped my eye and brush it away. "Just remembering a happy time with my mother."

"Happy? I had the impression she was the opposite of that."

I tilt my head in agreement. "Mostly. She didn't have the life she wanted. It made her bitter." I turn the bagel in my fingers. "But she was sometimes happy in moments, nonetheless."

Willow picks the toppings from a poppy seed bagel, narrowing her eyes. With her crazy hair and skinny arms, she looks like an elf from a children's story. Age has barely touched her. "When I think about her losing her whole music career like that, it makes me want to try harder."

I nod. "It drove your mother, as well."

After a long minute, she says, "Auntie."

Her tone brings my attention to her face. Her eyes are clear and sharp. "Do you think we might need to move some"—she glances at the couple across from us—"things around the apartment?"

A swell of furious emotion burns up through my chest, into my throat. I'm ashamed at my youthful actions, and horrified that she might be in danger, and terrified that I really am on the brink of losing everything I treasure. "Anything in particular?"

"Maybe the landscape in the parlor? The one with poppies?"

The Renoir. I force myself to keep my voice calm, even. "Perhaps."

"And the dove in the foyer?"

"The dove?" A pang shoots right through my chest. "Why that one?"

"You tell me. The agent was very interested."

For a long moment, I'm silent. The dove is one of Isaak's paintings, an original he painted when we were together. There are three others in the apartment, and they are not on their own valuable, but if the dove painting "attracts interest," I'll be in more trouble than I thought. I take a breath, discard the remains of my bagel. "Yes. And three others. Did he say when he would return?"

She shakes her head. "We need to have a serious conversation."

"We do," I say and pat her leg. "I promise we will. But first, let's make Sam our priority. We can't leave her here alone."

"Of course not. We can take turns. I'll hang around until the next round, but we need"—again she glances at the others in the room—"a plan."

"I'm working on that. You don't have to worry about it."

"Seriously?" She scowls at me. "Maybe next time I should just let him walk away with whatever he wants?"

"No! I just—" I feel winded. "I am not sure what to do right this minute. I need to talk to a friend of mine."

"Fine." She sighs. "Sam can't be alone. Will Asher help?"

"I don't think we should ask him."

"Why? They've been best friends since they were little kids!"

"Something happened a while back. They're not talking."

"Then how did he rescue her?"

I shake my head. "I don't know. Maybe she sent him a strange message too."

She presses her lips together. "I feel really awful about that. Why didn't I keep pounding?" She glances out to the hushed waiting room. "Because I was afraid of making people mad." Tears wash her eyes, and she blinks them away. "What if she had *died* because I was too afraid to make a scene?"

"Maybe she wasn't even there, Willow. I don't know what time Asher picked her up."

She nods. "You're right. No point making more drama here. I'm going to the ladies' room. Do you need anything?"

"No, thank you." As she tosses her oversize bag across her body, I say, "Maybe find a comb?"

She laughs and shakes her head. "I'm going feral."

As I wait for her, I open my phone, as we all do, habitually, to distract me, calm my jumpy nerves. In the back of my mind, I'm running scenarios, wondering who I can ask to help me, running through places I might go, and I click on my Instagram feed automatically, seeking the dopamine rush the comments give me. My latest shot is one of the early-morning Manhattan sky from yesterday, which feels about a million years ago. The back of my neck is tight, and my eyelids are dragging over my irises, as sharp as if they have pebbles under them. I close them tightly and lean my head against the wall, trying to calm my racing heart. I texted the lawyer this morning and haven't heard back yet, and I texted Miriam to let her know Sam is sick.

Restlessly, I open my Instagram. There are a dozen private messages, and I open the list, scanning for the name Isaak used. It is not there, but at the end of the list is another name. Noam Tal.

My heart leaps. **Ma bichette, you are not alone. This I promise you.**

Emotion swells up my throat, stings my eyes, and before I know it, tears are falling down my cheeks, hot and unstoppable. I dash them away, uncaring, and text back, How can I reach you?

But there's no reply. Feeling as if I might leap out of my skin, I text Miriam. Are you free? Need to talk. In person.

Chapter Twenty-One

Sam

It's hard to know what time it is, between the lack of windows and the ridiculous amount I'm sleeping. A nurse tells me at one point that I'll be moving to a regular room tomorrow, so I should just try to enjoy the quiet for now. "Quiet?" I echo ironically.

"Quiet," she affirms and bustles out.

As I sleep and wake, the game stays with me, almost haunting me with possibilities. I haven't had enough energy to do anything about it, yet, but the urgency with which it is presenting gives me a sense of faraway hope. It's possible I'm just consoling myself with something that's going to be completely unworkable once I see it without a fevered brain, but I don't think so. I trust this.

Trust my own creativity.

Willow comes in, looking like she rolled out of bed and ran here, her hair barely brushed, her T-shirt wrinkled. "Hey," she says. I see her hesitancy and think of calling her, calling her, calling her. So embarrassing.

"Hey," I say.

She stands at the side of the bed. Her tiny fingers curl over the bar, and I flash on her baby hands, the tiny oval nails that so charmed me when I first saw them. I couldn't believe how tiny her fingernails were.

She seemed like something delivered from another world, not the sister and playmate I'd been hoping for. "How are you doing?" she asks.

For a minute, I can't think of any way to answer. I close my eyes, and across the screen of my imagination runs a tiny being, a baby crawling into the woods of my game.

Huh.

Finally, I realize she is still standing here. I can smell the remarkably robust scent of her skin, a sweaty smell that manages to still be reassuring. I open my eyes. "I'm so tired. I'm sorry, I can't—"

"Sam, we love you. You don't have to do anything. We're doing the stuff right now, okay?"

I nod, and she rubs her hand over the round of my shoulder.

"We would sleep in here with you, but they won't let us."

"Don't stay overnight," I say. "Go home and rest." I tell a lie. "Asher said he'd come back for the night shift. You know he doesn't sleep."

"We'll see." A frown crosses her brow. "I think there's something going on with Gloria, so I might have to do a couple of things."

"What's going on with her?"

"Probably nothing," she says firmly. "And if it becomes something, I'll tell you. The only thing you're allowed to do right now is sleep."

And because even that small conversation has demolished me, I close my eyes. When I open them again, she's gone.

I page the nurse, and she comes and takes my vitals and hands me my iPad and tells me I need to eat, which I agree to try, but when she brings soup, it tastes like water. "You're not going to be able to leave the ICU until you can build up some strength," she says, so I drink it a spoonful at a time until most of it is gone.

My email list scrolls and scrolls, but I can't really read. My eyes are not willing, and maybe that's a good thing. There's something from Jared, but I don't open it. It seems too exhausting.

A doctor comes into the room, head bent over the chart, and I recognize him a split second before he recognizes me.

Eric.

Of course. He's a virologist, and this is his hospital, and I suppose meningitis qualifies. Not as exotic as the diseases he traveled everywhere to study, but not as common as some either.

He doesn't look up for a minute, and I wonder if that chart is mine or if he's still lost in a different case. He's wearing ordinary clothes, jeans and a sweater in many colors that I recognize from a trip we took to Scotland. It pierces me a little, and the day flashes over my memory, the long walk over the moor, a fish-and-chips supper in an ancient pub—

I tap my inner wrist. *Stop.*

Eric. We've been broken up for almost three years, and until this very second, I wasn't sure how I'd feel if I ran into him again.

Eric and I were together for four years, living together for three of those. Not married, not yet, but I had every faith that one day, when I least expected it, he'd fall on one knee at some dramatically romantic moment and propose.

It was a relationship that started all at once and flared into something amazing before either of us knew what was happening. It was wildly romantic, not like anything that had ever happened to me.

I thought it was real. I really did.

We met at a running event, a half marathon. He was a medic, and I had tripped over a rock at mile twelve and sprained my ankle. At first, furious that I was so close, I got up and tried to keep going, but I crumpled again a few yards down the road. Race assistants helped me to the med tent, and Eric was there, tucking a heat blanket around a guy shivering like he was dying.

I saw his hair first, brightest blond and not at all what I usually found attractive, but the color was so shiny bright in the tent and the curls so unruly that it was charming. When he straightened to turn my way, I saw an expression light on his face, as if he'd been waiting for me. I felt like I'd been waiting for him, like because I would meet him on this day when I had practically despaired of ever achieving the life

I hoped to have, a life with a husband and children in some ordinary suburb—it would be impossible to express how badly I had wanted that all my crazy not-suburban life—because I would meet him now, on this rainy day, I had not met anyone else, even though all my eggs were going to turn to dust if I didn't hurry up.

He looked at me. "Hello." His eyes were the palest possible blue; his nose was patrician straight, with a jaw to match. He'd grown up in Minnesota, though of course I didn't know that then, and everything about him was as hale and masculine as with any Viking. Aside from running, I was never much of an outdoor girl, but Eric grew up kayaking through the Boundary Waters, hunting deer, swimming in clear, ice-cold lakes. He loved the outdoors and being physical, and I learned a lot about that with him.

As he stands beside my hospital bed, what I feel is nothing.

I'm waiting for him to say something, and I wouldn't blame him if he turned around and walked right back out. I was the worst kind of crazy breakup ex at first. I just hadn't seen it coming, at all.

He didn't take anything except his clothes.

We'd been traveling in Vietnam two weeks before he left. I knew he'd been struggling with some work issues, a series of painful losses, but I just tried to be present, be with him.

And then he came home from work one day and announced that he was moving out. Like, out of the blue, just gone. At first, I was sure it was just a manifestation of his depression, that was my theory, but within six months, he *married* someone else. Someone I'd never even heard him talk about. She wasn't younger than me or particularly beautiful or anything, just another doctor he worked with.

They went to Africa with Doctors without Borders, and I really did kind of lose my mind for a few months, diving into grief and loss in a way that worried the hell out of my friends and Gloria, not eating, sending Eric a million letters, running so many miles I turned into a skeleton. Willow was traveling to Renaissance Faires with a Celtic band, so she didn't really notice it until she came home for a visit and saw how thin I'd become. She showed up at my apartment one night armed with a care package and didn't leave for three days.

Even now, the memory makes me smile. The vibrator she brought was alone worth the price of admission.

Eric is a specialist in infectious diseases, thus the travel to distant places, and thus it's not *that* weird that he would be my doctor.

It's still weird.

He stands beside the bed. "It is you." He frowns, his gaze collecting data—complexion waxy, rings below the eyes, lips chapped from fever. "I saw your name on the chart and couldn't believe it. How are you feeling?"

"A little better," I manage, but my voice sounds thin.

"Looks like you've been very sick."

I don't know what to say to that. My headache starts to thrum behind my eyebrows, down the back of my skull.

"Your fever is still pretty high." He frowns a little. "How's your headache?"

"Still there, but not so bad."

"Neck stiff?"

"Yeah."

He makes notes of various numbers on his tablet. Up close, I see that he has new lines around his eyes, and his cheeks are thin above the beard. He leans in. "Do you mind if I touch you?"

It's almost humiliating. *So crazy.* I was so crazy there for a while, so bewildered that I couldn't accept that it was over.

I lower my eyelids, shake my head. He picks up my wrist and takes my pulse, touches my cheek with the back of his hand, and then leans in. "Sorry." With his fingers, cool and professional, he checks my neck, palpating the muscles at the back. It means he bends over me, and I can smell his familiar scent. It assaults me, makes me wish I were not lying here helpless, with tubes and electrodes and whatever all over me.

I feel a crumpling in the middle of my chest—so much lost, so many dreams!—and keep my eyes closed as he kneads those tight muscles.

"Very stiff," he says, and I hear a gust of breath leave him. "You were lucky to get here when you did."

I open my eyes, but he hasn't gone that far away; he's still leaning closer than seems appropriate, his pale eyes full of concern. I ask, "What does that mean?"

"That you very nearly died, Sam. You have bacterial meningitis, which can be deadly in a very short time."

It doesn't mean anything to me. Not right this minute. I can't seem to care. "I don't know how I got it."

"We've seen a handful of cases in Brooklyn. Have you been down there recently?"

I start to nod, but the movement is so painful I halt and say, "Yes. Only a few nights ago, though. That seems very fast."

A shrug. "Not really." He straightens again, picks up the tablet, and makes a note. "We should probably get a history of your movements over the time between Brooklyn and getting sick."

"Jeez. I ran all the way from my apartment down to Gloria's. And I saw my dad. And I fed a bunch of homeless people."

A half smile quirks his mouth. "Doughnuts?" I've been buying doughnuts for the homeless ever since I discovered my gluten intolerance.

I allow a moment of connection. "Yes. Are they in danger, do you think?"

"Probably not. That's very casual contact." He's still scribbling notes with a digital pen. "Might need to let Gloria know."

"Oh my God! Do you think she's really at risk?"

He raises his head. "Not likely. But just to be safe. She is older."

"Don't let her hear you say that."

He smiles.

"My sister was there too. But my dad! My dad has little kids. We had coffee together at that place on Eighty-Ninth Street. By the park." My voice is ragged. "He's going to be so mad at me."

"It's not your fault you caught a virus."

"No, I know." But I'm thinking about my dad's face when he hears the news, and it makes my unsettled stomach roil unpleasantly. To distract myself, I add, "I was in Brooklyn for a release party for a new app. I mean, if I got sick there, other people might have too." I think of Jared. We had close contact at the party, and again at dinner.

He nods, writing. "Where?"

I give him the address.

"Anyone else?"

"Asher brought me in." My stomach flips. "He was at the party too."

"Okay." He pauses. "Are you two together now?"

I think of my dream, the house in Brooklyn, the little boys, and tears well up in my eyes. I look away, hoping they won't fall, and twist the edge of the sheet into a tiny tube. "Nope," I manage. "Still not." He was always weirdly jealous of Asher. "We actually had a falling-out a while back. I haven't been talking to him much."

"You and Asher?" His tone is just this side of incredulous.

"Yeah," I say, and it exhausts me to even think of it all. Our long history, our coming together, our terrible, terrible fight that broke us apart. "Me and Asher."

For a long moment, Eric rests his eyes on my face, taking in all my little tells, and I hope he can't read my longing, my wish to go back in time and keep my mouth shut. "And how's Tina?"

"She married Nuri and moved to Atlanta with him. They just had a baby."

That diamond-sharp gaze. The uncomfortable directness. "You must be pretty lonely."

The words are galling. I hate that he can see through me so well. That he knew me so well and still walked away so cruelly.

But instead of grief, what I feel now is a distant sense of outrage. It was cruel and I was blindsided. He doesn't get to be nice to me now and expect that I'll just be the old Sam who worshipped him.

"You know me," I say flippantly. "Lone wolf."

His smile is gentle. "You've never been a lone wolf," he says.

"Don't," I say. By which I mean, *Don't be kind, don't act like you know me, just . . . don't.* "How's Rachel?" I ask abruptly. His wife. The one he met only a few months after we broke up.

"Good. She's in Sierra Leone, actually."

"On a mission?" She's a member of Doctors without Borders.

"Yeah." He flips a piece of paper, flips it down.

Good, I think spitefully. *Serves him right.* "Are you still doing missions?"

"No." A wry smile as he admits, "Africa just about killed me."

"Too hot?" His intolerance of heat was a joke between us—I teased that his Scandie blood was too thick to tolerate it.

He raises his brows. "'Hot' is an understatement. But no, I contracted malaria."

"Malaria!"

"It was bad. I couldn't work for almost three months. Just knocked me out."

A ripple of pain moves over my eyes, and I close them abruptly. "I think the lights need to be off. Gloria turned them off, but the nurses turned them back on."

"I can fix that for you." The room went dark. "Better?"

A voice cuts into the quiet. "What the actual *fuck* are you doing here?"

It's my sister, coming in like a warrior queen, her hair flying. A part of me thrills to it.

"Willow," Eric says. "Good to see you too."

Her eyes narrow. "That's not exactly what I was thinking."

"I gathered." He looks at me. "If you need anything, just ring. I'm on call."

"Yes. Thanks." My eyes are closed, and some drug must be pumping through me, because I'm very sleepy. A movie reel of the game unspools, Willow in a breastplate and armbands, a warrior queen defending the kingdom.

"Are you okay?" Willow asks, taking my hand. Her fingers are cold and fierce.

Despite my wish to stay aloof, I cling to her small hand, pleased that she hates Eric, that she's here, that I'm not, actually, alone.

"Thank you, Willow," I say.

She brushes hair from my forehead. "It's all good, sis. Rest. I got you."

"Is my brain going to be okay?" I ask. Or I think I ask it; I don't know. The lake of sleep sucks me under.

Chapter Twenty-Two
Gloria

Miriam lives in the same apartment she bought in 1976, a two-bedroom her father helped her buy since nobody would have given a single woman a mortgage in those days. The best part of it is the light, which pours in through large windows, and the walls are filled with her own paintings and drawings of places she's visited around the world—watercolor-and-ink sketches filled with movement and light, and oils reconstructed from photos and drawings. She's dressed now in a bibbed apron and jeans, her feet bare, her hands stained with the paint I can smell.

"Come in, darling," she says, holding the door. "I've made coffee."

"I'm sorry to interrupt," I say. "Are you in the middle of an artistic fog?"

"I don't work in a fog," she says, tossing back her hair. "It's only for pleasure, and why would I make that more mysterious than having fun? Come in the kitchen."

The kitchen itself is a tiny galley, but the breakfast nook is open and airy with another big window looking out toward Park. It's a tall building with good views toward the city and the United Nations building, and I have always loved the light. She's set the table, as she does, with cotton place mats and napkins in a whirl of big, smeary florals in blues and purples. A trio of purple irises stands in a narrow pottery vase I recognize. "You picked this up in Fez, if I'm not mistaken."

"Good memory." She carries a silver pot over to the table, then swings around and picks up the tray of cream and sugar. "If you'd fetch the tray in the fridge, we'll be set."

We met the first day of training in 1967, each of us the tallest woman in the room until we met each other. She was a half inch taller but always thinner. In the bright light, I see every wrinkle on her face, and the crepey skin at her chest, and the softness of her jaw. Her eyelids are droopy, her fingers gnarled. Just like mine.

So much time has passed.

"Tell me everything," she says, pouring strong black coffee into teacups for each of us.

"Well, you know about Isaak's arrest. Have you heard that a British Air stewardess was arrested in Amsterdam?"

"No." She drops cubes of sugar into her cup. "That's not good, is it?"

"No."

I sigh, feeling my belly roil. "And this morning, an agent came to the apartment to talk to me. I wasn't there, obviously." I've already filled her in on Sam, and the thought of my niece is a weight pulling all my thoughts into it. I force myself to refocus. "But Willow said he was very interested in Isaak's painting, the one of the dove."

"Isaak's painting?" She frowns. "That's interesting, isn't it? I mean, why? He's never been known for his own work. Or at least *original* work."

"Right. I don't know, unless he just knew that was Isaak's work, and if so, it's a definite connection to me."

"Which they probably already know, or they wouldn't have bothered to show up in the first place."

"Yes." I stare out the window, watching a woman do a series of yoga poses in a modern, glass-walled apartment across the street.

"What do you have to worry about, Gloria? You didn't do the forgeries."

The woman across the street bends over into a triangle, lifts one leg. The thing is, none of the others know the full story. They all think they bought lost paintings for a song, paintings hidden away by the Nazis and then recovered through an art-theft ring in Israel.

Miriam knows the truth. A few paintings were discovered, and Isaak was involved in the sale of them, but then he had a very, very wicked idea: What if he painted fakes that were supposedly lost masterpieces? And what if I then carried those paintings around the world and delivered them to the buyers? I should not have offered them to my friends, but once they caught wind of the cover story, they were all eager to get in on it. Their husbands could more than afford it, and I . . . let them. They should not be in any trouble now—it isn't against any law I know of to buy a painting that looks like the painting of a master. Even Isaak's painting of them is in a gray area—he didn't actually forge any known work, only offered work that seemed as if it *could have* been a lost masterpiece.

"It seemed like such a lark," I say and rub my forehead.

Miriam stirs her coffee, picks up one of the sandwiches I brought over. "I think you need a lawyer, darling. A criminal lawyer, and a good one. Do you know anybody?"

"I found someone. Dani's husband referred him to me."

"Does she know the truth, then?"

I shake my head. "They're all going to be so pissed off at me."

She lifts a shoulder that's still straight and square. "They shouldn't have been buying stolen art."

"Reproductions," I say. "Maybe I need to let them know?"

"Might be dangerous to bring anything to light right now. As it stands, no one is going to realize any of them are connected. Better they should just lie low."

"You're right."

"Why don't you focus on getting your house in order, find a lawyer, and for God's sake, make sure that if they get a search warrant, there's nothing for them to find."

Ice water pours through my body, giving me a shudder. I think of the small, exquisite landscape in my parlor. "Yes. I'll do that." I swallow, meet her eyes. "I'm going to have to get out of New York."

Her eyes are suspiciously bright. She covers my hand. "I know."

Chapter Twenty-Three
Willow

I'm sitting in one of the chairs in Sam's room when Gloria returns. She is as impeccably groomed as ever, but I notice that she's forgotten to reapply her lipstick, and the lines around her eyes are more pronounced. "Come sit down," I say, patting the chair next to me.

She settles her oversize bag on the floor between us and sinks down. "How is she?"

"Okay. Her fever is better, actually," I say. "She was awake for a while when I first got here—and oh my God, guess who's her doctor?"

She shakes her head. "Who?"

"Eric."

Her eyes narrow. "No!"

"Yeah. He's a virologist, right? Isn't that the weirdest coincidence?"

"I hope that doesn't bring them back together."

"Ugh."

From the bed, Sam says, "I can hear you."

"I don't care," I say. "He was very, very bad for you."

Gloria stands. "How are you, sweetheart? Do you need anything? Some tea? Something to eat?"

Sam smiles very faintly. "No. I'm good right now."

I stand too. "Maybe some yogurt?"

She shakes her head. Tired, but a little color is returning to her lips. "I'm good. Really." She looks at me, at Gloria. "I'm so sorry I talked about selling the apartment, you guys. Seriously. I didn't mean it—I was just—"

"You were just coming down with meningitis," Gloria says. "Nothing to worry about."

Sam nods as if she's agreeing to a tall tale. Is there something going on with her that she's not talking about, in addition to the meningitis? I hate that she might have a burden she can't share. That Gloria won't talk either.

How will I get these two to open up?

———— ⁕ ————

Gloria sends me home to rest, and I go without argument, feeling the short night in the graininess beneath my eyelids.

As I leave the hospital, it starts to rain. This time, I have my good coat, but I still don't have my umbrella. Again. I can't afford to take a cab, and I'm feeling strung out and emotional and a little bit lost. It scares me that Sam is so sick.

She's always been prone to colds and flu, falling sick whenever her father was a particular bastard or when she was struggling with some social thing in her life. When Eric broke up with her, she was sick off and on for months. I worried so much that I came home from the Ren Faire to try to cheer her up.

This is worse. She is paler than her sheets, as if she's been painted on the bed. She can't stay awake, and she's . . . actually been kind of nice to me. *That's* scary.

What the hell was that bastard Eric doing in her room? And what happened between her and Asher?

Asher has been part of my life as long as I can remember. He's just always been there, a fixture, Sam's best friend. When I was little, he let me curl up next to him when they watched movies and were supposedly "babysitting" me while my mom was at a gig or out partying with her friends or just out cold in another room. Sam was never the warm and fuzzy type, but Asher was like my older brother. He played tricks on me with rubber spiders, but he also made sure we ate, bringing things from home that his mother had cooked for us, sweeping us back to his apartment on 72nd, where he lived with his family. His whole family—mother and father and five siblings and grandmother—and more books than I'd ever seen in my life, stacked in every room, lined up on a hundred shelves and piled up beside chairs. I loved it there. Loved everything about the big family: the noise, the fact that you were never alone, the smells of food cooking, the debates about politics or the news of the day. His mother taught English lit at City College, and his father ran a warren of a bookstore, three floors of magic below the apartment.

It was one of my favorite places in the world, and they accepted Sam and me as if we were naturally meant to be sitting at their crowded table. By then, Gloria lived with us and filled the apartment with her friends and music and energy, but it wasn't the same as a mom-dad-kids kind of family. I felt like I was living a TV show in their apartment.

Sam and Asher clicked because they were so weird, each of them in their own way. Asher a classic shortsighted nerd with troubled skin, a little bit of a belly, and a complete inability to play any kind of social game. Sam was too tall and too skinny and didn't care what people thought of her. She had weird allergies—like to marshmallows and avocados and latex, for example—and she hated the sounds people made when they chewed. Then as now, she was prickly and too truthful, and in Asher she had the kind of friend we all dream of.

As I'm watching the rain pour down outside the hospital door, I wonder if I should call him. See how things are between them, what happened.

Or maybe it's none of my business. I don't want Sam to get mad at me.

I should, however, make a point of going to see Asher's mother, Deborah. She'd never forgive me if I came home and didn't stop by.

As I'm debating whether to buy another umbrella in the gift shop for zillions of dollars or just try to run to the train, my phone buzzes in my pocket. I pull it out and look at the screen, pleased when I see who it is.

"Josiah," I say. "Hello."

"Hello." The voice is even better than I remember, as rich as butter. "How's your sister?"

"Terrible! Josiah, you will never believe it! She's in the hospital, with meningitis."

"For real? I had a student in one of my courses a couple of weeks ago with it. Must be going around. Is she going to be okay?"

"Yeah." My stomach hurts a little. "I think so. I hope so. I'm at the hospital right now—just came down from seeing her."

"Hey, well, maybe you're not in the mood, but I was going to suggest this afternoon might be a good time to jam."

The most urgent need I feel right this minute is to get online and start googling this whole art story. I'm anxious about G, about what might be bearing down on us, and I need more information.

But my stomach is upset from tension, and one thing I know is that I can't live on *my* nerves when both Sam and Gloria are in full-on freak-out mode. One of us has to keep it together. I know from experience that an hour of music will do more for my clarity of thinking than anything else.

I'll spend an hour with Google, then an hour jamming, then head back up to the hospital. Sam says she doesn't want anybody there, but that's a lie. She always thinks she has to do everything alone.

"I have to go back to the hospital later, but we can jam for a bit. Around two?"

"Great. I'll see you then."

When I get home, soaked to the bone, Jorge says, "Sweetheart, you forgot your umbrella!"

"I got used to Southern California." I give him a wry grimace and exaggerate swiping water off my face.

He reaches behind the desk. "Package for Miss Gloria. Hand delivered."

It's a big cardboard tube, with stamps and labels slathered over it. The tension in the back of my neck rachets up another two hundred million notches. "Thanks. I'll make sure she sees it."

Upstairs, the first thing I do is find my umbrella—the big black one—and prop it against the door so I don't forget it again. Shivering, I skim out of my wet clothes, take a hot shower to warm up, and dress in an oversize sweater and leggings and thick wool socks. The cats swirl into the kitchen with me, tails high, noses hopeful, and I put the kettle on to boil while I feed them their evening wet food. They have kibble all the time in the pantry, but twice a day, they get the good stuff. I stroke each high tail, gently tugging each one's feet off the floor, which they love. They're focused intently on the wondrous deliciousness of Fancy Feast, and I leave them to it.

I carry the mug of tea into the parlor and prop open my laptop on my knees. Google waits patiently as I try to think of the best search terms. Finally, I settle on *arrest in the art world* and hit enter.

The results are copious. Who knew how many art thefts and cons there were? I look around at the paintings in the room, the modern and the old, the sketches and watercolors and tiny scenes tucked in between the others. I've never thought to question any of them before, and now they're all suspect. That bold abstract—who painted it, and why did my mother buy it?

Or at least I think my mother bought it. I don't know, really, which ones she bought and which ones Gloria brought with her when she came to live with us after my mother died. I was only nine, so I hadn't paid any attention to the walls before that.

Sorting through the Google results, I click on the stories about what's happening right now. It's pretty straightforward: a guy was arrested a few days ago on charges of fraud and forgery of masterworks.

Heart in my mouth, I add Gloria's name to the search, and as the wheel spins as it collects my results, my chest aches.

Nothing.

I let go of a breath, then pull out the artist's name. Isaak Margolis. I click on images to see if there are more photos of him. There aren't that many. One is the arrest photo, and he looks blandly away from the camera, as if he's a sophisticate forced to wade through the masses. He's wearing a crisply ironed shirt and slacks, and his hair is truly magnificent, thick and curly, not entirely white.

His story is more interesting. Born in Israel to a mother who was a refugee from the war, he was a talented artist who attended the Avni Institute in Tel Aviv, then traveled to France to see if he could make his mark. He had several shows and a lot of critical acclaim but never seemed to click with buyers.

I am far more familiar with that scenario than I would like.

A few of his paintings show up under Images, a handful of dark landscapes, some scenes of a Middle Eastern market, and several portraits of women, clothed and half-clothed and entirely nude.

More than three-quarters of them have a face I recognize. My hands start to shake.

Gloria.

Gloria at the full apex of her beauty, buxom with a tiny waist and wide hips and red hair tumbling over white shoulders. She is utterly astonishing, and without prejudice, the paintings of her were his best work, especially a partial nude of Gloria looking over her shoulder with a whimsical smile, looking tousled and happy and ready to make a joke, but also very sexy. Her skin is infused with light, her eyes shining.

The evidence that she's connected to Margolis makes me feel sick to my stomach. I think of the woman in Amsterdam who was arrested. Will Gloria be arrested too?

Esme jumps up beside me and butts her head against my elbow. "Wow, baby," I say, skimming a hand over her back, "your mom was a bombshell back in the day."

Although Gloria didn't come up by name, her link to the artist is unmistakable and direct. Gloria was obviously important to him at some point, and I look back at the paintings around me on the walls. Are any of these his work? Does it matter? If he painted his paintings and they landed on the walls here, that wasn't a crime. Why would the agent want to talk to Gloria?

Aside from the little matter of the Renoir, of course.

I suddenly remember the mysterious package that was delivered today. By hand. I hop up, dislodging Esme, who stomps away in a huff, and go to the foyer, where the tube is propped against the wall. Rain is pattering on the skylight, and the clouds make the colored lights dim. I turn on the light to examine the tube more closely.

It's about four feet long and made of heavy-duty cardboard. Words in Hebrew are stamped along one side. One postmark says *Tel Aviv*, and another says *Paris*.

Tel Aviv. That's where Margolis is from. Did he send this? How could he have done it if he was arrested?

From my pocket, I take my phone and shoot a photo. This arrived by messenger for you, I text to Gloria.

When she doesn't immediately respond, and let's be honest, she can ignore a text for centuries, I send another: Also, where are you? Can we touch base?

Nothing. For a moment, I wonder wildly if she's been arrested at the hospital.

That seems unnecessarily dramatic. The agent this morning didn't seem particularly threatening. I'd guess he was trying to get some evidence without having to go through the bother of a search warrant.

I'll try her again in a little while.

One thing I can do right now is get some of this art out of sight. I start with the dove in the foyer and take it off the wall. It's surprisingly heavy, the frame from a previous style era, thick and baroque. For a moment, I can't think what to do with it; then I carry it to what would be a maid's bedroom, smaller than the others, with only a single long window. No. Too plain. Across the hall is Sam's old room, which is just an ordinary guest bedroom now. The closet is deep here, though, and I yank open the door, tug the string for the light, push past old coats and abandoned fashions to the very back, and tuck the painting behind everything in the deepest recesses. For a minute, I'm worried that maybe bugs or rodents could get to it, but it won't have to stay long.

Once I have the hiding place, I round the walls of every room, looking for the signature that means it was painted by Margolis. Gloria said there were four. I find another one in the parlor, a small but surprisingly light-filled street scene that makes me think of the Orientalists with its splashes of red and figures in Middle Eastern dress. It is hung too high for me to reach without a ladder. A third is tucked above where the Renoir—a freaking Renoir!—was, a portrait of a woman staring directly at the viewer, her face and head covered except for her eyes. I've always liked this painting; the turquoise of her head covering contrasts beautifully with the depth of her fathomless, mysterious, and—how do painters do this?—slightly amused gaze.

I take it down and carry it into the closet.

No matter how I look, I don't see the fourth one. I take a slow turn around the music room, checking all the paintings again. Who knows when the FBI guy will come back?

The light is gray and soft, and I swear I can hear my mother playing a melancholy tune on the piano. I sit on the bench and wait for it, but the notes fade away, leaving only the sound of rain pattering at the windows and the soft fuzz of treetops in the distance. I think of my aunt looking over her shoulder at her lover, and my mother writing her song, and my sister sick, broken up with her very best friend, and for a minute I wonder what any of this is all about. It makes me feel hollow.

Life. You're born and imagine a big life for yourself, and maybe you even have it for a minute, and then your lover turns out to be a thief, or you can't kick a bad habit, or your best friend finds another.

And just like that, there it is, the music, winding around the notes I heard in the greenhouse earlier. Mournful, but not exactly. I raise the lid of the piano and pick out a note. It's very out of tune, and I hum instead, drifting into my room to pick up my violin. I'm in soft-focus mode, letting the notes bloom, as I open the case, lift out the violin and my bow.

And there, on the far wall, is the fourth painting. It's a child sitting on a seawall, her dark hair blowing in the wind. I've always loved it for the peaceful tone, but looking at it now, I see the turmoil in the sea, the harsh violet shadows, clouds looming dark on the horizon. It's lonely. How have I never seen that before?

The music, says a soft voice that pulls me toward the music room again. It's my mother's voice, and I sense a spirit of encouragement. I imagine I can see her on the piano, her long fingers plucking out the notes that are just out of reach. I play what I've discovered so far and layer in a line of minor chords, reaching for combinations that suggest something . . . just out of reach.

In my back pocket, the phone buzzes. Gloria's face is on the screen, and I answer. "Thank God. Where are you?"

"I was reading to Sam," she says. "She's asleep now. Why don't you bring that package with you when you come?"

"It's too big. I can't carry it around Manhattan."

"Big?"

"As tall as my shoulder. Heavy too."

"Maybe I should come home and check it out. But I don't want to leave Sam alone for long."

"What's going on, G? Are you in trouble?"

A slight pause. "Maybe. But don't worry about it. I've got it under control."

I scowl. "You don't have to do everything yourself, Gloria."

She is startled into a laugh, then grows serious. "Truly, Willow, this is my problem, and I'll handle it."

I know that stubborn tone. With a sigh, I ask, "Do you want me to open it?"

"No. I'm pretty sure I know what it might be."

"What?"

"A painting. But I want to see it first."

"Like . . . stolen?" I whisper the last bit, my heart hammering away in my chest.

"No," she says definitively.

I nod. "All right. I've taken care of some things. The other ones."

Gloria is silent for a long stretch. "Thank you."

"You know I'm dying of curiosity now, don't you?"

"Of course I do." Her voice sounds lighter. "I'll explain everything, I promise. Just not right this minute."

"Should I bring you dinner?"

"I stopped on the way here to pick up some of Sam's favorites. I'll eat with her."

"I'll be there in a couple of hours, and you can go home."

"That's fine, Willow. It's all going to be all right, you know."

Is it? I wonder. But I say, "I know!" in the chirpiest voice I can.

Chapter Twenty-Four

Sam

Gloria more or less forces me to eat, then stays with me, watching the TV on the wall, not even checking her phone.

"Do you remember when you had your tonsils out?" she asks.

I haven't thought of it in a long time. I was fourteen, which was way older than is usual, and I felt embarrassed and weird. Gloria brought me strawberry ice cream. "Are you going to get me some strawberry ice cream?"

"I would be happy to."

"Maybe tomorrow." I'm itching to get back to my game. I'm relieved when a nurse comes in and tells her that visiting hours are over.

"Willow is going to be here in a little bit," she protests.

"You'll have to tell her she has to wait until tomorrow." The nurse adjusts my covers, smooths them tight.

"But—"

"Sorry, Mother. But your daughter is doing just fine."

I'm about to say that she's my aunt, not my mother, but something in Gloria's face stops me. Something a little lost, something maybe a little proud. It makes me feel vaguely ashamed that I always correct people when they get this wrong.

I take her hand. "Everything is going to be okay," I say.

She shakes her head slightly. "I don't know about that."

"Why don't you go do a series on some exotic plant in your greenhouse? Or go to a tai chi class? It will make you feel better."

She looks at me for a long, long moment, and I have the sense she has something on her mind. Something sad, which is really unlike her.

"What's up, G?"

"Nothing, darling." She squeezes my fingers. "I just don't want to leave you here by yourself."

"They'll be in with magic pills any second to knock me out."

She half grins, and I see how tired she is, how the wrinkles along her mouth seem deeper. "I'll be back first thing in the morning. Willow and I are getting your room ready so you can stay with us for a little while."

"G, that's not—"

"It's not up for discussion," she says, raising a hand. "I'm not letting you out of my sight until I know you're really better."

I don't really want to go to the apartment, which is a place I fought to escape, a place where I was largely unhappy, always longing for something else—my father, then my mother when I lost her. Some other version of myself, maybe, one who could navigate the world with the ease my sister and Gloria and my father did.

But in this, I can see she will get her way. I nod. "I'll see you in the morning."

"What can I bring you?"

What I wish I could eat are some fresh, hot doughnuts, the manna of the gods according to my mother, but of course I can't anymore. "Surprise me," I say.

"Done."

For a while, I sketch ideas in my notebook, but it's too hard to stay awake, and then they come and move me to another room, out of the ICU, but I still have a room to myself. The moving has made me feel more alert.

And lonely.

Loneliness has been my most devoted companion the past couple of years. You'd think I'd be used to it, but the manifestations can be so very humiliating. I lie on my pillows and stare at the ceiling, counting dots in the tiles, thinking of the calls I made blacked out by fever, begging for help from Gloria and Willow and my father and then even Asher.

I'm still desperately embarrassed by my hallucination about Asher and humbled that he still answered my SOS, but now that he's gone again, I wonder if we'll just go right back to where we were.

My phone is under my palm, and I pick it up. "Suzanne, I miss Asher so much!"

"I'm sorry, Sam. Do you want to talk about it?"

I hold the phone and stare up at the ceiling, remembering that I need to keep feeding the AI more history. "Yes. He was my best friend," I say.

"I remember. You met in third grade."

"Yes!" I forgot I'd told her that. "What else do you know?"

"The two of you established a company together called Boudicca, which is named for the game you created together when you were both nineteen. It became a big success." She continues on with the basic Wikipedia version of Boudicca, which is great. She's doing some learning on her own.

But personal learning is what I need to teach her now. "We were friends until we went to our friend Tina's wedding," I say, "and then we became lovers."

"I see."

"Just for the weekend, but it was great. I mean, really, really, really great, soul mates great."

"Do you believe in soul mates?"

"I don't know," I say, my voice hoarse. "I didn't think so, but I feel lost without Asher."

"What happened?"

"When we got back to the city, we had a terrible fight. I just got scared, I think. Afraid that I would lose my best friend, that he'd leave me."

"You have suffered many betrayals," Suzanne says. "It's understandable."

"Have I?" I ask.

"You have, Sam. Your parents were divorced. Your mother died. Your long-term relationship with Eric ended abruptly. It's not surprising that you'd feel frightened about a new relationship."

For a moment, I let that sink in. The ceiling is a soft gray from the light, and I think that I need to work on the way the app uses language. *Frightened* is too formal a word.

Or maybe it isn't. Maybe it's just right. She's certainly making some big steps forward in this conversation. I need to remember to keep giving her more of my history.

"But I lost Asher anyway."

"That must be very difficult. Is there anything you can do to heal the relationship?"

Is there? I have no idea. I miss him so damned much! It was hard when Tina left, but not having Asher in my days makes them feel like I've been sent off to some faraway land where I don't know the language of the locals. I pick up the phone and look at it, scrolling back through the period when I was out of my head.

I called everybody. Gloria, Willow, Asher, my dad.

And everybody called me back, except my dad. It sends a whirl of confused emotions through me, and I punch his icon with a glare. It rings four times and then goes to voice mail. "Dad, I think you might want to talk to me this time. I've been diagnosed with a contagious disease, and you need to be aware of the symptoms."

It isn't even two minutes before he calls me back. "Christ, Samantha, what are you talking about?"

"Hi, Dad. I tried you a couple of days ago, but I guess you didn't get that call."

"I'm sorry. It's just been one deadline after another, and I feel like I'm always behind."

"That's what having kids will do, I hear."

"C'mon, Sam. What's up? What kind of contagious disease? Please tell me it's not some new SARS."

"No, just run-of-the-mill bacterial meningitis."

"Meningitis?" he echoes, and to my deep satisfaction, there's a proper amount of horror in the word. "Are you sure?"

"Quite. I'm in the hospital, and if someone hadn't come to get me, I would have died by morning."

"Sam." His voice is hushed. "I'm sorry I didn't—"

"Don't," I say sharply. "The thing is, Dad, it's contagious, and I had coffee with you the day after I was at the party where they think I picked it up."

He's silent for a long minute. "I don't understand. You might have given it to me?"

"I don't know. Probably not, because they say it's not that contagious, but you need to be aware." I paused, trying to find the right way to say what I need to say. My headache is thrumming around my skull, and the light is bothering my eyes again. "It can be really bad for kids."

"Kids? You mean my kids?"

"Yeah, Dad." I rub the place above my eyebrow. "Your *other* kids might get it if you've picked it up."

"Oh my God. They're so little. What . . . ?" he splutters. "What do I do?"

"I don't know. I think they do a spinal tap?"

"Fuck! I can't believe you exposed me and my whole family!"

Tears sting my eyes. Tears that I never shed, that just keep fucking showing up because I'm not in control of my emotions, and it's both embarrassing and infuriating. "I didn't do it on purpose."

"I have to go. I have to call the doctor and find out what the hell we're supposed to do."

And he hangs up. I sit in the bed with my phone in my hand, utterly still. He's so bad at being *my* father that he's like a cartoon villain. I can see him in my imagination, drawn in Sharpie, his nose a straight black L, his eyebrows beetling down, a cloud above his head exclaiming, *Christ!*

"Suzanne," I say.

"Yes, Sam? I'm listening."

"My dad is a dick."

"What does 'dick' mean in this context? Penis?"

It makes me laugh. "Yeah, but a really bad penis."

"Noted."

I text Willow and Gloria to let them know I've been moved to a new room with longer visiting hours, in case Willow still wants to see me tonight. One of the machines starts to beep, and a nurse comes in calmly to check on me. Reads something, flips it off. "Give me the phone, baby," she says, and I drop it into her palm. Everything about her is round. Soft. She presses a button on the bed and makes it flatter, takes my temp. "You need to just let that outside world go. Hear me? He isn't worth it."

I close my eyes, nodding. It would be one thing if it were a lover, but you can't just get another dad, can you?

Chapter Twenty-Five
Willow

I'm still deep in the bowels of the internet, trying to track down definitions of crimes, going on my best guess of what might have happened here. What I discover makes it feel like anything could happen. If she carried contraband, she could go to prison for a long time. If she stole a painting, she'll never see the light of day.

I just don't have enough information to know for sure.

When the house phone rings, I realize it must be Josiah, and I leap up to let him in, opening the door so I can wait for the elevator. Anticipation zips around my body, restless pops of possibility. I'm half-worried that he won't be anything like I remember.

And then the elevator opens, and he's there, ducking under the low doorway to emerge into the corridor between apartments.

I noticed that he was quite tall before, with those beautiful long legs, but it's startling to see him in the environment I know, in a doorway I've crossed a hundred times. He's dressed in everyday clothes, jeans and a heathery sweater and a raincoat hanging from very broad shoulders. He's wearing the same knitted hat as the other night.

I didn't imagine anything. His cheekbones, his mouth, his sleepy tiger eyes. I take a breath. "Hi."

"Hey," he says, in that amazing voice.

"Hey. Come in."

He brings himself and his bass into the room, looking up at the skylight as everyone does, lifting his eyebrows. "Wow, this is the real thing, isn't it?"

No one comes into this apartment, especially anyone who lives in the city, and doesn't say something like this. "It is." I gesture. "The music room is this way."

He follows easily, glancing at paintings, but mostly just loping behind me, his feet light on the wooden floor. In the music room, he looks around curiously, noting the album and magazine covers, the framed original music. "Damn," he says, splaying his hand over his heart. "I wasn't expecting to feel such awe."

"Look around. I don't mind." I dip my head back to the piano, running another series, trying a minor slant. He rounds the room, looking at everything, his hands tucked behind his back as if he's in a museum.

"Do you have a favorite song?" he asks.

"Of my mother's?" I drop my hands into my lap. "Of course I love 'Write My Name Across the Sky.' I mean, it's her signature. It made her wealthy, and it still earns royalties."

He's listening with his head tilted slightly. He has that gleam in his eye that people get, men and women, when they get close to the big, big fame story of my mother.

"But?" he prompts.

"She sang lullabies to us." I run through the notes of one of them on the piano and sing along. "Those are the ones I most love. Sam, too, though it's hard to get her to talk about my mom at all."

He comes over, sits on the piano bench with me, and lifts his hands and plays a bass harmony to my notes. "This is 'The Rising Moon,' right?" he asks, referring to a song on her third and least successful album. He hits the notes more heavily, giving it the rock tone.

I nod, smiling, and my hands play of their own accord, embroidering the song. When I get to the chorus, he picks it up, and we sing together, his voice making my own plain one sound so much richer. The hairs on my arms stand up, and I look at him. He nods, very slightly. We finish the song and sit quietly, letting the sound fade. My heart is racing.

"This chemistry, the musical chemistry, is really something," I say.

"Agreed," he says, resting his hands on his thighs.

He's close, and there is an electric chemistry hanging around us, binding us. Is it music or sex? Both. I want to kiss him, and I don't. If it's music, I want that more than anything physical.

And again, I hear my sister's taunt, *I'm sure you'll find a guy to rescue you soon enough.*

There's a difference between rescue and partnership. On the piano, I play a small bar of the sonata. "I've been writing this thing for a few weeks," I say, then express a barely acknowledged ambition: "I'd really like to submit it to this major contest, and I think this"—I move my index finger between our chests—"feels like it could take it to the next level."

He nods. Just waits, his expression neutral. I suddenly think that I'm overthinking things, that maybe he's not one of those people who will sidle up next to me to get some reflection of my mother somehow. He's a professor, a musician in his own right, and—

"Maybe you can just be here now," he says.

"What?" I say mockingly. "Is that even possible?"

"I've heard it is."

"Huh." I look toward the window, instinctively taking in a breath and letting it go. It helps. As it always does. "Are you Buddhist or something?"

"Since birth, actually. My mother found the practice when she was a teen."

I was only kidding, but my curiosity wants more. "In Marin County?"

"Probably in San Francisco, I'd guess."

It makes him even more appealing. The Buddhists I've known are calm, thoughtful people, qualities I'm drawn to, and I have a sudden desire to just lean into his shoulder and rest my head there. It's such a strong urge that I have to duck my head to hide my longing. It would just be such a *relief*.

But isn't that what Sam sneered about?

I don't know. What I do know is that between the trouble Gloria's in and the worry over Sam's illness, I can't even think about whatever this is outside of the music. I focus on the keyboard, plonk a few notes.

Beside me, he's quiet. And then he suggests, "Why don't you play what you've written so far?"

"Good idea." I stand and pick up my violin, spend a few minutes tuning it. Josiah sits at the piano, waiting. Behind him are windows showing the building across the street, two windows lit in the dark afternoon, and a busy restaurant on the ground floor. In the distance is Amsterdam, a running river of taillights. My mother watches from an album cover, and I turn toward her.

I take a breath, close my eyes, and let the music rise through me, run through my veins and into my hands, and then emerge from the instrument itself. It's unlike music I've written before, woven with a thread of melancholy that surprised me when it first arrived.

As I play it in my mother's music room, though, I know where it comes from. It's the thread of loneliness every motherless child feels, a cry at night that goes unanswered, a longing that just cannot be filled by anyone else. I think of her pretty eyes and how rarely she laughed. She had tattoos for each of us, me and Sam, and I think of those now, feeling them in the notes. I think of her wild, raw voice, blazing so briefly across the heavens, calling to the lonely around the world.

I break off, a swell of emotion making me press a hand against my heart.

"Insight?" Josiah asks.

"Yeah," I say and lift the instrument again to finish.

Josiah moves into position on the piano and says, "Again."

I start at the top and play, and he listens, very softly adding under-tones here and there, and I see what he's doing, so I simply play it again, and then again, and by the third time, he's worked out a complementary line. "Do you have paper?"

"Right there," I say, pointing to the table by the window where I've left the tablet of manuscript paper out. "Old school, huh?"

"You too, I see." He holds up the sheaf I've been working on and reads it, nodding, then bends over and, faster than I can believe, scrawls a long series of notes, singing to himself the same way I do. "Play that midsection again." He hums and I pick it up, and he writes, then carries the paper to the piano but picks up his bass instead of sitting. "This is really good, Willow," he says.

I smile at him. "I had a feeling."

And then we dive back into the music, repeating the notes again and again, refining them. At some point, he starts to hum along, ges-turing for me to follow his lead, and I do. He sings the bass and I sing the melody, and I'm wishing for recording equipment because it's so damned beautiful.

"What are the lyrics?"

I lower the violin, look toward the window. Wait. A whisper comes, far away at the edge of everything, but I nod. "I don't know yet. But I will."

"When's the deadline?"

"Three days from now."

His thick dark brows rise, and he makes a soft whistle. "Let me see what I can do." He glances at his watch. "I've got another twenty minutes right now. Let's keep going."

I walk him to the door, feeling the buzz that means the work is good, that the music is working. "Thank you so much, Josiah," I say as he opens the front door.

"It's not a favor," he says, turning back to face me. "It's exciting to create something so powerful. I felt it the minute we started to sing together in Brooklyn."

"Me too."

He just stands there for a moment, and I realize that one of the things I am drawn to is his stillness. He only looks down at me, and I force myself not to look away because it's uncomfortable, but I can't resist crossing my arms over my chest.

He notices, gives a slight nod. "I'll call you when I've worked through my obligations."

And before he leaves, I really want to touch him, and my hand reaches out of its own accord and rests on his upper arm, just above his elbow. It halts him, and for a space of lost time, I think he might kiss me, or I might stand on my toes to kiss him, and I'm already half living it when he covers my hand with his and says, "Be here now."

I laugh softly, drop my hand. "I'll do my best."

Then he's in the corridor and pushes the button for the elevator, and I wouldn't want to be rude, so I stand at the doorway, waiting with him. Noticing things. His easy posture. His long throat.

The elevator arrives and he steps in, lifting a hand as the doors close.

I lean against the wall.

Gloria. Sam. Both of them need me.

Chapter Twenty-Six

Gloria

It's pouring still when I arrive home. Willow called to say she was going to run some errands and go to the hospital, so the rooms are empty. Oddly expectant. Eloise and Esme swirl into the foyer as I shed my wet coat and hang it up to dry. "Don't tell me those stories," I say. "I know Willow fed you." They mew, pitifully, as if to convince me of the story. I bend and stroke each back in turn, talking because they like it. "I think our Sam is going to be just fine. Her fever was down and she was eating like a soldier when I left. The nurse told me that's a good sign." I sink down on the worn velvet-topped bench to reach them more easily. They slink around my legs. "Poor girl."

I kick off my shoes and notice that Isaak's painting of the dove is missing. It makes my stomach twist, bringing home the mess I'm in. The package Willow told me about slants against the wall, almost unnoticeable in the gloom. Taking a breath, I stand and flip the light switch, which illuminates the six wall sconces around the circle.

It's a painting, I'm sure, in the heavy cardboard tube. How did he know where I live? I suppose it couldn't be that difficult to track me down if he already follows my Instagram. I wonder with a pained sense of thwarted possibility how long he's been watching. Why he never spoke up before this, when we might have had a chance—

No. I'm not going down that road again. Letting go of him the first time was one of the hardest things I've ever done. I missed him for literally years.

I lift my chin, square my shoulders. A long time ago.

Thinking of Instagram reminds me that I need to post something before bed. It's been a full day, and one of the things about the algorithms is that they like regularity. It doesn't matter if it's every two hours or every two weeks, but a pattern matters. Perhaps, considering everything, it's foolish to make a social media site my priority, but life is patterns, isn't it? Patterns and routines create sanity where nothing else can.

The painting leans against the desk, waiting. Lamplight spills down the brown paper side, catching on stamps and pointing out customs marks. From a container on the desk, I take a pair of scissors and slit the tape carefully, pulling loose the lid. For a moment, I hesitate, feeling a thousand emotions welling to the surface—hunger and lust and longing primary among them, all in tones of orange and red, tangled and knotted.

I take a breath and tug the canvas from inside. It's too large to open where I am, so I carry it into the dining room and let it unfurl on the gleaming oak table.

It's the painting I thought it might be. Me, at age twenty-seven, sleek and unmarred by time, my nude body insouciantly displayed as I lie on one side, head propped up on my hand, my hair loose. I touch a finger to the full, plump breasts. "I remember you." Touch my smooth thigh. "And you."

I remember lying on Isaak's bed, feeling hot and aroused and amused by both, as he painted and painted and painted. A sound of cellos plays behind it, full throated and somehow wise, the undertone to every memory I have of him painting.

Do you have to be young to be in love like that? Because I've never felt it since. Even now, the power of it can make my heart flutter.

Nothing like an old fool, I think, shaking my head as I roll the painting up again and carry it under my arm to hide it in my room for now. Will I show it to Willow and Sam? I'm not sure.

As I walk back through the apartment, I find the note that was enclosed, lying on the floor. A pale-blue piece of linen paper, with a single sentence in a hand I recognize so very well from all the letters he wrote, dozens and dozens of them, letters I still have in a box in my closet.

I have never forgotten you.

The handwriting, elegant and slanted hard to the right, wakes up memories I've kept buried for a long time. The whole of our intense, deep love affair tumbles into my body, memories full of color and laughter and sweet yearning.

And all of it is in the painting. Youth and passion and color and longing.

Oh, Isaak.

It comes to me that this is probably his very finest work. Considering the notoriety of everything that's happening, he wanted it safe, and the fact that it has arrived now means he must have known Interpol was closing in on him.

Does that mean he has planned for protections for me? How can I find out?

I walk around the painting, admiring the light, the vividness. It breaks my heart that his success will come now, so late in his life, when he will never be able to enjoy it. His arrest is accomplishing what he could not accomplish before: fame and recognition for his work.

Oh, Isaak, my love. I brush my fingertips over the lips of the woman in the painting.

Suddenly I have a great idea for an Instagram.

Digging in my closet, I use a stepladder to reach a high shelf and get the letters. I carry the box to the bed and take off the top, and at the sight of his handwriting on the envelopes, a twist of mingled pain and longing courses through me. Just that would make a great photo, the striped hatbox with letters inside, the elegant handwriting, the archaic stamps and airmail paper, so thin it's nearly transparent. I pick one up and feel a fine trembling in my limbs, feel a ghost of the fresh possibility that ran through me when I saw one of his letters on the table of my apartment when I arrived home from a trip.

I open the flap of one.

June 17, 1977

My darling Gloria,

Tonight, the sun is low on the sea, shining red and orange as if I've spilled my paint. I'm thinking of the night we walked for hours and hours, trying to learn everything we could about each other. Your little sister. My much-younger brother. Your love of hummus and lemons and flowers of all kinds. My love of the markets, the noise and color.

I wish you were here with me tonight. I don't know how I can bear to wait until next week. Always, our moments together are so fleeting!

I stop, a pain thudding through my chest so intensely that I'm worried for a moment that I might be having a heart attack.

But I'm not. These are just the ordinary feelings of a woman remembering her great, lost love.

It has been decades since I've looked at them, since I tucked them away here when I came to take care of the girls, and it won't serve me to read them right now. I might, one day soon, but I don't have the fortitude to do it now, to see my young and hopeful self through the lines. The great tragedy of aging is not the loss of the supple body but the illusions we are forced to leave behind, one after the other, like a string of pearls from a necklace. That all will be well, that dreams can come true, that we can always do what we wish, that sacrifice and sorrow are not inevitable.

For now, I carry the box to the music room and gently scatter a solid handful over the table, then zoom into the address from so long ago, *Gloria Rose, 919 3rd Ave, #12, New York, New York, USA 10022.* I shoot it, then the edges of the overlapping envelopes, then zoom in on the *Par Avion*, suggesting a long correspondence. So long. Almost sixteen years, all together.

The hollow ache returns to my chest. I wish I could see him just one more time. I didn't know I was harboring the longing until this all came up, and now it feels like I've been cheated of something.

In the end, I post only the *Par Avion* banner above my name and address with a lighthearted, **Remember the days when we received actual mail? Tell me about someone you corresponded with.**

I wonder if Isaak will see it.

My phone rings, and when I look at the face, I see that it's my lawyer. My heart leaps into a tangled rhythm, and my hands are shaking as I pick up. "Hello, Mr. Walters."

"Hello, Ms. Rose. I have found quite a lot of information. Can you meet me first thing, downtown?"

"Can we speak over the phone?"

"I'd rather not." He names a coffee shop, and I scribble the address down. "I'll see you in the morning at seven thirty."

I hang up, feeling jangled. Good news or bad? I wish he'd given me some hint.

Chapter Twenty-Seven

Sam

I'm restlessly drawing more ideas for the new game when a familiar voice says at my curtain, "Knock, knock."

I'm too drugged to hide my pleasure. "Asher!"

"Are you decent?"

"Not including my hair, yes."

He comes in carrying a white bakery bag. He's wearing a button-down with thin green and blue stripes that makes him look tan and vigorous. "Hey. How are you?"

"A lot better." I gesture. "They moved me to a regular room about an hour ago, to make room for some other patient. Which lifted my spirits because now I can have more visitors"—I'm babbling because he's here and I want him to stay and I'm afraid of doing something to send him scurrying off again—"like you." Quietly, I add, "I didn't think you'd come back."

He takes a breath. "Yeah, well." For a moment, that tension is between us, the loss, and then he wipes it all away and smiles. "Brought you something."

I peek into the bag, and even before I see them, I smell the yeasty perfume of glazed doughnuts. I look up—he knows I'm celiac, but has he forgotten?

"They're from Ruby's." A gluten-free bakery.

"Oh my God." I take one out and look at it, admiring the soft brown finish covered with thin sugar that's cracking here and there, flaking off to fall on my stomach. I hold it up to my nose and just barely lick the side. I close my eyes and focus on taking one bite, not too small, not too big, and letting the soft texture and sugary deliciousness fill my mouth. "It's so good."

He chuckles. "I can tell."

"Do you want the other one?"

"No! They're for you." He points to the end of the bed. "Do you mind if I sit?"

My heart aches a little as I pull my feet into a cross-legged position. I can't really look at him. I've been missing him so much, and it's so crazy that he's just—*here*, now. I'm afraid he's a figment of my imagination. He sinks onto the end of the bed, letting his feet dangle, and I look at his hand, strong and fine, with long fingers and good oval nails he takes exceedingly good care of. He has much better nails than I do.

I take another bite of the doughnut. "It was very nice of you to bring these."

"Everybody needs treats when they're sick." He swings his backpack off his shoulders, unzips the top pocket. "My mom sent chicken broth, no noodles."

I laugh. "Really? That is so nice!" Tears fill my eyes. I look away, hoping he hasn't seen.

He has. His hand circles my foot. Neither of us says anything. I hold the doughnut in my hand and the plastic container of soup in my lap. I will have some later.

"How is your mom?" I ask when I'm less stupidly emotional.

"It's been a rough winter for her. She lost a couple of friends last year, but I think she's shaking it off now."

I take another bite of the doughnut. "Willow will go see her soon, I'm sure."

"You should go too. She misses you."

I nod. A thousand words pass through my mind, words like *I'm sorry* and *please forgive me* and *can we start over?* I don't say any of them. I want him to sit right there, all night, all day. Not go away again.

"I've been thinking about your new game, Sam. And the business."

Here's something I can talk about without danger. I reach for the scribbled pages I've been working on all day when I'm awake. "I've been sketching out a lot. I think it's . . ." I flip through the pages, shake my head. "It has a lot of potential." I laugh, looking at the forest diagram. "No, it's really magical. I'm excited for the first time in ages."

"I think so too."

I look up. "Really?"

His dark eyes shine. "Yeah. Your notes were super crazy, but I could see what you have in mind. At least I think so." He takes out a notebook that's a twin to my own. We settled on these notebooks a million years ago, and they're still perfect for this kind of brainstorming. He opens to a page filled with lines of code in his precise, small printing alongside a clear drawing of a girl in a forest surrounded by little animals. "This?"

"Yes!" The vision floods back in, all kinds of Mylar colors, open world, the dark forest, the girl. Staring, I let it rise, coalesce. "A girl who learns she's powerful. But it's that setting, that—"

"I'd like to help you, if you'd be open to that."

I hardly breathe. "You're kidding."

"No. Let me help you get back on your feet."

A hole opens in the middle of my chest. He feels *sorry* for me.

"Look, I said that wrong," he says.

"It doesn't matter. I can do it on my own. It's a great idea, and I am a coder, too, you know."

"Hey."

I clench my jaw to keep my emotions in place. Meet his eyes.

He clears his throat, and I realize that he's hiding emotions too. He doesn't like this any more than I do.

So why haven't we solved this rift? For the first time in my life, I wish I had Willow's understanding of human dynamics, because then maybe I could fix it.

Maybe I should ask Suzanne, my AI app.

"I don't feel sorry for you," he says in a fierce, focused voice. "I'm furious that Jared wants to take the company, but I'm also . . . enchanted by this game idea. I'd really like to work on it with you. I think it will be even better than *Boudicca*."

Working with him again would be like the sun shining after months of rain. I downplay it with a wry smile. "We both know how much better it will be if you do the coding."

"We're a good team."

"Yeah. We are."

He smiles. "Feel up to some brainstorming?"

I smile back. "Yes."

He settles on the end of the bed, but that's kind of awkward, so eventually, I move over, and he sits next to me so we can see what we're each doing. Our arms are close together, our hips touching even if the sheet is between us, and it feels so normal, so good, that I have to force myself to just be chill.

He smells of himself, of the notes of childhood that comfort me, the endless nights we spent writing the game, changing it, and rewriting it, and at some point, I simply fall asleep slumped against his familiar shoulder. At peace.

Chapter Twenty-Eight
Gloria

What am I going to do?

Willow has gone to the hospital to take my place, and I'm ostensibly getting some rest, but I can't stop pacing. *What am I going to do? What am I going to do?*

The thought is a chant running through my mind over and over. I can't sleep, and I wander the apartment from room to room to room before finally going out to the greenhouse, where I stand barefoot in my pajamas and transfer seedlings from a long tray into small clay pots. I've strung fairy lights throughout to give a beautiful background to the night photos, and the soft white lights now ease me.

The baby plants, vigorous and yet so vulnerable, already have the imprint of their species on their tiny leaves, and I wonder about that—nature versus nurture, seeing the line between my mother and Billie and Willow, the music running through each of them like a powerful river, whereas I have never had a single note pop up in my head ever. Can't even imagine it. Music is born into you.

And whatever it is that makes it possible for Sam to create the complicated coding and visual work of making games must be inborn too. Where did that come from, I wonder? My father was a kind man, a good man, but he was never brilliant. I never knew my mother's grandparents, of course. They were lost during the war, but my mother spoke of them as intellectuals, bohemians.

I suddenly think of Sam's dad, Robert. He might have had a hand in that brain of hers too. He has a little boy who's just as strange and smart as Sam was.

Unlike the rest of them, I didn't get any big gifts. I'm pretty good at a lot of things—the photos and my plants. I can sing passably well and dance well enough to get compliments, but mostly I am friendly. My gift has always been an ability to be happy.

It sounds small until you live in the world for a while.

Despite my worry and the scythe hanging over my head, I am even happy in this moment. The lights make a bokeh background for the newly potted baby iron cross begonias with their amethyst swirl leaves. I first discovered the species when I was flying between Shanghai and New York. Unlike so many plants, the most beautiful parts of many begonias are their leaves, which can be ruffled, textured, colored, spotted, pointed, swirling. I brought them home for my sister the first time I saw them, because she'd just bought the apartment with its greenhouse and I thought she'd be as captured by their beauty as I was.

Billie, however, had no knack or desire for growing things. I took the begonias home to my own apartment when I saw that she wasn't taking care of them. I started collecting them, gathering the most beautiful forms I could find.

So many dazzling shapes and colors. I bend close to the iron cross and shoot the geometric texture running beneath the dramatic cross. As I bend, my back protests and I catch my breath, stand up. It eases, and I bend down again, this time more gently.

What am I going to do what am I going to do what am I going to do?

The story is all over the news now, not just the cable channels. Turns out some very famous people bought paintings from Isaak, thinking they were rare, undiscovered pieces, and although most of them are trying to distance themselves from their connection to Isaak, a few are outraged and stupid enough not to recognize that they look like idiots for buying fakes of paintings that never existed.

My incessant scrolling through the various stories revealed that the case broke, finally, because the offspring of a famous French actor discovered that the "lost" masterpiece they'd imagined would bring them a fortune turned out to be a forgery.

Tenderly, I transfer a tray of babies into a spot where they'll get indirect light for most of the day, and remember when he told me about his scheme. We were sitting on a dock over a lake in the mountains of Italy, eating strawberries from a bowl.

"What if," he said, "a cache of lost masterpieces had been hidden by the Nazis?"

I laughed. "How convenient."

He raised his eyebrows and laid out his plan. He would study various artists who meshed with his personal style and then create new paintings in their style and go through a meticulous aging process to give them the right patina.

And sell them.

I thought it was utterly brilliant. And honestly, it didn't seem like anything illegal, only slick. I agreed to carry the paintings he created in order to get them over international borders.

Such a lark!

And the paintings themselves made Isaak happy. He found some creativity in the work of copies by imagining what artists *might* have painted: a lost Picasso from the Blue Period, a Matisse window, a Van Gogh from the early days.

Now that the story has made international news, some of Isaak's own paintings are surfacing too. His Moroccan markets, especially, have caught the attention of the art world, and one sold for a rather startling sum out of a gallery in France.

I take a photo of the begonias for a future post, wondering if I can use the stamps and letter fronts in a series. The idea calls to me, and I head back inside to fetch a few of them.

It's only as I set up the shots that I realize how idiotic it is. Once Sam is better, I have to get out of here. Or if the FBI close in before that, I won't be here anyway.

But I'm here now. I have nothing else to do. It's calming my blood pressure. If I have to flee, I can line them up to post.

I sweep clean one of the photo work spaces I've set up and angle a ring light over the grouping of plants and letters, arranging and rearranging until I find one that suggests a story. I'm careful not to let any of the return addresses show, but the stamps are a rich tale on their own, and I let them tell it. A packet of letters from a long-ago lover, who wrote to me from Casablanca and Paris and Florence. The light is soft, and I'll enhance the aging with filters before I post. A little ripple of excitement breathes air through my worry, and again I imagine Isaak seeing my feed, seeing his letters.

It's hard to imagine him in prisoner clothing. He dressed with sartorial splendor, in the best fabrics—linen trousers and silk shirts, always with a handkerchief tucked into a top pocket. He liked hats, despite the fact that they were falling out of favor by then, and I can see him in a white fedora, standing on a cliff outside some mansion where we'd been invited to stay. It happened often—houses in southern France, in the Alps, in northern Italy, a place he loved.

We'd been together for six or eight months by then, and I was beyond smitten—he was unlike any man I'd ever met, polished, urbane, sophisticated, passionate. I loved his skin, the color of rich earth from his long days outside painting, and his snapping eyes, and his thick hair. I loved the way he kissed, long and slow and thorough, and the way he made love with hands and mouth and body, bringing me to such pleasure I would sometimes fall stunned and dizzy to his side after.

We had made love in a big four-poster bed, with winds blowing hard in the Swiss night and the fire snapping in a hearth so enormous as to be medieval. He propped himself on his arm and looked down at me, touching my nose, the round of my lower lip, the edge of a nipple. "I think of nothing but you," he said in his accented voice. "I've never had such a thing happen."

I swallowed. "It's the same for me."

"Is it, *ma bichette*? I can't think how you love a man like me when there are pilots and kings of industry seeking your attentions all the time."

"They're all like small boys," I said, touching his cheekbone. "You're the only man I've ever met."

"I am in love with you, my glorious Gloria. I have nothing to offer you, but I want you to know it."

I rose and pushed him back on the pillows, pressing my lips against his. "I don't want anything."

"No diamonds or promises?"

"No," I said and meant it. "Marriage is not for me."

For a long moment, he was silent. "But what of children?"

I shook my head, very sure. "No."

"You and I, we would have lovely children."

I smiled. "No doubt, but then we wouldn't have this." I reached over and placed my hand gently on his stubbled cheek. "This is enough."

"Do you love me?" he whispered.

"Yes," I said fiercely. "I have never loved like this in my life." I kissed him, lingering. "I never will again."

He kissed me back, and we touched each other's faces, eyelids and brows, noses and chins. "I love you," he whispered. "I love you. I will love you forever."

In my greenhouse, far, far away from that time and that place, I feel tears on my cheeks. How did I not realize that I would never stop missing him?

Chapter Twenty-Nine

Sam

Sometime in the middle of the night, I wake up disoriented in my hospital bed. For a long moment I lie there blinking, trying to remember why I'm here. I feel lost and overheated, and my mouth is very dry, the headache and stiff neck suddenly back.

My mom is standing beside the bed. It scares me. "Am I going to die?"

Her hand is light and soft as she brushes my hair off my face. Just like Asher does, or did. Like Willow did. "No," she says quietly. "You're going to be fine."

I close my eyes, and I can smell her, cigarettes and Jean Nate, which she liked for its fresh, lemony splash. It transports me to a time when I was small, before Willow arrived and ruined it all. I'm sitting in her bathtub, with bubbles boiling up around me. It must be summertime, because the glass bricks are aflame with sunset, which I always used as evidence that I should *not* be going to bed yet. *It's still light!*

And then I'm in a towel, and she's singing to me as she combs my hair, then weaves the wet mass of it into a braid that will make my fine hair look much fuller the next day. "Your hair is just like my mother's."

"She died," I supply.

"Yes."

"And you miss her a lot."

"Yes, I do. Every single day. She would be so proud of me for the music."

A sense of love and quiet moves through time from the heart of that child into me. As if there is a soundtrack that accompanies every scene and every moment, the ghost in my hospital room—or the figment of my imagination—starts to sing a ballad that was on her fifth album, *North Star*, about a girl who went to the city and succeeded, but war came and took it all away. She loved to sing to us, one on each side of her. I can feel her body, the spareness of her breasts, her slim arms.

The song has always been one of my favorites, too quiet for most of her crowd. "Willow sings this song," I say into the room and realize it's empty, except for that very sister, curled up like a little cat in the chair, covered by a coat. When did she get here?

I don't remember. Gloria was here at dinner, and then Asher, but then it's all dark. They must have given me drugs, which have now worn off. My head is pounding, not the way it has been, but enough that I wouldn't mind more meds. If I ring for a nurse, it will wake Willow. She's sleeping hard, her mouth slightly open. She looks about seventeen, and I feel a swell of tenderness.

When my mother first brought her home from the hospital, I thought she was like a kitten and would grow fast enough for me to have an actual playmate, but day after day, she stayed small, her voice wailing in the middle of the night. Wailing and wailing and wailing, as if she knew something terrible had happened.

That something terrible was my father leaving. He left when my mother was pregnant, when it came out that the baby wasn't his. I've never quite understood why she didn't have an abortion. The father was a passing interest, a musician she'd met on the road, and getting pregnant meant she had to skip touring for a year, more when Willow was an infant, and my father left her.

Maybe, I think now, in a disconnected way, maybe she was trying to stay clean. The idea slips into my mind like a little bird, fluttering around for a moment, then settling on a branch to look at me.

I was not the only thing in her life. Only one of them.

———— ❦ ————

Willow makes a sound in her sleep, almost as if she is singing, and I have to smile. It sweeps aside some of those old, old feelings, that sense of fury at Willow that grew as I realized that she was the reason my father left me.

I suddenly remember that they wouldn't let me stay alone in the room with her. I hated her screwed-up, screaming face. Her little red fists. Her thrashing legs.

A sense of horror rises in my throat. What if I'd actually hurt her?

Without her, what would my life be like? How much lonelier would I have been?

Gloria came to stay with us for the first time when Willow roared into the world. She swooped in wearing her stewardess uniform and pinned wings to my dress. She took me out every day to eat somewhere—a local diner we both loved, down to Midtown for hamburgers at a fancy steak house, ice cream, her beloved Russian Tea Room. I loved being with her, loved the attention she drew wherever we went with her red hair and friendly personality. So different from my small, punk rock mom.

In the hospital room, my head aches, and I'm worried that my brain is being eaten by meningitis, which I mistakenly googled.

Great.

I watch my sister sleep, thinking of that baby, then the little girl who followed me everywhere, all the time, exasperating, but also fun to play with sometimes. We built elaborate forts out of blankets in the dining room, the space beneath the table a faraway country. Willow was good at taking on whatever role I assigned her—cat or witch or mean sorcerer—and didn't need to be the star.

She just needed to be with me. She was the moon to my earth, circling me whenever I gave her space.

In return, I was mean. Often. It shames me now to think of the things I did, the ways I hurt her, deliberately.

In the soft light, her wild curls shine around her fox-shaped face and pink mouth. So pretty. Everyone always exclaimed over her when we were out: *What a pretty girl! What lovely hair! Such big blue eyes!*

People struggled to give me compliments, and it infuriated me, embarrassed me. It wasn't until later, when I grew to my treelike height, that people started asking if I was a model.

Gloria always believed in me, *saw* me. She told me I had the heart of a queen, and it was she who first told me about Boudicca, the British queen who staved off the Romans. Gloria praised my intelligence and my clear thinking, and she was the one who finally said, when I was twelve and in tears over my ugliness, that my hair needed to be short, which first of all freed me of all the fussing I hated but also made the most of my long neck and big eyes.

But I still didn't make room for my sister. There was always a wall, built of my resentment and pain. I had no idea how to dismantle it. Then or now.

Chapter Thirty

Willow

Sam is sleeping hard when I wake up. It's still mostly dark, but through the window I can see the first glimmers of dawn shining on the glass across the street. I need coffee and food, but I don't want her to think she's alone when she wakes up. Taking a sheet of paper from her notebook, I write HUNTING FOR COFFEE, BRB and fold it into a tent I place on her belly. The words are facing her.

In the cafeteria, I pick up some yogurt and fruit for both of us and start to grab some granola before I remember that it will crunch and the sound will drive Sam crazy. No popcorn in the movies, no slurping through straws, no mouth noises, period. Someone chewing gum can make her homicidal, and she wears earphones on public transportation or shopping. She hates it, and it embarrasses her, but she can't help it. It's the same thing some people feel when Styrofoam squeaks or nails scratch a chalkboard. Imagine if that sound happened every single time you heard another person eating.

Evidently, my grandmother was the same. Gloria said they always thought she was just a fussy Parisian, but turns out she probably suffered this same genetic thing.

Sam is still asleep when I return. I wish I could talk to her about everything that's going on with Gloria. We could use her brain.

But how unfair would that be? To weigh her down with something so dire when she's barely escaped death?

I leave the note propped up on her tummy and settle in with my phone and my yogurt to scroll through my email—nothing much—and Instagram. I haven't checked Gloria's feed for a couple of days, and it's as evocative and rewarding as ever. She has posted a beautiful series of begonia leaves, one of the fern in her bathroom, the one of me from the other day (I really need to do something with my insane hair), and some thoughtful shots of old letters.

They're hers, and I bet they came from that man, Isaak, although there's nothing to overtly link them on the letters. It pierces me somehow, and I nudge the emotion to see if I can discover why.

That she loved him, clearly, and left him behind. Was it for us, after my mother died?

A news alert pops up from the Huffington Post. **Authorities Trace Tentacles of Art Ring to New York.**

My entire body freezes. *Shit!* I open the story, leaning forward as if to see more than the text. There's a link to a video, but when I search my purse for earphones, I can't find them. I watch it without the sound. Some of it is the same video I've already seen, Margolis being arrested, the woman in Amsterdam.

There is also more, video of paintings, and in particular some of Gloria, the ones I found myself. I'm electrified, watching with a sense of the world tilting, rearranging what I know of my aunt, a woman who has essentially been my mother since I was nine years old.

One painting is highlighted, the one of her looking over her shoulder, and it's shown against some auctioneer. The story below says the painting sold for 800,000 euros.

A flush courses through my body, and I swear under my breath. I don't realize I've spoken aloud until Sam says, "What's wrong?"

"Um." For a minute, I waver over spilling the truth. She might really be able to come up with solutions. No. Right now, I can manage on my own. Protect her. I click my phone off. "Nothing. Just some bullshit with a friend of mine." I stand, tucking the phone in my pocket. "How're you doing?"

She notices the note I left on her chest and grabs it, smiling, and endures my hand on her forehead. "I think I might be better."

"I think your fever is a lot better." Her skin is faintly warm, but not like it was.

"Maybe I can get out of here today. I really need to get back to work. There's a lot going on." She swallows, with effort, and I pick up the hospital cup with its straw. With relief, she sucks on the water and adds, "I want to sleep in my own bed."

I raise a brow. "Don't get too carried away, now. You shouldn't be alone for a couple of days. You should come to G's so we can take care of you."

"Uh, no." She rolls her eyes. "I'm hardly an invalid." She touches my arm, a peace offering. "Thanks, though."

This vulnerable Sam is the one I love the most. I love all of her, prickliness and all, but this one is . . . easier. So I don't push the going-home request. No way G will let her go to her apartment.

If G is even here. The agent's avid eyes flash over my imagination. What if she gets arrested?

I force myself to focus on my sister, who is never needy and right now kind of is. "You want anything? I can call the nurse and get you some breakfast."

"I think it's coming." She points toward the corridor, where there's a clattering and voices, and a guy in scrubs and gloves comes in with a tray he settles on her table. Expertly, he gets her into a sitting position and rolls the table over to her. "Thanks," she says, looking at the very unappealing food. Eggs and fruits and oatmeal. When the orderly leaves, she gives me the oatmeal wordlessly, and I move it out of sight. Another of her quirks is that she hates the texture of oatmeal.

When I turn back, she's staring at the rest of the plate with sorrow.

"I'll get you whatever you want, sis," I say. "What sounds good?"

"Deborah sent soup. I want some more of that. Look in the drawer."

"Asher's mom?" She loves to cook for her family and has always fed everyone in her realm. I learned a lot about cooking from her, and her ability to bring us into her family, make space for us both at the table and away from it, made both of us stronger. I pull open the drawer to find a thermos. "Nice."

"Yeah." She twists off the cup and pours soup into it. I can see a faint steam rise from it. "This is probably what's making me feel better."

"I thought you and Asher weren't talking or something."

She bows her head, then thinks better of it, straightens. "We weren't, but he came back last night." Her eyes are vulnerable when she looks at me. "He's going to work with me on my new game."

"I didn't even know you guys had fallen out," I say. "It seems so . . . strange, Sam."

Her face falls. "Yeah."

"But it looks like it's on the way to healing," I say, bringing it back to the upbeat. "I'm glad." I'm eyeing the soup, and it's nice, but it's not enough calories for a woman recovering from a serious illness. "What else do you want to eat? Pears? Apples? Popcorn?"

"Nothing that is hard to chew. My teeth kind of hurt."

"Okay. I'm going down to the market to see what I can find." While I'm out, I'll call Gloria and find out what's going on. Make sure she's still safe. "I'll text suggestions, so keep your phone handy."

"Aye, aye, Captain," she says and falls back onto her pillows. Her short hair is mussed and crazy. I should comb it for her.

Her nurse bustles in. "Look who's feeling better!" she says.

I wave at Sam and duck out.

Chapter Thirty-One
Gloria

I'm up early to meet with the lawyer, but he calls at six thirty to say he has to cancel and can I come at ten to his office. "Can't you give me a clue of what I'm dealing with here?"

"It's complicated, and I'm sorry, but my daughter had to be rushed to the emergency room this morning with stomach pains. We think she might have appendicitis."

"I'm sorry," I say, and I mean it, "but am I in trouble? Am I going to be arrested? What should I do if the FBI comes back?"

"Be cooperative, tell the truth if they ask a direct question, but don't say any more than you have to."

I find I'm clenching my jaw and force myself to release it. "All right. I'll see you at ten."

I've just had a shower and am sitting down to my usual breakfast of a boiled egg and a slice of toast when Jorge calls up. "There's a fella here to talk to you, Miss Gloria. Agent Balakrishna. You want to talk to him?"

The FBI agent. My head buzzes, too bright and loud with fear. Is he here to arrest me? I look around desperately to see if I should put anything away, but Willow has been thorough, bless her.

I have no choice but to let him in, but first I smooth my blouse, a boatneck linen in turquoise. No jewelry yet, and no makeup, either, but I don't have time for that now. I do check the bra to see if it will be comfortable if I have to wear it for a while. It's not an underwire, so it should be all right, and the panties are simple briefs, so also comfortable.

But they probably make you change into prison underwear, don't they? I mean, I have no idea. Will I need socks?

My hands are shaking when I press the intercom button. "Send him up, Jorge."

And then I stand there, looking around the magnificence of the foyer with its bars of colored light falling from the stained glass. I look toward the garden and my greenhouse, and my throat is tight as I consider I might not ever see them again.

The bell startles me so much that I actually jump, and I'm flustered as I open the door to the agent. "Ms. Rose?" he asks. "I'm Agent Balakrishna, from the FBI. I'd like to ask you a few questions."

His ordinariness makes me think of traveling businessmen in their uniforms of golf shirts and slacks, and I find calm in donning my flight attendant persona, a pleasant demeanor hiding whatever I think.

We don't shake hands. "How may I help you, Mr. Balakrishna?"

"May I come in for a moment?" His jaw is so clean that it looks as if it were shaved five or ten minutes ago. His shirt beneath his coat is pressed impeccably. His shoes are shined.

Not one to miss details.

I swing the door open, trying to appear composed. "Of course."

He steps into the foyer and looks up at the stained glass cupola. "Remarkable. It was cloudy when I was here before. The sun creates its own magnificence, does it not?"

"Yes." My stomach is roiling, but I clasp my hands together in front of me, leaving them loosely linked. At ease. It gives me a focus point.

He takes his time, looking around at the paintings one at a time. "You might have heard the big story in the news about some art that's been discovered," he begins, not looking at me, and before I can respond, he adds, "I think you knew the artist, Isaak Margolis, didn't you?"

I swallow. This does not seem like a question I can really avoid, so I answer simply. "Yes. I knew him many years ago."

He turns to look at me. His eyes are very large, as if to see more than the average man. "You were lovers, isn't that right?"

I incline my head. "That's a very personal question, Mr. Balakrishna."

"My apologies." He steps forward to look at an abstract, then around at the walls. "Wasn't there one of his paintings here, in this alcove?"

"Yes. We're about to do some renovations, and we're cataloging all the works of art." The lie slips off my tongue without any conscious effort, and then I'm worried that it is a lie, and I smooth my hands over the fronts of my thighs. With as much dignity as I can muster, I say, "I don't mean to rush you, but my niece is in the hospital, and I'd like to get back to her as soon as possible. Was there something in particular you wanted?"

"Oh, I'm so sorry. Is that the lovely young woman who spoke with me before?"

I don't smile, but Willow has that effect on most men. "Not Willow. Her sister."

"Very well, I won't keep you long. I will simply ask you a few questions, if you don't mind." He coughs lightly. "Would you mind if I had a drink of water?"

"Of course. Please come with me." I lead him through the servant hallway to the kitchen and take a glass from the cupboard, a pitcher of filtered water from the fridge. "Ice?"

"No, no. That's fine, thank you."

I pour the water and wait while he drinks. The kitchen seems almost noisy with silence. Clearly he hasn't come to arrest me, or he would have done so already. Is the evidence too thin? Is it possible I might escape this whole mess somehow?

He's after something. That much is clear.

At last he sets the empty glass on the counter. "Thank you." From his pocket, he pulls out a small spiral tablet, and the gesture reminds me so much of Columbo I want to giggle. Is it on purpose?

Or maybe he's trying to disarm me, make me think he's foolish. Which is what Columbo does, after all. Bumbles around so brilliantly that he solves the murder every time.

I glance at my watch pointedly.

"How long has it been since you've spoken to Mr. Margolis?" he asks.

"Oh my goodness." I have to think about the year. Just before Billie died, we had a last, wild rendezvous that broke both of our hearts. "Twenty-five years or more, I'd say."

"And have you exchanged letters? Phone calls?"

"No."

"Do you know what he's been doing all that time?"

"No," I say again, simply.

"Did you know he was forging art when you were lovers?"

I take a breath. "Of course not." I frown. "Am I in trouble over this? Should I call my lawyer?"

"No, not at all. I'm finished." He tucks the notebook back into the depths of his pocket.

Relief floods my body, flowing down my spine so fast it makes me feel like I might faint.

Then he continues, "I wonder, though, if you'd indulge an art lover and show me"—he gestures toward the hallway, where a few paintings can be seen hanging in the gloom—"your collection?"

Clammy sweat breaks beneath my breasts and hair. How can I protect myself if I don't know what he's after? "I don't really think—"

"Please, madam. I have studied art my entire life, and rarely have I seen such a beautiful, modern collection. It will only take a moment, surely."

Cooperate, the lawyer said, but this is a fishing expedition. Do I allow it?

If this is chess, he's moved his rook straight out into the open, and I have no idea what he means to do with it. I am torn between wanting to appear to be cooperative and worrying that he's looking for some evidence I haven't hidden. My natural tendency is toward cooperation. "Perhaps just the parlor," I say. "Come with me."

The biggest painting is the iconic one of Billie, of her standing at the window of her music room, smoking. She's wearing a tank top, and all her tattoos show. The light shines softly on her face, revealing a pensive expression. In the shadowy background is a child playing violin. Willow, all hair and grasshopper limbs. Sam has always hated that she's not in the frame, and even when it was explained that she lived with her father for that period, it didn't help. Due to the early betrayals of her parents, she always saw the world as conspiring against her, and this was more evidence.

But the painting itself is magnificent. The agent is physically halted, and I hear him give a little "oof."

"It still can do that to me sometimes," I say. "Stop me right in my tracks."

"Did you know the artist? Karen Shroeder? This is one of her most famous works."

"We did know her. She was my sister's lover, I suspect. Billie seemed to love men and women both." I gaze at the painting, feeling the loss all over again. Forever, I will miss her. The world knew her as Billie Thorne, wild rocker, but to me she was Billie Rose, the sister I spent my childhood with, the only one who knew my parents and our little room at the top of the house that looked out over fields and hills in the distance. "It's one of my favorite portraits of her. She actually looks like my sister, not a rock star."

He is struggling for composure, but I see he's gobsmacked. "Billie Thorne is your sister?"

"Yes."

"She was . . ." He stares at the painting, and I see his throat working. Is he going to *cry*? "I don't know how I would have gotten through my adolescence without her music." He gulps. "Especially 'Write My Name Across the Sky.'"

I meet people all the time who tell me some version of this, but it is surprising coming from this buttoned-up agent of the law. How, I wonder, did he come to be standing here? It surely wasn't exactly what he had planned. Mentally, I'm framing a photo of him for my Insta, the black coat, the painfully well-shaved jaw, the fringed eyes. "Did you want to be a musician?" Those are usually the ones who loved that song, not realizing that it's not just about becoming famous but about longing for things just out of your grasp.

"No. I've always been intrigued by art, not music. The song just . . ." He pauses. "Inspired me. To dream. To try."

I nod, but again I wonder if he's just doing a Columbo on me, talking about my sister so I'll let down my guard. I look frantically around the room as he circles, looking at every painting. Is there something I've missed?

One by one, he examines the paintings in the room. I stand where I am, feeling my breath growing shorter and shorter in my ears, depriving me of oxygen, the oxygen I need to think. Wildly, I look around, wondering what he's looking for. All the paintings from Isaak are gone. The place where the Renoir hung holds a ghostly square for its return. He passes it, and I would bet a million dollars that he sees it, but he doesn't comment. When he has made his rounds, he stops once more in front of Billie's portrait. I look over his shoulder at the depth of color in her iris, the thing that makes her seem still alive. Samantha has those eyes, that clarity and depth.

How would all our lives be different if she'd lived?

I lead him back out.

"Thank you, Ms. Rose." Halfway out the door, he pauses. "One more thing—we are investigating all links to this case, and for now, you should not make any plans to leave the city."

My stomach drops all the way to the floor, and now I know this game of cat and mouse is going to lead to prison if I don't figure out how to get out of town. I wonder if my friend Sandro has received my fake passport yet. Tears sting the back of my eyes, but my voice is smooth. "Of course not," I say. "I'll be right here."

Chapter Thirty-Two
Willow

Out on the street, I try to call Gloria, but it goes through to voice mail. "Auntie, I've been reading the news about Isaak Margolis, and we really, really need to talk. Call me."

I find Sam some sweet custards and cubed watermelon and a spicy, steamy chai from a little grocer down the block. On the way back, I pick up some cheery yellow sunflowers, and my arms are full as I come back into the room.

"Willow!" Sam exclaims. "How pretty!"

The nurse is puttering around the tubes and machines, making notes on a tablet. "Very nice," she says. "I'll get a vase for the flowers, and then I want you to get out of here and let her sleep, okay?"

"But I just got back!"

She's a middle-aged woman with a punky haircut touched with the faintest blush of pink. "She can probably get out of here today if you let her sleep before the doctor comes."

"Oh! That's great news." The rush of relief through my body is acute, a shivery cold sweat that makes me realize I've been terrified. "Don't you think?"

Sam nods. I arrange the custards with a paper napkin and a plastic fork and the chai, which smells of good ginger and a fine snap of coriander. "This looks great."

"You're welcome," I say and step back, slapping my hands together. "Now, I guess I'd better get your room ready."

"No," she says without emotion, picking up her fork. "I'm going to my apartment."

"Not by yourself," says the nurse. "You can't be alone for a few days."

Sam rolls her eyes, then winces, touching fingers to her forehead.

I laugh. "Serves you right. I'll see you later."

By the time I make it back to the apartment, I'm practically asleep on my feet. Yawning, I wait for the elevator, and when it opens, Agent Balakrishna is revealed. His face brightens when he sees me. "Hello again."

"Hi." I'm suddenly wide awake, wondering what he's doing here this time.

"You look like her," he says, holding the door for me.

"Who?"

"Your mother."

It's not what I expected. "Um . . . thanks." The elevator door closes, and the car labors slowly up the six flights. Sweat has broken out down my back, and by the time the doors open on our floor, I'm feeling close to an actual panic attack.

"Auntie!" I cry when I'm inside the door. "Where are you?"

No answer. The cats are nowhere in sight, and I dash through the rooms, looking toward G's bedroom, where the door is standing open. Not there. Not in the parlor or the music room. "Gloria!"

I find her on the roof, without a coat, just standing there. Thank God. Against the sky, she looks sleek and tall, but there's something about her shoulders that makes me know she's not okay. "Auntie," I say.

She turns. Her face is bare of makeup, and her skin looks practically gray. I notice the brackets around her mouth and the lines in her cheeks and realize that seventy-four might look good on her, but it's still seventy-four.

"Are you okay?" I ask.

"For the moment."

"What did he want?"

She shakes her head. "Everything."

"What can I do? Tell me and we'll fix it."

"No." She smooths her hair. "I don't want you to worry about anything. I don't want you involved."

"You can't expect me to just sit by when you're in trouble. We need to do some research, get the paintings out of here—"

"Willow." She takes my arms. "This is not your concern. It's my mess, and I'll figure it out."

I scowl at her. "I'm not twelve, you know. And you don't have to do this all on your own." I take her arms. "I'm here for you. I'm your family."

I see her swallow, feel the taut worry in the tendons of her arms. "Thank you."

I shake her slightly. "Okay, I'm already dealing with one stubborn Rose female who refuses to let anyone help her. Can you not make me work so hard. Please?"

A welter of tears gives her blue eyes a dazzling aspect. She covers one of my hands with one of hers. "You're right." A slight raise of her shoulders. "I don't know yet. I have an appointment with a lawyer in a little while and should have some more information after that. The painting that was delivered is worth a lot of money, so it gives us some options. I just have to find a buyer."

"Can I see it?"

She bows her head. "No, I'm sorry. Some things are personal."

I raise an eyebrow.

"It was a long time ago."

I nod, letting it go. "Are they going to arrest you?"

"I don't know." She guides me over to the bench, and we sit side by side in the warming springlike air, looking toward the skyline to the south. "If he was going to, why didn't he do it today?"

"What did they arrest the other woman for?"

She glances at me. "You have read up on all of this, haven't you?"

I nod.

"She was arrested 'in connection' to the case against Isaak." She sighs. "So it could be anything, I suppose."

My stomach aches. "Which means it could be anything with you too."

"Maybe." She looks into the distance, maybe into the past, maybe looking for solutions.

"I saw some of the paintings too. Online. You were his muse."

She nods. "We were quite in love." The words are simple, but I hear the depth behind them. I think of the dashingly handsome man being led away in handcuffs.

"He's handsome now. I can't imagine what he was like forty years ago."

"He was—and is—good looking, but it's much more than that. A magnetism. Have you ever met anyone like that?"

I think of Josiah capturing the crowd with his amazing voice. I think of the way he moves, so easy in his skin. "Maybe."

We're silent for a while, and I sense that she needs this. Maybe she needs me to be here, in case she goes to jail. In case it all vaporizes. I imagine her in jail, eating crappy food, and it breaks my heart. "I'm not going to let anything happen to you, G."

She gives me a wry smile. "Wonder Woman, are you?"

"You'd be surprised." I switch directions. "They're going to probably let Sam out of the hospital today."

"That's wonderful news! And that's something you can take charge of. Get the bedroom aired and order some groceries. She might want you to go to her apartment and pick up some clean clothes and things like that."

"You can't expect me to just ignore everything that's going on with you!"

"Not at all, my love." She takes my hand, and I feel her bracelet cold against my inner wrist. "I want you to take charge of *everything*—your sister, the apartment, everything here, in this realm. That will free me to see what I can do about my problem. Can you do that?"

"Of course."

"Good girl. Now, let's get inside. I'm freezing."

The bedroom is dusty and airless. I strip the bed and toss the sheets and pillowcases in the washing machine, one of the great luxuries of the apartment, then carry the duvet out to the roof to air. Gloria is in the greenhouse, doing something with her plants, and it makes me anxious that she's doing that rather than addressing the whole mess. But she's set her boundaries, and I guess I have to respect them.

Except . . . how can she really do all of this on her own? Who do I know who is a lawyer or knows a lawyer? Sam would probably know someone, but she really doesn't need to be worrying about any of this.

I open the windows to get a cross flow of air, then vacuum and dust. In the back of my mind, I'm planning a handful of meals and snacks with a lot of nutrition, working with Sam's limitations and preferences. I wonder if she has any new ones, but rather than call and possibly disturb her, I call in the grocery list I've made. Easy soups, cheese, a rotisserie chicken to strip for the carcass and easy sandwiches. And junk food, potato chips and ice cream and root beer, which she's always loved. Maybe we can have banana splits.

I'm bending over, looking at the dates on pickles and chocolate sauce in the fridge (both well over two years expired), when a memory sprouts like a mushroom: A small me taking things out of the nearly empty fridge—a stick of butter, half a loaf of bread. I had to get a chair to turn on the stove, but I knew it had to be lit, so I called Sam to help. She was afraid of the stove, of that fast whoosh, so I exchanged places with her. She turned the knob, and I lit the match to start the flame. It didn't quite take the first time, and then the second match flared too much. I felt the fire against my face, but it was fine. I shook out the match and stood on the chair to butter the bread on one side, all the slices lined up on a cookie sheet. Sam gave me the sugar and climbed up to get the cinnamon from the spice cabinet. I slid the pan into the broiler, and we watched the butter melt and the sugar start to bubble. "Now," I said.

We took out the pan carefully and carried it to the tiny table in the corner. Dinner.

Sam caught sight of my face and started laughing. "You burned off your eyebrows, stupid!"

"What?" I reached up and felt the singed rows of hair, the tiny balls of hair left behind. My eyes stung with tears, but I just shrugged. "I don't care. I'm hungry!"

The memory swamps me with emotion. She's four years older than me. Why wasn't she the one operating the stove?

Except that I was taking care of her. Then as now.

I pour out the expired pickles and rinse the jar, feeling unnerved. I try not to think about those times. Before Asher. Before Gloria. When my mother was so sick, all the time. Sick, or missing, or nodded out on the couch. We must have had babysitters, but I don't remember them. Gloria stayed with us when my mom was actually out on the road, but when Billie wasn't touring, who took care of us? Mostly, it was just the two of us, me and Sam, making do.

I'm staring out the window, watching the river shift light streams, gray, silver, a dull gunmetal, and I want to go back in time and tell that little girl that it's okay. I want someone to do it. Someone to tell her that her eyebrows will grow back.

Sam didn't. I don't remember where my mom was. Or Gloria. I do remember that the burns, on the tip of my nose and my forehead, woke me up in the middle of the night. It felt like every nerve was wide open to the air, and I cried, careful not to turn my face to my pillow. I remember going to school the next day, and Ricky Rivera took one look at me and snorted. He called me Piglet for the rest of the year.

My left eyebrow never was quite the same, with a block right through the center that doesn't grow. I learned to color it in and eventually had a Ren Faire friend tattoo it back in place.

A long time ago, I think. Nothing to do with now. I rinse off the shelves of the fridge in preparation for the groceries.

Chapter Thirty-Three
Gloria

After Willow goes back inside, I breathe in the cool morning air and try to order my priorities.

Protect Sam and Willow and, as much as possible, the apartment, from anything that might transpire.

Protect the art, which is a legacy I do not want to disturb.

Avoid arrest and thus stay out of prison. Obviously. Like the woman in Amsterdam, I trafficked in stolen works of art, carried contraband across borders, aided and abetted a felon.

More than one count of each.

I will talk to the lawyer, but I can feel the urgency of the need to flee. I stand in the rooftop garden I have created and look south to the beautiful skyline I have loved for so long, and it feels like something is being torn from my body. I can't bear it. Not having coffee with Sam and Willow, or having lunch with my friends, or waking up to my cats slumped over my belly. Can't bear not having the greenhouse and all my plants, the apartment I vowed to die in.

My beautiful, beautiful Instagram account. It's very small in comparison to the loss of the girls and the apartment and my beloved greenhouse, but it still grieves me deeply. All my hard work, all my connections. It has given me so much joy.

But I would rather leave it all behind than go to prison.

The lawyer calls me again as I'm heading inside. "Look, let's just do this over the phone. My girl has gone to surgery, and I can't leave her."

"I understand."

"It appears that the FBI has not yet found enough actual evidence to arrest you—yet—but I'm betting the next move is a search warrant. Do you understand?"

My throat goes dry, but I scratch out, "Yes." I tell him about the visit this morning, and he swears under his breath. "All right, then. You might need bail."

I blanch. "Bail?"

"What sort of assets do you have that you can use as collateral?"

My mind whirls. "An apartment, I suppose, though it's not in my name. Art."

"If you flee, you'll lose whatever assets you've posted; do you understand?"

The box around me closes in, tighter and tighter. "I do, thank you."

"Call me if they come back. In the meantime, get your affairs in order in case."

"In case," I repeat.

"Yes."

I hang up, my hands shaking, and look around the garden. I can't use the apartment or the collection for bail because I might very well need to flee.

Which means I need to act before they come back with a search warrant or, even worse, a warrant for my arrest.

The noose around my neck cinches, and I run through the possibilities. There's only one that makes sense. I need to run, and soon.

I gather up the letters and the nude painting, now in a much less substantial tube, and head for Miriam's place. She's calling the others too. I'm also going to have to tell them the truth, which I'm not at all looking forward to.

It's a nice day, the sun burning off the fog, offering hints of what spring might look like. The expressions of people on the street reflect that, a certain lack of tightness, a chipper step, a jacket shed and tossed over a shoulder. In a couple of months, the cherry trees will start to bloom, and spring breezes will blow away the harsh gloom of winter. It is one of the very best times in the city, spring. Full of hope and possibility.

When I first came to the city at eighteen, it terrified me and thrilled me in equal parts, but within days I'd fallen entirely in love, and unlike Joan Didion, I never wanted to leave the party. I have visited cities all over the world and spent substantial time in many of them. I love Hong Kong and Vienna and Paris at certain times of year, but none of them have ever held a candle to New York. Even now, when billionaires are trying to buy up everything for themselves, it remains a beacon for the world, for the families who scrape and save to make the journey from the only country they've ever known to look for a dream and then work three jobs to afford a tiny place on the outskirts, a place they share with five or six others. It's a beacon for the oddballs, for the passionately creative, for the intellectual.

It's always that beacon. For me, it was flight school and the possibility that a girl from a farming town with two traffic lights and five churches and not even a cinema could see the world. The *whole* world.

For Billie, it was the city of music, where she found her people in the rock and punk scenes, where she discovered she loved singing and heroin, and women as well as men, and living on the edge. We scattered her ashes from the Brooklyn Bridge. It was the only possible choice.

My mother would have been so much happier if she'd married a man from the city instead of the rangy farm boy, kind but unimaginative.

I've wondered so many times why she didn't leave him and seek her fortune. Perhaps if she'd not given birth to us, she could have.

The cab pulls up in front of Miriam's building. I pay and gather my things. For a moment, I stand on the sidewalk, watching people hurry on their way, more of them on the sunny side of the street. A work crew has set up cones around a hole in the road, and a man in an orange vest directs traffic around it. It pierces me, all of it.

My city. My home. Leaving it will shatter my heart completely.

I head upstairs to Miriam's, and she opens the door the minute I knock, swinging it open to show our dwindling little group arranged on her midcentury turquoise couch. Sunlight cascades in through the floor-to-ceiling windows, splashing on the bamboo floor. We're old now, all of us, with our spindly fingers and thin hair, but each one of them is so dear I nearly fall to pieces right there. I want to take a picture, and on impulse, I drop my burdens on the floor and pull out my phone. "Miriam, go sit on the arm."

"Not for Instagram. Not anymore," Angie says.

"No." I raise the camera and shoot sideways to get the whole picture. Miriam leans in, her long legs as graceful as ever. Dani's hair flames against the light, and her ice-blue eyes capture the center of the frame. Next to her, Fran looks 101, but she still mugs for the camera, and Angie wears a purple-and-green knit only she could pull off, her feet crossed at the ankles. I shoot three in a row to get a few options, all on Live mode.

"Turn off your phones," I say.

Dani rolls her eyes, but they all do as I ask.

"I think I should post it," I say. "I've posted us all dozens of times, and it will be weird if I suddenly stop." Admiring the photo, I'm mentally composing the caption. *What fifty years of friendship looks like.*

"Don't," Angie says. "Wyatt is losing his mind over all of this. He follows you."

"He does?" I'm pleased before I realize how exhausted she looks, and that brings me back into the present moment in a way nothing else could have. I pick up the letters and painting and sit down in the circular yellow chair.

"I got something in the mail." I pop the end from the cardboard tube and gently pull out the painting. Looking at it again makes my heart ache.

"Jesus," Dani says. "I know I saw it when he painted it, but I was young then too. You're so gorgeous."

"I was so jealous," Fran says. "He worshipped the ground you walk on."

"Maybe," I say, struggling to hold up the massive canvas. Miriam comes over and helps me carry it to an easel fitted with binder clips, then rolls the easel over where we can see it.

We all stare, Miriam and I standing, the others sitting, and look at my nude self in the bright light of the apartment. I feel airless and lost, thinking about all the time that has gone by, but also about how near those days feel, as if I could just step through a curtain and be there, my young self, looking both modest and terribly sexy.

"He's an exquisite painter," Miriam says and walks closer. "Look at these flesh tones, how many colors he used." She stays there, looking intently with the eyes of an artist. "It's terrible that he couldn't find his audience then."

"He's finding it now," Dani says. "Did you hear that Sotheby's sold one of his paintings of the market for eight hundred thousand dollars?"

I nod.

"Why did he send it to you?" Angie asks in her raspy ex-smoker's voice.

"To sell," Dani says. "She's going to need some serious money for lawyers and defense."

I swallow. Bail was bad enough, but imagining a trial, the jury staring at me, makes me feel sick.

"I'm not going to sit here and wait to be carted off to jail," I say, and I sit on the chair again, folding my hands. "That's why I'm here. I need help. And you all need to make sure the paintings are . . . um . . . nowhere to be seen."

"Already done," Dani says.

"Good."

"What do we do with them?" Fran asks. "They're bulky."

"Take them off the frames," Miriam says dryly. "Then you can roll them up just like that."

"Oh. I see." She shifts her lower jaw back and forth, a side effect of a medication she takes, I think, but it's distracting. "What about the other one?"

I can't remember who has what. "Which one is it?"

"The Pissarro."

I take a breath. "It's a fake, so just treat it the way you treat the others."

"What? It's not a fake."

"It is, actually." I lift my chin, spill the truth. "They're all fakes."

A hushed silence greets this information, and I feel the soft purple wall coming up. "I hope you're kidding," Angie says. "We paid half a million for the Gauguin."

The *supposed* Gauguin. The story was that someone had discovered a Paris apartment, a Nazi headquarters, and inside had found a stash of paintings, most of them from the pointillist or impressionist periods.

"Perhaps those of us who purchased works of art we believed to be stolen, lost masterpieces should be a bit less judgmental, hmm?" Miriam says. "I knew mine was a fake, actually, but it was so beautifully done I wanted it anyway."

"Oh, sure you did," Fran says, rolling her eyes. "Miriam always knows everything."

"Just art," she returns calmly, then stands. "I've made tea. Will you help me, Dani?"

Dani stands and flings me a look I can't quite read. Somewhere between disgust and admiration.

The rest of us sit in the silence. I look at my hands, folding and refolding, then out the window, searching for Yoga Woman, but the apartment is empty today. A bird flies by, and in the distance, I see the contrails of a plane lingering in the high blue sky.

"How could you lie to us?" Angie asks softly.

"I don't know," I say honestly. "I mean . . . I could offer excuses, but I don't have any."

"Did you even think about it?" Fran asks.

"Would it really make it any better if I had?"

"Oh my God!" Angie spits out. "You are so insanely selfish. You always have been."

"Pot, kettle," I return. "You sure didn't win any awards for altruism, Miss I Stole My Billionaire Husband."

She rolls her eyes. "From his *third* wife. Believe me, I was pretty sure it wouldn't last."

I laugh. "So that makes it okay?"

Fran says, "It does, actually." She leans forward. "Without those paintings, I'm going to end up in some horrible nursing home, alone."

Her husband is quite ill, in a nursing home. She's the only one of the three who didn't marry a wealthy man. Her husband is a kind, good man, but he didn't make millions. Her apartment is a good legacy, a two-bedroom in the East Forties, but she'll have to sell it. My stomach rumbles again.

"Look. I know you don't have much. The reason I brought the nude is because it's his best piece, and it will sell for a lot of money. We can split it, five ways."

"You don't need it," Fran says. "You have all your sister's royalties. I still hear that damned song practically every day."

"There isn't that much anymore, actually, and it belongs to Sam and Willow. Once I disappear, there will be no way to access it. I have to have cash."

Miriam settles an enameled tray on the coffee table, and I remember the day she bought it from a market in Hong Kong when we first started flying. The memory brings a jolt of spice and cacophony with it.

"I am sorry for the lies," I say. "But let's just work out a plan, all right? I need to get out of the country, and you all need to hide the paintings."

"Where?"

Angie frowns at the tea. "I'd rather have wine."

"Help yourself. It's in the fridge."

"Safe-deposit box should be fine for now."

"Really?" Fran asks. "That seems . . . iffy."

"It will do." She offers me a cup, but my stomach is so wretched I just shake my head. As if she knows, she offers me a cookie instead, and I take it, nibble a small corner. "In the meantime, I've contacted a couple of friends who should be able to negotiate a quiet sale of the portrait."

"You can't just *go*," Fran says. "Leave Sam and Willow? Your beautiful apartment? Your greenhouse? How will you stand to live without your greenhouse?"

The knife in my gut cuts straight downward. "I don't have a choice." With a small, bitter smile, I add, "Funny that it takes such a long time to find out what really matters."

Miriam snorts. "You wanted to fly, and you did—for almost thirty years. Don't discount that. Having that life gave you this one."

"Wise Miriam," Dani says, and this time, there's no sarcasm.

We spend the better part of two hours working out details, and on the way out, Miriam hugs me hard. "I will miss you more than I can possibly say."

"How will I get through my old age without you?"

"We'll figure something out. Mysterious meetings on faraway shores. Coded letters."

I rest my forehead on her shoulder, unwilling to let go. "Something."

Out on the street, the sense of breaking, of loss, follows me to the curb, where I hail a cab that sails over to pick me up. A young man with thick dreads woven with green and red and yellow threads gives me a smile. "Good evening, beautiful lady. Where am I taking you today?"

I give him the address and stare out the window.

I don't want to leave.

But I don't know how to stay.

Chapter Thirty-Four

Sam

I'm dozing, my mind filled with thoughts like soap bubbles, bouncing, bumping each other, iridescent and insubstantial. For a moment, I'm with the game, the powerful visuals of a girl navigating a challenge, wearing the uniform she chooses.

Boudicca crosses my heart. It's safe for the moment, but I have to get this game to market fast.

Then I'm thinking of my mother's apartment and my old bedroom.

Then it's Asher and the strange hallucination I had about us being married. It was such a sweet, soft vision; my ovaries are still aching with the wish for those beautiful boys. Asher's boys. Mine.

Asher has been coming in every few hours, day and night, as if I really am his wife and he doesn't want to leave me alone. Or rather as if we are the best of friends and he's realized that he almost lost me.

That he would have lost me if I hadn't sent that SOS. What possessed me? I still don't know.

When he's here, I try to just let it be, our easy connection. I try not to think about that last, awful fight or, even worse in its way, the long weekend that led to the fight. We spent approximately fifty-six hours in bed. *Literally* in bed, ordering food from room service, and the rest of the time having mind-blowing, endless sex. We were both raw and sore by the end, laughing about it but still unable to stop exploring each other's bodies, as if both of us had been imagining it for twenty years.

I had not been. But Asher had. He had been in love with me for decades by then, a fact I had known and conveniently ignored. I loved him, but I had never been in love with him, and when we fell into bed at Tina's wedding, I thought I was maybe just lonely. Recovering from the relationship with Eric.

Or so I thought.

But that weekend.

That weekend. In my wide-open state, where all my walls have been demolished, I think of that first kiss, Asher leaning in, a little tipsy, his thumb tipping up my chin ever so slightly, and then his mouth was on mine. I had not realized his lips were so lush, that he would taste so right, like dawn, like the sea, like wedding cake, and I fell into it with abandon.

That kiss. It went on and on and on, my back pressed up against the wall outside my room, our pelvises moving in ancient rhythm, his hands neatly on my waist. I kept thinking I should stop, break away, laugh it off, but I couldn't stop.

I just couldn't stop kissing him. He couldn't stop kissing me.

I realized that I was in love with him. Had been in love with him for a thousand years, maybe always, and had never let him in because . . . because what if he stopped loving me? What if then I lost him completely?

That weekend, all my illusions were shattered. Our union went so deep, so fast, so far—

And then, when we got back to the city, everything broke into a million pieces because I was terrified. I lashed out. As I do. As I've been doing for years and years.

How can I stop? How can I stop shoving everyone I love away from me?

A voice says my name quietly. "Hey, Sam."

I jerk my eyes open to find that it's the doctor, who is Eric. I feel weirdly revealed, with tears at the corners of my eyes and the awareness of the thin covering of the hospital gown over my otherwise-naked body. It didn't bother me the first time, so I must be feeling better.

I try to sit up a little more demurely, but his hand settles on my shoulder. "You're fine. Sorry to wake you."

"I was only dozing. Are you here to let me go?"

He smiles. "Are you ready?"

"More than ready. This is not the most exciting place on earth, I have to tell you."

"By design." He places the tablet on my rolling table. "How are you feeling?"

"Good." I sit as straight as I can, hoping my eyes look bright and shiny.

"Is it all right if I touch you?"

"Yes." But this time, it's a lot weirder than last time. My body is all reactive and strange, and I have to look away as he palpates my neck, my lymph nodes. "Still a bit stiff. Do you have any headache?"

"Not much. Is my brain going to be okay?"

"Yes. It should be fine. You do have to take it easy for a while, however, Sam." He gestures to the notebook and scrawled notes on my lap. "New project?"

"Yeah. It showed up with the fever, believe it or not."

"That's great, but as I recall, you can spend a lot of time on a new project. You can't do that right now. You're going to have to let your body heal."

"That's reasonable. I just want to be home."

"Is there anyone who can stay with you?"

I narrow my eyes. "Did you talk to my sister?"

"The crazy tiger woman?" He grins ruefully, and I love the intelligence in his eyes as much as I ever did. "No."

"She wants me to come to the apartment so she can take care of me."

"That sounds like a good idea."

I frown, but a part of me wonders if this might be the chance. The way to start practicing letting down my guard.

"Poor Sam," he says, meaning exactly the opposite. "A lot of people would be grateful under the circumstances."

I roll my eyes, and just as it did with Willow, it makes my head hurt. I make an involuntary noise and press my fingers to the place. "They hover."

"It's good for you. Did you talk to your dad?"

"Yeah. He was just as mad as I thought he'd be."

"It's not your fault."

"Tell that to him."

He tucks the tablet under his arm. "I'm going to let you go on the condition that you are released to your aunt and sister. And I will check."

"Fine. How long do I have to stay?"

"Until I am convinced you're actually safe on your own."

"How are you going to figure that out?"

"I remember where Gloria lives."

For a minute, I let that sink in. "You make house calls?"

He holds my gaze, and all at once I see the regret and hope in his face. "For you, I will."

I don't know how to respond. The craziness of losing him ripples through me, the times I called and called and called, the number of times I ran by the hospital, all the awful, ridiculous things I did as a grief-crazed ex-lover. I just look at him for the longest time. "Okay," I finally say.

His hand curls around mine. "Take care. I'll see you soon."

Then he's gone, and I'm frowning at the door when Asher walks through it. He has a bag of food in his hands and a cup of chai I can smell across the room.

Everything about him is as welcome as dawn. His unruly curls, his serious eyes. After thinking of the weekend of the wedding, I particularly notice his mouth, such full lips. "Hi!" I say, sitting up, and the gown slips on my shoulder. "Would you help me with this?"

Wordlessly, he places the bag on my lap, the chai on my table, and robotically ties the gown at my neck. His fingers brush my nape, and it's ridiculous, but I'm aware that my nipples are visible beneath the thin cotton, and now that it's in my mind, I can't stop remembering how it was to have him kiss me that way, against the wall—

"You're going home, huh?" he says, and there's something off about his tone. He isn't meeting my eyes.

"Yeah. But only to Gloria's. I'm not allowed to be on my own yet." I open the bag and find my all-time-favorite vegan cheeseburger on a gluten-free bun. "Oh my God! You are the absolute best, Asher." Pulling it out, I ask, "Do you want half?"

"No, I'm good." He takes a breath, his hands in his pockets. Again I look at his mouth and wish we could kiss, that he could lie down here beside me and we could just kiss and kiss and kiss.

And then he looks at me, and I can see that his wall has come back. "I have to go, actually."

"What?" A hole is punched through my heart, and I don't know where it's coming from, and maybe I'm reading too much into his kindness. "Really? You can't even stay just a little while?" Tossing aside all the rules we've had between us, I reach for his hand. "Please?"

"Sam, I just—this was a bad idea, for us to be friendly again."

Tears spring to my eyes. "No, Asher. I have missed you so much it's like I lost a limb."

"Me too." His hand lies limply beneath mine.

I pick it up and place it against my cheek, holding it there until my skin melts into his palm. It connects me to all that's real and right with the world, as if his skin is an electric current that smooths all the wild electrons in my body and puts them in order. "Then don't go."

"Are you seeing Eric again?"

"What? No!" I drop his hand. "He's my doctor."

"That's a little weird, don't you think?"

"Yeah, I mean, of course. But he's one of the best virologists in the city, this is his hospital, and I didn't choose to get meningitis."

"You just don't have a lot of perspective about him."

I narrow my eyes. "I *didn't* have perspective. That was years ago."

"Two years."

"Almost three, actually, but what difference does it make? Everybody makes an idiot of themselves once in a while."

"Yeah, they do," he says and presses those beautiful lips together. "Including me." He stands there, and I can feel the conflict in him. "I was doing really well, and I don't want to go down this road again." He spins on his heel.

"Wait. Are you *leaving*?"

He turns at the door. "Yes. I'll call later to see how you are."

"Don't you think you're being a little unreasonable?"

For the longest time, he stands there, and I feel the intensity of his gaze on my face, my body, and the heat of our tangling rises up again, limbs and skin and tongues and breath, all of us, all of him, all of me. I think of our long, long hours of working on one game or another, of the past days, when he's been so present and I realized the depth of my loneliness without him.

"No," he says at last and turns to go.

I'm suddenly four years old, and my father is carrying his suitcase from the bedroom to the front door. In the background, a baby is wailing. I'm running, trying to hold on to the suitcase, cling to his legs. *Don't go, don't go, Daddy, please don't go.*

"Wait! Asher, please." My voice breaks a little on the last word, and it stops him.

He takes a breath. "What?"

"I didn't mean it, all those things I said."

When we got back to the city after the wedding weekend, he wanted to come inside and stay with me. All the way up the stairs I'd been feeling more and more emotional. By the time we got to my apartment, I was a Tasmanian devil of terror, lashing out savagely, protectively.

"I just got scared."

"Yeah, I get that." Unmoved, he raises his eyebrows. "I think you did mean them."

"I was afraid. Afraid that if we kept going, I'd lose my best friend."

He lifts his chin. "Thing is, Sam, you called me—what was it? 'Smothering,' was it?"

"I didn't mean it, and you know that."

"I don't know that."

"You were brutal, too, you know." Tears sting my eyes. "You were meaner than I was."

He ducks his head. "Self-defense."

"Can't we just let go? Start over?"

"No, Sam," he says, and his voice is certain. "I just can't do it."

All the emotions that have been shaken loose by this illness rise up in my throat, spill from my eyes. "Please," I whisper.

He turns away.

I scramble to come up with an errand. "I need one of my notebooks. You're the only one who can get it."

"Sam, this is—"

"You said you would help me save Boudicca." I swallow. "I really need your help. Please."

For a long moment, he says nothing. His head is bent, his body still. Everything about him feels like the most precious detail of all time—his shoulder. His forearm, covered with silky black hair. His nose.

At last, he says, "All right. Tell me where it is. I'll bring it back later."

"Thank you."

He only nods, and I wish I had the brainpower to say something, make this go back to the ease we were feeling, the simple connection. "Don't . . . ," I begin.

"Don't what?"

Everything I can think of to say sounds like something you'd say to a lover, and he's my friend. I just shake my head. "Nothing. Thank you."

Chapter Thirty-Five
Willow

When I was fifteen, I wrote in my journal that I wanted to have a life in music, make money, and *be happy*. That last part really mattered because I'd seen that my mother was not. I didn't know why, back then, only that what I saw was that she loved music and loved her work but wasn't happy anyway.

Make music. Make money. Be happy.

I'm thinking about that triad as I work on the homey chores of readying the apartment. Gloria has to take care of some business she would not share with me, but she took the painting with her. The work makes me feel as if I have some control over something. Being busy helps calm my anxiety.

I've finished the bedroom—made the bed with fresh, sweet-smelling linens and even dug out the vacuum cleaner to give the floors a quick once-over. I like household work. I love the sense of putting things in order and the solid feeling of accomplishing a task, and I've also learned that my creativity simmers wildly. Taking a shower, washing dishes, cooking—all those tasks give the muses room to play without me examining them too closely.

And it's the same today. I keep hearing the sound of my voice mixed with Josiah's, mixed with the bass and the violin, all of it winding together, smooth and rich and original. That sound tickles the composition I've been working on for months, sails into it like ribbons of rainbow light. Yellow underlining those notes, purple swirling around the lower register, lending it value.

When the cleaning is finished, I start the soup. Often, I play music, but today I don't want to interfere with the music in my mind, so I hum to myself, capturing a phrase here, another there.

I strip a rotisserie chicken, putting the meat into a bowl to be chopped. The skin and bones go into a heavy pot, one of only three in the kitchen, all of them very dusty before I got started. I roughly chop onions and carrots and celery and toss them on top of the carcass; add whole peppercorns and a few cloves, fresh rosemary and thyme, and salt; and turn the flame to low.

The actions, easy and familiar, calm me. It's been a while since I had a kitchen to cook in, the last one belonging to the boyfriend who kicked me out a couple of months ago after a spectacular fight. I didn't like him that much anyway but convinced myself his flaws were bearable, given that he was a music exec who could get my album made.

And he did. Turned out he wasn't all that enchanted with me once it flopped.

The lockout, however, was extreme and humiliating, and he meant it to be both. I arrived home to find my meager belongings outside the gate with a sign over them that said, **FREE**.

Luckily, it was a neighborhood where no one needed free anything. I stuffed everything into my bag, shaking the dirt off delicate blouses and panties, my hands trembling with humiliation and a sense of being really stupid.

What I think now, chopping thyme finely, is that we were using each other. I wanted the record deal. He wanted a young woman on his arm. It was never love for either of us.

I'm not sure it's ever been love for me, ever. I think of the way Gloria looked when she spoke about Isaak, and that's never been how I felt. Relationships have always been surface, secondary to my relationship to my music. It always felt like men were the enemy on some level, that if I let them in, I'd lose . . . something. The music. Myself.

Where did I pick up such a destructive idea? My mother, most likely. She didn't want a man in her life. I never saw Gloria get caught up in a relationship either. And Sam—well, Sam has other issues. She can't let *anyone* in.

I look out the window toward the river. A tugboat pulls a barge through the water. A plane circles low, coming in for a landing at LaGuardia. I can see lights on in the cabin windows and wonder if someone is looking down to my window. I wonder if that's going to be Gloria, flying away. It cracks my heart open to think of it, and my anxiety starts to ramp up again.

Be here now. The green scent of parsley beneath my knife fills the air, and I taste a leaf meditatively.

I need to be here now. In this space. Working on this music.

Josiah's low voice moves through my body, rousing a sensation that's almost sexual and yet both more and less. I close my eyes, let the music rise, let what I feel move in me however it likes. I taste the buttery bass of Josiah's voice across my tongue, catch the flavor of the violin, the bass, and my own voice sweetening it all.

A chord plays, slides over my skin, into my belly, as vivid as a touch.

I have no idea how long I stand there suspended in the sound, the power, but it's a long while, a long time of making love to the music in me, a long time lost in the beauty of that.

When I open my eyes, I laugh. What *is* this?

As if it's been waiting for me to notice, a new measure of music surfaces, layered and magical, and it has more than just violin and voice. I hear a recorder and a low swell of bass guitar or maybe bass violin. For a moment, I stare out the window, listening, my hands still on the knife, enchanted.

Urgently, I pour water over the carcass and spices and aromatics in the pan, wash my hands, and carry my violin into the music room. In one of the drawers of an antique desk, there are pads of manuscript paper, and I slap one down on the desk, pick up the violin, and begin to reel in the notes in my head, getting lost in the melody and the sounds and the possibilities.

Happy.

When everything is ready, I call Sam. "When are they going to let you out?"

"I just have to wait for the official paperwork. I'm starting to worry that it won't be until tomorrow."

"I'll be there in a little while, then, bring you some good food. Do you want a book or anything? Some magazines?"

"No. I just want to get out of here."

"I know." I can't think of what else to say, except, "Everything is ready for you here."

"I don't want to go to the apartment. I want to go to my own home. My own bed."

I nod, chewing my lip. "Maybe it'll just be for one night. You're getting well really fast."

"Why don't they just let me get well enough to go home here?"

It stings. "You'd rather be in the hospital than be with us?"

"Not that. Don't misinterpret my words. I just want to be home."

She's sick, I tell myself, and she's not one to mince words on her best days, but she's been so much kinder since she's been sick that I am stung by her surliness. "Okay," I say in a mild voice. "Is there anything I can do?"

"Don't get that hurt tone," she says with fierce irritation. "This is not actually about you at all, Willow."

I think about the soup on the stove, the fresh linens, and I feel like an idiot for, once again, thinking we would have a normal relationship. "I'm not hurt," I say. "Sounds like you want to be alone, so I'm going to give you some space—"

"Oh my God! Will you stop with the California speak? You can come over if you want, or stay home if you'd rather, but you don't have to make it all peace and love and groovy."

I'm standing in the thickening gloom of the parlor, feeling something hot and prickly in my throat, between my ribs. Words, incoherent and tangled, can't make their way to my tongue. "Call me if you need me, Sam."

When I hang up, I stand there stinging, feeling four years old, or seven, or twelve, at the mercy of my sister's sharp tongue. *Oh, stop being such a baby! I was only teasing!*

Why do I even keep trying? She is *so* mean, and she obviously doesn't like a single thing about me. And yet I keep trying and trying and trying.

Obviously I can't abandon her when she's sick and lost and having so much trouble, but one of these days, I promise myself, one of these days, I'm going to stop being her punching bag.

Taking a deep breath, I raise my hands over my head and go through a sun salutation, clearing bad energy, letting good in. *Breathe out anger; breathe in love.* I do one, two, three and by number four have started to believe. By six, I'm a lot better.

On number nine, I hear Gloria come in.

I meet her in the foyer. She looks worn and drawn as she hangs up her coat. "It smells wonderful in here, sweetheart. What are you cooking?"

Without knowing I'm going to say it, I blurt out, "We need to get the paintings somewhere safe."

She sighs and tosses hair out of her eyes. "I need a drink. Let's go to the parlor."

I trail her into the old-fashioned room, sit while she pours a measure of whiskey into a crystal glass. This is all Gloria, never something my mother did. I don't think she drank much at all. "Do you want something?" she asks.

"No, I have a lot to do. So do you, actually."

She sinks in her favorite chair, the cozy Grandmother chair with rose chintz next to a glass-topped table with a good lamp. I know that it looks through the window to the rooftop garden. She takes a sip and stares into the distance. I've never seen her look so tired. It scares the hell out of me.

I feel a sense of urgency and stand. "Come with me. Bring your drink."

She follows me down the hall to the spare bedroom, where I've stacked up the paintings I hid. "I looked up how to get them out of their frames." I gesture at the small layer of canvases on the bed.

"Wait." She takes her phone out of her bra. "Turn your phone off."

"What? You think they're listening?"

"I think they can listen, and I'd rather not give my thoughts away."

"Okay." I take my phone from my back pocket and turn it off. "I thought I could take them to Sam's place when I pick up her clothes. Tuck them under the mattress."

For a moment, Gloria looks at them. Then nods. "If you need money, they'll be worth a fortune after all of this." She pulls the little girl out of the stack. "Don't sell this one."

"You sound like you won't be here. You're only seventy-four, G."

"Just letting you know," she says mildly.

I stare at her for a long moment. "What's going on? Why are you talking like I'll never see you again?"

"Willow, there's no way to predict any of this. I'm in a lot of trouble."

I start to roll them up, all in a stack. "I don't understand why you'd be in trouble. You didn't forge the art."

"I carried it. I sold it."

I blink, stunned. This is worse than I imagined. But still. "Isn't there a statute of limitations on a crime like that?"

She spreads her hand. "Maybe? I don't know. They're very aggressively prosecuting the woman in Amsterdam, the British Air flight attendant. I looked it up, and it's not good."

"Did you know her?"

"No." She's gazing backward in time. "I knew there were other women in his life."

"Were there other men in yours?"

She looks up, amusement on her mouth. "Yes. None of them were Isaak, but we didn't have an exclusive relationship. I wanted it that way."

"You did?"

"Don't sound so surprised. I didn't want to get married, and back then, that's what happened. You got serious, and then you got married, and then you found yourself with a bunch of kids and no way to fly." She shakes her head. "I didn't want that life."

"You did it when my mom died. And we weren't even your kids."

She leans forward, brushes her palm over my cheek. "I loved you. I wanted to do it then. I was a lot older." She swirls the liquor in her glass, looks up at me. "I *chose* you. Both of you. I should have done it sooner."

I touch my eyebrow and realize what I've done. "Why didn't you?"

"I don't know, Willow. It's tricky, with an addict. She would do all right for a while, a month or two or three, and I'd think she was fine. I mean, I didn't think I could just swoop in and live in her house and take care of you girls."

"What if you had?"

Her smile is sad, but she meets my eyes. "I've asked myself that question a million times."

It's dark outside the windows, and I can't sit here with this much sorrow in my belly, so I gather the paintings. "It's all water under the bridge now. Thanks for coming when you did."

"I love you, Willow. You are the daughter I never had."

"Just me?"

"No, of course not. Sam was older, more resistant. But both of you."

"It doesn't seem like she loved our mother at all, though."

"Oh, no. That's not true at all. She adored her."

I narrow my eyes, trying to think of one time I remember Sam showing affection or love toward our mother. Granted, I was only nine when she died, but I can't think of anything but fights and Sam's sharp tongue and slammed doors and fury. "If you say so."

"When Sam was small, your mother was married, calmer. Clean. She didn't do any heroin for several years. She and Sam were a team, mommy and baby."

The vision of it nearly breaks me in half, little Sam in my mother's lap, laughing, playing, cuddling. "Poor Sam." I hug Gloria. "What are you going to do?"

A ripple of resistance moves in her body, and then she tells a truth. "Right now, I'm going to take a bath. And you should check on your sister."

Chapter Thirty-Six

Gloria

I've just dabbed oil into my skin when the buzzer rings. My heart freezes, and for a long moment, I don't even move.

Here it is.

Before I answer, I shimmy out of my robe and into a nice pair of underwear and one of my better bras and a comfortable pair of slacks and a sweater in case I have to wear them for a while. I find socks, too, in case my feet will be cold. I imagine jail to be all concrete. Freezing.

The buzzer rings a second time, with more urgency, it seems. "Yes?" I answer.

"I'm so sorry, Ms. Rose," says one of the new guys. I can see his face, too thin with a prominent chin, but I can't seem to remember his name. Jason, Jacob, Jared. One of those nineties names. "The FBI is here with a search warrant."

A cold wash of relief moves through me. Not an arrest, then. At least not yet. Or can they arrest me right on the spot if they find something incriminating?

"Hold on, I'm getting dressed," I say, then dial my lawyer.

He picks up. "Gloria. What's up?"

So casual, I think, as if we're going to talk about the weather. When did everyone start talking like surfers? "The FBI is downstairs with a search warrant. What should I do? Am I going to get arrested?"

"Doubtful. Just be cooperative and don't lie, but don't volunteer anything. I'm in Long Island City on another case, so they'll be done by the time I can get there, but call me the second they leave."

I nod, pressing a palm to my roiling belly. "All right. Thank you." I hang up and pick up the house phone. "Okay. Send them up," I say calmly. My hands are shaking. I look around the foyer, and there's nothing here to worry about. Willow has taken everything with her in a backpack. The depth of my relief runs down my spine with cold fingers. So smart, my Willow.

Agent Balakrishna leads a pack of two women and a man. They're all insanely young, not a single one past thirty-five, with blank expressions and hands folded. "Ms. Rose," he says, holding up a warrant. "We're here to search your apartment for possible art forgeries and other stolen contraband."

My stomach gurgles, which I hope they can't hear. "Come in. I do hope you won't make a big mess the way they do on TV."

"That should not be necessary," he says, and I do think he means it. "Will you step out of the way and allow us to do our duty, please, ma'am?"

I gesture toward the parlor, where I just spoke at length with Willow about hiding everything. "I'll be in there."

I don't dare have another drink, for fear of making a misstep, but I sit in my chair and listen to them going through the rooms, through closets, drawers. I can see down the hall, and several paintings are taken into the foyer, but from this distance I can't make out what they are. The team is efficient, calm, businesslike.

I'm going to need a new phone when I leave, I think absently, and when the phone is back online, I open my Insta, the first thing I do anytime I pick it up. There are 831 comments on the begonia series and 24,907 likes. I scroll through some of them.

The light! I wish I had your eye!

I've grown some rhizomes but never from seed. Bravo.

You inspire me!

I love your greenhouse, and I asked my son to help me build one. He's coming over later today to measure!

That one makes me smile, and I give it a heart, but I also open the reply box and tap out, That's wonderful! Please post a photo when you get it going!

My heart plummets once again, because where will she post? Here to this account I'll never be able to use again?

I'm shaky and look toward the noises the agents are making.

How could the universe be so very cruel as to take all this *now*, when I mind so much? When I've finally found a life that means something? I've always loved the girls, but they were not my life, the meaning of everything. We're supposed to feel that way about our children, as women, but how many of us really do? Love, yes, love madly, kill to protect.

But childhood is fleeting. A relationship with a child is a rich and rewarding thing, but it is a relationship and therefore simply a part of a person's life, not the whole.

With my Instagram, I discovered a way to be *useful*. Helpful. I know I'm helping other women with this account—maybe even some men—inspiring them, like the woman with the greenhouse, to do things they haven't articulated, or maybe haven't had the courage to claim. I'm telling them all that it's perfectly reasonable to expect to have a full, interesting, exciting life after seventy.

I will be letting them down, along with Willow, Sam, my friends, and, most of all, myself.

But no whining. I click the phone to dark and fold my arms over my knees. This is all my own doing.

Balakrishna carries something out of the dining room, a fairly large painting, and places it with the others the agents have brought out. They can't mean to take them out of here in their frames, can they? I stand up and walk briskly into the doorway of the foyer. "Why are you taking these?"

"I believe several of them are forgeries, actually." He lifts his chin, and I see that beneath the appearance of softness is a spine of titanium, and he takes his job seriously. "They will need to be authenticated."

The one he holds is a piece Billie bought on tour in the early eighties, one of the first paintings she picked up after buying the apartment. It's not anything I ever paid much attention to, a minor painting by an artist I don't care much about. Another one, propped up in the chair, is a drawing by Duncan Grant, the Bloomsbury artist. "That one is not a forgery," I say definitely. "I bought it myself, in a fierce auction."

He gives me a bland look. "It will be authenticated."

"Please be careful with it."

"Yes, ma'am." One of the agents comes in and asks about the room I call the parlor. He nods. "Will you wait elsewhere, Ms. Rose?"

I nod, take myself to the small kitchen, and turn on the kettle. A big pot simmers on the back of the stove, filling the air with the fragrance of Willow's magic—herbs and chicken and whatever else. I peek in and see rounds of carrot floating. It smells like healing, like hope, and I scoop out a small bowl for myself, then sit at the table to eat it while agents go through my precious, precious things.

Willow, my love, I think, stinging. *I will miss you. Sam, I will miss you too. Kitchen, I will miss you. Teaspoons I bought on eBay, I will miss you.*

I feel empty. How can I start again, so late?

Chapter Thirty-Seven
Willow

Sam has called ahead to have the super let me into her apartment so that I can get some clothes and toiletries for her.

The apartment is in disarray, untouched since the night she went to the hospital by ambulance. A small table has been knocked over, the bed is a tangle of covers, and there are take-out boxes on the counter, reeking. It's going to take me a little while here, I can see.

First things first. I unzip the backpack and take out the hoodie I stuffed in on top. Rolled up inside are the paintings, the entire lot of them, and it's surprising how little space they take up, considering how much they're worth.

Which is a silly thought. Jewels are small too. Computer chips with secrets.

Shaking myself, I look around the place slowly. The loft is open, with lots of industrial-looking furniture, open shelves, not a lot of hiding space. I said I was going to put them under the mattress, but that would be too obvious. I open the cupboards in the kitchen, looking for possibilities. She doesn't have much in the way of cookware, but the shelves are stacked with books and clothes. I could stash the paintings behind some of them, but that wouldn't feel very secure.

The high, narrow closet in the bathroom has potential. The cupboard rises all the way to the top of the sixteen-foot ceilings, and if I could find something to stand on, I could hide the paintings all the way in the back of the top shelf. From here, it appears to be empty.

Still too obvious.

Holding the rolled-up paintings in the crook of my elbow, I return to the main room and look at everything. The TV is hung on the wall with a metal arm to move it various ways. Shelves hold stacks of video games and several gaming systems.

Nervous frustration raises the tension in my neck, and I nearly jump out of my skin when someone knocks on the door. "Willow!" a voice calls. "I came to help you."

I'm still holding the paintings, and I don't know where to put them, so I stash them back in the pack, hurry to the door, and unfasten the locks.

Asher is standing there, looking so fit and trim my mouth drops. "Hey! You look great."

He gathers me up in a bear hug that lifts me completely off my feet. "I've missed you so much, kid!"

I hug him back, almost teary with the pleasure of his brotherly scent, the feeling of safety he brings with him. "Me too."

He puts me down, and I wave him in. "Did Sam send you? She's getting impatient, but I wanted to straighten things up a little." I gesture behind me.

"Yeah." He makes a face. "I'll help. She just wanted me to get one of her old notebooks. We're working on a new game."

"That's great," I say, but I'm trying to think what to do with the paintings now. I can't exactly hide them while he's here.

He runs his fingers over a row of notebooks on the shelf opposite the bed. Pauses, flips one open, slams it closed. "Oops. Diaries. I need work notebooks."

"Sam keeps a diary?"

"Yeah, she has since she was a kid. You didn't know that?"

"No. She really doesn't seem like the journaling type." The multicolored row of volumes is one of the most tempting things I've ever seen. What would it be like to see behind my sister's walls? What has she written in them? What has she written about me? About her dad and Asher and—

"Don't even think about it," Asher says.

"I would never," I lie.

"Me either," he lies back.

"What do you think she writes about?" I ask as I strip the bed.

Asher finds another shelf of heavy-duty spiral notebooks and takes a couple down, opens one, puts it back, opens the other. "Bingo." He shucks his jacket and lays the notebook on top of it, then comes over to help me with the bed. "What does anyone write about in a journal? Feelings, observations, resolves."

"Do you keep one?" I shake the pillow out of its case.

"No. I did for a while in high school, but it was all about the same subject, all the time, and I just got tired of myself."

I smile. "What subject? How to get into video game design school?"

He scoffs, tossing a pillow on the couch. "Hardly. It was always Sam. Sam, Sam, Sam."

For a moment, I stare openmouthed. "What?"

"C'mon," he says, gathering the sheets into a ball and carrying them around the corner. He opens the bathroom closet and takes out fresh linens. "Everyone in the tristate area knew I was in love with her."

"I didn't."

"You're kinder than most people," he says, tossing me one end of the fitted sheet. "You take people at face value."

"Do I? That's a nice thing to say." We stretch the sheet, very sensibly white, high–thread count cotton, and fit it over the corners. I shake out the top sheet, and he grabs the other side.

He gives me a half grin. "You've always been the nicest of all of us, including G and me and everyone in my family."

"Well, I don't know that it's done me a lot of good." I frown, shaking a pillow into a fresh case. "But don't get me off track. You were in love with Sam in high school?"

"High school, middle school, grade school, college." He scowls. "This is weird. I don't want to talk about it."

I shrug, pulling the duvet up and folding the top neatly. I'm intrigued and have to give this some more thought. How did I never notice?

When did he stop?

Together, we clean up the apartment for when she returns, and I gather underwear, toothbrush and toiletries, and some comfy pajama bottoms and T-shirts, which I neatly stack on the bed while I try to decide what I should do with the paintings. Asher washes the dishes, fills a trash bag, polishes the sink, and then just stands there with an expression on his face that I can only call sad.

"What's up, big brother?" I ask, touching his upper back.

He starts a little, as if he'd forgotten I was there. "We haven't been talking," he says. "Did she tell you?"

"Gloria did. But you're the one who got her to the hospital, right?"

He closes his eyes. "Yeah. Barely. She was so sick when I got here, out of her head. It scared me so much."

My gut lurches. "I know. I came by here, too, but I was too afraid of her getting mad at me to call the super." I cover my belly with a palm. "I would never have forgiven myself if she had died because I was afraid of her."

He touches my hand. "It wouldn't have been your fault, Willow."

I shrug. "How did you know to come if you haven't been talking?"

"SOS." He gives me a rueful little smile. "From the Batman movies, a signal that we needed to come now. Right now. I tried to call her back and just couldn't rouse her, so I used our old Friend Connection, and it said she was home."

He doubles over, his elbows hitting the counter with some force, but he doesn't even seem to feel it. He buries his face in his hands, pushing his glasses up his forehead. He is silent, almost as if he's holding his breath. "She nearly fucking *died*."

My body reacts with a rush of nausea, and I have to breathe slowly, in, out, in, out, to halt it. The comma of his back clearly expresses grief, shock, horror, and I move a little closer so I can rub my hand on the place between his shoulder blades. That's when I realize he is silently crying, his sobs so small and intense that it almost breaks me too. "She didn't, though," I say quietly. "You saved her."

"I almost didn't come. I thought it would serve her right."

I'm not following this exactly, but I keep my hand on him, proof that I'm here and listening and it's okay.

"And then I got here, and she's babbling about being married and who is going to take care of our kids, and . . ." He takes a deep breath, makes himself do the man thing and stop feeling the full roar of his grief. "She was so sweet, so vulnerable. She forgot everything that has happened and somehow made up a story to fit why I was there, and it just broke my damned heart."

I nod. Listening. Confused, but that doesn't matter. He just needs to say whatever it is that's bugging him.

But he stops talking, straightens up. "Sorry." He takes off his glasses and wipes his face with a paper towel. "I'm such a fucking idiot."

"Uh . . . how?"

"Do you know who her doctor is? Of all the people in the world? That bastard Eric."

"I know! Right? I chased him out of her room when I saw him. How dare he?"

"Yeah, well, I think—" He halts, shakes his head. "Never mind. I'm just not doing all of this again."

"Okay." I hold up a palm. "I'm sorry, but I am completely lost. Doing what?"

"I want to get married, have kids. I'm forty years old, and I don't want to be a grandfather dad. I want to be a dad-dad."

"That makes sense."

He bows his head. "As long as Sam and I were 'best friends'"—he puts the words in quotes—"I was never going to look for a woman who wanted to settle down. I'd just keep . . . hoping."

"That Sam . . . ?"

He gives a humorless laugh. "I know. Pathetic."

I scowl. "So you told her you didn't want to be friends anymore? Broke up?"

He nods. "And you know, Willow, it's been good for me. I've actually been dating, sometimes anyway. And going to the gym, and eating right, and treating myself the way I always should have, instead of pouring the best of me into Sam."

"You do look pretty good."

"Thanks. You don't, by the way. You look half-starved."

"Thank you." I shrug. "It's been a rough few months, but it's better now that I'm home." I fold my arms. "Except that my sister, who still hates me, is sick, and my aunt is in trouble."

"Trouble?"

"More on that in a minute, but Asher, what happened to you and Sam?"

His expression is sad. "Ask her."

I nod slowly and change direction, thinking of the paintings. I make an executive decision. "I need your help with something."

Chapter Thirty-Eight

Sam

It's well past dark by the time Willow loads me into a cab bound for the apartment. She brought a notebook, the excuse I had for getting Asher to come back to the hospital, and it irks me. That she interfered with my plan. "I wanted Asher to bring that to me," I say, and even I am embarrassed by my petulance.

"I'm sorry." She clears her throat. "He . . . uh . . . had something to do for Gloria."

I lift my head. "Gloria? What?"

She takes in a breath, sighs it out. "It's complicated, and a long story." She looks toward the hallway. "I don't want to tell it here."

Even in my weary bad mood, I feel a whisper of worry. "Is she in trouble or something?"

"Kind of." She touches my shoulder. "Let's focus on getting you back to the apartment, and then we can talk."

I want to push for more, but it takes all my energy to walk with her to the cab, then stay upright and not crumple over sideways into her lap. My head hurts, and a slight roar has filled my ears, as if I'm wrapped in cotton balls. Lights reflect off the wet pavement, and the sharpness is too much.

I close my eyes.

"Asher said you guys broke up as friends," Willow says next to me. "What happened?"

"I don't know," I say. My head rocks back and forth against the back of the seat. It's weirdly soothing. The traffic is heavy and full of honking horns and tires swishing and the sound of the rain. I think about telling my app everything and not Willow, and it seems absurd. "That's not true. We had a really bad fight after Tina's wedding."

"You've had plenty of fights."

"Not like this one." It flashes through my memory, full of hurled shouts and misunderstandings on both sides and so much hurt. "We said things we can't take back."

"What things?"

I shake my head, but I think of the insults I flung—*needy, cloying.* I squeeze my eyes tight. *Fat.*

So fucking mean.

She's silent. "Why *then*? What happened at the wedding?"

I flash on sleeping against his chest, waking up to make love again. "So many things."

"Like?"

"I can't talk about it."

"Wait," she says. "Did you guys have sex?"

I squeeze my eyes tight. "Yes, and it ruined everything."

"Was it the sex, or did you shove him away?"

"Don't." I hold up a hand. "This is none of your business."

"Maybe not." She takes my hand and draws me down until my head is cradled in her lap, and I feel like a woman in a Pre-Raphaelite painting. She strokes my forehead with cool fingers.

"Will you sing to me?"

And of course she does, a lilting lullaby about a girl who can't marry the love of her life, so she weaves him a shirt of the hair she cuts from her head.

"You have a real pretty voice, young lady," the cabbie says over his shoulder.

"She made an album," I say, half-hypnotized by her fingers, her sweet voice. "You should buy it."

"Is that right?"

But I drift off, and the next thing I know, Jorge is holding an umbrella over my head as I get out of the cab, his strong hand hard on my arm. It's a cold, hard, miserable rain, and I'm glad to get inside. Willow comes behind with all my things. "Thank you, Jorge. I'll get her upstairs."

"Hey, how's your auntie doing? All those paintings—" He tsks.

"What?"

"Never mind," Willow says, and I see her give a hard look to Jorge, shaking her head fiercely at him.

The simple trip from hospital to here has taken all my reserves, and I lean against the wall of the elevator, staring at the polished brass decorations, which are just the same, as if nothing ever changes inside this cramped, ornate cage.

Hmmm, says my creative brain, tucking that away. *An elevator toward new things . . . ? A place of return?*

Willow hustles me in, and the apartment looks messy, with empty picture frames stacked up against the wall and a coat knocked down from the tree. Willow says "Shit" under her breath and picks up the coat while still holding on to my arm. "Gloria! We're home."

I'm dizzy, but I right myself with a hand to the wall, surveying the disarray. "You said Gloria is in trouble," I say. "What kind of trouble?"

Willow pauses. "Let me get you to your room and find G, and then I'll tell you everything."

"Tell me."

Willow raises her eyebrows and takes my arm. "You're the color of the moon. You need to lie down."

The journey from the hospital was as arduous as climbing a mountain, and I feel like I might pass out. "Okay. I need to lie down."

"Lean on me."

So I do, and she walks me down the hall to my old bedroom, where the sheets smell fresh and crisp, and the light from the stained glass lamp I've always loved shines on the nightstand. A water bottle is there, and my brush, and as I fall into the bed, I feel her cover me up. "Thank you," I whisper.

Willow sweeps her hand over my hair, touches my earlobe just as my mother used to, and I want to weep for missing her, Billie, who has been gone for a thousand years. *Why don't any of the ballads resurrect dead mothers?* I wonder.

Then I grab Willow's hand. "Promise you'll come right back."

"I promise."

Chapter Thirty-Nine
Willow

I find Gloria in the greenhouse, of course, where she's writing frantically on a piece of paper. Loud classical music is blasting on the speaker system she installed a couple of years ago. And I do mean she installed it. It's the kind of thing she does so often, reminding you that she's not only a knockout and really smart and funny and a million other amazing things, but she's also handy and likes doing that kind of work.

"What are you doing out here?" I ask. "Did Balakrishna take the paintings?"

"Yes." She straightens, gestures around the greenhouse. "I'm making lists of what to do in here. You know most of it, but—"

I feel winded. "Are you going to be arrested?"

"Very likely."

"But surely you won't be there long. We can bail you out."

"Maybe. It's possible the bail will be quite high, considering the possibility of flight risk."

"We'll just tell them that you have this apartment and me and Willow, and where would you go? Surely. You're seventy-four. What judge would keep you locked up?"

She smiles sadly. "I'm sure they will just believe us if we're earnest enough."

I sink onto a bench. "I see what you mean. But G—"

"Shh." She raises a hand. "Let me get this written down while I have a chance."

The greenhouse for her is what music is for me, the calm amid the storm. "What's this?" I ask, jumping up to sit on a wooden table. The sprouts are small and colorful.

"Begonias. I ordered a bunch of seeds a few months ago, and they're all coming up at once." She doesn't look at me. "They like to be damp but not too wet, and they like light but not too much direct sunlight."

"Like . . . all begonias?" I ask with a grin.

"Smart aleck." Her hair is a bit disheveled, and her lipstick wore off a long time ago, and she actually looks her age, the LED grow lights exaggerating the lines on her cheeks and around her eyes. "They're going to be so pretty, wait and see. I ordered them all the way from China."

I can't bear to imagine her in jail. A Leonard Cohen song, "Suzanne," pops into my head, about a lost woman who gives a man tea that comes all the way from China. I start to sing it.

It makes Gloria smile, which was my whole aim. "Is your sister settled?"

"Out cold."

"Poor baby. This is hard on her need to be independent."

I nod. "What happened to the paintings, G?"

She sighs, resting her wrists on the edge of the potting area. "The FBI took them."

"Will they be enough to arrest you?"

"No. Not those," she says. "Strangely," she adds, brushing hair off her forehead, which leaves a streak of dirt behind, "I've been thinking of my mother. I can't imagine what her life was like during the war." She continues, "Six years, her parents dead, and all she had was her beauty and her wits. When I think of her, I'm just so sad that she didn't get anything at all of the life she wanted."

"But she made you and my mom really fierce, right? And then my mom had two fierce daughters, and you made us even more so."

"Did I?"

"Of course! Imagine if you hadn't been around, G? Who would have taken care of us? What would have happened?"

She nods thoughtfully. Goes back to scooping potting soil into small clay pots. I watch her free a seedling from a plastic tray and nestle it into the pot, carefully tapping down the soil around it. "See how gently I'm doing this? You see people smashing the dirt down really hard, but it just needs to be firm enough for the plant to stand upright. The roots need space to grow."

"That makes sense." I pause. "Are you scared?"

"Of course."

I stare at her, unwilling to give up without a fight. "Isn't there a statute of limitations on something like this?"

"There must not be. I googled it, but with international law, it's murky. I mean, they've arrested Isaak and the woman in Amsterdam." Delicately, she shakes excess dirt from the roots of a seedling, tucks it into a pot. "No more. I hate that you're involved even a little bit."

I touch her arm. "Come on; let's get some supper. You might as well eat."

We're setting the table in the kitchen, that old red table that's so homey and so ugly, when the bell rings. It's Asher, who comes in with a spring in his step. I open the door to him and touch my lips with one finger to indicate silence. He nods.

It really is remarkable how much more of himself he is. Always a slightly chubby kid with pasty white skin, his only beauty in those days was his big, dark eyes, hidden behind thick glasses.

Now he's just grown into his own aura or something. He's still not thin, but he's fit, solid looking, and his hair is a little long to give the curls some room to be themselves, and he wears glasses that complement his features—a nose that's aggressive but not too much so, a great wide mouth with big white teeth. He dresses better, too, in hipsterish-but-not clothes that seem as relaxed and high quality as he is himself.

"What?" he asks.

"Nothing."

"Is Sam here?"

"She's sleeping, really hard. Do you want to eat?"

"Bloom's?"

"No. Me."

He laughs. "Of course."

My phone buzzes against my butt, and I pull it out, see the name on the screen. "Go on into the kitchen," I say. "I'll be right there."

He amiably heads through the hallway, because no one but us ever takes the servant hallway.

I answer the phone. It's funny that he's calling, not texting. "Hey, Josiah."

"Hey. How's your sister doing?"

"Good. I got her home, anyway."

"That's great." A small pause. "I worked out some free time in my schedule, and I'm free tonight if that works for you."

I look over my shoulder, toward my family, the women I love, who are both in crisis. And yet what would it hurt to play some music? I can't do anything for either of them, frankly. What I can do is something for myself.

And really, we're all in charge of our own happiness.

"It's a little bit crazy here, but I'd really love it if you can come over. I might not have a ton of time, but—"

"We'll do what we can," he says in his calm way.

I flash on his hands, flying over his bass, and the sound of his voice. "Right." I swallow. "Come whenever. I'm here." I give him the address.

"I remember."

Because of the looming trouble, the meal with Gloria and Asher feels precious. Rain is pouring outside while we sit in the badly lit kitchen, eating soup and bread while Sam sleeps. It's cozy, quiet, and I wish for music. "Why don't you have a Bluetooth speaker in here?"

Gloria dabs her mouth. "Because I'm almost never in here, my love."

Asher chuckles.

"Fair enough," I say. "I'm going to get one."

"Oh, you're staying?" Asher asks, inclining his head.

I shrug lightly, looking through the window of the back door to the rooftop and the rain and the shadows of plants and the glow of fairy lights in the greenhouse. "I miss New York. I miss . . . this."

"I thought you loved LA. You were out there for a while. I thought you'd end up staying." He butters a slice of bread, not the good sourdough I sometimes got in LA but a genuinely decent french bread. "You always raved about the weather."

"You can get tired of sunshine," I say. "I need some storms and gray miserableness to think."

Gloria laughs. "I know what you mean."

"I don't," Asher says. "Stick around for another month, and you'll see. It's been miserable."

"Yes, but soon it will be April," Gloria says, "and that's a lovely, lovely month here." Her face looks abruptly, painfully sad.

I touch her hand. "It is."

The wail cuts into the quiet like the cry of a banshee: "Willow!"

I bolt from the table.

Chapter Forty

Sam

When I awaken, my mouth is dry, head aching. At first I have no idea where I am; then I recognize the particular arrangement of windows with light coming in from the busy street below. My bedroom at my mom's apartment.

I have to pee. This is the first time I've had to do anything on my own, really, and I consider using my phone to call Willow. No. The sooner I get my act together, the sooner I can get out of here.

What I forget sometimes is how great this room is. Windows along the south wall. A big, very soft bed that I have always loved, a bed for the princess and the pea, my mom said when she bought it. Teasing me. That couldn't have been long before she died.

Don't, I tell myself and roll off the bed, plant my feet on the old rug that covers bare wooden floors. From the direction of the kitchen or maybe the parlor, I hear voices, and it's oddly comforting. It gives me courage to stand up and shuffle to the door, then out into the hall, and then, leaning on the wall, into the family bathroom, which is one of the most beautiful bathrooms I've ever seen. It's getting pretty dated in some ways, but another skylight allows buckets of light to flow in, and the tub is gigantic, and there are built-in drawers beneath the linen cupboard. That cupboard in itself is a huge luxury.

It's a relief to sit on the toilet. I close my eyes and rest there. Long enough to gather my resolve again. It's better being up. My head is slightly less buzzy, but I do have a headache, and it seems like it must be time for medicine, though I have no idea what time it actually is.

Suddenly, I remember the empty picture frames and Willow's hints that Gloria is in trouble, and I realize that she never came back to tell me what's going on.

Probably because I've been asleep all this time, to be fair. I'll ask her about it now. I want to be included in whatever this is.

But as I wash my hands, I realize that I'm very dizzy. It feels less like the illness and more like the shakes I get when I've forgotten to eat. Which happens more often than I'd like to admit. How long has it been since I really ate something? I probably need food. Tea.

On shaky legs, I open the bathroom door and, holding on to the wall, shuffle back out. The hallway looks a million miles long, and I really am feeling extremely shaky. To avoid falling, I slide down, back against the wall, and muster up my voice: "Willow!"

It comes out as a croak.

I lean my head against the wall, remembering when I came home after living with my dad for the first time. He'd taken an apartment in the neighborhood so that I could walk back and forth to my same school, and I loved living with him. It was a small place, just a one-bedroom with a futon in the living room, where my dad slept, and a galley kitchen, where I made my own cereal before school, careful not to wake him up. Evenings, we cooked together, and I did my homework at the table while he wrote up interviews. He wasn't famous then, but he had made a name for himself.

"Willow!" I cry, but it is still such a small sound in the vastness of the apartment with its endless, creepy rooms and dark hallways. As a child, I absolutely refused to enter the servant hallway from the foyer—I was positive ghosts lived there.

Like the ghost of my mother, who sits down beside me now. I can't really see her; I just feel her presence. Comforting. Infuriating. "Go away," I say without energy, my eyes closed.

After my parents were first divorced, I lived alternately with my mother and father. My dad fell in love with a woman—not Brittney, his current wife, or the one before that, or maybe even the one before that—and it was suddenly quite difficult to care for me and do his job, so I was sent back to my mother full-time when I was six. I begged and cried and threw the only fits of my life, but I couldn't change the outcome. I came back here, to Willow and my mother and the lonely, lonely rooms. Later, I lived with him again, off and on, whenever it was convenient, mainly.

Now I think, *Where was Willow when I was with my dad?*

How could I have never asked this question before?

As if the thought has conjured her, she's suddenly beside me in the dark, cold hallway. "Sam, oh my God!" She presses her hand against my forehead. "You're burning up. Let's get you back to bed."

I try to comply, but she's as wispy as the ghost on my other side. And then there are solid, strong hands. Asher's hands. "C'mon, Sam. Let me help you up."

He tucks my arm around his neck, his arm around my waist, and he walks me back to my room, which isn't nearly as far as I thought it was. "Don't be mad at me, okay?" I say as he tucks me back under the covers.

"I'm not mad at you." He presses his palm to my cheek. "It's never that."

Willow brings pills and a cup of water, and there's something I want to ask her, but I can't remember what. My mother sinks down on the bed beside me and curls her body around mine. She starts to sing softly, and I am swept away.

Chapter Forty-One

Gloria

A text comes in at eight fifteen p.m. It's ready.

I text back. I'll be there in 20 min

Willow is in the music room, working out the sequence of a series of notes and breaks. The music is her way of coping with the stress of everything. I've heard her working on the same phrases since she arrived. On the violin, on the piano, humming under her breath. It's both melancholy and hopeful, though I could never tell you why, and I find myself humming along as I walk down the hallway.

I stop at Sam's room and poke my head in. She's asleep again, and Asher is reading in an overstuffed chair that used to be in the parlor. He lifts a hand, and I leave him to his watch. At the music room I wait at the door so that Willow can surface in her own time, and as I stand there, I see my mother playing the piano my father bought for her, a used and battered upright, and I see my sister curved over her guitar. Their bodies blur together, become a column of sound and time connecting the generations. Who was the first one, I wonder? The first to play a harp or sing a cantata in some medieval room? Or perhaps it stretches further, to the Romans or the Babylonians or a Neanderthal who discovered a rhythm on an animal stomach.

And into the future, I hope. I hope they will have children, my girls. Samantha, particularly, for although Willow is a nurturer, it is Sam who burns for a baby.

Is it wrong of me to wish children on them? I don't know. Ambition and children are not always the best fit, not for women. I had to choose one or the other, and I chose my work. Billie was careless. She wanted music but let her body dictate the direction of life.

But where would my life be without these girls?

Probably a lot like Miriam's, which is a lovely, good life. She has companionship and the satisfaction of her art and probably lovers now and then, though she doesn't speak of it, never has.

But I think of Willow as a ten-year-old, all eyes and hair, playing her violin for a recital and bringing down the house. I think of Sam, so very, very angry at her mother, her father, her sister, because every time she settled into a stable life, some adult took it away from her.

Thank heaven for Asher. For Willow, even if Sam doesn't really appreciate her the way she should.

In the music room, I listen for a moment. "I love this piece, Willow."

She raises her head. "Thanks. I've been working on it for a couple of months, and it's finally coming together." Her hands fall to her lap. "I'm going to enter it into a competition, but it needs to be in by the day after tomorrow."

"Good," I say and mean it. I want her to have something to distract her. "Promise me you'll get it in, will you?"

She frowns. "Why?"

"I need a promise, Willow. Cross your heart and hope to die."

"But—"

"Promise."

She nods, draws a cross over her heart. "I promise. A friend of mine is coming over in a little while to help me finish. You think that's okay?"

"Why wouldn't it be all right?"

"Well, because . . ." She gestures toward me. "You. Sam. Everything."

"She'll be okay. It will be good for her to not be completely in control of her entire world for five minutes."

"What if she bolts?"

I shrug. "She bolts."

"Well, that makes me feel like a bad sister. People are more important than music."

"Don't do that, Willow. Your goals are important too. Play the music. It'll be fine." If she's busy, it will make my next steps that much easier. I cross the room and kiss her head. "Anyway, I have to go out for a while."

"Now?"

"I won't be long. Good night."

The rain has stopped, leaving behind a crisp, fresh cold. Everyone complains about rain, but I love it and always have, and I focus clearly on where I am right now, in this minute. Walking in the neighborhood I've loved for twenty-five years. The shimmer of traffic lights on the street, flowers in the window of a bodega, a tiny man in a perfectly tailored suit and a cane making his way down the sidewalk one slow step at a time.

My world. With my phone camera, I shoot a dozen photos. Pressing them into my heart.

At the church, I head down the stairs to the basement, where Sandro awaits. "Hello," he says as I enter. He looks so much better than he did when he first arrived, when he had been starved and beaten in his home city of San Salvador, then walked for more than three thousand miles with a ragtag group of teenagers to help find them asylum. As a priest, he had a better chance of shepherding at least a few of them through, and that was all that made it—three, plus Sandro himself.

He has a suitably sober expression as I sit down, suddenly feeling the weight of everything fall on my shoulders, bending me over like an old, old woman.

"I'm so sorry," he says in his soft accent.

I bury my face in my hands, willing all the sorrow to stay right where it is, below the surface. "It's my own fault," I say and raise my head. "No whining."

He gazes at me with kindness and takes my hand, saying nothing. I think of Tuesday mornings here, when we feed sometimes hundreds of hungry people. He is such a calming, peaceful presence that it seems that every week we prepare everything much more smoothly than should be possible and feed far, far more than the ingredients would suggest. A small miracle.

"This man must have been very special to you," he says, "to risk so much."

I shake my head, look at the ceiling. "I was a little bit mad, maybe."

"So it goes." His gaze is always so clear and straight. "We fall in love. It's what we do."

"I suppose." I take a breath. "I guess that's one thing about the priesthood, huh? It spares you that, at least."

"No, it does not," and there is the faintest sorrow in his words. "And when one falls, we betray vows to God himself."

"Where is she?" I ask quietly.

His smile is crooked, sad. "I don't know. It seems she was not so serious as me. I left the priesthood, and she left the city."

"No!" I'm aghast. "That hussy!"

He laughs, as I meant him to do. "She was not who I thought," he admits.

"You're not a priest?"

"Not anymore. Only a servant of God, where he needs me."

"Why does everyone think—"

"I cannot convince them, so I let it stand. Even though I do not offer any of the sacraments or homilies or any other thing a priest does, they don't believe me."

"I think I just assumed."

He nods. "Father Anselmo gave me shelter, and in return, I help him in whatever ways I can. I cannot return to San Salvador, and here, at least I can offer my service to the community."

Of all the things I've heard or felt today, this one makes me ache more deeply than any other. He's an exile because his land is being destroyed by gangs. I'm to be exiled because I was a foolish young woman. If he can bear it with grace, I can certainly do it myself. "Thank you for sharing that with me."

He reaches into a bag and brings out a manila envelope. It contains a passport and other documents in a new name. I hold it for a moment, then open the flap and look at the passport, American, in the name of Gertrude Fernsby, which makes me smile. It sounds like the name of an armchair detective, but the photo is mine, as is the driver's license, which gives my home address in Eastchester. I stare at them for a moment, then nod.

This is how I will spare the apartment, spare the girls, spare my friends. I will flee before they can arrest me. "Thank you."

He hugs me, and then I hurry back out into the rain. The sooner the better.

Chapter Forty-Two
Willow

As I go over the notes and bridges and arrangements over and over, I'm thinking about Gloria and the trouble she's in, and I realize I haven't talked to Sam about it yet either. First thing, when she wakes up the next time. She's getting stronger, but it scares me how weak she is, like a character in a historical novel, Marianne in *Sense and Sensibility*, falling apart.

Except that it's always been me, the younger sister, who's held the center. Which is funny, because not only am I the younger sister, but I'm also small, not to mention blonde and wispy. People discount me. Manic pixie dream girl, as Sam always says, but I'm not. Nothing like that. By nature, I'm less like my lost mother and my delicately wired sister and much more like the sensible Gloria, who sees what needs doing and just does it.

The music loops back and back, looping around my mother and her longings. Her women and her men, her drugs. Why didn't the music sustain her the way it has sustained me? For me, music has been at the center of everything my whole life, a solid core of love that I could count on no matter what else was happening. Not to bring in money, although I know I will never starve as long as I touch it, but a thing I can love and trust completely, more of a friend than any other thing in my life.

I wish my mother had trusted her gift.

It's while I'm in the depths of these circling thoughts that Josiah arrives. He's dressed nicely, in a pair of slacks and an oxford shirt beneath his camel coat, his hair combed out into a natural, dots of water crowning it like a halo.

He's looked different every time I've seen him. This is the professor side, and I think of him in front of a classroom teaching—what? I haven't asked yet.

Before I can, he closes the door behind him and turns, and I haven't stepped back and nearly stumble in my haste to do so, and he catches my waist in one big hand. "Careful," he says, that voice rumbling through my body, my neck and elbows and hands.

"Sorry," I say a little breathlessly, stepping back and smoothing my blouse. "Come on in."

I lead him back into the music room, and I realize I've forgotten to take his coat, and I can't seem to get my shit together, because now the scent of his skin is mixed with the heady scent of rain, and lamplight is catching in those little diamonds in his hair, and I haven't been so flustered by a man since . . . I don't know when. "Can I take your coat?"

"Sure." He sheds it. "I can—"

"No, it's all right; I'll hang it up in the hall."

"Or I can do it."

But I've already got it, holding it close, and I hurry out, bending my nose into the collar before I reach to hang it on the hook by the door.

I startle when he says, "I forgot my phone in my pocket."

It's dim in the hall, so he can't see my blush, but I know he saw me smelling his coat. It's so junior high. I don't do this, get flustered around men. Not any of them.

And yet here I am, looking up at him like I don't know the first thing about sex or men or how any of it works.

"It's in my pocket," he says, pointing behind me.

"Oh. Sorry." I laugh and move out of the way; in fact I take myself all the way back to the music room because I'm both embarrassed and afraid I might start giggling to make it worse. I cover my mouth as he comes back in, looking up at him, and he's inclining his head. "Something on your mind, Willow?"

I let myself laugh, then, laugh out the stress and the longing and the everything, and he lets me, rolling up his sleeves, opening his instrument case. He sits on the bench by my mother's albums and waits for me.

Finally, I'm finished and wipe away laughter tears. "Whew. Sorry about that."

"I don't mind." In the lamplight, his eyes are as dark as a lake, fathomless. Glittering.

I take a breath. Truth always wins. "You probably get this all the time, but you fluster me a little."

His hands rest on the bass and the bow, and for a moment, he doesn't say anything. "I've been flustered since I walked into the pub and saw you sitting there with Paige."

"Oh." A swell of happiness wells in my chest, and then I remember the reason I wanted him here in the first place. "But the music," I say. "I'm afraid of . . . ruining that part."

"Agreed," he says and holds my gaze as he lifts his bow. "Let's get to work."

Something easy runs through my muscles, my throat. "Are you always so mellow?"

"Mostly. Not everyone likes it."

"Really?"

A shrug. He skims the bow over the E string and makes a tuning adjustment. "Some people need drama."

I laugh and roll my eyes. "Not me." I pick up my violin and skim my bow over the strings, listening to him do the same, and we come into harmony. "Were you teaching today? You have that professorial look."

"Yes, a seminar."

"What do you teach?"

"Oh! Writing. I'm a poet. I thought I told you that already."

A soft blue puff of light zaps me. "A poet. Can you write lyrics?"

He reaches down into the bag at his feet. "Yes." He hesitates a moment, then hands over a piece of paper. "It's a work in progress, but I started hearing it when I left and jotted some notes down. I was thinking of your mother, and your album, and the way you looked when you talked earlier."

I read the scribblings, and they're a play on my mother's song "Write My Name Across the Sky," an echo of love from the other side of the universe. It's only two verses and clearly a rough draft, but it's right enough to make tears rise. "I think we can work with this." I don't wipe the tears away as I lift the violin, allow my mother, my wish for her, my longing for her, to fill me up, and I pour that emotion into the mirror of her longing all those years ago.

And it's good. It's really, really fucking good.

Chapter Forty-Three

Sam

When I next awaken, the meds have taken hold, and I feel like myself again. Asher is asleep in the chair, covered with a blanket he must have taken from the foot of my bed. He's kicked off his shoes, and his feet are propped up on the ottoman, and I don't want to wake him, but even my teeth are floating. As quietly as possible, I swing my legs out of bed and wait to see how it feels to sit up.

Pretty good.

I stand. Wait. Still okay. No dizziness. I touch my head, and it feels like my fever is totally gone.

Good. I walk toward the door, carefully checking my status, and I feel pretty much like myself. Normal. Except—jeez. I'm *starving*.

"Sam!" Asher is at my side. Takes my arm firmly. "What are you doing? Why do you think I'm sleeping in your room? Because it's comfortable? I can tell you it isn't."

"I'm seriously fine now."

"Let's just not test that too much, huh?" He opens the door and offers his arm, elbow out, so that I can walk beside him. The hallway is lit by a single gloomy light, but it's better than the darkness earlier.

"I used to think a goblin lived in that closet," I say, pointing.

"I remember. And ghosts in the servant hallway."

I laugh a little. "I forgot you'd know all that."

"You thought everything was haunted. Good thing you grew up and found a use for that imagination."

"Yeah, I guess so." I don't mention the fact that I've been sensing my mother. It seems like too much of an omen that I might die.

He leaves me at the door. "I'll be here, so don't get all brave if you have a problem."

"I promise," I say, but if I had a problem with the toilet, I'd rather dunk my head than have anybody help me, much less Asher.

Luckily, it's not a problem. I wash my face and hands, drag a brush through my hair, and catch a whiff of my body. "Ugh. I think I need a shower."

I look at myself in the mirror. Can I ask him to do that? Wait while I shower? My eyes stare back at me, and I see the lust in them, the longing I feel to push him into a position where he'd put his hands on me and then maybe remember—

Don't be stupid, I say to my reflection. It's entirely a mental exercise, because I will quickly be out of energy entirely. The shakiness I'm feeling is all about starvation.

I open the door. "I am so hungry I could eat that troll under the stairs."

He grins, holds out his elbow again. "Let's get you some food, then."

The apartment is quiet. I didn't look toward Gloria's room, but Willow's door is closed, so she must be asleep. "What time is it?"

"Just after two a.m."

"Huh. I slept a long time." In the kitchen, I head straight for the fridge, but Asher blocks me, points me to a kitchen chair. The harsh overhead light does neither one of us any favors, tinting his skin with a greenish tone. I'm glad I at least brushed my hair. "Did you eat earlier?"

"Yeah, Willow fed us all."

"All?"

"Yeah, me and G and some guy who played some music with Willow."

"And I slept through all of that?" Something snarky tries to push through, and I'm not quite successful in pushing it back. "What guy?"

He takes a pot out of the fridge and ladles soup out of it. "I don't know. Josiah? Sounded good, though. I mean, really good."

I roll my eyes. "She's only been here five minutes, and already she has a new boyfriend."

He crosses his arms over his chest. "Why are you always so mean about her?"

"I'm not."

"Yeah, well, who made you this soup? Who went shopping so that you'd have your very special things?" He pops a cup of rice pudding on the table. "Who made sure that your bed was fresh and you had people around to take care of you?"

I look at him, feeling emotions rise all too quickly to the surface. "Sorry. You're right. I don't know why."

"Maybe give it some thought while you're recovering, huh?" He takes the bowl out of the microwave and sets it in front of me, then takes out a sandwich wrapped in the distinctive Bloom's paper and plops it on a plate. I'm watching his hands, big and competent, and bend in to eat the soup.

Which is so amazing I make a little sound. "How does she *do* this?"

He meets my eyes, and I realize he's not wearing his glasses, which means I can see those luxurious lashes and the slight tilt at the corners of his eyes and the fact that he has laugh lines. "Maybe tell her that tomorrow, huh?"

"I will. I promise." I look away, worried that he's going to see all the things I'm thinking on my face. We eat in silence. A siren goes by beneath the window, and then another. An accident on the West Side Highway, I think.

"A robbery on Ninth," Asher says.

"An old man with a heart attack."

"A fight at an after-hours joint."

I smile. He meets my eyes and takes a bite of his sandwich. After a minute he says, "A woman with meningitis alone in her apartment."

"I'm so lucky you came."

He closes his eyes, and because he's not wearing his glasses, I see the single tear at the corner of his left eye.

I stand up and come around the table and pull him close. His forehead lands between my breasts, and his hands fall on my hips. I bend my face into his thick, beautiful hair, and it smells of him and sunshine and a memory of a picnic long ago in the Sheep Meadow at Central Park, with a basket packed by his mother, so lovingly, enough for me and Willow and Asher. Willow idly played her violin, and Asher and I lay side by side, and it seemed that maybe life would be just fine.

Now in the kitchen in the middle of the night, he says nothing, but his hands are tight on my sides, and I can feel the tension in his neck, his shoulders, as if he has to maintain iron control or he'll shatter. I hold him and let him rest there, knowing he cannot bear to show me tears, even though I can feel them against my skin, soaking through my nightshirt. "I'm sorry, Asher," I say, and I don't mean for getting sick and calling him in the middle of the night.

I mean, *Sorry for all the things I should have already said I was sorry for a million times. Sorry for the way I treated you, sorry for taking you for granted, sorry for pushing you away, sorry for the terrible, terrible, terrible things I said . . .*

Gently, he pulls me into his lap, still keeping his head low. I rest my head against his shoulder, and we just sit there together, not talking. Not kissing. It's all unsaid, the press of his forehead on my neck, the feeling of his ear against my fingers, his hand on my waist, mine around his shoulders.

"I was so afraid you'd die."

"But I didn't," I say, and this time, I do kiss his forehead.

For a long minute, he allows it, and then he says, "You need to eat. Or you will never get well."

Chapter Forty-Four
Gloria

From my bedroom, where I am attempting to compress my life into a suitcase I can roll away with me, I can hear the low murmurs of Willow and her friend working on their music. It brings bittersweet memories of Billie doing the same thing with one or another of her musician friends, sometimes a member of one of her bands. None of the bands stuck. They always started because they admired her work, her voice, her talent. They all devolved to wanting to prop her up on the stage like a Barbie doll, exploiting her looks instead of giving her space to grow fully into her own gifts.

Willow is tougher than Billie by far. Some of it is the luck of being further along the path of feminism, but a lot of it is the simple clarity Willow brings to her life. She thinks she's confused, but she has always focused clearly and without angst on giving voice to the music within her. From the time she was small, she knew she was born to make music, and she has simply . . . done it.

I love that she's back in New York, which is really her place. LA pretends to be a land of eccentrics, but it's not. It's a land of youth and vitality and sunshine, while New York is a land of brains and accomplishments. Too much about money these days, but that seems to be a disease that has infected the entire world.

I sort through panties and bras, T-shirts and slacks and socks. From my bureau, I take a photo of Billie and me when I was about ten, in Montreal with my mother, who took the train there just to hear her native language. In it, I'm too tall and too thin, with my hair pulled back into a braid. Billie is more serious, looking directly into the camera as if measuring the intention of the photographer. My mother sits beside us, extraordinarily beautiful even in her vast unhappiness. In this one photo, she's smiling, her lips red and full, and she has a beret on her head. Billie and Willow both take after her in their small build, their birdlike bones. Samantha and I favor my father, and I at least inherited his red hair.

I take the photo out of the frame, take a picture with my phone, and tuck the original into my suitcase. There are four other photos, and I do the same with each: Miriam and I in Egypt on a camel, the Pyramids behind us; a black and white of the view from Isaak's flat in Casablanca, with rooftops and palm trees; and one of Sam, Willow, and me at Coney Island not long after Billie died. They were both so desperately sad. All of us were. But that day, eating cotton candy and riding the Ferris wheel and trying to win at carnival games, we were happy.

Eventually, we all recovered. More or less.

Winded, I sink onto the bed. I do not want to go. *I do not want to go.* The loss feels like it's shredding something within me.

But life doesn't care if you like something. It gives you choices. It's up to you to decide which things are right for you. I cannot bear the thought of jail, and I do not want my youthful errors to cause any trouble for the girls.

When I finish the packing, I tuck my suitcase into my closet and head for my greenhouse, where I write instructions for Willow and a letter for Sam and practical details about finances. Miriam will handle getting the nude sold, and that should both finance my long-term travels and give Sam and Willow each a bit of a cushion, as well as making up for the harm I did my friends so many years ago.

At 3:00 a.m., after a few hours of sleep, I make my way silently out of the apartment, ride the elevator down for the last time, and slide by the new overnight man, who only lifts a hand as I walk by. We don't know each other. I don't come in and out at this time of day. "Do you need a cab?" he asks, not getting up.

"No, thank you." I've already called one, and I see the yellow body waiting outside. "Penn Station," I tell the driver. My train doesn't leave for hours, but I couldn't have left when everyone was awake, and besides, I wouldn't put it past Balakrishna to have me watched. Less likely anyone would be paying attention in the middle of the night.

I hope I'm correct.

Chapter Forty-Five

Willow

In the morning, I carry my violin and a big mug of tea out to the greenhouse, where I won't disturb Sam, though I've left the door propped open a little to both circulate some air for the plants and give myself access to the sweet freshness of morning. It's going to be one of those lusciously soft almost-spring days. I can hear birds celebrating in the trees of the rooftop.

I'm feeling giddy and hopeful, all caused by Josiah and the music, and it spills over into the trouble facing Gloria. I can't believe anything bad is going to happen to her. The paintings are off site. She's seventy-four. They'll give her bail, and one way or another, we'll raise it.

If it comes to that.

In the meantime, I have one more day to finish this piece by the deadline. To warm up, I run through a series of practice pieces, work a little on Beethoven's Violin Sonata no. 9, which I've been learning over the past couple of months for the exercise. My muscles are a bit fatigued from all the work last night, and I smile. It's been a while since I felt so optimistic about my work. In some part, it's due to Josiah opening something in me, and his lyrics are so incredibly beautiful that I can't wait to see what else we'll come up with.

We didn't kiss last night, although the possibility hung between us for two hours. Neither of us made that move, and that also felt right. There's time, if it comes to that.

But mainly, this morning I feel good because of *me*. Because of something new growing in me, like a fern unfurling, like an orchid sprouting stalks of buds that will bloom slowly, one at a time, over a long stretch. I feel it in a looseness in my body, in a sense of space in my mind. I'm so glad to be home, but even that isn't it.

It's just me. It's like my skin finally fits again after the awful episode with David that undermined my confidence.

It isn't until I am about to go back into the kitchen and make some breakfast that I see the envelope tucked between the pots of new begonias. It's a simple white envelope with my name on it, and the instant I see it, I know she's gone. "Oh, Gloria," I say aloud, pressing the envelope against my chest.

Setting my violin aside, I sink down on one of the iron chairs she keeps out here, heart pounding, and open it.

Dearest, dearest Willow.

I know you won't be happy, but I've decided to take matters into my own hands. I don't know what the authorities can/will do to me, but I abhor the idea of jail and rather than take a chance, I'm heading out of Dodge. When I feel it is safe enough, I'll find a way to let you know I'm all right, but in the meantime, don't worry. I'm an experienced traveler and I know the tricks.

Talk to Miriam at some point soon; she will have information for you. She can also help with some of that other unfinished business. I've left instructions for the greenhouse and the schedule of the garden (spring is almost upon us, and there is a lot to do!). If you need help, hire it. I've left a couple of names in the greenhouse notes.

One more thing. I've left my phone in my bedroom, for obvious reasons. I would love it if you could continue to post to my Instagram for me, at least for a little while, to keep up the appearance of my presence in New York. I've left all the pertinent details with the phone. I think you might have fun with it.

You are coming into yourself so beautifully, Willow. Trust that. Trust yourself. I can't wait to see what comes out of this period in your life. From where I stand, it looks fertile and magical and full of possibility. Enjoy it.

Take care of your sister, and the apartment. One day, we'll all be together again. I love you more than I can possibly say.

Aunt G

My hands shake, and I wonder where she is right now. How lonely she must be! It breaks my heart.

I carry my violin inside and lay it down on the dining room table on my way through to Gloria's room. Sure enough, the bed has not been slept in, and the phone is right there on the nightstand. A neatly printed list of instructions sits below it, and I type in the passcode, then the Instagram log-in. She hasn't posted since last night, but her photo stream is full of possibilities.

I sink down on her bed, scrolling through them, clicking to go full screen when I get to a series of the TWA crew, what's left of them. I remember when there were seven or eight who would show up at Gloria's dinner parties, all very glamorous and charming, making the other guests laugh. These few are the only ones left. The photos are wonderful, almost staged in the midcentury room, with all of them posing for the camera as if for a magazine spread, ankles crossed, backs straight. I post one of them, trying my best to imitate Gloria's voice, and add a bunch of hashtags. Wherever she is, she'll see it and know that I got the letter and her phone.

And now I realize that I've never told Sam about what's going on, and now Gloria has left without even consulting her. Damn. She's not going to take this well.

Gloria, Gloria, Gloria, I think, looking around her room. A dirgeful sound echoes through my mind: *Empty, empty, empty.* Will I ever see her again?

I realize that I haven't eaten since last night. Sam will need to eat, too, and Asher, if he's still here. Humming under my breath, a tic that I've had since childhood to calm myself when I'm sad or anxious, I close the door to G's room and head for the kitchen to make some gluten-free blueberry pancakes. Sam has always loved pancakes, and I found a very good recipe for gluten-free. I can do nothing to help Gloria right this minute, but I can cook for my sister.

I imagine her happiness, and it lifts my spirits.

Chapter Forty-Six

Sam

Asher is gone by the time I get up. I would have left, too, if I had to smell me any longer. I desperately need a shower, so I gather up some fresh clothes—just yoga pants and a T-shirt and a pair of thick wool socks—and make my way down the hall. I feel like an old person, walking so slowly, my hand on the wall, and it makes me irritable.

So when Willow appears, taking my arm, she bears the brunt of it. "I've got it!" I say, yanking my arm away.

Which totally overbalances me, and I nearly fall. She crosses her arms and inclines her head. "How's that working for you?"

I lean on the wall, sweaty and out of breath. "For fuck's sake. This is ridiculous."

Willow offers her hand. "Shower?"

Meekly, I take it. "Yes, please."

"I want you to sit down, though, okay? I'll wash your hair if you want."

It's humiliating to think of my little sister seeing me naked. I know I'm bony at the moment, and I really don't want her to feel sorry for me. "I can wash my hair."

"Okay."

I think of what Asher said last night, that I need to be nicer to her. "Hey, the music sounded really good last night."

"Yeah?" She's surprised, I can tell. "Thank you. I'm kind of excited about this piece."

"Who's the guy?"

"Josiah. I met him at a gig in Brooklyn a few nights ago." She lets go to allow me through the door first. "The night you got sick, actually. He was with me when I checked on you."

A slither of nastiness passes through me—mere days in the city, and already she has a new guy hanging around—but I let it just keep going. "He's a good musician too."

"Yes. He grew up in Ren Faires, on the circuit. Isn't that funny?" She pulls back the curtain and turns on the shower.

I cross my arms. "I can do this part, okay?"

She narrows her eyes. "Mmm. I don't think so."

I bow my head, embarrassed.

"I've seen your skinny ass before," she says, reaching in to test the water. "Feel that. Too hot?"

I stick my hand in. "Perfect." Still, I stand by the shower curtain in my disgusting T-shirt and sloppy sweats. I smell like a goat, but—

"How about this," Willow says. "I'll close my eyes, but you can hold on to me while you sit down. I mean, it would be kind of ridiculous for you to fall and crack your head open, and then I have to call an ambulance, and then everybody will see you naked. Not just, you know, your sister, who took baths with you in this very spot a hundred million times."

I smile reluctantly. "Okay."

She closes her eyes and stands by the front of the tub like a guard. I shuck the T-shirt and sweats. Out of the corner of my eye, I see my practically breastless torso and the outline of my ribs, and I flush, thinking of my father saying once that a woman didn't look like a woman if she was flat. I reach for Willow's hand, and she's steady as a tree, but it's hard to step over the edge of the claw-foot, and I nearly slip. "Help more, please," I whisper.

She's right there, helping me step over the edge and then sit down. "My eyes are still closed, but sis, I am seriously jealous of your calves."

Safely on the floor of the tub, I turn my face to the water, letting the spray wash away the sense of helplessness, the sweat of sickness, the alcohol wipes, and the tangled dreams. I think of being in my apartment, sick and knowing I needed help and so afraid and lost and lonely. A hole opens in my chest, and I squeeze my eyes tight.

I'm so tired of being alone.

Willow is tidying the vanity, humming loudly enough I can hear her. I can smell the bleach wipes she's using, and I get a flash of her in an apron in an old farmhouse, making things nice.

She loves making a home, making people comfortable and keeping them fed. I don't think my grandmother did. I think it was forced on her and she was miserable, just as Willow would be if she didn't have the outlet of her music.

I look for the shampoo, but I don't see it. "Is there shampoo out there?"

"Yes. Do you want lavender or dandruff?"

I laugh. "Lavender, please."

"Do you want me to do it?"

For once, maybe I can let go of things. "Yes, please."

"I'm still closing my eyes."

I close mine instead. "You don't have to."

The sweet scent of lavender fills the air as she pours it onto my scalp. Her fingers are powerful from all the violin work, and I won't lie: it's heaven when she starts to massage my head, across the top, down the sides, behind my ears, to the nape of my neck, which has been so sore. I groan quietly, try to stretch a bit, and stop when I find the lingering stiffness. Her fingers navigate right to it, and I can't help making another little noise as she works on the knots and cords.

"Keep your eyes closed," she says and pours water over my head, once and then again.

"Thank you," I murmur.

"You're welcome."

———— ◦◦◦◦◦◦ ————

After a breakfast of blueberry pancakes, I wrap myself in a thick sweater and sit outside in one of the alcoves Gloria has created. The air is mild, and sunshine pours into the space, promising fresh starts. In one of the planters, leaves are springing up—flowers Willow would know. She and Gloria share the love of growing things—handed down from the farmer side of the family, no doubt.

I wonder where Gloria is. She's been out all morning. Maybe that's normal for her. How would I know? I never visit. Just this minute, I can't remember why. G would be glad to have me anytime. She and I were best of buddies first, long before she took an interest in Willow, visiting her friends in their modern apartments and country houses. Dani's house had a swimming pool, and she let me swim while they drank cocktails on the patio. Willow was too small to come with us, to swim without supervision, not that my mother would have cared, but G was mindful of things like that.

Again it flutters across my mind: Who was taking care of Willow? Was there an au pair or a babysitter? When we were small, my mother was certainly making plenty of money to cover such a cost.

I'll have to ask Willow.

A breeze moves over my face, and I'm thinking maybe I'll be well enough to go home by tomorrow or the next day. Get back to normal life.

Willow appears. "You have visitors."

I get to my feet. "Who?"

She raises an eyebrow. Just one. "Your dad," she says, "and his wife."

"What?" I halt, look toward the door.

"Yeah, I thought it was a little weird myself. Do you want me to tell him you're not feeling well enough for visitors?"

For a single moment, I wonder what that would feel like. But I shake my head. "I exposed him to meningitis. I should find out if he got tested."

"But why is Brittney with him?"

"Who knows?" Willow sticks with me as we enter through the dining room, and it makes me think of her warrior attitude toward Eric at the hospital. She's got my back, always. How have I never appreciated that?

We make our way to the parlor, where the painting of my mother looms over everything.

"How are you, sweetheart?" my dad asks, getting up. I wave him away and take a seat below my mother. Willow stands beside me, no less a warrior for having no weapon but her cold gaze and perfect beauty.

A flash of my developing game floats through my mind, attached to a violin.

"What's up?" I ask.

"We just wanted to come see how you're doing," my dad says. "Brittney was worried that you might have gone home alone, but they told us at the hospital that you'd come here with Willow and Gloria."

"They told you that?" Willow asks.

"I am her father," he says.

Brittney looks nothing like a real estate agent, all coiffed and pressed. She has long dark hair she wears shiny straight. Her face is pretty but not overly made up. It's a natural kind of West Coast beauty, all health and intelligence. I'd probably like her if she weren't my dad's wife and the mother of the two kids he stuck with. "We wanted to let you know that your dad was tested," she says, "and he shows no sign of the virus. We'll keep an eye on the boys, just in case, but the doctor didn't seem to think there was any realistic risk."

"That's good news." I don't see them often, only at birthdays and the like, but they're sweet, lovely children. "How's Nathan doing? School-wise?"

"Good," she says, and I can tell by the way she folds and refolds her hands that this is not entirely true. "We're going to take your advice and try to just treat him like an ordinary kid."

"He can always come hang out with me," I hear myself say. "I can give him some weird stuff to do, with computers and programming. Keep him busy for a little while, anyway."

"Really?" Brittney glances at my dad, back to me. "That would be really nice of you."

For the first time ever, I want to be alone with her, hear more about what's happening with Nathan, who is a kid I really like. I like both of them. They're blameless in everything.

Like Willow, a voice says quietly in my heart.

Brittney adds, "He's struggling a little, if I'm honest. He doesn't always read social cues that easily. And he's"—her mouth gives a kindly smile—"a bit of an odd duck."

"I don't know anything about that," I say dryly.

She smiles.

Remembering how miserable school was at times, how hard it was to fit in, my dad always this urgent presence, I say, "Let me know."

Willow continues to stand there, and although it occurs to me late, I finally think to ask, "Do you guys want something to drink? Cup of tea, maybe?"

"Oh, no thank you." My dad leans forward. "We were hoping maybe you'd show Brittney how amazing this place is."

My body goes completely cold. Next to me, Willow says, "We aren't selling this apartment."

"Of course not!" Brittney smooths her palm down her jeans. "I'm sorry, that was terribly rude." Her cheeks are so pink I feel bad for her.

"It's just that places like this are so rare now, and I've always wanted to see the garden. It's fairly famous."

"Is it?" I ask.

"G-L-O-R-I-A," she sings. "Her dinners in the nineties are the stuff of legend."

Willow frowns. "Really?"

"Oh my God! Do you guys really not know this?" She pulls out her phone, swipes up to get to the internet, and types something in. She's smiling with such delight that I feel halfway forgiving, not that I'm going to forgive my fucking dad. "Look."

She shows a page of search results, essays and photos and—I take the phone. "Wow. I remember this guy." I show it to Willow.

"That's Gerald," she says. I'm surprised to see her wipe a tear off her cheek. "He had the best laugh."

Brittney nods. "Gerald Vanderhoof. He was a great writer, a social commentator, and he loved Gloria. Unfortunately, he died of AIDS."

I feel a little slip of time, a swell of pain or memory that slaps me from nowhere. Gerald, always inserting himself between me and the old man who talked with his mouth full; Gerald, who brought me headphones so I could drown out the horrific sounds of people eating so that I didn't have to leave the table. Another person who had my back, always.

Maybe I've not been as alone as I always thought. "He was a nice man." I hand the phone back to Brittney. "I had no idea. I'll have to look up some of those essays."

Willow's phone buzzes in her pocket, and she tugs it out. Inclines her head. "Sorry, I have to take this."

"I'm fine."

She hurries outside.

For a moment, my dad and Brittney and I sit there. I know what will get rid of them, which is all I want to do now. "I'll give you a tour if you want."

"Great." My dad claps his hands.

"Are you sure you're strong enough?" Brittney asks.

"I'm okay. It's not like a castle or anything." I stand. "We call this the parlor, and it's a better room than the living room because it has some light and, obviously, the french doors to the garden." I'm not sure which way to go, but since Willow went outside, I turn right out of the parlor. The next door is the living room, and I notice that it seems like some of the paintings have been moved around or something. "This is the living room, and it's never been used much."

Brittney pauses at the doorway. "Do you mind?"

"Go ahead."

She steps in, almost reverently, and looks around, at the paintings and walls, then up to the ceilings. "This seems to all be original."

"Pretty sure it is."

"Remarkable." She looks at the floor, shakes her head. "Parquet."

"Is that unusual?" my dad asks.

"In this condition, it is. I mean, it needs work, but it's pretty well cared for."

I feel my dad adding up the figures in his head, and annoyance snaps at the back of my neck. "The music room is down here," I say, herding them down the hall. Willow's violin is on a stand, and papers are scattered all over the grand piano. It's very much a working space. "You're not the musician, are you?" Brittney asks.

"No, Willow. She had an album out recently."

"No kidding. Would I know it?"

I meet her eyes. "Maybe. She's a folk musician."

"Such a waste," my dad mutters.

"What do you mean?" I ask, more snapping along my nerves.

"She was a prodigy. She could have done anything, but your mom just kept protecting her from the public."

"You say that like it's a bad thing." I cross my arms. "She wasn't a commodity, something to make money on."

"That's not what I meant."

I feel a wave of heat, maybe anger or something like it, coming over me. "Look, I just don't think I can do this. I don't *want* to do this."

Willow shows up at the door just as my father says, "I'm sorry, Sam. I didn't mean it. Just let Britt see the rest, will you? It's a big deal to her."

"That's all right," she says. "We can come back some other time."

"I think that would be best," Willow says. Her face is performer blank, and I think she must be furious. She takes my arm. "Come with me. I'll be right back, you two."

As we walk down the corridor to my room, she says, "No offense, but that was a very tacky land grab."

I don't say anything. She's right.

"Asher's back. I'll send him down."

"Okay." I sink on the bed. "Where is Gloria?"

"Uh, we need to talk about that, but give me a couple of minutes."

"Talk about what?" I ask sharply. "You never did tell me what's going on."

"I know, there hasn't been time, but I will. Let me just go get rid of them, okay?"

I feel a ripple of warning. "Is Gloria sick or something?"

"No. That's not it. I'll be right back."

I nod, thinking of my dad, bringing his wife, the real estate agent. Talking about my sister like she was a check to be cashed.

But where is Gloria?

Chapter Forty-Seven
Willow

My blood is humming as I pop into the kitchen to tell Asher that Sam's in her room. He's helping himself to the deli turkey and pickles in the fridge, and I can tell he, too, has showered.

"Did you take care of our little issue?" I ask quietly, meaning the paintings I handed over.

He gives me a sideways grin. "I did, Inspector Gadget. It's all good."

I let go of a sigh. He's wearing a lavender shirt, loose cut, that shows off his skin tone and dark hair. "I like that shirt," I say.

"Thanks. My sister."

I smile. "Is she the one responsible for the difference in your clothes?"

He gives me his side grin. "Is it that obvious?"

I shrug lightly, turning on the teapot, feeling bubbles in my head, my throat, and I'm ready to burst. "Guess who just called me?"

He spreads mustard over a sturdy slice of bread. "Who?"

"*Rolling Stone*!" I squeeze his arm and make a squealing noise. "They want to interview me! And not part of some retrospective or anything about my mom—I asked—but because somebody there is a big folk fan and they love my album."

He hugs me. "That's terrific, Willow. I'm so proud of you!"

I suddenly remember Sam's dad. "Uh, Sam is in her room, if you want to go down there."

"How is she?"

"Much better, but she might have overdone it with her dad." I scurry down the hall, but Robert and Brittney aren't in the music room, where I left them. Their voices come from another room, and I follow them through the parlor out to the garden. They're standing there, admiring the view, when I come out.

"Sorry, Willow," Robert says. "I just wanted to show Britt the garden. She's heard so much about it."

"I follow Gloria on Instagram," Britt says. "It's such a great narrative—she has such a full and beautiful life."

"Instagram is supposed to look like that," Robert says.

Pain runs around my ribs; I've got to let Sam in on what's going on before she finds out some other way. The anxiety makes me antsy. "It is," I say, crossing my arms. "But her life really is like that. Brittney, do you want to see the greenhouse?"

"I think we've overstayed our welcome," she says. "Another time, maybe."

I give Robert a look and lead them through the kitchen, through the servant hallway to the foyer, and just as I'm about to go back to the kitchen, the buzzer rings. I answer it. "What's up?"

"An FBI agent by the name of Balakrishna is here. Shall I send him up?"

Shit. For a moment, I'm totally frozen, wondering what I should do. What's right? What's going to protect Gloria? How far has she gone?

"Sure. Why not."

Before I can turn around, there's another buzz. "Miss Willow, a doctor is here to see Miss Samantha."

Next there will be dancing lions and acrobats. "Okay. Him too."

My stomach flips a little as I think of Gloria and what I should say to the agent. What does he want this time? I pull my hair away from my face and secure it in an elastic, glancing in the mirror by the door. Even without makeup I can see that I look better, that the hard months of the fall and winter are falling away. There's color in my cheeks, hope in my eyes.

Rolling Stone. The thought shoots through my terror.

My mom was on the cover of *Rolling Stone* in 1979. Her song "Write My Name Across the Sky" had just gone platinum, and she'd just returned from a wildly successful tour. It might have been one of the best times in her life. She was living in the apartment, making it into her place, writing a ton of songs. The article talked a lot about her influences and her music and performing but not much about her writing, as if it was the least important thing about her. Sam's dad had written it, the second one he'd written, and he was clearly enchanted by her, by her potential.

The cover shot is dramatic and beautiful, Billie sitting in a blank area, her knees up in front of her and her beautiful long-fingered hands, covered with rings and holding a cigarette, draped over them. Her neck is long, her head cocked at an angle. She had cut her hair by then, and it clung to her head like a cap, leaving the entire focus on her enormous eyes, lined heavily in kohl, penetrating and steady.

Sam's dad married her, and they had Sam, and my mom was in a good place for a while. She went on tour and had that fateful fling with some random musician, and I was the result. Robert spent the rest of her life punishing Billie and Sam.

Mostly Sam.

A knock on the door startles me, and I swing it open to reveal both Eric and Agent Balakrishna, who is freaking me out, and it makes me fluttery. He looks grim, and I wave him inside, looking at him from the corner of my eye.

"Hello," I say, "come in, both of you." Eric carries a bouquet of flowers, lush pink and white peonies he must have paid a fortune for,

Sam's very favorite in the world. Asher will hate that. I give him a glare. "I'll take those and put them in water."

He holds on to them. "That's all right. I'd rather give them to her myself."

I can't exactly rip them out of his hands, though I want to. To Agent Balakrishna, I say, "Will you sit down and give me a moment? My sister has been quite ill, and this is her doctor."

"Of course, of course." He sinks down on the bench as if he's a good student and looks up to the stained glass.

"This way," I say to Eric.

He follows without speaking. I poke my head into her room. Asher is sitting beside her on the bed, both of them leaning against the head-board, their feet in front of them. He's kicked off his shoes, and they lie akimbo on the floor. "Sam's doctor is here," I say and leave them, hurrying back to the foyer before Balakrishna can start snooping.

"Sorry about that," I say. "How can I help you?"

"It's perfectly all right. How is your sister?"

"Improving, thanks." I find myself folding my arms defensively and force myself to stop, tucking my hands in my back pockets.

"I'd like to ask Ms. Rose a few questions, please."

"She isn't here."

"When do you expect her to return?"

I shrug. "She doesn't check in with me. I have no idea."

"Will you call her, please?"

Her phone is in my back pocket, and I have no idea if the ringer is on or off. I can't take the chance. My hands are shaking so much I have to shove them in my pockets. "Is she in trouble? Does she need to call a lawyer?"

"That's up to her, of course. I only want to ask about a few of her movements some years ago."

My throat is so dry I have to cough. "Again, I guess you need to come back another time, because she's not here."

He measures me for a long moment. "Very well." He offers me his card. "Please have her give me a call when she returns. It will only take a moment."

I nod.

As he's about to leave, he turns. "The painting of your mother—would you ever consider selling it?"

"No," I say. "It means a lot to all of us."

"Of course." He lifts a hand in farewell and ambles out.

For a long moment, I stand with my back against the door and try to think. Can I get a message to Gloria somehow? She needs to know that he's onto her.

It occurs to me that Balakrishna admired the painting of my mother before, so it has to have been with Gloria. I hurry into the parlor, and there it is in all its splendor. The light is good, making her eyes shine, a hint of a smile on her mouth, as if she liked who she was looking at. Rock star Mona Lisa, I think, and hold up Gloria's phone. This is the image that should have been on *Rolling Stone*. It reveals a lot more about her.

I snap the photo, then sit in Gloria's chair and edit the shot. I have to think about how to get the message through that Balakrishna is asking about her without giving anything away. During the happy days. To the world, she was a rock star. To me she was my little sister. I sometimes think maybe she should have disappeared. Maybe it would have saved her life. This painting is much admired, but we'd never sell it. #rockstarmonalisa #billiethorne #sisters #art #love #missyou #alliswell #rockon

I post it.

A DM pops up, sending my heart skittering. Can she see me? I click to open it, and there are dozens of messages, but the one that just came in is from Malachi Renoir, and it's such an absurd name I click on it just to see what the troll is saying.

Ma bichette, it says. All is well. You are safe.

Is it her lover from long ago? It makes me ache, both because he sent it and because she will not see it, and I'm mulling over how to handle that when Asher storms up the corridor. I jump up to follow him into the foyer, where he picks up his coat and shoves his arms into it. "I have to go to work," he says.

"What?"

He sets his jaw, shakes his head, and I step out of the way so he can dramatically yank open the door.

"See you later," I say.

"I doubt it." He slams the door.

Chapter Forty-Eight

Sam

Ten minutes earlier

I am dozing when Asher comes in. I only know he's there because he sits beside me on the bed and strokes my hair. It feels like my dream, and I turn. "Hi."

"Hi. You can sleep if you want."

"No, I just didn't want to talk to my asshole dad."

"It was nice of him to make sure you're okay."

"It would have been nice if that's why he was here, but he brought his wife, the real estate agent, to see the apartment."

"Whoa. Ballsy. Is Gloria going to sell?"

I glare at him. "It's not hers, actually. It belongs to me and Willow."

"But she lives here. You can't sell it out from under her."

"I know that. I was just—" I shake my head, trying to wiggle away from the shame of my motives. "I might have mentioned to my dad that my business was in trouble. I was hoping he'd maybe offer me a loan, but instead, he told me I should sell the apartment."

"Sam!"

"I know, okay!" I look at him. "I wouldn't do it. I just—I talked to G and Willow about it, and they lost their minds, and I wouldn't do it anyway."

"You sound a tiny bit unsure of that."

I pluck at the bedspread. "Maybe. I mean, it's a big apartment for one person."

"Two. Willow lives here too."

"Still. Two people in all these rooms? What a waste!"

He's very still. "I don't like this side of you, Sam. Gloria loves this place. She would hate to leave it."

"I know." I bend over and put my head in my hands. "I just don't know how to make Jared go away."

"That you want him to go away is a pretty big sign that you don't want to sell."

I let myself smile. "Maybe. That was also the night the idea for the game showed up."

"Let's make that happen, then." He reaches into his leather satchel and brings up his laptop, then settles back against the headboard. I scoot back with mine, and we sit side by side, opening our machines in tandem. His thigh is hot next to mine, and I have a sudden memory of how it felt against mine when—

Focus.

But it's hard when he smells so good. When all I really want to do is slide down and bring him with me so we can kiss. And more.

"Let's go back to the branches of play in the forest," he says, tapping out some notes with his keys.

I look up at his face, the profile I know so intimately, his heavy eyebrows, the beard, his remarkably lush mouth. My own mouth purses with the wish to kiss him, and he looks down at me. For a long second, that's all we do: imagine kissing each other.

And then, miraculously, he does. He lifts a hand and slides it along my neck, then my jaw, and bends close and kisses me very, very gently. I close my eyes, afraid to breathe, and then he does it again, deeper this time, tilting his head, his thumb at the edge of my jaw.

So gentle.

We might have continued to kiss like that for a while—a long while—but there's a sudden, sharp knock at the door, and Eric walks in, as if it's his house and he has a right.

Asher and I break apart, but we're awkwardly leaning into each other, and I can't meet his eyes because I'm still feeling dizzy about the heat of his arm against my shoulder.

"Hello," Eric says. He's carrying a bouquet of peonies, and the sweet scent of them fills the room. "I thought you might like something to cheer you up."

"Beautiful," I say, "thank you." Rote words, but I hope they don't sound that way. I'm about to say he can take them to Willow and she'll put them in water, but he presses them into my arms. Automatically, I bend my head into them, inhaling, and I feel Asher move next to me, standing up.

"Can you give us a minute, Asher? I'll just do a quick exam and be out of your way."

"He doesn't need to go."

"Oh, no, that's fine," Asher says. "I'll just be on my way, get out of your hair."

Two red patches burn on his cheeks, a hectic color that shows only when he is very angry or very aroused. I don't think it's the latter just now. I hold out my hand. "Will you stay?"

But he has already snatched his coat from the foot of the bed. "I'll see myself out."

I think I hear the sound of something tearing inside of me, but it's hard to locate because Eric is leaning in. "How are you feeling?"

"Much better. I'd like to go home."

"Not yet." He listens to my heart through the V of my T-shirt. He's close, and I see the little crisscross of scars under one brow and notice that his lower lip is quite chapped. It always stayed that way.

He puts the stethoscope away, then asks, "May I check your lymph nodes?"

I nod.

He sits down on the bed and moves the bouquet out of my arms, which makes me feel weirdly revealed, although I felt perfectly comfortable with Willow and with Asher. I can't look at him as he palpates my lymph nodes under my neck, down the side, then—"Lift your arm, please"—under my right arm, then under my left, which makes me squirm a little.

Eric smiles. "You always were the most ticklish person I've ever met."

I look up, frowning. He's looking at me like he sees me, and he's really too close. I can't move back because I'm against the wall, and of course nothing will happen because he's married and this is a professional visit, but the intent is there anyway. I recognize and remember it. I narrow my eyes. "What are you doing?"

"What do you mean?"

I push against his shoulder. He eases back, but the look in his eyes doesn't change. "I'm not an idiot."

"That's the last thing you are." He sighs and looks at his hands. "I made a big mistake, Sam."

"What?" I raise a hand. "Okay, no. We aren't doing this. You need to go."

"Sam—"

"No." I toss the flowers at him and pull my knees up to my chest. "Go."

"But I'm your doctor."

"Send the info to my regular doctor. I'll text you the info."

"You fell in love with Asher, didn't you? I knew you guys were more than friends."

I think of that kiss, that moment of beginning that is now ruined. "We aren't even friends anymore," I tell him again. I rest my forehead on my knees. "Please just go."

Chapter Forty-Nine
Gloria

In my hurry to leave before Willow knew what I was doing, I failed to realize that by leaving my phone, I would be leaving not only my Instagram and a way they could trace me but also all my contacts, access to my email, and—worst of all—music.

So with my little drugstore phone in my bag, I look out the train window and watch the scenery go by. We travel along the Hudson River for a long time. There is still snow in the shadows as we go north, but the trees have a soft glaze of green along their tips. The forests here are thick and mysterious, and I can close my eyes and feel the cold air collecting along the ground, feel my childhood feet kicking up thick piles of leaves, smell the spicy humus composed of earth and worms and layers and layers and layers of leaves.

Such a long time ago. It strikes me that Billie would be seventy now. Hard to imagine.

The farm where we grew up wasn't far from here as the crow flies, straight west, in a hollow of the Catskills. It was never a particularly successful farm, but it produced plenty to feed us.

All I dreamed of was leaving. Billie and I both spun tales of what we would do when we got to New York City, how we would live. She favored the idea of a shared apartment, but I wanted to just get out by any means necessary. We both flew away, rarely to return.

Even now, the idea of returning makes me feel panicky, as if the land itself might rise up and capture my ankles and I could never leave again.

The rolling, beautiful hills rush by, and I wonder again why my mother never left. Was she serving some misguided notion of loyalty? It wasn't like she hid her misery from my father. He suffered her sharp tongue the entirety of their marriage, bearing the brunt of her disappointment on his broad shoulders. I have no idea what his motives were. He never talked to us, never really talked to anyone, so I didn't know him at all.

But now, with time on my hands and the land that he loved (I did know that much) right over the horizon, I wonder about my taciturn father. I can call up his big hands, with blunt nails and marks of all kinds from the hard work he did. His hair was thick and dark, falling over his forehead like Elvis Presley's.

He was among the Americans who first freed Paris, then went on with the troops to the Battle of the Bulge and the liberation of the camps. It couldn't have been easy on him, and then he married a startlingly beautiful Parisian, who must have seemed to him like a fairy queen or an angel. He brought her back to New York, and like in a ballad, the angel turned into a shrew.

Why do people do what they do?

A prick of irritation snaps behind my eyes. Why do people put up with so much, or rather, why do they settle for so little? Did my father love her so much it was all worth it? Or did he just not know how to get out of it? Why didn't my mother take her beauty and her talents to New York or Montreal and try to make the life she wanted?

Trees whoop by, whoop whoop whoop, and then the water appears again.

My mother couldn't leave again, couldn't face another hard road. At least at the farm she had food and clothing and enough luxury that she wouldn't suffer. My father had his land and a wife so beautiful everyone envied him and two little girls I'm pretty sure he loved.

And my mother breathed her hunger for more into her daughters, and Billie in turn breathed it into hers.

I close my eyes, wondering what those two beloved nieces of mine are doing. Have they discovered my departure yet? Is Sam still improving? I am not a weeper, but tears sting the corners of my eyes. How did I get here, running away like this?

Why do people do what they do?

I think of Isaak, the last time we were together. A little older now, weary. He was nearly arrested in the early nineties and had to go underground. Before he did, he called me late one summer evening. I had my own apartment in New York by then, nothing quite so grand as Billie's, but nice enough. When I answered the phone, I'd been watching the last of the colors fade from the sky outside my window, the pinks and peaches turning paler and paler until all was a soft gray.

"Hello, Gloria," he said. "How are you?"

I smiled. "Isaak! How wonderful to hear your voice."

"Yours is one of my favorite voices in all the world. I miss it very much."

We had not coordinated one of our trips in quite some time, almost three years. I'd stopped carrying contraband years before—thus his need to seduce someone else into doing it, a fact I knew and ignored. We'd never been monogamous, after all.

I'd started flying less often to faraway destinations, partly to help out sometimes with Sam and Willow, but I still loved the adventure and freedom of flying. I hadn't yet realized how erratic Billie was, how unreliable her nannies and babysitters, who were often hangers-on who wanted to partake of the drugs she kept in such vast quantities. She'd always liked drugs, all kinds of drugs, from the early teenage years on, when she'd stolen bennies out of my mother's medicine cabinet, but she seemed to stay fairly sane. Her first stint in rehab was long before she had her first smash hit, and I lost track of how many times she went back, got clean, held on for a time, fell back into her habit. In between she married Robert, had Sam, wrote more than a dozen perfect songs, and sang them. Had Willow. Got clean for a solid eight or nine months, went on tour—

Why hadn't I just gone to live with those girls long before Billie checked out? Why did I just keep looking the other way?

Isaak said, "I am going back to Casablanca in two weeks. Will you meet me there?"

It had been such a long stretch between, while he lay low, and I'd missed him far, far more than I wished. If I met him again in our old stomping grounds, I feared it would be more pain than pleasure. "Oh, Isaak, we are beyond all that, don't you think?"

"Are we, *ma bichette*?" He paused, and into the silence fell memories and longings, the yearning I felt, even then, to press my body into his, to feel his lips on my hair. "For old times' sake, hmm?"

I thought of the moments we'd first danced, of the hours we'd spent in his apartment, making love and eating, me posing while he painted. I thought of a thousand kisses, a hundred belly laughs. I swallowed. "All right."

I flew in on a Thursday evening, and we met at a tiny bar near the sea. He still looked marvelous, in a linen shirt, his hair thick and silvery. My reaction to him had not changed in the nearly two decades I'd known him, and when he took my hand and kissed my fingers, I damn near caught fire on the spot.

It was worth it, that trip. We walked on the beach and feasted on tagines and skewers of chicken shawarma and drank buckets of wine, then wandered back and made love. Perhaps it wasn't as vigorous as it had been, but we still meshed. Later, we lay in moonlight, his fingers splayed over my belly. "I'm going away," he said.

"You are always going somewhere," I laughed. "Where this time?"

"This is different," he said gravely. "It's time to truly disappear."

"Ah," I said, understanding that it was law trouble. I pressed my hand over his. "Will you call me sometimes?"

"I was rather hoping you might like to go with me." He rose up on his elbow. "I have loved you for decades. I know you love me too."

"I do," I said, "but my answer has never changed."

"Why must you cling to this idea that the only good life is an independent life?" He flung himself away. "We can be happy in our old age."

"I can't live in exile, Isaak. I loved you and I always will, but—I love my life, my nieces, my sister, my job. All of it."

"How much longer will you be able to hold on to that job with your back issues, kitten? Hmm?"

I took a breath. "Not long. But I still need to be close to my nieces."

"Bring them, then. Your sister is an addict—she cannot care properly for them."

"How do you know that?"

He made a noise. "I read the papers."

In that single instant, I knew I'd been lying to myself. "I have to go, Isaak."

He tried to stop me, cajoling and pleading, but I suddenly knew I'd been letting the girls and my sister down completely. I could find a desk job with the airline, move into the spare bedroom, be a steady presence in all their lives. The urgency of doing this swamped me so acutely that my hands shook.

Before I landed again in New York, Billie was dead of an overdose.

Watching the landscape of the Hudson Valley flash by the windows, I suddenly know what I have to do. What I should have done all along.

The conductor announces the next station, and I put on my coat.

Chapter Fifty

Willow

My mood is all over the place after Balakrishna leaves, swinging wildly between terror and anxiety over what might happen to Gloria, excitement about the *Rolling Stone* interview, wild hope about the new piece, and fear that everything is going to fall apart any second.

The only answer is to play music. I run through all my practice pieces, play a few of the songs on my album, and then, for no reason except that I'm in her music room, I start bowing the melody to my mother's most famous song. So much hope and passion in that song. It's mighty and full of power, and she sang it with her signature voice, husky and beautiful, almost whispering at times, then belting out those famous lines.

Still bowing, I wander down the hall to look at the painting of her. It's enormous and one of the best pieces Karen Shroeder ever did. She was known for her color work, layer upon layer upon layer to render light and glow unlike any other portraitist. The thing I love the most is the slight, knowing smile. It shines in her eyes, and if you look closely at the pupils, you can see Shroeder.

It reminds me that she was happy sometimes.

And just like that, I hear a new song. The melody first, and a sentence—*my feet are on the ground and my head is in the clouds*. Parts, too—for me, for violin, for recorder, for flute, for two voices, winding together. I think of Crosby, Stills, and Nash and their exquisite harmonies and alliteration in "Helplessly Hoping," and I wonder if there's any chance Josiah and I can ever capture something so timeless and perfect.

I pull out my phone and text him. When will you be here today? I'm anxious for us to finish the first piece.

For a long minute, nothing. Then three dots tell me he's typing.

As I wait, I head into the kitchen, filled with a swelling, excited energy, and start pulling out vegetables, herbs, and the chicken stock, but that's not going to do it tonight. I call Bloom's and order apples, gluten-free flour, butter, sugar, cinnamon, and a dozen other items.

My phone buzzes. A couple of hours okay?

Great

He sends back a laid-back emoji version of himself in a suit and glasses, smiling with thumbs up. It's silly and cartoony, and I love that he doesn't take himself too seriously to do something like that.

To direct my energy, I start the soup, then am diving into a gluten-free pie crust when the other groceries are delivered. Sam *loves* apple pie, and I make a version with caramelized apples and lots of ginger that she'd walk a hundred miles for. The careful mixing, the rolling, and the smell of apples ease the agitation in my neck, and after I get it in the oven, I wander outside and admire the low clouds pillowing the tallest buildings in Manhattan. Their weight lends luminance to the world below, as if capturing the light and possibility and reflecting it back down.

I wonder where Gloria is. How long it will be before I see her again. How can I communicate with her?

How will I know if she's safe?

Chapter Fifty-One

Sam

As soon as Eric leaves, I call Asher, but he doesn't pick up, and I curl up in bed, feeling weepy and lost. It occurs to me that I've done more of that in the past few hours than I've done in a week. I fall asleep.

For a long time. I can tell it's been hours by my dry mouth, by the shift in the light in my room. The air smells of apple pie, and I know Willow has made it for me. For one moment, I think about how kind she's been since the start of all this.

For God's sake. All these stupid emotions.

I have to stop sleeping. It's been a strange relief to take a break from all the hard things in my life, but enough already.

I stand up and stretch hard, and my energy is decent. I patter out to wash my face and brush my hair, then go in search of that pie.

I look at my phone, and nothing has come in. I'm not sure what that was with Asher, the bad mood, but I'm clinging to the kiss. If he kissed me, there's hope we can fix this, that we can make that vision I had come true. Maybe we can bring those beautiful boys into the world.

How did it take me so long to realize that's what I wanted? Why haven't I fought harder for him before this? I know he loves me. I know we can work this out—but the effort is going to have to come from me.

Willow is in the music room, scribbling. "Is that pie going to be ready soon?" I croak.

"Yes!" She leaps up, and her hair is springing out from her head in that kinetic way, escaping from the ponytail to do whatever it likes, making her look like a girl Einstein. "It's been cooling for more than an hour. Come on."

Impulsively, I hug her. She's small and finely made, like a bird, and I wrap my arms around her tightly. "Thank you for taking such good care of me," I say. "I don't know what I would have done without you."

Her arms are tight too. "I love you, sis. I was so afraid you'd die."

"That's what Asher said." I let her go, and we head for the kitchen. "Did he say anything when he left?"

"Not really," she says, but there's a slight twitch to her mouth. "Just that he had to go to work."

I nod, look at my still-blank screen. "I tried calling him, but he didn't pick up."

"He probably has a lot to catch up on."

The pie is sitting on the counter, the crust lightly, perfectly browned, little bits of caramelized juice oozing out of the little design. It smells like everything good ever made, and my stomach growls, loudly. "That is a work of art."

Willow chuckles. "I ordered ice cream too."

I hear Asher in my head saying, *Who made sure that your bed was fresh and you had people around to take care of you?* "That's really nice, Willow. Thank you."

"Of course." She reaches into a drawer for a knife. "I had to go through the entire fridge and throw everything out. Gloria doesn't keep anything in this house, I swear. It's ridiculous."

"My apartment is like that too." I shrug, reaching for plates in the cupboard.

"You don't really need anything, do you?"

"I do. I need coffee and sugar and milk and maybe some cookies."

She cuts the pie and carefully lifts a slice out. The apples are stacked like in a photograph. "I keep a pretty full pantry." She twists her mouth. "Not that I've had a kitchen much in recent years."

I carry my plate to the table and sit down with a glass of water. "Yeah, what happened with David? I thought you'd found somebody good there. Money, prospects."

"Yeah." She gives a humorless snort and licks pie off her finger. "Too bad he was also a total dick."

There's something about the angle of her neck that makes me think she's underplaying that. I give her a minute to say more, but she doesn't. "I'm sorry," I say.

She shrugs and sits down across from me, digging into the pie. "Oh my God!" she moans. "This is delicious!"

I dig in myself, and it's a mouth explosion—sugar and spice and the crumbly flaky crust and apples that are not too firm, not too squishy. I make a noise of pleasure, covering my mouth and nodding.

She clicks her phone on, a kindness to help hide the mouth noises, and it's playing one of our mother's songs. "I love this," I say. "I remember her practicing it. I must have been really small, because my dad was around, and he applauded."

"That's a great memory."

I nod, and we listen together for a little while. She says, "That phone call this afternoon? It was a reporter from *Rolling Stone*."

"Really?" The first comment that comes to my lips is faintly sarcastic, and I hear it with a sense of startled recognition. Instead I say, "An interview or something?"

"Yes!" She taps her feet on the ground in a staccato rhythm. "And it's not even a retrospective about Mom or anything. It's about my album!"

"That's great, Willow." I look at my phone again, and there's nothing. I open the message app. Still nothing. I realize how rude that is and turn it facedown. "Sorry. When will you do it?"

"Like tomorrow, actually."

"Wow!" It suddenly occurs to me that I haven't seen Gloria all day. "Where's G? Have you heard from her?"

She looks at her own phone. "Shit." She presses her lips together. "We need to talk about this."

I set down my fork. "She's dying."

"No." Willow takes a breath, touches her napkin to her lips. "She's gone."

"What? Gone where?"

"I don't know that part." Then she tells me a story about the FBI and paintings and Gloria's involvement in an ancient crime.

A familiar sense of resentment wells up. "Why didn't you tell me?"

"You haven't been exactly up to it."

"But maybe I could have helped! You didn't even give me the chance."

She blinks. "I'm telling you now."

For long moments, I let the silence stretch between us, fighting the irritability that has been my defense for decades. I take a breath, then let it go. "Okay, give me all the details, and then I'm going to do some research."

I see the relief in her face, the easing of her shoulders as she lets go of her defenses. It sears me, that she has to erect a shield against me.

"Thank God." She hugs me. "I knew we needed your brain."

We spend an hour going over every single thing that's happened. On my laptop, I type the names, the dates, the various visits of the FBI. "And Miriam knows what's happening?" I ask.

"Yes."

"I need her number."

Willow pulls a phone out of her back pocket. "This is G's phone. She left it."

"Good." I move it close to the computer.

"How can we communicate with her?" Willow asks. "I want to let her know that Balakrishna was here this morning."

I frown. "There's Instagram, but we'd have to be really careful. She won't be able to sign in to her account, or they'll be able to locate her. Let me think about it."

The house phone rings. "Damn," Willow says. "That's probably Josiah. He took the day off to work with me on a piece I'm trying to get into a competition tomorrow. Maybe an hour or so?"

A new flare of annoyance runs over my nerves, and I have to fight it back down, fight against flinging out a comment about hooking up with a new guy.

From somewhere, maybe from the part of me that feels loved in this moment, I think, What if it were my work project that needed to be done by tomorrow? "Okay. I'll go back to my room and work on the rest of this."

"Thank you."

In my room, I get dressed in a pair of jeans and a long-sleeved sweater over a T-shirt. It's cold in the apartment, something else I'd forgotten. High ceilings, all those windows, ancient insulation. What I don't have is a pair of socks.

From down the hall, I hear voices, alight with happiness: a very deep voice, another man's, and Willow's laughter. She's so easy with people, I think, digging through my bag. I wish I could be.

My phone flashes on the bed, and I grab it urgently. It's a text from Tina. You haven't checked in! Are you alive? Is everything okay?

I curl up on the chair by the window, looking out toward the street as I text back. FaceTime?

In the music room, they begin to tune their instruments. Someone playfully runs through a series of notes on the piano, and someone sings alone, not Willow, but a very rich voice. It's beautiful.

My phone flashes with Tina's face, and I answer. "Hey," I say.

"Thank God! I've been worried that I hadn't heard from you. How are you?" She frowns. "*Where* are you?"

"My mom's apartment," I say, "and I'm doing pretty well. I'm going to be fine."

"Good. Jeez, Sam, your text scared me half to death. Meningitis?"

"I know. It was pretty bad. But thank God for Asher."

"So you guys are talking again?"

I lift my shoulders, allowing a small smile. "Yeah. It's crazy."

"Silver linings, right?"

"Maybe." I think of him falling apart—in his dignified way—in the kitchen last night. His tears against my neck, his hands on my waist. Our kiss today. "I hope so."

"Wait." She peers at my face. "Oh my God. Did you guys have a fight about being *together*, together? Is that what the fight was about?"

"I still don't want to talk about that." Down the hall, the music weaves together, spinning out something like a reel, but not exactly. I cock my head, listening. "It's enough that maybe we can fix it now."

"Thank goodness. You really look a lot better than the last time I saw you."

"That was the night!"

In the background, a baby starts to wail. Tina looks over her shoulder. "Dang. I've got to get him, sweetheart. I'm so sorry! I'll call you back in five minutes."

"No, that's okay. I'm going to go listen to my sister play. We can talk later."

"Sure? I just have to get him on the boob."

I grin. "I'm sure. I'll text you later."

"'Kay." She blows kisses, and the screen goes dark. I look at it for a minute, then pull up Asher's number. I listen to his voice say, "Hey, this is Asher. Leave a message."

"Hey, Asher. Sam again. Just wondering when you're coming back over. I'm feeling a thousand times better, so maybe we can get a lot done. Oh, and my sister is playing with that guy from the other night, and it's crazy good. You should hear it."

I hang up, trying not to think about him looking at the phone and my name and choosing to let it go to voice mail. Maybe he's just in the middle of a meeting or something. Or writing code—

Anxiety rises in my torso, filling all the cavities. Something is wrong again.

I shove the knowledge away and rub my gut, aware of a knot living there. In my imagination, I see Eric putting the flowers in my arms and me bending down to smell them, automatically, not because of anything particularly compelling but because that's what people do. I have no feelings for Eric whatsoever.

Stop.

I don't have any socks, and Willow's child-size socks will never fit, so I head down the hall to Gloria's room. The door is closed, and I knock, but there's no answer, so I poke my head in.

She's clearly packed up everything. I step into the room. There's nothing in the sock or underwear drawers, and the shoes are depleted. The emptiness hits me like a rock to the middle.

I frown and head back to the music room in my bare feet. The door is open, and a river of music pours out—violin and a piano and two voices braiding together in a way that makes my heart ache. I stand in the doorway, watching, a wild emotion rising in response to the music.

Because I'm analytical, I try to figure out why. It's melancholy, but more than that, I can feel a story of something in it, something I should recognize . . .

At the piano is a long-limbed Black man in a toque, bending into the music, nodding. Willow leans close, fiddling mournfully. The music pauses, and their voices take up the melody, only the piano flowing beneath it. They lean into each other, and their voices lace together, rising on a column of light and sound.

The man is looking at Willow, whose eyes are closed as she sings, her violin in her hand, her bow in the other, and I feel the sexual tension in the room, like a first kiss, like hands on bodies, like all the longing in the world.

How does she do that? I watch and watch, and I just can't see where it comes from. My mother did it, too, every time she was onstage. You just couldn't help but look at her, at her hair and her mouth and her body. Willow wears a T-shirt and jeans, and she's like a dancer in her movements, the sway of her head, the lift of her chin.

She opens her eyes, smiles at the man, and he smiles back slowly, full of heat.

I roll my eyes, irritated again, and this time, I let it rise. Here she is in her full stun mode, the manic pixie dream girl, representing all those dreams a man can't reach without the help of his little magic girl.

Fuck that.

I whirl and head for the kitchen, my feet cold, which is also kind of her fault since she forgot to bring me socks. In the kitchen is the pie she made, but I can't even imagine taking a bite. A thousand emotions are rocketing around inside me, and I can't get a handle on any of them.

Why are you always so mean about her?

Why am I? Something shakes loose inside me, and I see myself standing in the doorway of the music room as my mother invites Willow to sit beside her on the bench of the piano, asking her to do something on the keys. I see the baby in a blanket, so tiny and wrinkled and not at all the full-grown sister I thought I was going to get.

I stare out the window, letting the feelings rise. So much jealousy! I felt lost and left out, and honestly, I was.

But it was never Willow's fault.

My phone vibrates in my pocket. Asher! I yank it out, and it is a message from him.

I'm sorry, Sam. I just don't think I can forget all the things we said to each other. I have to have a life, and to get there, I can't be around you.

Blinking, I read it over and over, my ears roaring.

Another text comes through. I'm sorry.

Every good emotion in me shatters. Of course. There was no way this stretch of peace was going to last.

It never does. No one ever stays. Not with me.

Chapter Fifty-Two
Willow

The jam session with Josiah is off the charts, and it takes my mind off Gloria and the impotence of not knowing what to do. We burn through a bunch of folk songs we both know, just to warm up, and then some jazzy improv; then we get into the new song. I play it through, at least the main themes, and then we improvise, improve, deepen. I didn't anticipate the voice part, but it's as thrilling to sing as it is to play. "I'll never be able to play *and* sing this," I say, scribbling some notes on the composition, "but we can record in a couple of tracks or hire someone to come in and do other parts."

"What if you take the piano and I take the violin?" Josiah says.

"We can try that, for sure."

"Before we wrap it up, come sit down a minute," he says and moves over on the piano bench. He pats the empty place, and suddenly all the things I've been tamping down swirl up, waking up the cells in my body.

"I might be a little sweaty from all this," I say.

He makes a face. "I don't care." His hands are on the keys, and he starts to tickle them slightly. I slide in beside him. Our thighs touch, and I'm aware of the scent of his hair and the laundry soap he uses and, below all that, the alluring notes of skin and man.

He plays something I know, sweet and melancholy, a song I've heard a million times. My mother's most famous song. He begins to sing words I've heard over and over and over until they practically have no meaning.

I stood in your shadow; you glowed so bright
I rode along; you were the captain of the flight
You were the sun and I was the moon
A tiny crescent that vanished at dawn
I was just a sliver of reflected light.

I never knew how big the world could be
So much bigger than my eyes could see
I was just there, baby
I was nowhere, baby
But now it's mine, my sky, my reality

Look up, you'll see me now
I ain't following you no more
Look up, I'm gold and silver
Shining like a star
You can't steal me from myself
You can't put me on the shelf
Don't ask why
Just write my name across the sky.

His deep baritone travels through my entire soul, touches places I didn't remember existed, and I think of my mother, dreaming of such a big life.

"It's a man's world; it's just the way things are.
"Stick with me," you said, "I'll take you far."
But I went my own way, baby
I knew that someday, baby
I would spread my wings and I would soar

I'm way above the clouds, looking down
You're just a tiny spot on the ground
I won't ever, ever need you
If I squint I can barely see you
If you're looking for me, well, honey, I'm long gone

Look up, you'll see me now
I ain't following you no more
Look up, I'm gold and silver
Shining like a star
You can't steal me from myself
You can't put me on the shelf
Don't ask why
Just write my name across the sky.

Emotion clogs my throat, and I can't speak.

He drops his hands to his lap. "I really like you, Willow."

"Me too, Josiah. I mean, I'm so attracted to you. But—"

He inclines his head. "But?"

I let go of a sigh, and all the mean things Sam has said come tumbling back into my mind. "The music. It might mess up the music. And . . ." I take a breath. "I just don't want to be that manic pixie dream girl anymore," I say and look at my mother's face on the wall. "Like Billie."

He nods and picks up my hand, holds it between his own. "What I see is the queen of fairies, but you have to feel it yourself. Take your time."

A light bursts within me, scattering through my body, lit by his comment and a vision of myself as a queen, powerful and whole. "I do sometimes feel quite royal," I joke.

"Your majesty." He chuckles and lifts my hand to his lips, pressing a kiss to my palm. His mouth is as soft as I expected. He smells faintly of rain, and the air shimmers between us, full of promise. Potential. So many things.

From the doorway, Sam says, "Oh, for fuck's sake."

I surface so fast that it gives me a headache, holding on to Josiah's hand for safety as I turn my head to look at her. It only takes a glance to see that she's in a brittle mood. I don't even know what I see, just that some part of me contracts. "What's wrong?"

"Never takes long to find a new guy, does it." She shakes her head, laughs with a mean bark. "Really, Willow, the queen of fairies? What a joke. You, in charge of anything?"

I wince, as physically taken aback as if she's slapped me. For a moment, I can't even think of a way to respond.

Josiah moves close, as if to defend me. His arm touches mine, and I'm grateful.

"What's going on, Sam?" I ask.

"Oh my God. Isn't it obvious?" She's vibrating with tension but glares at Josiah.

I look at him. "I'm okay. You'd better go."

"Are you sure?"

I nod.

"You know where to find me." He touches my arm.

I cross my arms as he leaves. "What is wrong with you?"

"I'm sick of you always being the one who gets everything."

"What are you even talking about?"

"Why do you always fuck every guy that comes through? Why do you have to do that?"

I blink. "I don't know what your problem is, but I'm not doing this." I shake my head and head out of the room, trying to get around her. "You're not going to just attack me for no reason."

"Don't just walk out on me!"

I swing around, a flickering blue flame kindling in my fingertips. "What do you want, Sam? Just tell me. I've bent over backward trying to make you comfortable and happy while you're sick, but it's never enough. Nothing is ever enough for you."

"Maybe if I ever *had* enough, it would be. Some of us don't get everything we want with the snap of our fingers."

"Oh, like me?" I shake my head. "Everything I own fits into an overnight bag. I arrived here with nothing."

"Poor, poor Willow." Her words are sharp and bitter. "What did you *think* would happen if you spent your life at Ren Faires instead of a job?"

"It was a job! I got paid and everything. Just because it's not your idea of what work looks like doesn't mean it isn't actually work. My band was one of the most popular on the circuit, but did you even know that? Take any time to notice?"

"It was a Ren Faire band, Willow! That doesn't mean anything in the real world."

"Oh, because *your* world is so grounded in reality. You write video games. How is that real life?" I frown. "And by the way, I do know your company is in trouble, because unlike you, I do pay attention."

"That's none of your business! How dare you?"

"I just set up a Google Alert with your name and business." I shake my head. The flames are licking up my arms, lapping the edges of my ears. "I wasn't prying; I was trying to participate in your life!"

"Maybe I don't want you in my life! You're the reason my life got fucked up in the first place."

"Oh. My. God! You're not seriously using something that happened when I was a baby to justify the reasons your life sucks?" I step forward.

"How about you're an aloof weirdo who makes it impossible for anyone to get close to you!"

"At least I'm not a thirty-five-year-old teenager fucking everything that moves."

"I'm not fucking anyone, for your information, but even if I was making myself a man sandwich with twenty guys, don't you think slut shaming is a bit beneath you? Oh, wait." I pause, exaggerating a thinking gesture. "There's nothing beneath you, is there?"

"Back off!" she cries. Her chest is splotched with red. "You don't know anything. Everybody has loved you your whole life. 'Willow's so good at violin. Willow's so pretty. Willow's so nice. Willow, Willow, Willow!'"

"No chance anyone would ever call *you* nice, that's for sure."

"Yeah, well, maybe there's a reason I'm mean. I had to develop a hide like an armadillo just to get by. *You* didn't get left every time you turned around."

"That's true," I say, very still. "And now you're alone, just the way you like it. No one to complicate your perfect plan."

"That's not true!"

"Really? It was only an accident that Asher got your text. Your best friend moved to Atlanta, and the only people who came to see you at the hospital were Gloria and me. Your dad only came by because he wants the apartment."

"At least I have a dad."

"Oooh," I say mockingly, "that hurts. I'd rather have no dad than have an asshole for one. He uses you, manipulates you."

"Just like all your little boyfriends use you! Do you think that guy wants to make music with you, Willow? Did you learn anything from Mom's life? He'll just prop you up to be the figurehead and fuck you until he's tired of it and then wander off to the next girl. Although I think you're getting a bit long in the tooth for the 'girl' bit."

For a moment, I stand blistered and on fire, my heart pounding so hard I can hardly hear anything but Sam's evil words. I take another step forward. "First of all, it's not sex you're seeing between us; it's music. Second, I'm not my mother, and it's not the seventies."

"Yeah, right. Music. That's what it looked like, all right."

"You have felt sorry for yourself your whole life. Poor Sam, too tall and all those allergies and, oh, don't forget, too smart to deal with the real world, poor dear."

"I didn't choose any of that."

"No, but you didn't have to make it the center of everything either. You did have your dad. Who did I have? When you were with your dad, there was someone to feed you. Give you a bath. Talk to you." I shake my head. "Why do you think I need a full pantry? Why do you think I learned to cook?"

She blanches, and I see the sword has sliced neatly through her argument. "You had Mom. And Gloria. And all those babysitters."

"Yeah, Sam. How do you think that worked out?" She starts to say something, but I hold up a hand. "No. For once, you listen to me. There was nobody here for me, not even my sister. You took every chance you could to humiliate me, embarrass me, needle me, get me in trouble."

"I did not."

"Oh yeah, what about when I burned off my eyebrows? How about when I got locked out on the roof for a whole night and you wouldn't let me in?"

She looks away. "I was a kid."

"Yeah. You were. But you aren't now, and you're still mean and petty and horrible to me." I pick up my violin bow. "You're mean and petty to everyone, and it's getting you exactly the life you deserve."

She slaps me. So suddenly, so hard, that it makes my ears ring. I gape at her, my hand over the place that stings.

I shake my head. "I'm done."

I grab my violin and leave.

Chapter Fifty-Three

Gloria

It takes me less than two hours to return to Manhattan, a trip that took five hours on the train. By the time the Lyft drops me off, I've been up for nearly thirty hours, not counting naps on the train. I let myself in and call out, "Willow? Sam! I'm home."

The cats come tripping into the foyer on their pretty little feet, and my heart swells to quadruple its size. I sit down on the bench and bend over to pet them. "Hello, my sweet girls." Esme butts her cold nose against my wrist, and Eloise twirls around my ankles. "I'm glad to see you too. We just haven't spent enough time together lately." Esme squeaks her agreement.

Sam comes into the foyer, barefoot and draped in an oversize sweater, and rushes across the space to fling herself into my arms. "Gloria!" she cries.

I wrap my arms around her, eyes closed, smelling her hair. Emotion wells in my throat. "Oh, my dear, sweet girl. I love you so much."

She clings to me, hard, very unlike her, but I revel in it. "I thought you were gone," she says. "I don't want you to go anywhere."

"Me either," I say quietly.

She lets go finally, her hands still on my shoulders. We are face to face, the tallest women around most of the time. "But I thought you were in trouble?"

"I am, but I don't want to run. That's not my way."

She tightens the sweater around her middle, and I see now that her eyes are swollen, as if she's been crying, and the illness lingers in the paleness of her skin. But she says, "I don't think you have to run. I've been going over scenarios, and I think there might be a way out."

I kick off my shoes. "I called my lawyer on the way home. He does think there're some possibilities. Why don't you show me what you have in mind?"

"Yes. Let me get you a cup of tea. Are you hungry?"

I blink. Sam thinking of someone else's needs? "That would be great," I say cautiously. "Let me go wash my face." Then I realize the silence. "Where's Willow?"

She looks over her shoulder toward the music room, and I see something in her expression, but I'm not sure what. "I don't know." She heads for the kitchen. "I'll make you some tea."

I wash my face, grateful for my own space, for my beautiful bathroom, for the fern in the corner. *Please,* I think.

Sam is hunched over the kitchen table, nibbling a cookie. I smell chamomile, which she's made properly in a sunny ceramic pot. More cookies and a pile of grapes are arranged on a plate. "This looks lovely, Sam. Thank you."

"You're welcome." Her eyes are almost a neon blue when she looks at me. "You're very important to me, Auntie. I'm sorry I don't say that more often."

I pat her hand. "Thank you."

"Now," she says, opening her laptop with efficiency. "Let me show you what I found."

She's searched every case of this nature, including variations in a dozen ways, and has come up with a plan that has genuine merit. Together, we call my lawyer, and by the time an hour has passed, it seems I might actually get out of this.

By the time we're finished, I am beyond exhausted and stand up to go to my room. It's odd that Willow is still gone. "You have no idea where Willow is?"

Sam bows her head. "No. We had a fight."

I sit in the chair, taking this in. "It must have been quite a fight for her to leave you alone."

She's plucking a loose string at the end of her sleeve and suddenly bends over, putting her face in her hands. "It was awful."

I sigh. Willow would not attack or fight unless Sam started it. "Do you want to tell me about it?"

"No." She rubs her forehead. "I don't know why I do this, why I'm so mean to her. Asher even commented on it."

"If you're looking for absolution, sweetheart, you've come to the wrong person."

She looks up. "I don't think I want absolution. I want to stop doing it." She swallows, unravels a row of her sleeve. "I did it with Asher too." She clenches her jaw to stay in control, but I see the tears in her big blue eyes. "At Tina's wedding, we got together, and it was . . . amazing."

I wait.

"And then we got back to the city, and he wanted to stay over, and I just got so scared that we'd ruin everything, our friendship, that I started a fight, and it got way out of control." She closes her eyes, touches her eyelids. "So, so out of control."

"That's why you haven't been talking?"

"Yeah." The string from her sleeve grows, unraveling, unraveling. "And then, I mean, when I was so sick, I had this hallucination that we were married and we had two little boys, and I must have texted him the SOS, because that's how he got to me." She pauses. "Before I died."

I rest a hand on her shoulder. "Are things fixed, then?"

She shakes her head. "No." The word is hushed. "I thought they were. I thought we could move forward. I mean, we've been best friends for decades. How can we just not be anymore?"

"Do you want to be friends, or do you want to be lovers?"

"I want us to be married," she cries. "I want to have babies and live in Brooklyn and have meals together every night."

"Have you told him that?"

"No. What if he rejects me?"

I shrug. "Nothing ventured, nothing gained." I brush hair from her face. "Have you ever talked about your fight?"

"No. How do you even start a conversation like that?"

"You could start by apologizing."

She looks at me. "I have."

I incline my head. "Really?"

She bows her head. "Not really." She gives me a thin smile, then gives a hard sigh and squeezes her eyes tight. "Oh, how am I going to fix things with Willow? I said awful, awful things."

"Why?"

"What?"

"Why," I repeat. "Why did you say such awful things?" As she considers, I pick up the teapot and pour a cup, then offer it to her.

She sips. "That's so soothing."

"Mmm. Why did you get so angry with Willow?"

"It was this whole awful thing this afternoon. My dad came over with his wife, and Asher got mad when Eric came over, and then he left, and then Willow was just in the music room, and—" She lowers her eyes. "I was jealous. So jealous. She makes life look so easy."

I don't say a word. The back of my neck is aching from the tension of the past forty-eight hours, and my eyelids are grainy over my irises, but I wouldn't miss this moment for the world. Sam has needed to come to this place for literally years.

"How do I stop doing this, G? The people I love the most in the world are mad at me. And they have every right to be."

"First of all, you need to talk to them, each of them, and take ownership, apologize, and make amends."

"How?"

"I don't know. That's up to you." I pat her knee. "And then, my dear, I think you need some counseling. You do have abandonment issues, with good reason." I touch her hair, tuck a lock behind her ear. "If I could go back in time and fix things for you, I would. But I can't. Only you can do that now." I pause. "You might need some anger management too."

"What? It's not like I'm beating people up."

"Not physically."

"Oh," she says softly and bends her head.

"You need to get some rest," I say, standing. "And I need to get ahold of Willow."

"Okay." She holds the cup of tea between her palms. "Thank you."

I brush her cheek. "Of course, my love."

Chapter Fifty-Four

Willow

When I leave the apartment, I don't really know where to go. The day is breezy and sunny, so I just start walking aimlessly south toward Midtown, taking pleasure in the anonymity of the crowds, people busy on their way to something.

At first, anger carries me along at a fast pace. I'm walking to calm myself, to get myself back into my body. I'm so angry with Sam, and I'm worried about Gloria to a degree that makes me feel like I'm walking on coals. Where is she? When will I see her again? How can I get a message to her?

Music and walking are the only things that will help. On my earphones plays a list I've assembled for such times, a combination of fast and slow violin, in all sorts of modern and historic compositions. Lindsey Stirling, Bach, and Paganini, the madman. A little of everything.

Listening to violin reminds me of what I'm here to do. I mean, I knew when I was a little kid and Mom fit that tiny one-eighth size into my hands and showed me how to rosin the bow. I was starstruck, right from the start.

That's what I want to think about. Violin.

But my mother was my teacher at times, and it's that I remember now, stomping toward Central Park with a mad violinist in my ear. My mother fitted that violin in my hand, nudged my elbow higher, and picked out a simple series of notes for me to play, and I tried to reproduce them. She wore tiny skull earrings and a long feather clipped into her hair.

"That's so good, Willow! I just have a feeling you're going to be really good at this."

"What am I going to be good at?" Sam said, coming in to slump in a chair.

"Everything," I said. And that's all I remember.

Poor Sam. Tears sting my eyes, because I do understand why she's so hostile, but at the same time, my body feels scored with slashes, her cuts true and deep. A manic pixie dream girl—I have played that role many times, trading the illusion of myself for a sense of security or a boost in self-esteem or—whatever. An album.

She's not wrong. That sticks in my throat, makes it hard to swallow.

I reach the park and realize I don't want to go wandering through all those pathways and sidewalks. I'm getting a little bit cold and hungry, a state I often knew as a girl. Where can I go?

But I realize I've walked right where I need to be. My feet have carried me to Lachman's Bookstore, the shop Asher's dad runs, a place that gave me great comfort when I was a girl.

I sidestep the main door and pause in front of another one, smaller, next to the nail salon that used to be a barbershop. I ring the bell, and a woman answers, "Hello?"

"Mrs. Lachman, it's Willow Rose. Can I come up?"

"Willow! Of course, dear." The buzzer rings me in. The stairway smells familiar, slightly mildewy and warm, and my body eases immediately. Mrs. Lachman opens the door at the landing of the third floor and ushers me in. "It's so good to see you, Willow," she exclaims and waves me into the main room, the living room with comfortable, overstuffed furniture. A golden retriever leaps down and comes over to greet me. "This is Herman. Be nice, Herman."

I open my palms to let him sniff them, then scrub his silky head. "He's beautiful."

"Come, sit," she says. "What would you like? Coffee? Lemonade? Maybe." She holds up a finger, opens the fridge. "Yes, lemonade. Soda?"

She will not settle until I choose, so I say, "Coffee."

"Good choice. It's chilly out there. Your nose is red."

I touch it. "I didn't realize."

She makes a pot of filter coffee by rote and stands beside it, one hand on her hip. Her blouse is a camel color, tucked neatly into her jeans, and her salt-and-pepper hair is short, where it used to be a heavy black pageboy. Otherwise, she looks very much the same. "How are you, Willow? I bought your album and loved every note. Tell me everything. How's it going?"

"It's been very up and down, but that's the music life, right? How are you? The kids? Mr. Lachman?"

"He's downstairs. You'll have to say hi before you go." She peers into the distance. "Everybody is good, you know. Doing their thing, I guess. Everybody is married but Asher—and hey, he told me Sam's been sick with meningitis! Is she all right?"

To my absolute horror, tears well up in my eyes and spill over before I can do a damned thing to stop them. Mrs. Lachman is right by my side before I can blink. "I'm sorry; she's not okay?"

I nod. I can't talk about Gloria, which is part of this, but I can talk about Sam. "No, she is. We just had a really, really terrible fight." I squeeze my hands together. "Said terrible things, things we can't take back."

She pats my shoulder and says nothing. Goes back to the coffee maker and stands there. "She had a bad fight with Asher a while back too. He hasn't talked much about her since then." She looks at me. "Do you know what happened?"

I shake my head. "Sam never told me. I only found out they weren't speaking when I saw him in the hospital."

She pours two mugs of coffee and carries them over to the table, then gets a half gallon of milk out. "Sorry, I don't have cream." She sits down, her rangy hands palm down on the table. "What's going on with poor Sam?"

"Poor Sam?" I burst out. "Poor *Sam*? She said horrible things to me, and she is always mean. And not just a little mean. Really mean. Always, always, always. All I've ever wanted was for her to just love me, and all she does is sneer." My voice breaks a little on the end. "I'm so tired of poor Sam."

Mrs. Lachman smiles faintly and covers my hands with one of hers. "She has a tongue as sharp as a serpent's tooth. I'm sorry she attacked you."

"But." I roll my eyes.

"No but. She needs to learn how to deal with her emotions so she doesn't cut everyone off."

"I don't know how she's coping without Asher," I say, and it strikes me that she's *not* coping very well.

"Nor do I." The buzzer rings twice, and then we hear footsteps on the stairs. "I believe that's him now. He's coming over for dinner."

He comes through the door, and at first he's perplexed, then frowns. "Is Sam all right?"

"Yeah, fine, why?"

He can't quite meet my eye, and I think of him storming out of the apartment. "Just wondering."

"Asher!" his mother says. "Did you have a fight with her too?"

"Too?" He points to me. "You did?"

I nod, but now I'm wondering if . . . "You fought?"

He shakes his head. "Not exactly. We've just had really good boundaries until the past few days, and they're all broken. I'm trying to get mine back in place."

"Boundaries? What's going on with you two?"

He closes his eyes. "Nothing. I mean, I just can't get into it. But maybe she was pretty upset at me."

I'm thinking about the flow of the day. Giving her a shower, and she was so embarrassed by her body, which really is awfully thin. Her father showing up, not to see her but to bring his wife in to see if she could sell the apartment. Eric showing up. Asher storming off.

Then my little band playing so cheerfully, and my good news about the reporter, and the discovery that we'd hid everything from her. For a good reason, but still. We left her out.

Damn. I close my eyes. "I have to go."

My phone rings in my pocket, and I stop to look at it. Unfamiliar number, so I ignore it. Then I remember that Gloria doesn't have her phone, so she might call me from anywhere. Urgently, I say, "Hello?"

"Willow," she says, "I need to know where you hid the paintings."

Behind me, I hear Asher say, "I need to go talk to Sam."

"Wait!" I cry, phone down. "This is G."

Understanding dawns. "Ah. The paintings?"

I nod.

Chapter Fifty-Five
Sam

After a shower and a quick nap, Gloria leaves to meet her lawyer, and I'm alone again. It feels very, very, very empty here, and my heart is hollowed out, too, and I lie on my bed with headphones on, Tupac turned up high to drown out the voices in my head. I can't sleep. The words I flung like knives at my sister echo.

Why am I so mean?

The fight with Asher was the same kind of fight—he wanted to stay, to kiss me and sleep with me, in my apartment, and I suddenly couldn't breathe. Literally.

Tupac is too intense, and I scroll through my music and settle on Keb' Mo'. The quiet bluesy sound eases my nerves, clears some space for me to really think.

Fact: I'm in love with Asher. How did I not know that before the wedding when we got together? If I look backward, I see him in every single frame of my life—eating dinners of takeout while we worked side by side on a game; falling asleep on his couch or he on mine before waking up and starting again; attending bar mitzvahs and weddings and graduations; being happy and being sad.

The day my mother died, I was over at Asher's apartment, playing *Final Fantasy*. His mother appeared at the door of his bedroom and just stood there for a long, long moment. "Samantha," she said, "I need to talk to you, honey."

I don't know what I thought it would be, but I said, "Hang on just a minute. I've got to—"

"Now, Sam," she said.

I gave Asher the controller and stood up. He, alerted by something in his mother's voice, followed us out to the hall. "I have terrible, terrible news, sweetheart," she said, her hands on my shoulders. "Your mother is dead."

The words didn't mean anything. I looked at her face, but it didn't make sense. "No, she's fine. I saw her this morning."

Mrs. Lachman nodded. "I know. She was fine this morning, but now she's not. I need to take you home."

Asher stood beside me. "I'll go with you."

I reached for his hand, and he gave it, and I stood in the hallway hearing words that made no sense. That very morning, my mother had been drinking coffee in the kitchen and smoking. I hated her smoking, hated it so much, the way it clung to the walls and my clothes, and I'd asked her a million times not to do it, and now, in middle school, I was very aware that people could smell it on me sometimes.

When she asked for a hug that morning, I waved my hand in front of my nose. "No. You really need to stop smoking. It smells disgusting."

She leaned back, her foot on the chair. "Fine. I love you anyway," she said.

"Whatever." I slung my pack on my shoulders and left. Behind me, my mother had called, "Have a great day, sweetheart!"

When I got home with Asher and his mother, Willow was inconsolable, howling. She was the one who'd found Billie, overdosed on her bedroom floor, and called 911. Jorge, who was a young man then, had stayed with her until Mrs. Lachman arrived and Gloria could be called.

Asher stayed with me through the whole crazy night. Social services wanted to take us at least overnight, but Mrs. Lachman wouldn't let them. She called my father, who came over and stayed until Gloria arrived by air the next morning.

What I remember is Willow, rocking on the floor, and Asher sitting down beside her, putting his arms around her and letting her cry. She cried and cried and cried and cried. I just kept thinking of Billie that very morning in the kitchen, giving me her little smile. Patient. Never minding.

She loved me as I was. The recognition breaks my heart, coming so late.

In the end, we all curled up on my bed, me and Asher and Willow. She slept between us, only nine to our much more mature thirteen. But over her head, Asher held my hand. "It's okay, Sam," he said. "It's going to be okay."

Of course it never could be, but it felt like it might be, if I could just reach out.

Then and now. Reach out and let them in. Both of them.

I just don't know how. My mind keeps giving me ridiculous romcom setups that are completely out of character, grand gestures of all kinds, but that's just not me. I'm not a grand-gesture kind of person.

I can only be myself.

It takes some time to get myself dressed and together enough to go out, but I am stronger, and there's no one here to stop me. I take a cab to Asher's apartment and knock on the door, but he isn't home.

It's only then that I realize I've left my phone behind.

For a long moment, I wonder what I should do. It seems humiliating to wait, but I've come all this way. Like Gloria, I don't want to run. I'm tired of running.

Awkward as it may be, I sit down beside the door. To wait for him.

Chapter Fifty-Six
Willow

Asher hid the paintings in the bookstore, of all places—a very good hiding place, since it's a warren of aisles and dusty alcoves and so many books. It's a bibliophile's dearest dream, and I have trouble just walking through the aisles behind him, my eye caught by this or that.

I take the paintings back to the apartment in my backpack, according to Gloria's instructions, and Asher comes with me. We ride the train side by side, silently. "I don't think I can stand for Sam to keep doing this to me," I say at last. "I mean, I want to stay in New York, but if I have to deal with my sister all the time, I just don't think I can face it."

"I get it," is all he says. His fingers tangle and untangle in his lap.

"You've put up with her shit forever, Asher. How did you do it?"

He shrugs. "She's never mean to me, well, mostly not. She saves that for you."

A wave of sadness crashes over me. "But why?"

"Because she has to be mad at someone, and you will never leave her."

"I *will* leave her," I say. "I'm tired of being her punching bag."

"You need to tell her that."

"I think I did." The fight comes back to me in bits, the shouting, the splotchy color on her chest.

"Then you have to give her room to figure it out."

"What if she never does?" I whisper.

He smiles down at me, my big brother all my life. "She's a pretty smart cookie."

I narrow my eyes. "Did you just say she's a 'smart cookie'?"

He laughs. "I did."

Gloria has just come out of the shower when Asher and I arrive. Her hair is wet and slicked back from her face, and she's cloaked in a dressing gown. I hug her hard. "Oh my God, I'm so glad to see you." I breathe in her smell, the feel of her shoulders. "Are you okay?"

"Well, for today. I'm not out of the woods by any means."

"What are you going to do?"

"Leave that up to me." She pats my arm. "Where's Sam? I thought she'd be with you."

I feel a sudden hush over my nerves. "I don't know. I haven't talked to her. We had a big—"

"Fight, I know. She told me." G frowns.

Asher comes out of her bedroom. "She left her phone behind."

"I think we have to find her." I'm gutted by a hollow sensation, worry and anger and love all mixed together. "Shit. She does like to make it hard, doesn't she?"

His expression telegraphs the same emotions I'm feeling. We're frozen for a moment.

"What are you waiting for?" Gloria cries. "Go find her!"

Chapter Fifty-Seven

Sam

I'm bored waiting for Asher, leaning against his doorway. I pull my knees up to my chest and think of my dream of Brooklyn and boys and Asher cooking dinner.

Footsteps on the stairs alert me, and I stand up, smoothing my clothes and hair. Asher emerges from the stairwell, and I can see his glasses are smudged, his hair completely wild. I want to smooth it down, offer him a cleaning cloth. "Hi," I say.

"Hi." He pauses, a few feet away.

"I came to—"

"Let's go inside."

His face is the most beautiful, most dear, most amazing face I have ever known, and I stare at him for a long moment. "I love you, Asher," I say. "I mean, not love you like a brother but love you, love you. I'm *in* love with you."

I'm trying so hard not to cry, but it feels like all the tears I've never shed are pouring out of me all at once. Not noisy but copious, pouring and pouring. "I am so sorry for all the awful things I said to you after the wedding. I didn't mean them. I just panicked."

He's just standing there, listening, and I can't figure out what his expression means.

"That's all," I say, dashing water from my jaw. "I just wanted to tell you the truth. I don't know how to make amends or some big gesture, but I had to tell you what I really feel, because this past year has been absolute hell. I miss you every single minute, every single day." I swallow, take a breath, and let it go. "It's like the world has no color without you in it."

He is still just standing there.

"Okay," I say. "I'll go. I just wanted you to know." I start to duck away, but he catches my arm.

"Sam."

I look up, and he takes off his glasses, and his big dark eyes are as wet as mine, and he bends in and presses his forehead to mine. "The first time I saw you was in third grade. You came into the classroom with a chip on your shoulder and your hair all limp and sat down beside me, and I knew you would be my friend forever."

He kisses me, very, very gently. "All those years, I dreamed so many times of you confessing something like that to me, realizing that you loved me as much as I loved you. When we finally got together at Tina's wedding, it was such fucking magic. It was a thousand times more powerful than I thought it would be, and I thought about it a lot, let me tell you."

His hands are in my hair. Tears are still pouring out of my eyes, so many so many so many, and they're soaking the front of my shirt, but I don't care.

"I just wanted to revel in it a little bit. But . . ." He straightens. "I'm not going to put up with that evil tongue. I don't want to feel that way, and even if it means we have to walk away forever, I'm willing to do it."

I reach for him. Touch his face, hold his neck. "I know. I really do. I do know I have to make amends and I have to change my behavior, so I promise I'll find a therapist and maybe some anger management or something. I promise," I say again and bow my head, and now it feels like all of me is going to break into pieces, as if all the moments I never acknowledged are rising through me, and I bend into Asher's chest and let them come. "I've just been so angry for so long," I manage.

He holds me, kisses my hair. "I know, Sam. I know."

After a long time, we go inside, and he pours me a tall glass of water. As he offers it to me, he says, "I was wrong to desert you. It wasn't fair to abandon you the way I did. I knew you were lonely, and I knew you were struggling, but all I could think about every time we were together was how much I wanted to be with you. I couldn't figure out how to be okay with that."

I drink the water, cold and refreshing. "You did the right thing. You were right. I was never going to get it as long as you were in my corner." I laugh a little. "As it is, it took a near-death experience."

He smiles, wipes a tear off my eye. "Let's call your sister. She's looking all over for you too."

Chapter Fifty-Eight
Willow

It's late when Sam comes in. Asher called to let me know she was all right, and I could finally let down my guard a little. Gloria is asleep in the other room, assuring me that she is not going to be carted off to jail anytime soon, though I'm going to be very curious to see how she manages that.

But she's Gloria. G-L-O-R-I-A. She can do anything.

I'm in the parlor, watching it rain and listening to my mother's best album on the very good stereo. Asher called to let me know Sam was with him, and I thought I would come in here and work on the piece for the contest, but I have to admit it's not going to be finished in time. Just . . . no way. I should have been spending twenty-six hours a day on it if I really meant to enter, but between Gloria's crisis and Sam's illness, I've barely had three or four.

And I could not have made any other decision. There will be other contests.

New albums. Just because one release was a flop doesn't mean they all will be. This is what I'm meant to do, and I'll keep going, no matter what.

I have all of Billie's music on digital, but there's a depth of sound to an album that's worth the effort of a turntable sometimes. I'm listening to her sing another song about a woman losing a game to a man or being tricked by life, and I'm thinking of Josiah's rich baritone singing the words to her famous song, as an offering.

As if my thoughts have called him, my phone buzzes, and I see it's him. "Hey," I say.

"Hey." That bass rumble moves through my body, pools in the region of my heart. "I just wondered if you're doing all right. If you want to work on the music some more?"

I run my thumbnail down the seam of the pillow. "I'm good. I'm not going to be able to finish in time for the contest, but I don't think it matters. This connection, I mean"—I feel my face get weirdly hot— "the music we can make, is bigger than a contest." I pause, and when he doesn't say anything, I add, "I mean, if you're interested."

"I am interested. Let's see where we can take this thing."

"Yes." In the hallway, the door slams, and I look over my shoulder. "I have to go."

"Maybe we can jam a little tomorrow evening? You can come here if you like."

"Absolutely. Let's do it. See you tomorrow."

Sam comes in as I'm hanging up. She looks pale but happy. "Is it all right if I join you?"

"I don't know. That depends on whether you're going to call me a bunch of names or not."

She looks down. "Not."

"Okay, come on in."

On the stereo, my mom sings about dancing even when the world doesn't dance with you. Sam settles on the couch. "I'm sorry, Willow. I didn't mean any of that."

I shake my head. "You don't have to apologize. I know you didn't mean it."

"I am sorry, though. I'm sorry for all the times I've done that, just taken my anger out on you." She swallows. "You are one of the best people on the planet. You're good and kind and real and authentically, completely yourself. I don't know anyone else like you."

I blink, feeling my soul rise and expand and fill the room, dancing like the little mouse in Angelina Ballerina. "Wow. That is by far the nicest thing you've ever said to me."

"I love you more than anybody in the world. You know that, right?"

My mom's voice, bluesy and rich, weaves between us, binding us together, and I cross the room and sit down beside her, flinging my arms around her shoulders. "You have to stop yelling at me like that. It takes me days to get over it, and I think really hard about every single thing you say."

"You do?"

"Of course I do. You're my big sister. I look up to you. You're the smartest person on the planet, so if you say it, it must be true."

She laughs. "I wouldn't go that far." But she lifts her arms and hugs me back and whispers into my hair, "I am so sorry."

I close my eyes and breathe in her smell. "It's okay."

Our mom's voice winds around us, drifts through the room on waves of color, a dusky purple, a waft of white.

"Asher told me about the paintings. What's going to happen to Gloria?"

"I guess we're going to find out."

Chapter Fifty-Nine

Gloria

One week later

Dani's husband has been involved in much sketchier deals than this one. I meet him at his club at 7:00 a.m. It's a dying-world kind of place, all heavy woods and velvets and hushed quiet, the realm of kings.

Matthew sits by a long window that overlooks the park. He's wearing a well-cut black suit with a crisp white shirt, his white hair combed back from a face that's stern but still very good looking. He stands when I approach the table and gives me a kiss on the cheek. "Hello, Gloria. You look remarkably well."

I sit, adjusting the gauzy white scarf I've draped over a turquoise linen dress with buttons up the front. Men can never resist the suggestion of all those buttons. "You mean, considering everything?"

He cracks the smallest of smiles. "Indeed."

We order coffee and an assortment of fruit and small, elegant pastries. The coffee arrives in a silver pot, and I pour out of habit, offering sugar cubes. He takes two, and I pour the cream.

"Remarkable that you remember," he says.

"I never forget such important things," I say with a wry grin. He flew with us a great deal, sometimes twice a week, for years. As I stir my own coffee, I ask, "You've spoken to Balakrishna?"

"I have. He agreed to meet us here to spare you the embarrassment of being connected to Margolis, but he does seem to have a favor to ask of you in return."

On the way home from the train, I thought about Balakrishna's passion for art and his love for my sister's work. I started to wonder if there might be a way to make a deal, to give him a way to solve his part of the case while granting me my freedom. When Sam found correlations in old cases, my lawyer and then Matthew helped me work out the details.

I shrug. "I'm in no position to refuse, considering."

"You brought the key?"

"Yes." I reach in my bag and pull out a medium-size manila envelope with a heavy clasp that holds a key to a safe-deposit box in a very large, and therefore anonymous, bank.

"Good." He raises his hand and waves at someone, and I stand as he does, both of us waiting for Balakrishna. To my surprise, he's dressed in a pin-striped suit, dark charcoal and pale gray, paired with a light-pink shirt. His shoes are expensive, polished.

"Well," I say under my breath.

"He doesn't look like an FBI agent."

I step forward with an outstretched hand, and he takes it, shakes as if man to man. "Hello, Mr. Balakrishna," I say.

"Adhita, please," he says and rounds the table to greet Matthew. "Hello."

"Please sit down."

We settle, and a silence falls around us. "Would you like coffee?" Matthew asks.

"Certainly. Thank you."

I guess he will take it black, but he surprises me and adds three cubes and a substantial amount of cream. Seeing me watch, he inclines his head. "I grew up on masala chai, which is very sweet."

"Ah."

He takes a sip of coffee, then reaches for his briefcase and withdraws a sheaf of papers. "This is our written agreement," he says, placing it in front of me. "It grants full immunity from all charges stemming from this case, in return for the recovery of the lost Renoir."

Matthew takes it and reads the clauses, flips up the page, reads more. "Very good."

I sign where I'm asked, then pick up the envelope and place it on top. "Thank you," I say.

He inclines his head, all professional bearing, but I notice his hands are trembling slightly as he places the materials back in his briefcase. "I won't keep you," he says. "It has been quite interesting to meet you, Ms. Rose."

"You too." Relief is pouring through me.

"If you should ever consider selling the painting of Billie Thorne, I humbly request that you ask me first. Is that possible?"

Whatever I thought the request would be, it wasn't this. "I will, but I doubt my nieces would ever let it go."

He nods and looks down, and I see the emotion there.

"But if you like, I would be happy to show you her music room properly at some point."

"Would you?"

I nod. "Of course." With a smile, I add, "You know where to find me."

"Yes," he says and stands. "Thank you." He gives a rather formal bow.

"Adhita," I say as he's about to go. "I hope you will take your time. At the bank."

He gives me the faintest tilt of the head, and I see his eagerness. The pleasure he will bring to holding a work of art that he will then return to the world. "Yes. Yes, I will."

When he leaves, I look at Matthew and hold out my own hand, which has a visible tremor. "I've been so afraid that something would fall through."

"I was fairly certain it would be all right." He selects a small twisted danish. "I have other news, as well."

"Oh?"

"The painting. The nude?"

"Yes, yes. Has it sold?"

"It did," he says. "To a collector who was always a rather large fan of the portraits of you." He passes me a check that makes me blink.

"Well, then." I pick it up and tuck it into my purse, thinking it will be great fun to split it with the girls. After a moment, I ask, "Any news about what they're doing with Isaak? Will they send him to prison for a long time?"

"I don't know. It seems there has been some trouble with the evidence." He shrugs lightly. "Time will tell."

Time will tell, I think and look out to the treetops sliding into their spring jackets, the tulips sprouting in planter boxes, and the moment is ordinary and precious beyond words.

But not pictures. I pick up my phone and take a photo.

Spring in New York City.

And I'm here, in it.

Chapter Sixty
Gloria

Several months later

On a soft June day, I'm deadheading flowers in the pots along the rooftop garden. Clouds, blown by a wind high above the earth, make shadows as they move across the sunlight. I'm lost in the task, enjoying the view across the river, taking pleasure in the scent of lemon geraniums and a pot of pink carnations. I pluck one and tuck it behind my ear.

"G?" Willow calls. "You have a visitor."

Miriam was going to bring me some lemon marmalade she's made. "Send her back," I say and clip a frond of rosemary, which I lift to my nose. In the distance, a plane takes off, nose pointing up to the heavens. Such a great life.

A sense of hush catches my attention, and I'm aware of a presence, and I turn.

Isaak.

For a moment, I can't breathe. My mind can't comprehend his presence, and as if he knows, he only stands there, a faint smile on his wide mouth. He wears a crisply pressed shirt and beautifully cut trousers with a crease. His hair is thick, curly, mostly white, and his hands are in his pockets.

My breath catches. The face is dark and craggy, heavily lined, his nose more aggressive than I remember, his mouth wide and sensual. But those eyes, those eyes . . .

"You are still so beautiful," he says, and the voice, too, is what I remember, so rich and lyrical.

My hand flutters up to my throat. "Isaak," I whisper. A thousand moments rush through me, moments of love and longing and loss, moments of laughter and pure connection and ecstatic pleasure. But always, always, always this wild longing.

"Ma bichette," he whispers and pulls me into his arms.

Something I've been holding together for longer than I can remember, longer than I can calculate, years, decades, centuries . . . suddenly shatters. I bend into his neck and break into pieces.

"Oh, my love," he says, his arms strong around me, bracing my body with his own as I weep, soaking his shirt, my body shaking with my emotion. He strokes my hair, holds me, murmurs soft things, nonsensical things.

I raise my head at last, slapping away tears even as new ones pour from me, like a river suddenly unfrozen. "Isaak," I whisper and touch his face, look into his dark, dark eyes.

He kisses me.

The first kiss is gentle, a greeting. We pull away, look at each other again, and then there is simply no question—he crushes me close, and we kiss as if we are twenty, kiss and kiss, our bodies pressed hard together. It's as if no time has passed. It is just the same. Always the same.

"How long will you be here?" I ask.

His hands roam restlessly on my back, awakening cells I'd forgotten existed. "As long as you'll allow me to stay."

I close my eyes and hug him with all my being.

There is more than one way to love a man the whole of your life.

Epilogue

Sam

Five years later

"Does everybody have what they need?" I ask. "Once I sit down, there's no way I'm getting up again."

"Get off your feet, Sam," Tina says. She and Nuri have moved back to New York after four years in Atlanta. "Your ankles look like peaches."

I snuggle into the couch between her and Asher, on my right. In his lap, my daughter Mia offers me a Cheerio, and I open my mouth happily. She's three, the very image of my sister with her wild curls and big eyes, and adores her father. Since my entire lap is taken up with her sister, still inside but due in four weeks, I'm just as happy to have him hold her for now.

Asher and I bought the brownstone last year, with money from the second game in the new series from Boudicca, which landed on the top-ten lists of every gaming magazine and website out there, blowing our first release, so long ago, right out of the water. Our team is powerful in more than one way.

Gloria, sprawled across the chair she's claimed as her own, shushes us. "Here it comes."

On the screen of the television, a woman in a caftan walks up to the microphone. "The nominees for best folk albums are . . ." She reads them, and the last one is *My Sister's Dreams*, by duo Willow and Josiah.

The album, their second, has done remarkably well, a crossover success with the muscular backing of such superstars as Lucinda Williams and Patty Griffin. The sound is intensely original and fresh, and people can't get enough of it.

We all cheer. Mia throws Cheerios in the air, and Asher cracks up. One lands in my hair, and I toss it back at her, grabbing her hand to pretend to munch it.

"And the winner is . . . *My Sister's Dreams*."

Gloria leaps to her feet, still amazingly fit for her age, and dances and cheers. Isaak has come to live with her in New York, but his gout has flared up tonight, so he stayed home with the cats he adores and texts every few minutes. "I knew it, I knew it!"

The camera zooms in on the duo. Josiah bends down to scoop Willow into his arms and swings her in a little circle before he sets her down.

The two of them make their way up to the stage, holding hands, both of them beaming.

Willow takes the mike. "We are staggered and so very, very thankful for the reception to this album." Cheers and whistles break out, and she laughs, completely at home on the stage. "I'm grateful to all of you, and to my partner"—she raises their joined hands—"because it was magic from the first night we sang together." She pauses and looks into the camera. "I also want to thank my aunt Gloria; my mother, the great Billie Thorne; and most of all, my sister, Samantha, who has been my most beloved friend all my life. This is for you, Sam!"

I rub my belly and grin like a crazy person. Asher rubs my upper shoulders. "That was beautiful."

Next to me, Mia toots a little tune on the harmonica she discovered last week and will not put down. I look at Asher. "Did she just play the first bars of 'Mary Had a Little Lamb'?"

"I did!" she cries and does it again.

"Brava," Gloria says, clapping. "Brava all around. Excuse me. I have to go call Isaak."

Briefly, I feel my mother, happy at last, cheering all of us. I rub my belly and realize the new baby will be called Billie.

On the television, Josiah holds Willow's hand and raises the award high in thanks, and Mia toots her harmonica, and all is well.

All is well.

The End

Acknowledgments

I could not be on this journey without readers, and all of you make my life so very rich. Thank you for your notes and letters and Instagram posts and private messages. I love walking with you.

Deepest thanks and gratitude to my entire publishing team: my agent, Meg Ruley, barracuda, wise woman, and as bighearted as the world; Alicia Clancy, editor extraordinaire; Tiffany Yates Martin, dev editor, who makes me swear as I polish; Danielle Marshall, especially for that amazing conversation we had one day in New York City; and Gabe Dumpit and the marketing team. Also thanks to my friends, who see me through the hard days. You know who you are.

Big, big thanks go to my longtime friend Judith Arnold, author of the Bloom series, who wrote the lyrics for the song "Write My Name Across the Sky," copyright Barbara Keiler. Find her at JudithArnold.com.

And always and ever, thanks to Neal Barlow for holding up the tent while I'm lost in the writing. And to Rafe, for keeping my feet warm.

About the Author

Photo © 2009 Blue Fox Photography

Barbara O'Neal is the bestselling author of fourteen novels of women's fiction, including *The Lost Girls of Devon*, *When We Believed in Mermaids*, *The Art of Inheriting Secrets*, and *How to Bake a Perfect Life*. Her award-winning books have been published in more than a dozen countries, including France, Great Britain, Poland, Australia, Turkey, Italy, Germany, Israel, Croatia, Russia, and Brazil. She lives in the beautiful city of Colorado Springs with her beloved, a British endurance athlete who vows he'll never lose his accent.

To learn more about Barbara and her works, visit her online at www.barbaraoneal.com.